The
Dreamweaver

The Story of Mel Fisher
and his Quest
for the Treasure
of the Spanish Galleon
ATOCHA

by Bob "Frogfoot" Weller

The DREAMWEAVER

cover design by **Melinda Smith**
Charleston, South Carolina

cover photo by **Theo Westenberger/Gamma Liaison**
New York City, New York

most interior color photos by **Pat Clyne**
Key West, Florida

Typesetting by **En Rada Publications**
West Palm Beach, Florida

prepress production by
Ad Pro Graphics, Inc.
Charleston, South Carolina

manufacturing consultation and production by
The Charlestonian Press, LLC
Charleston, South Carolina

wholesale distribution by
Sunshine Distribution, LLC
Columbia, South Carolina

Fletcher and Fletcher Publishing, LLC

Post Office Drawer 22828, Charleston, South Carolina 29413

First Printing, First Edition

Other books by Bob "Frogfoot" Weller

"Sunken Treasure on Florida Reefs"
ISBN 0-9628359-1-9

"Famous Shipwrecks of the Florida Keys"
ISBN 0-9628359-0-0

"Galleon Hunt"
ISBN 0-9628359-2-7

"Shipwrecks Near Wabasso Beach" (co-author)
ISBN 0-9628359-4-3

ISBN 0-9628359-5-1 (Hard Cover)
ISBN 0-9628359-7-8 (Soft Cover)

Library of Congress Catalog-in-Publication data;
Weller, Bob "Frogfoot"
The Dreamweaver

Edited by Ernie "Seascribe" Richards

ACKNOWLEDGMENTS

The author would like to acknowledge the original Mel Fisher tape interviews conducted by Wendy Tucker. They provided much of the information on the early years of the Fisher family. I want to thank Deo Fisher for inducing me to write *The Dreamweaver*, a task I thoroughly enjoyed. Deo provided much of the information that has been previously screened from public view, the insight that made the book more personable.

I have worked on the salvage sites of the 1715 Spanish galleons for eighteen years, and during that time have come to know Kane Fisher as one of the most dedicated salvage masters in the business. He is the embodiment of his father, and there is no doubt that the Fisher legacy will be carried as long as Kane can cast off the dock lines and head to sea. His input to the book has been responsible for the on-site operation that puts the reader "on the bottom" as treasure is being recovered.

Kim Fisher provided much of the information on the recoveries during the years prior to the *Margarita* discovery as captain of the *Southwind*. Syd Jones shared with the author his "favorite" wreck site, the *Santa Margarita*. Syd was responsible for recovering a considerable amount of treasure from the site as captain of the *Swordfish*. He was responsible for many of the details in the *Margarita* recoveries, second only to the *Atocha*.

With author Eugene Lyon's permission, some extracts from his book *The Search For The Atocha* were used to detail many of the time periods that were missing in the taped interviews with the Fisher family. Gene is an excellent writer and one I have great respect for.

Taffi Fisher has been great. Her help in writing *The Dreamweaver* is evident with the many personal "peeks" into the Fisher family life. Her collection of photographs of the treasure years should give every future salvor the adrenaline necessary to head for the Spanish Main.

Finally, Mel Fisher had the patience to sit through countless taping interviews, doing his best to recollect facts and happenings that took place so many years ago. It was as rewarding to him as it was to the author, because as he recalled the highlights of the past thirty years his eyes would light up, and the smile never seemed to leave. He has become a legend in his time, and it was a pleasure to work with him as *The Dreamweaver* was written.

Mel Fisher, Age 12.

THE DREAMWEAVER

Table of Contents

PROLOGUE

It was an occasion for celebration. Brightly colored flags whipped briskly in the breeze, while booming ceremonial cannon fire rang in the ears of the excited citizens of Havana as they crowded the docks to wave good-bye. The annual Spanish treasure fleet had hauled anchors and was proceeding past *El Morro*, the grim stone fortress that guarded the entrance to the harbor. It was September 4, 1622, and well into the hurricane season.

The sailing had been delayed for weeks at Portobello as more than 100,000 silver coins and over 1,000 silver ingots were loaded on board. Another delay occurred at Cartagena, where more silver coins and bars --as well as over 20,000 pesos in gold bars and discs-- were logged into the manifest. It was August 22 when the fleet finally reached the docks at Havana. Last minute cargoes of copper slabs, baled indigo, tobacco, and more private treasure found room aboard the galleons which were already seriously overloaded.

Pilots of the galleons had generally disagreed on a sailing date, feeling that the danger of a hurricane was too great to risk losing such a huge treasure now carried by the flotilla. The final decision was made by the fleet commander, the Marquis of Cadereita. He had considered the conjunction of the moon, which greatly affected the weather. This was the time of the new moon when the Earth, sun, and moon were in "conjunction". If bad weather prevailed, he would delay sailing. But on September 4, the day before the conjunction occurred, the weather looked promising. His decision was to sail.

There was another urgency to sail as well. The King of Spain was, as always, in desperate need of the gold and silver. By 1622 the financial straits of Spain were stretched to the limits. The Fugger family of Augsburg had financed Spanish wars and religious expansion, but in 1607 a suspension of debt payment by Philip III drove the Fuggers out of royal finance. In 1621 Philip III died, and his son Philip IV became king. The thirty-year religious war between Protestants and Catholics in the Holy Roman Empire had already begun, and Philip IV needed the

1

galleon treasures to support Spain's efforts in this war. The fortunes of Spain literally rose and fell with the flow of precious metals from her overseas empire.

It took more than an hour for the fleet of 28 ships to clear the harbor. Once they had formed into a sailing order, the *capitana* led the fleet off on a north-by-northwest course that would carry them to the Gulf Stream. Once there the current would give them an additional two knots, which would boost them homeward. By sunset they had reached the center of the Gulf Stream, but the weather had changed. The deep red sunset and a bank of clouds that began to pile up to the southeast gave the pilots their first uneasiness. Unknown to them a hurricane had formed and was rapidly moving along the Leeward Islands.

As darkness descended upon the fleet, topmast lights were lit as ships tried to maintain position. But now the gusts of wind began to toss the ships about. Long, undulating seas made it difficult to maintain their course. Before morning the winds had increased and were now whipping the tops of the waves into a white froth. The *almiranta* of the fleet, *Nuestra Señora de Atocha*, positioned in the rear of the flotilla, had to reduce sail by morning in order to weather the storm that was now upon them. Deck cargo had to be secured and cargo hatches firmly lashed down as the day darkened and the weather worsened. By noontime the winds had shifted to the east and reached gale force. No longer could they see other ships in the convoy. The mainsail was lowered and secured, and the foresail alone kept her bow into the wind.

Now the sea boiled around the galleon, her yards disappearing into the green water that began to wash over her waist. Great seas swept all around, and flying spray obscured the horizon. *Atocha* plunged into each wave, lifted up on a crest to roll wildly into the next. No longer could the galleon be steered. With the tiller lashed in place, the whipstaff disconnected, each huge wave sent shudders through the *Atocha* hull. Below decks was turmoil. Olive jars filled with water or oil were sent crashing about. Passengers and crew alike suffered wholesale seasickness, holding onto anything solid. Now they were at the mercy of the sea. The struggle to stay afloat went on, but only thoughts of survival put seamen through the motions of working the ship. The winds had moved around to the northeast, and now the fleet was being driven relentlessly towards the dreaded Florida reefs.

By first light of dawn on Tuesday, September 6, the *Atocha* had reached the shallows near the deadly coral rocks. Her stream anchor had been deployed during the night, and now as it struck bottom, the two main bow anchors were dropped in an effort to keep the galleon from being driven onto the "dragon's teeth". Fifteen foot waves had carried away the foremast and rudder, and now her bow carried the brunt of each wave. The anchor lines, stretched tight as a bowstring, soon snapped with a loud report, and *Atocha* became part of the mountainous waves breaking on the reefs. Captain Bernardino de Lugo, gunnery captain aboard *Atocha*'s sister ship, the *Santa Margarita*, was able to see *Atocha* "rise up, strike a reef, and sink shortly thereafter." The *Margarita* soon afterwards parted her own anchor lines and was dashed against the reefs four miles away.

By a twist of fate, the *capitana* and nineteen of the ships in the fleet were driven southward and passed west of the Dry Tortugas into calmer waters. One vessel, *Nuestra Señora de la Consolación*, was lost in deep water. One of the larger *naos*, *El Rosario*, was driven onto the reefs near Loggerhead Key in the Tortugas. A *patache* sank nearby in front of Loggerhead Key, and a small Cuban coast guard vessel sank near the Marquesas Keys. A morning calm found debris, floating trunks, barrels, masts, and a few survivors.

Of the *Atocha*, sunk in 55 feet of water, only her mizzenmast protruded above water. To it clung five desperate souls, thankful to have survived. One of the merchant vessels, the *Santa Cruz*, had weathered the hurricane and, now loaded with 68 survivors of the *Margarita*, approached the sunken *Atocha*. The five men --a seaman, two apprentices, and two black slaves-- were taken aboard the *Santa Cruz*. All trapped below decks, 260 souls were lost aboard the *Atocha*. The *Margarita* had lost 143 as her hull disintegrated against a sand bar.

When the news of the disaster reached Havana, Gaspar de Vargas was commissioned to locate and salvage the sunken galleons. Within a week he had outfitted five vessels and sailed for the area near "the last key of the Matecumbes." He soon located the mizzenmast of the *Atocha*, but was unable to retrieve the treasure from her hold because the hatches were so securely fastened. He recovered two small bronze cannon from her stern castle, buoyed the wreck site, and then turned his attention to locating the *Margarita*. He searched in vain for any visible signs of the *Margarita*, then finding none, he sailed westward towards the Tortugas.

On the reefs of Loggerhead Key de Vargas found the *Rosario* in ten feet of water, her keel broken and badly holed. Her crew and passengers were huddled on Loggerhead, along with the survivors of the *patache* which sank nearby. He brought them aboard his salvage vessels, then went about the task of salvaging the treasure from *El Rosario*. The hull was burned to the waterline, and the one million pesos in silver bars and coins were recovered. Just as the recovery was completed, a second hurricane --more powerful than the first-- swept over the area. The salvage vessels were barely able to stay afloat, protected somewhat by Loggerhead Key. The treasure and survivors were taken to Havana, and preparations were made to return to *Atocha* with explosives.

Unknown to Gaspar de Vargas, the second hurricane had separated the upper deck structure of the *Atocha* from the hull and sent it dancing over ten miles across the waves, strewing the bottom along the way with coins, gold bars, jewelry, and artifacts. The hull --nailed to the bottom with almost forty tons of silver, fifteen tons of copper ingots, and sixty tons of ballast stones-- remained in deep water. When the salvage ships reached the Matecumbes they could find no trace of the *Atocha*. The buoys were gone, as was the mizzenmast. De Vargas and his men dragged the area for weeks without success. They also could find no trace of *Santa Margarita*.

By February of 1623 the Marquis de Cadereita sailed to the Matecumbes to take personal charge of the salvage operation. He was under great pressure from Philip IV to recover the treasure, and he thought that his presence might inspire the team of salvage divers to work even harder. They named the last of the Matecumbes "Marquesa Key" after him. But the *Atocha* still eluded them. For several months they would row four hours to the potential site, drag the area for several more hours, then return --

exhausted-- to their base on the southwestern tip of Marquesa Key.

Without a trace to show for their efforts, they returned to Havana. The site of *Nuestra Señora de Atocha* slipped into archival history...a history of galleons with manifests of gold and silver lost on the wicked reefs of Florida, waiting for a modern day salvager to recover them.

A SAILOR'S PRAYER

A stout Ship
And loyal Crew
A strong Wind
The Sea and You
O Lord
To Guide us.
Amen.

1...HONEYMOON OVER KEY WEST

F og had settled over Key West Harbor sometime during the night. At first light, only the tops of masts stood above the gray mist that hid the row of sailboats anchored near Wisteria Island. Like Mokojumbies, those West Indian gremlins, the fog seeped under window sills and doors, bringing a damp chill to the morning. Somewhere a boat engine gave a wake up call as it sputtered to life. A pelican sitting atop the piling at the head of Duval Street raised its head with thoughts of an early morning breakfast. Stretching a wing, then a leg, it seemed satisfied that everything still worked. With a heave, he left his perch and disappeared towards the engine noise that now had settled into a low, resonant vibration as it warmed up.

In the cockpit of the boat a lone figure bent over the raised hatchway, his flashlight checked the bilge. He dropped the hatch, moved to the stern, and snubbed in the mooring line of the rubber boat that had drifted under the dock during the night. The sleek lines, and a row of dive tanks along the starboard rail, set the boat apart from the shrimpers that shared dock space. The *Greyhound* had been running dive charters out to the reefs for several years, ever since the SCUBA craze had made fish out of couch potatoes. Ed Ciesinski was well known around the Key West docks as a good underwater man. A reputation well deserved.

He untied the canvas cover over a small compressor and began filling the tank with gasoline, when he heard cars drive up. "Must be my charter, and they're early," he mused to himself. "What a gung-ho bunch!" Along with car door noises and trunks being opened, came voices that were obviously eager. Steps above him on the dock caused Ed to put the gas can down. A tall figure emerged out of the fog. "I'm looking for Captain Ed Ciesinski." Ed wiped his hands on a rag. "You found him." And he reached up to shake hands.

The tall man smiled, "I'm Mel Fisher. I hope we're not too early." "Not at all. Come aboard." More voices came from the dock, and Mel turned to help a stunning redhead step aboard. "I want you to meet my wife, Deo." Ed couldn't help feeling that this would be a pleasant trip. The young lady he shook hands with wore an infectious smile, one that seemed to lift the fog from the deck of the *Greyhound*. Soon others were gathered on deck, introducing themselves and arranging the growing pile of gear that was being passed down from the dock. "You can stow your gear in the forward cabin," he said, motioning toward the bow of the boat.

Ed couldn't remember all of their names; "Doc Mathison, Jim and Bobby McNeff, Rod White, Dennis something --Thor Brickman was the big guy-- and others he would get to know over the next few days. Mel was their leader and spokesman; he was the one who had called the day before to arrange the charter. He had asked, "Do you know of any wrecks we can dive on?" Ed had assured him that he could put his group on a number of wrecks. There were fourteen divers in the group, and Ed half hoped they could handle themselves. Wreck diving wasn't the safest activity for new divers.

By the time the gear was stowed and everyone had a hot cup of coffee in hand, the fog lifted, and Key West Harbor began to stir. Other boat engines sounded across the water, and several pelicans now paddled near the stern, casting an eye for a bait fish or two. Sea gulls circled the dock, a sort of screeching plea to feed them as well. The dock lines were thrown off, and *Greyhound* backed out of the slip. With both engines turning over smoothly, Ed eased his bow towards the open channel, making sure not to cause a wake. As the sixty-foot charter boat moved into the channel between Cable Island and the Duval docks, Mel, Deo, and their group lined the rails. This was Key West. This is what they had traveled clear across the United States to see, to be part of, to share in an underwater adventure. It was even better than they had anticipated, and their enthusiasm was beginning to show.

The channel took them between Western Head and E. Triangle, where the bottom rose to a varicolored display of reefs and sea life. The water was crystal clear that morning; it was almost as if the *Greyhound* were floating on thin air. Fish, used to the boat traffic, seemed not to move as they passed over. A few of the coral heads rose to the surface, and Ciesinski moved closer to the center of the channel. Five miles from the harbor the sea buoy

7

marked the drop-off to deep, blue water. *Greyhound* turned westward on a course that would take them seaward of Sand Key.

Fisher's group began to relax; before long, bathing suits and sun lotion were the plan of the day. Mel and Doc Mathison moved up to the cockpit, and Ciesinski anticipated what they had on their minds. "I thought we would check out the wreck of the *Dominguez* first. It's just a ballast pile, probably still has a lot of bronze spikes and pins about, but not much else. It's only fifteen feet deep there, gives everyone a chance to get wet." Ed thought to himself it would also give him a chance to check out the divers. As he spoke, the rest of the group gathered around, sitting on the deck or leaning in through the hatchway --all eager to find out where they were going.

"After the *Dominguez* I think we can reach the *Valbanera* before dark. Give us a good start on diving in the morning." Mel asked, "What can you tell us about either wreck?" "Not much on the *Dominguez*, sank too long ago for much in the way of information. But I do know a bit about the *Valbanera*." First Ed mentioned that the *Valbanera* was one of the worst disasters, in terms of lives lost, off the coast of Florida in many years. It was a fairly large, steel-hulled vessel, 399 feet long with a 48-foot beam. Built in Glasgow, Scotland, in 1905 for a Spanish company, it carried cargo as well as passengers from Europe to the United States. It was in 1919, the year after World War I ended, that the *Valbanera* left Spain with 400 passengers, 88 crew members, a cargo of wine (mostly bad) and liquor. Among the passengers were some undesirable women, as well as a few prisoners, that Spain was shipping off to Havana, Cuba. After leaving Havana, the ship was scheduled to continue on to New Orleans.

The voyage was uneventful until the vessel approached the coast of Cuba on September ninth. It was hurricane season, and a full-blown tempest was approaching the eastern end of the island. Captain Morton had *El Morro* in sight, but because of the increasing winds he decided against trying to enter the harbor. Instead, he made the fateful decision to try and ride out the hurricane at sea. He turned his ship to the southeast and headed for Key West. There was an indication that the storm might pass into the Gulf of Mexico.

For three days he rode out the mountainous waves in the Bahama Channel. Like most fickle hurricanes, this one did not take the expected track, and the *Valbanera* was caught on the windward side. The last message heard from the ship was radio contact with Key West, when the ship's radio operator asked if there were any messages for the ship. Ten minutes later, when radio Key West tried to raise the ship...there was no answer.

A week later, on September nineteenth, the United States Sub-Chaser *203* and the Coast Guard cutter *Tuscarora* found the *Valbanera* sunk on the east side of Rebecca Shoal Lighthouse in the Dry Tortugas. It lay in forty feet of water on a bed of quicksand. No bodies were discovered in or near the wreck site. Divers were sent to explore the wreck and found no structural damage that might indicate that it had struck a reef. Also, because boat davits were still in place, no effort had been made to lower the life boats. It was assumed that all passengers and crew went down with the ship when it sank suddenly and without warning. "The ship is nothing more than a hulk now; past hurricanes haven't treated her very kindly. Still, it's home to a lot of fish, so it should be an interesting dive."

Ciesinski did his best to answer all their questions and still steer a course towards the "Quicksands", the location of the *Dominguez*. This area is a twenty-mile shoal in fourteen feet of water, stretching west from the Marquesas Keys. It is called the "Quicksands" because of its composition of sand and shells, constantly on the move by current and wave action.

By noontime they could see the bottom color change as they approached the shallows of the Quicksands. Taking bearings on a spar buoy on the edge of the shallows, Ed spotted the gray smudge on the bottom marking a pile of ballast stone. He circled to the west and dropped anchor, letting *Greyhound* drift back over the top of the pile. "Get your gear on, we're here!" The group needed no persuasion. They were already pulling on fins and spitting into face masks.

Mel had a contract to film a movie --for the Voit Company-- about a diving vacation. By the time he had unpacked his camera,

9

the rest of the group was already in the water checking out the ballast pile and looking for souvenirs. Ciesinski was in the water with them, like the shotgun on a stagecoach, keeping a careful eye out to make sure no one got in trouble. Mel and Deo helped each other with their SCUBA tanks, and they dropped over the side together.

It wasn't a large ballast mound, and sand had drifted over much of it. But here and there were signs of timbers and encrusted metal objects. They could see clouds of sand being fanned away as the divers probed for the prized green bronze spikes or pins that held the hull together. Mel began filming as they swam down the pile, pausing to get close-ups of each diver. Before they reached the end of the mound, Mel and Deo were joined by a large school of tuna. This was great stuff, and as Mel filmed away the fish seemed to cooperate by joining in a circle about the pair of divers.

These were large tuna in the sixty-pound class, and there must have been several hundred of them in the school. Mel and Deo were enjoying the fish parade until the circle began to tighten. It was then that they realized just how large the fish were. Soon the circle was less than six feet in diameter. It was wall-to-wall fish, with big eyeballs, all more than curious about these strange manfish with one eye and two big tails. It was the snapping of their tails as the fish closed in that finally made Deo give the sign "Let's go up!" Mel later mused, "Those fish don't realize just how good they are to eat."

Unknown to Mel at that time, less than three miles to the east, in fourteen feet of water, lay a huge galleon anchor. This anchor, half buried in the sand, would be the clue to one of the richest sunken Spanish treasures in modern history. One that would make Mel Fisher a legend in his own time. The Atocha *would sleep for another 32 years.*

It was late in the afternoon when Ciesinski called the divers back to the *Greyhound.* "We want to make anchor on the *Valbanera* before it gets dark." Reluctantly they all eased back aboard, handing up their tanks and equipment. It had been a great day, a free-spirit sort of day. The water was clear, a lot of fish in the area, and they had managed to recover a few bronze spikes as souvenirs. It was their first *old* wreck dive in Florida, and one they would not soon forget. But this next wreck site was a big one, and they were just as excited, even though it wasn't old and full of gold doubloons and pieces-of-eight.

They hauled anchor, and the captain headed westward toward Rebecca Shoal Light, some ten miles distant. As the sun began its disappearance act behind the horizon, Ciesinski throttled back and let his boat coast up near the hulk of the *Valbanera*, now visible below them. The anchor chain rattled in the hawse as he backed down to let out enough scope. The engine coughed a bit as power was shut down, and suddenly things were quiet. The light on Rebecca Shoal had just illuminated, swinging the 360-degree arc to warn vessels of the shallows and casting shadows as it passed across *Greyhound*.

It was time to sit on the stern, a cold drink in hand, and talk about the day. The Fisher team was enthusiastic, no doubt about it. Everyone had something to say, it was a matter of getting a word in edgewise. But they were a very comfortable group --of course Mel was their leader-- and they listened as he and Deo recounted their experience with the parade of tuna fish. In almost no time the smell of dinner broke up the confab on the after deck. Ed had managed to spear a few hog snapper for the evening meal, and there's nothing like fresh fish to whet the appetite.

Over dinner his passengers shared their enthusiasm with Ciesinski, and although he had become used to it over the years, this charter seemed a little different...better somehow. These divers bubbled, and it seemed to emanate from their tall, rangy leader, Mel Fisher. He was satisfied that these divers knew what they were doing; they had been well trained. He decided to relax on this trip and have fun just like the rest of them. It *had* been a good day.

That evening, after the rest of the divers had called it a day, Mel and Deo sat near the stern rail enjoying the sounds of the sea. "It was a great day. I'm glad we decided on Key West for our honeymoon." Mel nodded, "It's been quite a week."

The wedding had taken place in California just the week before, and it had been a dream wedding. The Wayfarers Chapel was the perfect setting for Melvin Fisher to take Dolores Horton as his bride that June day in 1953. High on the bluff at Portuguese

Bend, the chapel was designed by Frank Lloyd Wright, a man who loved the sea very much. The chapel was built of glass! The walls, the ceiling, even the door was made of glass. On a clear day you could see Catalina Island twenty miles away. For the wedding the chapel was lit with sunlight, and the waves of the Pacific Ocean sounded like a choir of baritones as they rushed against the ledges below.

The Wayfarers Chapel at Portuguese Bend.

The pews were filled with a happy crew of divers from all walks of life. They were there to cheer on their leader, "Fearless Fisher". Over the past several years Mel had managed to lead southern California into a new era of underwater exploration. Through a sports television show he hosted, he had literally picked hundreds of armchair enthusiasts out of their seats and put them in underwater dive gear. Mel had the talent to develop the hopes and dreams of young and old alike. He had the physical ability and the lack of fear to challenge this new frontier. It took someone of his caliber to lead the way, and he did.

California coastline as seen from Portuguese Bend.

Although Mel was the leader of this joyous group, this was "her day". Dolores "Deo" Horton, a gorgeous, flaming-red-haired beauty, could draw everyone's attention the instant she stepped into a room. She matched Mel's charm and wit, and she had the physical ability to stay with Mel in his underwater adventures. Born and raised in Montana, a long ways from the ocean, Deo felt right at home when her mother and sisters moved to the west coast near Los Angeles. She had met Mel when her mother, Aunt

Billie, and Uncle George bought the Fisher chicken farm, and Mel agreed to stay on for awhile and teach the family how to run the business. He had set up a dive shop in one of the sheds out back, and Deo had a chance to meet many of the divers when they came to fill their air tanks or to buy spear guns that Mel made in his spare time. When Mel introduced her to diving, she took to it like a water-baby. It was this mutual love of the ocean that was the chemistry between them.

After the vows were spoken, the photographs taken, and congratulations extended, Mel and Deo were standing in a circle of friends. Looking at the glass walls that surrounded her, Deo prophesied, "It looks as if my life will be an open book!" If she had realized how true that statement would turn out to be, it's not likely that she would have changed a thing.

There *was* a honeymoon. Mel and Deo had decided that the warm, clear waters of Florida would be just the right place to get their life together started. The Voit Company, a manufacturer of diving equipment, heard of Mel's plans and offered him a contract to do some underwater filming while in Florida. The movie was titled, "The Other End of the Line", and it was about a couple on a skin-diving vacation. Mel and Deo both thought it would be a great way to commemorate their honeymoon. Then there were the members of the "Sharks Underwater Adventure Club" of divers that Mel had started. It was an opportunity for them to get in some great diving in Key West, and Mel had managed to arouse their adventurous spirits. So by the time the bags were packed and diving equipment loaded in cars, the caravan to Florida counted fourteen enthusiastic people, singing and having a good time.

Mel never really made plans, he sort of let things happen. He had a basic idea: drive to Florida, go diving on some old shipwrecks, and have a good time. Come back to California when you run out of money. The group really didn't care; Mel was a lot of fun to be around and, after all, things usually worked out for the best. Mel makes trips fun. As they traveled eastward he talked about his adventures in Tampa Bay, when he saw his first shipwreck treasure. Standing there on the St. Petersburg pier one day he watched a diver come to the dock, obviously from a shipwreck "somewhere out there". The diver flashed a few old coins, teased Mel's fantasy, and then was gone. Up until that time Mel was noted as a spearfisherman, the "guy who went further out and brought back bigger fish". He had gotten into underwater photography just so everyone would believe the size of the fish he was spearing. But now it was sunken treasure that became the driving force in his life. He thrived on adventure, and he could weave a story around whatever he did, making the people around him want to share in the adventure. He was a "dreamweaver".

The miles melted behind them. Even the flat, endless plains of Texas never put a damper on the joyous mood they were in. There were never-ending numbers of cows on both sides of the road. Mel had everyone counting cows, ten points for a black cow, twenty for an all white one. The side of the car reaching 1,000 points first was treated at the next lunch stop. By the time they reached Louisiana, Mel and Deo had the song "Tell Me Why" down pat. Mel sang baritone, and Deo sang alto. The rest just joined in where they could. Mel probably had a hundred songs he knew by heart, and he was determined to sing them all.

Then they were crossing the state line into Florida. After a free glass of orange juice at the welcome station, there suddenly seemed to be palm trees and orange groves on both sides of the highway as far as the eye could see. The air was fresher, and the windows were rolled down to flush out the bayou dust. The singing continued until they reached Weeki-Wachee Spring.

This was their first sample of absolute under-water visibility, where young mermaids performed submerged endurance tests with ballet precision. Standing in a tunnel-like structure with thick glass windows facing a performing pool, the group enviously watched as the girls pirouetted and spiraled with flawless ease. It seemed that they never had to take a breath of air. Mel was busy filming the performance, and when it was over the divers were ready to head down the road. Seeing action under water merely whet their appetites. They were eager to get wet.

The Tamiami Trail led them along the perimeter of the Everglades to the outskirts of Miami. Then ahead of them lay Florida City, the gateway to the Florida Keys. There is something magical about the Florida Keys. The emerald islands, connected by short spans of concrete and steel, seem to skip over the water

15

as they curve like a scimitar westward. On either side of the highway the water was so clear it seemed as if there was no depth at all. Colors changed only as sand pockets or patches of eel grass turned the water from green to blue. Small clusters of fish or lobster traps stood back from the road, lining canals that protected the small boats from sudden storms. In 1953 most of the Keys were barren of commercial buildings. That boom would take place many years later.

And then they were in Key West. It was a small town in terms of size, but still the largest community in the Keys. At one time it was the largest city in Florida, a thriving salvage headquarters for "wreckers", who made their livings from ships driven ashore by storms or poor navigation. By 1819, the Navy had stationed a squadron of ships there. It was a clean town, a busy cross-section of shrimpers and charter-boat captains, with a downtown section that touted such notables as Ernest Hemingway, James Audubon, and the Truman White House. Neat shops were crowded into alleyways and along tree-lined side streets that made finding them as much fun as browsing through them.

But the Fisher group had other plans, diving plans. They stopped by a local dive shop and asked who was the best charter-boat around. The answer, "Ed Ciesinski". Mel called and arranged for the charter.

A slight breeze had sprung up, and the *Greyhound* swung around a bit to the north. The couple on the stern were roused from their reverie. Somewhere a ballyhoo skimmed across the water making a skipping noise. The moon had suddenly appeared from behind a cloud; the only other light came from a night lamp somewhere below deck. Mel put his arm around Deo, "It's going to be a long day tomorrow...but it'll be hard to beat today. Whatta day!"

It was very early morning, the sun wasn't two fingers above the horizon yet, and decks were still damp with dew. Other than the solitary figure on the stern, the *Greyhound* sat motionless on a flat, calm ocean. The water was crystal clear, and Mel could see the outline of the *Valbanera* below him, still cast in shadows. The wreck was a large one. The stern sat up on the edge of the bank in 25 feet of water, while the bow angled down towards deeper water. Mel guessed about 45 feet deep where the bow seemed to slip out of sight. Rather than put a tank on, he decided to snorkel the wreck and check it out before the rest of the group rolled out of their sacks.

Mel had his favorite underwater camera with him. He had captured the imaginations of thousands of Californians with his movies, and he was always extra careful in handling it. The bright yellow case had never leaked, probably because he always made sure that the gaskets were coated with silicone grease and the fittings were snug. As he dropped off the stern, the splash of this new visitor brought instant attention to the fish population of the wreck site. And this was a wreck site that was home to thousands of fish. Other than the concrete piers under Rebecca Shoals Lighthouse, it was the only obstruction in a flat, sandy bottom that stretched for miles in all directions. And so Mel's first glimpse of the bottom was of schools of fish that seemed to lie in motionless layers.

The *Greyhound*'s anchor line led off towards shallow water, and even that was surrounded with fish. Below him was the stern section, and although the shadows were misleading, the wreck seemed to stand off the ocean floor almost fifteen feet. Looking down the side of the wreck he could see shapes floating in and out of the hull near the sandy bottom.

Taking a few deep breaths, he settled to the sea bed and began filming the sweep of the stern where storms had scoured a trench along the port side. What surprised him was how tall the metal plates and framework of the ship looked to him as he stood on the ocean floor. The water plays tricks that way. There were holes in the sides, filled with shadows, through which he caught an occasional flash of tail. He had quite a surprise when he reached 'midships. Here the plates were worn off several feet above bottom, either by storms or rust. The ribs stood as sentinels, and to Mel they looked like stalls in a barn. And in each stall was a large jewfish --motionless, except for gills which opened and closed like trap doors. Jewfish can weigh between fifty and 500 pounds --or heavier-- and each of these *Valbanera* custodians weighed somewhere in the middle.

Mel was reminded of the first time he ever put a tank on and dove beneath the bridge between Tampa and St. Petersburg. It was black down there, and as he hung on to the concrete pilings to get his bearings he was suddenly aware of *large* shapes very close to him. When he could finally see, they turned out to be monster jewfish. The fish here on the *Valbanera* were small in comparison, and he could *see* these jewfish. It was a time when he wished he had a speargun instead of a movie camera.

The more he thought about it, the more he wondered if he just might be able to get a jewfish with his bare hands. They certainly were not afraid of him. They hardly moved when he swam over the stalls; only their eyes followed him. He was above a jewfish that had his head sticking out of the wreck by several feet, and Mel decided to try his luck. He reached down with one hand and quickly grabbed the fish squarely in each eyeball with his two fingers. He had braced himself for a sudden whiplash and frenzy of activity, and he was surprised when the large, eighty-pound fish just seemed to quiver in his hand. Mel was able to swim it to the surface and heave the fish into the rubber boat tied astern of *Greyhound*. By this time some of the other divers were up and moving about. Someone hollered from the stern, "Where's your speargun?" He replied that he didn't need one, and he pedaled back toward the bottom. By this time the other fish had headed for deeper water and parts unknown.

Mel began filming what was left of the shipwreck as he swam towards the deeper end. The shadows were still there...and a bit more foreboding. The hull was open, but dark inside where walls and overheads still remained intact. As he peered inside, a sudden swirl of sea growth was the only indication that he had disturbed another custodian. Without a tank on he decided not to try filming inside until later in the day.

He was now near the bow of the ship. It was deeper here, the bottom slanting away to a hazy blue. The bow section was host to a large school of fish that hovered like a leafless tree halfway between the sea bed and the surface. At first Mel paid no attention to them; he had seen quite a bit of fish activity already that morning. He moved along near the bottom, filming close-ups of sea growth that clung to well-rusted angle-iron stanchions. When next he looked up, the school of fish was close at hand, and it was then that he realized just how large a school of fish it was. "It seemed like there were at least a thousand of them, all...large...barracudas!"

These fish seemed to have no fear of "Fearless Fisher". In fact, they were too close for comfort. Barracuda are known for their underslung jaw and toothy appearance. Without moving, they look menacing. Suddenly, Mel was aware that what had attracted their attention was the yellow camera case he held in his hand. All eyes seemed to be riveted on it, and without warning one of the larger 'cudas took aim at it as he flashed through the few feet that separated them. Mel jerked the camera case away, and instantly the two of them were eye to eye. It was time to head for the surface.

Mel had a seventy-foot lanyard that he had tied off on the yellow camera case. He let that out as he kicked his way to the surface. On the bottom there were now several large barracudas nosing at the camera case. "Better that than me," Mel mused as he headed back to the *Greyhound* some 200 feet away. The school of barracudas followed as he made his way to the side of the charter boat. Once there, he pulled in his seventy feet of line and, literally, threw the camera case into the boat. In one leap he was in the boat as well. It was time for breakfast. *His* breakfast!

Even though it was still early in the day, Mel had stories to tell around the breakfast table. Afterwards the group was even more eager to get in the water and check out the wreck site. They were in for a great day. The fish seemed to follow each pair of swimmers wherever they went. Lobsters waved antennas at them from under collapsed metal plates. Gorgonia and sponges had covered all available growing space, adding some color to the rusting hulk.

Visibility under water was over a hundred feet. Every once in awhile there was excitement as a large shark would swim through the site. Some of the gray shapes remained just beyond the shadows until midday; they seemed to have someplace else to play until just before sunset. For those that remained in the water as the sun began to bleed all over the horizon, it was unnerving to see so many sharks converge on the wreck site. They were hungry and were foraging for supper. It was time to call it a day.

The following morning Ciesinski moved the *Greyhound* out to deeper water near Cosgrove Shoal. Here larger fish were to be found. When it came to spearfishing, Mel was quick to declare, "It isn't sportsmanlike to spear fish while using SCUBA gear." In deeper water it became a game of stalking the fish and holding your breath long enough to get a good shot. The shoal dropped off from shallow reefs to a sandy, sloping bottom 120 feet deep. The water was clear enough to easily see the ocean floor, and Ed was right. There *were* a lot of large fish in the area.

Mel located a large jewfish about one hundred feet down the shoal and was able to put a spear in him. The fish was large enough that Mel wasn't able to wrestle him to the surface in one breath. By the time he came to the surface and relocated the fish, it had moved under a ledge even deeper. Although Mel felt he was not a "hot shot" diver, it was just too deep for him to get. Thor Brickman swam over and saw Mel's dilemma. With a nod, he headed for the bottom, grabbed the spear and fish, and swam back to the surface. Mel could only shake his head, "Whatta guy!"

A little later they located a large ten-foot shark that had settled in the reef. Mel had developed a new CO2-powered speargun that he wanted to try out. Finning down to one side of the ledge, he took careful aim and fired. The spear hit the shark, but not fatally. The shark came out from the ledge, shaking its head and more than a little upset. Mel had carried his yellow movie camera with him...on the end of its lanyard. The shark grabbed at the camera, and the tussle began. The spear had caused enough damage that after a few minutes it was all over, and Mel was able to tow the fish back to the boat.

The shark event had caused enough excitement for the day, and soon the anchor was hauled. It was a long trip back to Key West, and Ed wanted to make it before nightfall. When they reached the docks, everyone seemed reluctant to say good-bye. They had enjoyed this trip with Ciesinski, and like all good memories, they wanted this one to last as long as possible.

Most of the group had to return to other commitments in California. Mel, Deo, and another couple had a few days left, and they took the short airplane ride to Bimini. There wasn't that much to see in Bimini. There was the boat trip to *Sapona*, the famous "Cement Wreck", a 2,700-ton concrete hull used as a rock carrier during W.W.I. It was grounded in 1926, just south of Bimini near Turtle Rocks. In the years following her grounding she became a haven for bootleggers, who used the ship as a liquor warehouse and a private club, and finally a target for W.W.II bomber training. The bottom around the wreck site was bare, just sand and the scraps of practice bombs --quite a letdown after the trip with Ciesinski.

Mel and Deo took the boat around to the west side of Bimini. Here the live reefs provided a bit more to see. While swimming, they noticed fish with a flat spot at the top of their heads, about a foot long, and very curious. It wasn't until one attached itself to Mel's back that they realized these were remoras, fish that clung to sharks with their suction-cup heads. Deo pulled the fish loose, and they were about to make a joke of it...when the big sharks suddenly appeared! These sharks were more than curious, enough to have the Fishers call it a day.

The rest of the afternoon was spent walking the beach, hand in hand, enjoying the warm sun. The honeymoon was coming to an end, but not really. The next day they did head back to California, but for the Fishers, the honeymoon has never really ended.

2...MEL'S AQUA SHOP

The trip back to California seemed longer somehow. On the way, the newlyweds had a lot to talk about. Mel needed to start a business of his own, something that both he and Deo could enjoy. He had never worked for someone else, other than the U. S. Army during W.W.II. Working on someone else's time wasn't in the cards. He had started a small diving equipment store in one half of the feed shed on the chicken farm. It was small, twenty by twenty feet, with no windows and a single door, but it was the only place near Los Angeles where divers could get their air tanks filled. At the time, spearing *big* fish seemed to be the challenge for couch potatoes, so Mel designed, built, and sold CO_2 spear guns. His first display case had been made from a spare window and plywood. But the business he generated from a single case was enough to make Mel realize that this could be successful as a full-time venture.

He made more money selling equipment, filling dive tanks, and manufacturing spear guns than his family ever did selling eggs. He had started the "Sharks" diving club, and with the weekly television show he hosted, the demand for diving equipment and supplies opened the door Mel needed. He and Deo decided to build a shop that catered only to divers and diving equipment, close to the ocean so that when divers called to ask about the weather, they could look outside and give an "on the spot" report. That turned out to be a pretty good deal.

In 1953 the city of Torrance, California, was small, surrounded by fields and rolling hills. It was here that the Fisher chicken ranch was located. The coastal highway, Route #1, was just a few miles away. To the south was Palos Verdes, a big mountainous bluff that jutted out into the Pacific Ocean. From the road, a slippery path meandered down the rocky cliffs to the water. This was Pt. Vicente, where kelp beds teemed with fish, and the rocky bottom was home to abalones and lobsters. It was the closest location to Los Angeles not affected by tidal runout, so underwater visibility was good most of the time.

On any given day highway Route #1 was lined with parked cars, and divers dressed in dry suits managed the long climb down the cliffs. Mel began his search for a good store location along the highway towards Los Angeles. Redondo Beach was the first good-sized town, and he and Deo took down the addresses of all vacant lots that looked promising. A stop at City Hall, and a look at the public records book, provided the owners' names. He sent cards to all the owners, asking each if his lot was for sale --and the asking price. At first it looked hopeless. A small thirty-by-hundred-foot lot was priced at $10,000, and this seemed to be the going price for property so close to the ocean. It was more than Mel could afford.

As luck would have it, a woman living in Indiana had two lots, both close to the ocean. She would sell both parcels for $5,000. Mel immediately sent her a check, for $1,000, and a promise to pay the balance shortly. He ran an ad in the local papers advertising the second lot for $5,000, just half the normal price. At that price he was able to sell it within days to a contractor, and he sent the balance to Indiana. Now he owned a lot, 1911 South Catalina Avenue, and it hadn't cost a cent. It was a time when Redondo Beach was beginning to stir. Condominiums were being built overlooking the ocean, sand dunes were replaced with stores, and the population movement to California had begun.

Mel's time at Purdue University during the war had been in the engineering department. His stint in Europe during W.W.II was rebuilding everything that had been knocked down as the armies swept through France. Putting his experience to practice, now that he had the land, he was sure he could build the store himself. With Redondo Beach at the beginning of a building boom, the city inspectors, and the building codes, were pretty strict. You had to have a California building contractor's license to build. Mel didn't have the money to hire a building contractor. With some persuasion, the city officials advised him that with a homeowner's loan, Mel could be an owner-builder. However, he would first have to have an approved architectural drawing of the store he intended to build. After a round of meetings with local architects proved rather disappointing, he was back in the starting box. The lowest bid for a simple plan was that magical number...$5,000.

Throughout Mel's life it seems that when adversity comes in the front door, his best ideas are right behind. A few days later Mel and Deo were driving down one of the main streets in Redondo Beach when they saw a store that looked like what they had in mind to build. They introduced themselves to the owner and asked him if he still had the plans to his store. When advised that they were still around somewhere, Mel offered to buy them. The owner declined. "Oh, I'll just give them to you. I don't need them anymore." The Fishers were jubilant. With these plans in hand, the building inspector told them they could get started.

Mel never did like money, but it always took money to do what he wanted to do. It would take quite a bit of money to build a store, money he had very little of. He still had the small shop in the feed shed, and he kept it open every evening from 5:00 to 8:00 p.m. It gave the divers time to get off work, drive over for a tank refill, or get whatever they needed. During the day the Fishers rented a boat on shares and dived for lobsters.

The Humboldt Current begins in the Arctic and sweeps along the west coast of the United States. By the time it reaches California it has warmed up a bit...to as much as 50 to 55 degrees Fahrenheit. That is still cold by all stretches of the imagination. Someone told Mel that if he put lard all over his body, it would keep him warm. The Fishers tried that, but it not only smelled, soon everything on the boat was greasy...and what a mess to clean up! Someone else suggested that they drink honey. "All that sucrose will give you the energy to keep you warm." But it didn't. About the only thing that kept the Fishers in the water was two pairs of long-handled underwear under a homemade dry suit of rubber. On top of that they wore a pair of coveralls and a pair of leather gloves. The lobsters had stickers and spines that could tear a rubber suit, or easily put a hole in it. The last thing you want in cold water is a suit with holes in it. Mel and Deo never had a dive trip when their suits didn't flood out and nearly freeze them to death.

Together they went out to Santa Cruz Island, one of the offshore islands just to the north of Los Angeles where few boaters or divers ever go. It was virgin territory, with big potholes and ledges everywhere, and these potholes were full of lobsters. Each ledge or pothole would have a hundred or more lobsters in it. It looked like a barbed wire fence with all those antennas sticking out from under the ledges. With a SCUBA tank on, Mel would make the rounds of each hole. Grabbing a lobster in each hand, he would pass them up to Deo, snorkeling on the surface. She would dive down, take them from Mel, and drop them in the boat. By the time she swam back, Mel would have two more ready to hand up. If a lobster swam away, it was usually to the other side of the hole. Mel would get it on the second time around.

Mel holding a lobster worth 10 concrete blocks.

Going from pothole to pothole, by the end of the day they estimated there was over a thousand pounds of lobsters in the boat, not leaving much room to move around in.

Then it came time to sell what they had caught. They took the gunny sacks full of lobsters back to the commercial fish market in San Pedro and were offered fifteen cents a pound. Mel and Deo decided that it wasn't worth freezing to death in the cold water for fifteen cents a pound. They drove to one of the fancier restaurants along the highway into Los Angeles. There the owner offered them 75 cents a pound, and they were in business. He also offered to buy all they could catch, but he wanted them brought in alive. Building a live tank wasn't a problem, so the Fishers were now in the lobster business!

With the lobster money they ordered concrete, and soon the foundation for the store was poured. Then it was out catching more lobster. Next it was a load of concrete blocks and, with his father's help, Mel built the retaining wall behind the store. The next boatload of lobsters bought the concrete blocks for the first wall of the store. As Mel would catch lobster, he began to mentally count concrete blocks. At 25 cents a block, with every lobster he caught he would say, "That's gotta be worth six blocks. And this one has to be worth seven blocks!" It became a game of how many concrete blocks they had caught each day. After that it was another load, another wall. Then two boatloads of lobster later the roof trusses were delivered. Another time they put a front on the store.

Mel swapped some diving gear to a plumber, and then they had running water; it was spear guns for the glass in the front of the store! The cement man was converted to diving --with a bag full of equipment-- for putting in the sidewalk. It took six months, but at last the store was completed. The final touch was when Mel traded a tank and regulator to an artist to paint a large underwater mural on the side of the building. It was a diver with a tank on, replete with mermaids and a treasure chest. Below the mural were the words, "Go underwater and really live!" The sign over the store read *Mel's Aqua Shop*.

It was the spring of 1954, and it had been a long winter for Mel and Deo. But they had finished the project, and it was open for business. In the morning there would be a line-up waiting for Mel to open. It was a success from the very first day. He began to handle every name brand of dive gear, as well as the spare parts to support them. Then Bel Aqua, a local manufacturer, made sheets of their foam neoprene rubber available to the Fishers. Bubbles of air would trap themselves in the neoprene and keep the divers warm. Mel wasn't the first to build a "wet" suit, but he knew a good thing when he saw it. Soon he had members of his family cutting out patterns and gluing wet suits together. It was the first attempt to customize wet suits, and it put a lot more divers in the water. As they soon found that they wouldn't freeze in the first few minutes under water with a wet suit on, there was a scramble to get on the list to have one custom made.

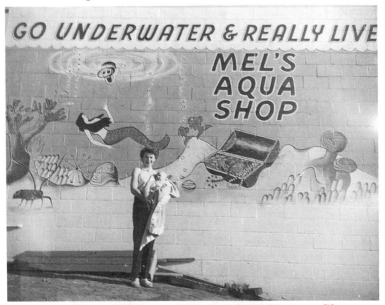

Deo Fisher holding son Dirk outside Mel's Aqua Shop, Redondo Beach, California.

Suddenly SCUBA diving was becoming very popular. Each week, Mel had quite a number of people wanting to learn about this new underwater sport. He decided that it was time to put a training course together. He made an underwater training movie entitled *Blue Continent,* a movie that is still used today by U. S. Divers, Inc. At first the course was three hours long and taught simple snorkeling techniques and clearing the face mask. Soon the demand for a more technical SCUBA course developed into three nights of class work, including pool training.

Before the year was out the course was five days long, cost $35, and included a certificate that said the students had completed their lessons and had passed a written test. It was the first diving school in the country, and Mel found the classes filled almost the day that they were announced. He had to hire and train additional instructors so that classes could be held every day, every night, and on weekends. Before long there were fifteen instructors working with Mel in what became an almost full-time job. For his water work, rather than the cold Pacific, he rented the pool at the Hermosa Biltmore Hotel. Several years later Mel estimated that a total 65,000 certificates had been earned by students who had successfully completed the training. The courses also helped to sell a lot of diving equipment.

Mel's parents, Earl and Grace Fisher,
getting an introduction to the wet world.

Earl Fisher filling up SCUBA tanks at Mel's Aqua Shop.

Somewhere along the way Mel taught his mother and father to dive. Earl and Grace Fisher loved it, but Earl had one problem.

His face had a few wrinkles, and this made the face mask leak continuously. He finally said, "The heck with it!" and decided that filling air tanks in Mel's Aqua Shop was the next best thing to being under water. On the other hand, his mother had no problems; Grace looked much younger than her years. She was an attractive woman that was still in good shape athletically. She was thrilled when Mel made her a model in one of his TV movies. Even "Aunt Marion" decided to try the underwater routine. She loved it as well. There was little doubt that this was becoming a family affair.

Mel and Deo wanted to raise a family while they were still young and the children could share in all the fun they were having. In 1953 Dirk, their first son, was born. In 1956 their second son, Kim, was born. All would become important parts of the Fisher legend that was beginning to grow. Mel had been married previously, during W.W.II, for only a few months. From that marriage his son Terry was born. He lived with his mother until years later, when the thrill of underwater discovery provided the magnetic attraction that would draw Terry back to his father.

Mel's Aqua Shop seemed constantly filled with customers. With a captive audience, it was an opportunity to offer them more than just diving equipment. Soon Mel was selling surfboards, underwater photo equipment, wet suits, and then...gold dredges. Gold dredges came about when Mel was trying to come up with new ideas for audience interest on his weekly TV show. Diving for gold in California rivers seemed like a good idea. Always a promoter, on one of his shows he took a five-gallon bucket --filled with black dirt in which he had sifted in about twenty ounces of gold dust-- and he dumped the whole lot on a table for everyone to see.

"There are all kinds of valuable things in this dirt. If you want to learn about the black sands and gold diving, come down to the Biltmore Hotel in Los Angeles tomorrow night, and I'll show you!" The next night, when he pulled into the parking lot, it was full. The hotel lobby was jammed with people, all standing around waiting for Mel's lecture on how to find gold in rivers. The hotel manager was less than thrilled with everyone milling about. Mel asked if he could rent the ballroom, and the manager was glad to get everyone out of his lobby. They filled the ballroom to overflowing, and it was another night of dream weaving.

Dredging in the Yuba River for gold.

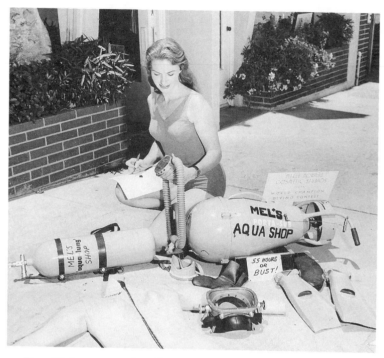

Deo Fisher preparing for an underwater endurance swim.

Mel decided to build dredges and sell them to the customers who were now calling every day about rivers full of gold. Soon Mel was taking groups on three-day trips, to Mexico, or up in the Sierra Madres. They lugged the equipment on their backs --up mountains and along unbeaten paths-- to dive in ice-water streams. It didn't matter if they found gold or not, it was a lot of fun. Evenings spent sitting around a campfire listening to stories about spearing fish or the thrill of making underwater movies converted many more of Mel's followers to this underwater world.

By this time, Deo had become at home under water. It was October, 1958, and the Fisher family had increased in size when son Kane added another branch to the family tree. Deo wanted to help Mel in promoting SCUBA gear, and what better way than to get women involved. In the late 1950s, few women enjoyed this underwater wonderland. The wet suits were bulky, the water was cold, and large predator fish seemed to be on everyone's minds. It was a sport, supposedly, for he-men only. That would change.

Deo Fisher under water at Hermosa Ocean Aquarium.

The Hermosa Beach Aquarium was involved in "Island Days", a seaside festival, and they approached Deo, suggesting that she could set a new underwater endurance record. Earlier that year a young lady by the name of Jones had set a new record of just over 48 hours. This had started a *ripple* of interest in SCUBA by the "opposite sex", and Deo wanted to make *waves*. The Merle Norman Cosmetics company offered to pay all expenses, and this set the wheels rolling. The Hermosa Ocean Aquarium tank was the right place to attract national attention, and the aquarium cooperated by shuttling the larger fish to another tank. They also installed an underwater outhouse...of sorts. They could not, however, warm up the water in the main tank. Deo started her underwater marathon about noon, on a Friday, looking at an entire weekend to break the old record.

The tank was only ten feet deep, so none of the diving diseases were a problem. The Fisher family and friends began a 24-hour vigil outside the large glass windows that were part of the tank walls. Mel had a number of filled SCUBA tanks sitting near the ladder to the top of the tank. Every two hours he would swim a fresh tank down to Deo and help swap out the empty one. At first it was fun and exciting, with crowds of onlookers waving at Deo through the glass windows. But soon the hours began to unravel very slowly. To pass the time away she would play Chinese Checkers with Mel or one of the family friends, using hand signals to indicate moves. Later, Mel brought a masonite board with weighted chessmen, and then Deo had all kinds of company on the bottom, as they tried their hand at underwater chess. The first night wasn't so bad --with all the lights on it was hard to tell the time of day-- but still the hours seemed to pass very slowly. Then Deo got the shivers. Even with a wet suit on, the water was almost twenty degrees cooler than her body temperature, and she began to feel it. Only by staying on the move was she able to keep her fingers and toes from going numb. Mel swam hot water bottles down for her to stuff in her wet suit, and she was able to keep going.

On Saturday came the feeding experiment. It was easy to eat bananas, but other food had to be made into mush and put into plastic squeeze bottles. And when it came to a carbonated drink, such as a coke, she had to drink it by holding the can down and letting the drink rise up. The hardest problem of all was holding her breath while she swallowed. Every once in awhile Mel would slip a milkshake into a squeeze bottle, and for that she gave him a "thumbs up". When it appeared as though Deo needed stimulation, Mel combined a little Canadian Club with honey in one of the squeeze bottles. Because Deo drank very little alcohol, it opened her eyes like a shutter.

The first major problem arose when it came time for relaxing. Deo couldn't just stretch out on the bottom, she couldn't keep swimming around in circles for hours at a time, and kneeling was out of the question. So Mel rigged...a hammock on the bottom. It was great publicity, too; swinging in a hammock in California was the thing to do. Because it was an underwater hammock, it made great publicity, and the Hermosa Aquarium sponsors loved it. There was another problem, however, when Deo kept floating off her underwater bed! Mel solved that problem by draping a weight belt over her waist.

The news media were having a field day. A local TV station decided that an underwater interview was in order. Soon a reporter, armed with a slate, a marking pen, and a borrowed SCUBA tank, was sitting on the bottom with Deo. With the TV cameras trained through the glass window, they made TV history with the first underwater interview. Mel set up a television near the window that evening so she could watch herself being interviewed on TV. What a blast!

Towards Saturday night, after a day and a half without sleep, Deo found herself slipping off into a doze. Suddenly she would be gasping for air as the mouthpiece slipped out of her mouth. After swallowing a bit of aquarium water, she resolved to keep moving about, inspecting every inch of bottom in the tank. It was this constant motion that would help Deo lose nine pounds of weight during the more than two and one-half days under water. "The best diet I ever went on!"

Deo had been under water 48 hours when Mel decided he had better have a doctor check her out, just to make sure that everything was O.K. She looked great, seemed to be holding her own, but just the same it would make everyone more comfortable knowing that she looked as good inside as she did outside. Mel called a local doctor he knew who said he would be more than happy to check Deo out. He had been watching the endurance record on television and wondered how anyone could spend that much time under water without getting waterlogged. The doctor was rather elderly and had never been under water with a SCUBA tank on. It didn't take long to train him. Either he was a good student...or else Mel was a good instructor.

Before long, the doctor had settled to the bottom of the tank alongside Deo and had a stethoscope pressed against her wet suit to listen to her heartbeat. He must have been surprised that he could hear through all that neoprene, but in any event he was satisfied with what he heard. Next he took her pulse, looked into her eyes, and began inspecting the skin of Deo's hands. It was then that he suddenly became evidently concerned. It appeared as if she had super-dishpan hands. The doctor thought that she would be permanently affected by the long submergence; after all, not many people had spent days under water before.

He grasped Deo by the arms and motioned her to the surface. Deo knew instantly that he wanted her to end the endurance dive, and she also knew that she hadn't yet broken the record. She shook him off and indicated that she was not going to give up the dive. Mel was also on the bottom, and she "sign-languaged" to him that she felt just fine. Mel took the doctor topside, and after a discussion they agreed that as long as Deo was breathing O.K., and her pulse and heartbeat were normal, she should continue with the dive. But for a few minutes it appeared as though the dive were over.

Then it was Sunday, and the home stretch was in sight. Deo read from soggy books and magazines, some of which came apart under water and floated away. Mel had all three sons outside the tank, and Kane had just taken his first steps at ten months. They were a great inspiration to this 23-year-old redhead, and she beamed. This day passed more quickly than her first day, and just at noon time, when she broke the existing record, her five-year-old son Dirk swam a rose down to her. The crowd outside the tank shouted and applauded, letting her know how terrific she was. It was enough to keep her on the bottom awhile longer. In fact, it was just at sunset when she finally rose to the surface, somewhat wrinkled by the 55 hours and 37 minutes that had shattered the old underwater endurance record. It was a new record for both men and women! After two and one-half days of silence, the applause from everyone gathered around the tank was deafening. But she loved it! The Fisher family had a great deal to be proud of.

36

3...CALIFORNIA SHIPWRECKS

By the middle 1950s shipwreck salvage was big news. Art McKee had become famous as "Silver Bar McKee" with his recovery of three large silver "loafs" off Gorda Cay in the Bahamas. In the Florida Keys it seemed that shipwrecks lay on every reef. With the advent of SCUBA gear, it opened the door to exploration of these ballast piles spearfishermen had managed to stumble upon. They began to find some great artifacts, as well as silver and gold coins.

There were stories of the sunken city of Port Royal, and of entire Spanish treasure fleets sunk along the coast of Florida. There were also rumors of Spanish galleons of the Manila trade route that had managed to sink off the California coast. The cover of *Life* magazine pictured a beautiful emerald cross, later known as the "Bishop's Cross", recovered by Teddy Tucker. He had retrieved it, along with some significant artifacts, from the *San Antonio* in Bermuda waters.

This was the incentive that Mel Fisher needed to become a serious player in the salvage of sunken shipwrecks. During his honeymoon he looked at shipwrecks as a background for underwater films. There were large fish that inhabited the wrecks, and there had been the thrill of the hunt in spearfishing the big ones. Now there was an entirely new horizon, one with an even more promising reward at the end of the treasure rainbow. But he was soon to learn that it would never be as easy as it seemed.

One day a customer came into Mel's Aqua Shop and said that he had located some cannon. The exciting thing about the discovery was that they were directly out from the Palos Verdes Estates, just a few miles away. Somehow the newspapers heard about the discovery, and the 'phone began to ring off the hook. Mel went to check it out, and sure enough, there they were, all covered with seaweed and coral. The next step was to charter a boat and go pick them up. He asked the captain to pick him up at the Redondo Beach pier for the short ride to the site. Television crews and newspaper reporters got word that the cannons were about to be brought up, and they crowded around Mel at the pier, asking to go along. "No way! We're keeping the wreck a big secret!" There were thoughts of Spanish gold doubloons and silver pieces of eight just lying on the bottom.

It didn't take long to get to the site, and with a few of his divers helping him, Mel raised two of the cannon to the surface. Rather than taking them back to the Redondo pier, he motored around to San Pedro harbor instead. They tried to be secretive about it, but the news media watched the change in plans and were there in San Pedro to greet them. The cannon were loaded on the back of a truck and taken to the end of the Redondo Beach pier where the public could get a good look at them. That night, on the local television stations, was footage of Mel "raising coral encrusted cannons from an ancient shipwreck."

Mel with anchors recovered from wreck sites along the California coast.

Newspapers carried the story the following day, and soon there was a steady stream of visitors. It wasn't long before the pier began to charge admission. Caught up in the fanfare were archaeologists from the Smithsonian Institute who traveled from Washington, D.C., to check out this latest recovery. They chipped away some of the coral, cleaned much of the seaweed off the relics, and then announced that the cannon were "circa 1894 sewer pipes!" What a letdown for the treasure hunters.

But there were other known shipwrecks for them to cut their teeth on. Nearby was Anacapa Island, and on the land side was a side wheeler that had sunk in the mid-1850s. One report had it that fifteen years earlier some divers had recovered a pile of gold coins on the site. Mel began running groups out to the wreck, letting them fan the sandy bottom for souvenirs. The next step was spending hours in the Los Angeles library, reading through old newspaper accounts of shipwrecks. Before long Mel had a file of them, never realizing just how many wrecks there were along the California coastline.

One wreck, the *Valiant*, was sunk near the dance pavilion on Catalina Island. It lay in ninety feet of clear water, where it had become a showplace for divers. The first dive Mel made on the wreck he noticed the two large monel propellers which were still in place. It became a group project to recover these propellers. They brought back some large wrenches but couldn't budge the nuts that held them on their shafts.

On the next trip Mel brought some primacord, detonating cord that exploded at the rate of 2,500 feet per second. First they tied a fairly heavy rope to the heavy monel screw. Then Mel wrapped the primacord around the prop in the direction opposite to how it normally turned, pulled the cotter key out of the shaft, and fired the primacord. The force of the explosion drove the propeller off the shaft and left it swinging at the end of the rope. The divers were able to bring it into Avalon Harbor, where it was lifted out of the water. It was the most excitement that Avalon had in years. Newspapers ran photos of the group holding their prize. It was later sold for scrap monel.

But there was another one to be recovered. They went through the same procedure, but with no thought about the rotation of the screws. Two propellers normally rotate in opposite directions. Mel wrapped the detonating cord in the same direction as he had on the first one. When it exploded, the result was that it only tightened the prop more. They were out of primacord but resolved to come back the following weekend. But the following weekend was too late. The publicity had brought out other interested divers, and they beat Mel to the second propeller.

Mel with underwater camera during filming of
Blue Continent.

In the weeks to come Mel was able to take some underwater footage on the *Valiant.* He filmed Deo, one hundred feet deep, sitting in the bath tub and scrubbing her back. Next they discovered a safe underneath a tangle of iron plates. Before they could bring the crowbars to move the plates, someone else had taken the safe. And then there was Al Capone's shipwreck. Mel found accounts of it in the library. Al had transformed a wooden-hulled coaster into a luxurious gambling yacht, then anchored it three miles off Seal Beach. In 1929, outside the territorial waters of the United States, gambling was legal.

The Los Angeles area, with its large population, also became a target for illegal liquor smuggling. Between gambling and illegal booze, the bureaucrats had their hands full. At one time the governor of California tried to board Capone's yacht and personally serve Capone with a court order to stop gambling. Capone promptly threw a net over the entire boarding party and ordered them off his boat. There was soon another gambling ship, run by a gangster of sorts, anchored nearby in Santa Monica Bay.

A fierce competition for gambling bucks promptly led to violence. About 2:30 one morning, the other gangster put an explosive device against Capone's yacht and blew it up. It quickly sank to the bottom. Turnabout was fair play, and the following night Capone and his henchmen sank the other gambler's ship. That ended channel gambling for the time being. When Mel first brought his diving groups to these sites, they found artifacts all over the bottom. On Capone's wreck Mel was able to recover a cash register, as well as a chuck-a-luck machine, a slot machine, and a roulette wheel. The cash register still had money in it.

Somehow modern wrecks had no fascination for Mel Fisher. Spanish galleons and gold doubloons were a challenge...to research, to locate, and to recover. Rumor had it that several rich Spanish galleons had been lost along the California coast. According to some accounts, one of the first pirates operating in the channel off Santa Barbara was an Englishman by the name of George Compton. In the 1750s Compton's targets were the galleons that sailed each year from Manila to Acapulco with spices, silks, ivory, porcelain, and worked gold. Intricate gold flower chains and engraved gold rings were highly prized by the Europeans. The Chinese had little regard for gold, but desired of silver. At the trade fair in Manila they would barter their goods for silver, and the Spanish conquest of Mexico and Peru had produced an unbelievable flow of that metal. So the exchange brought China out of the closet...into a world trade relationship.

Dirk Fisher at age three.

Because Spain's known enemies remained in the Caribbean, the Manila galleons sailed with little armament and few fighting men.

The space was used to carry supplies and goods on the long three-month great circle voyage that carried them near the Arctic, then down the west coast to Acapulco. As they approached the southern coast of California the galleons would use the Channel Islands, Santa Catalina, San Clemente, San Nicolas, Santa Cruz, and Santa Rosa as landmarks. It was near Santa Cruz that Compton lay in wait for the galleons. In 1753 he sighted the galleon *San Sebastian* and gave chase. For awhile the Spaniards were able to outdistance Compton, but near the north end of San Clemente Island the pirate ship caught up with the galleon and sank it. Mission records indicated that Compton was a rather cruel and barbarous captor when it came to the survivors.

Another rumor persisted for years that the Spanish galleon *Santa Rosa* had sunk in 1717 on the reefs of Bishop Rock, south-southeast of Cortez Bank. And as always, the romance of Spanish treasure overcomes rumor. Once a rumor starts, it's as good as cast in bronze. Rumor persisted that two Spanish galleons had sunk near Catalina Island. One was supposed to have been on the north end of the island, the other somewhere between the island and the mainland. Mel began taking student groups out to the island, and over a period of time they scouted the area completely. No trace of a shipwrecked galleon was ever found. They did find other shipwrecks, some that had never been located before. But the dream of Spanish gold was never realized. Still, it had been fun, and each hunt became another notch of experience.

Not all dive trips were fun, though. The first of these occurred when Mel organized his first serious treasure hunt. Mel was well into his TV host show, "High Road to Danger". The producer wanted some footage of a treasure hunt and was willing to pay all the expenses. At the time, the galleon with the most publicity was the rumored *Santa Rosa* off Cortez Banks. Because the banks lay almost 125 miles off the coast, it took a larger charter boat and a good-sized crew to get there.

In planning the search, Mel built an underwater sled sixteen feet long. Built into the sled were the electronics that would help them detect metal under water. To make the electronics watertight, but still visible, Mel set about building a plastic dome. Taking a dishpan and some Plexiglas, he heated them together in the oven, shaping the plastic until it formed a dome. A flange around the bottom allowed them to bolt it to the sled. It would keep the clock, depth gauge, and electronic equipment dry...to a point.

On the back of the sled they installed a large, four-foot-diameter sensor loop. With a loop that size they hoped to locate any ferrous objects --such as cannon or anchors-- at least fifty feet away. Across the front of the sled was a "windshield" that gave some protection to the underwater movie cameras and the diver. With this equipment they felt they could find the galleon if it were there on Cortez Bank.

Around Bishop Rock the water drops away fairly abruptly to a depth of 100 feet. If the galleon had struck the rocks, it would have settled to the bottom at that depth. The sled was designed to run at a depth determined by the speed of the towing vessel. With about 600 feet of line between the charter boat and the sled, Mel was able to maneuver the sled towards the bottom. Just as he leveled it off, the plastic dome imploded with the pressure. As it did, it sucked the mask right off Mel's face, knocked the SCUBA mouthpiece out of his mouth, and cut his face up a bit. Besides having the shock of his life, water was being forced up his nose as the sled was still moving forward at a good speed. He was able to grab his mouthpiece, and he headed for the surface. This ended the sled project, but the hunt was still on.

With the 600-foot line anchored in one spot, they put a knot every fifty feet. Then divers with tanks on began a circle search. As each 600-foot circle was completed, they would move the line. It wasn't long before they determined that the metal detectors were going to be useless. The Bishop Rock area had quite a few highly magnetic rocks that drove the detectors crazy. But the visual search began to pay off. Not with parts of a Spanish galleon, but with pieces of the ship that the rock was named after. In 1812, the *Stillwell S. Bishop* bilged herself on the rock, scattering ballast and wreckage all over the area. As the divers swept through, they began to recover bits and pieces of the wreckage. Two of the better artifacts were the compass and the binnacle. The movie was successfully completed, and for years the Los Angeles TV audience was treated to Mel's adventures off Cortez Banks.

His second hazardous episode involved a purported Spanish galleon sunk off the eastern point of San Miguel Island. Here again, Mel chartered a boat and, with a group of divers, headed for San Miguel. It wasn't the complete search that Mel had attempted on Cortez Bank, it was directed more towards underwater movies. It started out great. First the school of curious seals became underwater models as they pirouetted about. Then the "sea horses", or walruses, were on center stage. They were rather large and even more curious than the seals. They began to circle the divers until they formed a solid wall...above, below, and all around. Later the movies proved rather frightening, but at the time it was an interesting experience. The walruses never once touched the divers, but everyone was relieved when they headed for the surface without a problem.

Then the storm hit. They had all gotten back aboard the charter boat before the black clouds swept across San Miguel Island. Lightning began flashing all around; it was almost continual daylight, even with black clouds that blocked out the sun. The unthinkable happened next. A sudden, brighter than usual flash...the sound following was instantaneous...and the boat was struck by lightning! The first casualty was the radio, then the boat turned sideways to the waves, and a huge one broke in the side window. Deo quickly pushed a chess board up against the broken glass and kept the boat from filling up with water.

The waves seemed to get higher, and the troughs were too deep to get the boat turned around so they could head for shore. Instead, they rode out the storm by heading into the waves and finally came out of it somewhere near Port Hueneme, considerably north of where they had started. Near shore were huge kelp beds, and these seemed to dampen the huge waves that were still rolling across the channel. They anchored inside the kelp bed, and with the radio dead they couldn't let anyone know they had made it through the storm.

As it turned out, they had been discussing the storm on the radio with the Coast Guard, advising how dangerous it was and how big the waves were, when the lightning struck. The Coast Guard heard the crash of lightning over the radio, then silence. A cutter was dispatched, but the charter boat couldn't be located. They did find some driftwood and assumed the boat had sunk. The Fisher's baby-sitter, "Aunt Marion" Unger, was listening to the local news when she heard that "the Fisher boat had been sunk in the storm with no trace of survivors." This caused a wave of anxiety and emotion in the Fisher household.

In the meantime, Mel, Deo, and another couple, Pat and Jackie McConkey, decided to swim to shore where there was some solid ground. The rest of the crew said they would take the boat back south when the storm let down. They swam ashore, with a few pieces of clothing tied up in a watertight rubber bag. Getting through the breakers was a feat in itself, then there was the long climb up the side of the cliff. They were at Gaviota, just north of Goleta, where the cliffs extend seaward. They could see a lighthouse not that far away and decided to walk to it. As they crossed an open field, they heard a noise behind them. It was a bull, who was sure that these strangers were not his favorite heifers.

He came charging across the field for a closer look. Mel thought that it might be his red jacket that had attracted the bull's attention. He took it off and turned it inside out; it was red on the inside as well. Then it was a race for the creek. They made it, and apparently the creek was the dividing line of the bull's domain. He stopped and snorted a few times, then trotted off to probably brag about the escapade to some young bulls watching nearby.

At the lighthouse, the keeper and his wife gave them hot coffee and peanut butter sandwiches. They talked about the storm, and after awhile the keeper drove them to Lompoc --the nearest town-- which wasn't much more than a village nestled at the base of the mountains. From there they hitch-hiked back to Los Angeles, arriving a bit tired and disheveled. When Mel and Deo walked in their front door, they were surprised to see Aunt Marion in tears. She exclaimed, "What are you doing here, you're supposed to be dead!" She was trying to muster up courage to tell the Fisher children what had happened to their parents. That evening there was a celebration of sorts, but the storm would not be soon forgotten.

↗

4...TORTUGA VOODOO

"Let's go on a treasure hunting vacation!" Four people sat around on the floor of the Fisher residence at 117 Via Pasqual in Torrance, California, when this impromptu announcement was made. Hal and Carol Corbett were over visiting that evening --no one is quite sure what brought up the subject-- but around the Fishers it seemed that sunken treasure was a common language. They had all been working hard and decided they needed some time away from city hassle.

Deo pulled a Coffman treasure atlas down from a closet shelf and opened it up. Coffman had more fantasy than fact in his atlas, but that's what dreams are made of. There were many "X" marks on Coffman's maps, so the group decided to pick an area scientifically. "Let's blindfold Mel and let him pick a spot!" So that's the way it happened. With a handkerchief snug over his eyes, and the book rotated a few times, Mel put his finger down somewhere on the map. It landed directly on Silver Shoals.

After picking a date they all began making preparations. In fact the more preparations they made, the more excited the treasure hunting vacation seemed. So exciting that within days at least twelve other divers had heard of the trip and signed up to go along, each sharing the expenses. There was no doubt Mel had the ability to conjure up treasure fever in others. The Dreamweaver was at work.

Mel flew to Miami to find a good charter boat. On the Miami River was a 65-footer, the *Kilroy*, that seemed ideal for what they had in mind. By the time the rest of the group arrived, Mel had supplies and equipment on board ready to go. They navigated down the Miami River, past Key Biscayne and the stilt houses that were becoming a common sight in the shallow water beyond. As they reached Fowey Rocks lighthouse and turned southeast, the blue waters of the Gulf Stream were not as calm as the travel magazines pictured them.

The Atlantic Ocean was a bit rough that day, and the channel crossing was not a piece of cake. It was after dark when they reached Bimini and the Bahama Banks, where the water was a bit calmer. The Fisher party settled in for the night as the captain carefully navigated his way through the clusters of small islands. Before dawn they reached the Tongue of the Ocean, a deep part of the Bahamas between the Berry Islands and Nassau. It was rough. The waves and ground swells began rocking the 65-footer around like a long-necked bottle, shaking everyone awake.

Mel and Deo Fisher with gear for Tortuga trip.

By first light the group was seasick, each wondering if they would ever cross this treacherous part of the ocean. In the late afternoon the Nassau lighthouse was a welcome sight, and they motored into the harbor with a sense of relief. Docking the boat became their first problem. The captain had never been to Nassau before, so he wasn't quite sure where to tie up. He also had not counted on the strong current that runs in the harbor when the tide is in full swing. He lined up with the dock and started his approach when an engine shut down. He had difficulty restarting the engine, and before realizing what was happening, they had shuddered into the dock...and a real plush-looking yacht tied up alongside. When the rushing for lines and fenders was over and the boat securely tied to the dock, they had to face the owner of the yacht, who was now glaring at them from the teak deck of his previously undamaged property. There was quite a dent in the yacht's hull, accompanied by some paint that didn't quite match his own glossy white. To say the least, it was not a very auspicious arrival for the treasure hunters.

It was several days later that they had their sea legs back, sufficient supplies on board to make the next leg of their journey, and extra fuel to reach Great Inagua. As the adventurers left Nassau Harbor their only concern was if fuel would be available at Matthew Town in Great Inagua, some 360 miles away. The chart didn't show much in the way of a harbor or docks, and it was a long way from nowhere. The next stop was Haiti, about sixty miles from Great Inagua, and they were even less sure of what was available there.

Initially they had intended making the trip over open water, but after the rough crossing at the Tongue of the Ocean, they decided to stay in shallow water up on the flats. From Nassau it was a beautiful trip south along the chain of Bahama Islands. Each was a picture of what they had dreamed of back in smoggy Los Angeles. Sandy beaches, palm trees, crystal-clear blue water, and flying fish bounding across a flat ocean. Everyone spent his time sunning on the open deck or hanging over the bowsprit watching the fish dart along the bottom.

Every once in awhile a pod of dolphin would settle in just ahead of the bow. The playful porpoises would dodge from one side to the other, jumping above the wake. Finally tiring of the game, they disappeared astern, and only their dorsal fins --seemingly in formation-- would break the glassy surface that stretched in all directions. It was idyllic. The trip was now becoming a pleasant experience as the divers began to look forward to the Silver Shoals and the treasure that they were sure just lay waiting for them.

The next day the boat reached Great Inagua, the last island in the Bahama chain. Here the salt flats were located, and as they anchored in the protected area to the north of the island tip, they noticed some commercial activity near shore. No docks are located at Matthew Town --a small cluster of whitewashed buildings and narrow dirt roads-- but they were able to locate some Bahamians willing to bring fuel out to their boat in 55-

gallon drums. There was nothing of interest ashore, so as soon as the fuel was loaded on board they raised anchor and headed around the tip of the island into a chop that gave them some idea of what lay ahead. The sixty miles to Haiti would take them longer than they had bargained for.

Not only was the Windward Passage rough, but halfway to Haiti the engines stopped. No one on board was mechanically minded, so they tried second-guessing what was wrong. The first thing that came to mind was water in their fuel. Not being pumped from a regular storage tank, it was a strong possibility. The fuel filter was drained repeatedly, lines cleared, and finally the engines were purring again. The group made landfall before dark and was able to dock that evening at Le Môle in Haiti. The next day, refueled and re-provisioned, they left dockage and, keeping within sight of land, they made the short trip to the island of Tortuga.

Heavy seas were breaking on the eastern side of the island, so the captain decided to anchor up on the lee side; he had had enough of rough ocean. It was a nice looking island, mountainous and covered with trees and dense foliage. The water near shore was crystal clear and not deep, and it wasn't long before someone on the bow spotted a small ballast pile. It was their first wreck, and soon they had their gear on and were over the side. It was a small wreck, and with not much of interest. Probably a small island schooner. It would have been too much to expect that treasure was that easily found.

The girls on board had a nickname for the boat captain. It was "Captain Tuna." They came up with it from a TV commercial about tuna..."Chicken of the Sea." It seemed to describe this particular captain who apparently was uncomfortable at sea on his own boat. Now Captain Tuna began to live up to his name. He had studied the charts of the Silver Shoals, and knowing that the seas would not be particularly calm in this area, he announced that he would go no further. Mel had his work cut out for him. He was a salesman and did everything he could to convince the captain that it would be a safe trip. For three days they argued, and the captain refused to budge. Mel offered to take the boat himself, leaving Tuna on Tortuga and picking him up on the way back to Miami. No deal. Finally the divers gave up and decided to enjoy Tortuga as long as they were already there.

The island of Tortuga is steeped in voodoo religion. The group soon determined that, when they visited the small native community that nestled in the south end of the island. They also learned a great deal about the island history. During the seventeenth century the island became a haven for pirates preying on the Spanish treasure fleet as it sailed up the Windward Passage. It is recorded in history that a small group of pirates, in a rowboat, boarded a large Spanish galleon in the middle of the night as it sailed between Tortuga and the mainland of Haiti. The Spaniard was on its way to Havana, and it was loaded with treasure. With no enemy ships in sight, the watch on board the galleon was relaxed, and the captain and his officers were having wine in the wardroom. The pirates silently boarded the stern and quickly took the captain and his officers prisoners. The crew could do nothing except obey orders to give up the ship.

This small band of pirates became almost legendary for their exploit, and piracy grew by leaps and bounds. Tortuga was later raided by the Spanish, scattering pirates...but only temporarily. They returned to build a fortress that kept future raiders at bay. Deposed seamen of all nationalities made their way to Tortuga to "join up." Along the way they even set up a "pirate government", but soon gave that up as a bad idea. All of this *did* cause the Spanish to alter the route that the treasure fleet took from Vera Cruz to Havana; thereafter they sailed around the western end of Cuba and Point Antonio, hugging the coast to Havana.

Another claim to fame for the island was the origin of the term "buccaneer." The first inhabitants made a living hunting down wild pigs, smoking them on a grill or barbecue in dome-shaped huts called *boucanes*. The strips of meat were sold by the *boucaniers* in bundles of a hundred for six pieces-of-eight. As the hunters became pirates, they were called "buccaneers."

The island itself was called Tortuga because it resembled a great sea tortoise, called *tortuga del mar* by the Spanish. The north end of the island was very mountainous and full of rocks. It seemed that the roots of trees wrapped themselves around the rocks for survival. The south end of the island was the only

51

inhabitable area, and there was a small harbor with two entrances. It was here that most of the island's inhabitants lived. And before the Fishers were to leave the island they would be subjected to the ways of voodoo, the religion on Tortuga.

The people on the island of Tortuga are very poor. They live by the sea and what little can be harvested from the rocky soil on the south end of the island. So when Captain Tuna dropped anchor in the small harbor, the charter boat was soon surrounded by canoes filled with local inhabitants offering pineapples and coconuts in exchange for clothes, candy, or just about anything that could be spared. Tuna made the mistake of allowing the natives to board his boat, and while he was bartering for some fresh fruit, he found the natives rummaging around on his boat and stuffing anything that wasn't nailed down into their bags. When he asked them to leave, they made believe that they couldn't understand English. After a day or two of losing tools that he could not afford to replace, he tried to keep the devils off his boat. Finally, in desperation, he fired a pistol in the air. Afterwards they remained in their canoes alongside, trading at arms length.

One thing that seemed to hold everyone's attention was the drums. They were beating constantly, spooky and a little frightening. It was later determined that the drums were a major part of the island voodoo religion. The inhabitants also used drums to communicate across the island; telephones hadn't quite made it to Tortuga by the mid-1950s. When Fisher's group first visited the small village they noticed drums everywhere. In fact, some were ten or twelve feet in diameter. As they watched, a small, dwarf-sized native who was quite a gymnast used the drums like a trampoline. He bounded from one to the other, actually playing voodoo music as he went.

The day before the divers planned to head back to Miami, four in the group decided to check out some caves up in the side of the mountain. The buccaneers supposedly stashed their booty somewhere on the island, and they didn't want to miss a chance at discovering a hidden chest of gold and silver. One of the four, Joan Shaw, was a high school friend of Deo Fisher, and she promised they would be back before dark that night. It was after sunset, and before long it was pitch black around the island. They began to worry about their four companions, knowing that it would be easy to get lost in the dense underbrush that covered the sides of the mountains. Then the voodoo drums started.

Everyone in Mel's group came topside when the drums moved down to the water's edge. Before long they could hear the "splish-splash" of paddles, or hands, as the drums now moved out over the water towards them. It was so dark the Fisher team could not see the canoes, but soon they realized that canoes were all around them. Captain Tuna had the men break out their weapons, some even had spear guns, and line the rail in the event that the natives tried to mob them.

Suddenly everything went silent. No one spoke, each straining to see or hear something, anything. They no longer could hear the sound of paddling, or even whispers, and thankfully...the drums were silent as well. It was fifteen, possibly twenty minutes when they realized the boat was drifting out to sea! The natives had cut their anchor line and made off with the boat's anchor.

It was frustrating; nothing seemed safe. Tuna was ready to head back to Miami that night, but with four people still on the island, he couldn't. Mel wasn't sure if they had gotten lost, or possibly kidnapped, but everyone was concerned. The next morning they checked the village out...but still no signs of the missing treasure hunters. It was about 2:00 p.m. when the truant divers suddenly appeared on the dock, waving to be picked up.

It was a relief to have them back on board. They had quite a story to tell. They had visited several caves up on the side of the nearest mountain facing the sea, and on the way back they stopped at a Catholic monastery. As it turned out there was a monk who lived there and spoke excellent English. He had built a large stone house which served as a clinic, and he was studying zombies. At the time there were at least a hundred zombies living on Tortuga, and he was attempting to figure out why they believed in the supernatural power of reanimating a corpse. These people acted as if they had their souls stolen by sorcery. He had hopes that he could cure these poor devils of the malady.

Deo's classmate's husband was a doctor, another of the four who had taken the cave tour, and he became quite interested in what the monk had to say. So interested in fact, that before they realized it, the sun had gone down. The monk advised them against trying to go down the mountain in the dark and offered them a place to spend the night. They accepted. Too bad none of them understood drum talk, or they could have signaled the boat where they were.

As Tuna made preparations to leave the island, Mel asked if he could run a magnetometer survey along the edge of the island. Some day, conditions changing, the group might want to come back and dive any wrecks they might find. Mel and the others strung out the "mag" and started a slow, systematic survey on the west side of the island. They were getting "hits", or anomalies, on the magnetometer, and when they did, one of the divers would throw a weighted buoy over the stern of the boat to mark the spot. Mel intended to come back after the survey and dive each hit to see if they had an old shipwreck. Most everyone was watching the mag readout, when someone turned around to look over the stern. "Hey, they're stealing our buoys!" Sure enough, the first buoy they had dropped was about a mile away, and a dugout canoe had already picked up that buoy and was heading back to the beach. At the next buoy they could see a canoe alongside, and someone was pulling up their float. The last buoy they had dropped was about half a mile astern, and already a canoe was closing on that one fast...they must have been desperate for lobster trap lines.

This was a signal to Mel's group that it was useless to do much more in the way of treasure hunting, so reluctantly they let Captain Tuna head his boat back to Miami. The trip had been exciting, certainly different, and the adventurers could yarn ashore about this one for some time.

5...LEOPARD RAYS DON'T PLAY

Mel, Deo, and Doc Mathison were in the Virgin Islands making underwater movies --some planned, some not so planned. Mel had received a contract from Pan American Airways and Jantzen Swimwear for some underwater footage titled *Wings Over and Under Haiti*. The waters around St. Thomas offered better subject material than Haiti, and as long as the movie was exciting, it really did not matter where it was taken. One of the exciting sequences they had in mind was filming sharks in a feeding frenzy. Easier said than done. First they had to locate sharks, bait them, then film them...without becoming part of the feeding frenzy. Without a shark cage, that wasn't an easy job of casting.

The Virgin Islands offered just about everything an underwater movie enthusiast could ask for. Crystal clear water, an abundance of sharks, and a nice vacation place with great shopping in Charlotte Amalie. When Mel arrived in St. Thomas he learned that Peter Gimble's yacht *Melindie* was available for charter, along with a French captain. The film crew struck a deal and moved their gear aboard. The local dive shops were a big help in directing them to the best shark holes around St. Thomas. After buying a few provisions and checking the charts, they headed out of the channel, past Waters Island, turned north, and set a course for Savannah Island about fifteen miles away.

The Virgin Islands are made up of a number of small islands grouped around the island of St. Thomas. To the west, and across a twenty-mile channel, is the island of Culebra on the eastern extreme of Puerto Rico. To the east is the island of St. John, and just beyond is Tortola, Virgin Gorda, and the rest of the British Virgin Islands. The islands rise up sharply out of the deep, created by volcanoes many years ago, and, unlike St. Thomas, many of the islands have little or no vegetation on them. Such is Savannah Island, fairly small, void of vegetation, deep water on all sides but with a small sheltered cove and sixty feet to a sandy bottom.

A young diver by the name of Slaughter had made quite a name for himself in the Virgin Islands when he reduced the shark population by at least fifty, using an explosive head at the end of a bang-stick. One of the major magazines carried a feature article on his exploits, and it is quite possible that the shark population around Savannah Island had a grudge to settle with anything resembling a man-fish.

Mel, Deo, and Doc Mathison in British Virgin Islands.

By noontime the Fisher group had anchored the Gimble yacht inside the cove. This day had begun with the catching of bait fish. Reef fish, when caught and strung on a long line tethered to an inner tube, make excellent bait fish for sharks. Before long there were several inner tubes, each with tethered fish at the end of fifteen feet of line, being pulled in every direction. The inner tubes started inside the cove, near where *Melindie* was anchored, but before long the action moved out into open water. Mel, Deo, and Doc Mathison were in hot pursuit, lugging underwater cameras and waiting...watching...for large gray shadows to come up out of the deep water. And they were not disappointed.

Soon the predators were there, circling the fish now desperately trying to get away from that bobbing nemesis that held them to the surface. With cameras filming the action, the sharks "rolled for dinner"! Too quickly it was over. There were too few fish and too many sharks, and soon they were joined by more dark shapes that seemed to come from nowhere, attracted by the sound of the reef fish as they tried to escape. Suddenly, the sharks turned on each other, thrashing and biting, and the area became a feeding frenzy that Mel hadn't counted on. It was only then that the film crew realized what potential bait *they* were and that the sharks were hungry!

The divers could see the yacht anchored inside the cove, but it was now too far away to even consider outswimming a pack of hungry sharks. The nearest haven was a rocky ledge where Savannah Island seemed to drop into the sea. It was about four feet below the surface and covered with spiny sea urchins. Even this was better than being served up for dinner to a pack of hungry sharks. In what seemed like an eternity they made it safely to the ledge and scrambled up. Now, surrounded by sea urchins, they seemed safe and secure. Mel first spotted the big shark taking aim on them, and it was coming like a freight train, its jaws wide open. There was a mad scramble off the ledge and up the steep rocks out of the water. They made it just in time and had a close look at a six-foot gray reef shark as it barreled across the narrow ledge the swimmers had just vacated.

Suddenly forgotten was the reef covered with spiny sea urchins. Not until they were high and dry did they realize how many urchins they had stepped on or brushed against in their mad scramble. The divers sat for the next hour or so pulling the black needles out of their feet, legs, and hands. Many of the spines broke off under the skin, reminding them days later, as the wounds became painfully infected, of the close call they had at Savannah Island.

While in the Virgin Islands Mel wanted some movie footage of shipwrecks. It seemed that all the television stations back in California wanted footage on shipwrecks. One of the better known wreck sites in the Virgin Islands is the *Rhone*. The *Rhone* was a British ship launched in 1865 to serve as a mail-carrying passenger ship in Caribbean waters. With two masts and an abundance of sails, she also had a coal-fired steam engine to push her through the water at eighteen knots. At 310 feet in length and forty feet wide, she drafted at 2,738 tons and could carry 253 first-class passengers, thirty second-class, and thirty third-class. On her maiden voyage from Southampton to South America she had to make a stopover in the Virgin Islands for more coal. Arriving on 2 October 1867 with a full complement of passengers and loaded with mail, she anchored outside Great Harbour, Peter Island, just across the main channel from Roadtown. Captain Wooley anchored her alongside her sister ship *RMS Conway*.

Supposedly, the hurricane season was over. So, when the barometer began to fall dramatically, Captain Wooley believed it only signaled a high wind out of the north. He decided he would up anchor and head for more protection across the channel near Roadtown, where the hills would provide more shelter from high winds out of the north. Before he could move, a strong wind -- reaching hurricane proportions-- came out of the northwest and blew for over an hour. The *Rhone* faced the wind with her engine running at full power and was able to keep from being blown onto the rocks of Peter Island. When the first assault of the wind died down, both the *Conway* and the *Rhone* got underway and headed for Roadtown. The *Conway* made it, but the *Rhone* snagged her 3,000-pound anchor on the bottom and had to abandon it, along with 300 feet of chain. Without an anchor to hold her, Wooley decided the only chance he had against the wind was to head for the open ocean through Salt Island Passage.

But now the hurricane came out of the southeast, and the Salt Island Passage was a mass of boiling, foaming water. With little visibility, the *Rhone* headed for the opening, and just as it seemed she would make it, a stronger blast of wind hit her, and she was driven onto Black Rock Point, the westernmost tip of Salt Island. Her superheated boilers exploded as the cooler Caribbean waters hit them, and the *Rhone* broke into two pieces. She sank immediately in 82 feet of water. Only 23 crewmen and a single passenger survived. The hurricane cost over 500 lives in the Virgins and as many as 75 vessels foundered on the rocks or were sunk at sea. It was a devastating hurricane.

After the hurricane passed the *Rhone*'s stern lay in forty feet of water --her bow in deeper water-- with her hull rolled to the starboard side. Over the years the wooden deck disappeared, and the stanchions projected above the sandy bottom like sentinels. Large sections of the wreck remained intact, including the bow section, boiler machinery, and the ship's propeller. It was an ideal wreck site for the Fisher group to film.

To obtain good underwater footage you need clear water, sunlight, and the water must be calm. Even a slight ocean breeze can cause a surface chop that makes underwater filming shadowy and less than desirable. In the shark scenes off Savannah, Mel did not have the ocean "surge" to worry about. That's the movement over the bottom as ocean swells roll in from deep water. It moves swimmers and equipment like Ping-Pong balls in a high wind. Mel wasn't prepared for any of this as they anchored the Gimble yacht near Salt Island that evening. They could see the dark shadow of the *Rhone* near their anchorage, but they could wait until morning before their first dive.

Before breakfast the next morning, Mel was suited up, and with a speargun in hand he rolled over the side and began a swim the length of the wreck site. Like many wrecks this ship had become an artificial reef covered with marine vegetation. Large schools of colorful fish had made their home in the *Rhone*, and they seemed to be everywhere. Other large fish also made their home in the *Rhone*, as Mel was soon to find out. The rakish bow section was still intact and in deep water. It had become a condominium for jewfish, and even without a SCUBA tank Mel was able to dive the 84 feet and do a little exploring. As he checked it out he met up with a rather perturbed 350-pound jewfish which had taken up residence there. With the sudden presence of this man-fish the jewf .h thumped hard, thrashed his tail, and created quite a stir of sediment as he moved back inside the hull. It was too large a fish to spear at that depth without a tank of air, and without an underwater camera there wasn't a reason to disrupt the morning tour.

As he swam the length of the *Rhone*, Mel was joined by an entourage of curious fish. This was their reef, and not too many fish with one big eye and two tails came to visit. It was rather peaceful that morning, the sun just getting above the eastern end of Salt Island and making rippling shadows of the jumbled iron beams and machinery below him. It was breakfast time, and Mel headed back towards the yacht anchored some 300 feet away. Suddenly the swarm of colorful fish that had been following him flashed away. A larger, dark shadow now followed his fins as they pumped him along the surface. It was when the shadow moved up alongside him that he was suddenly aware of the largest barracuda he had ever seen. Mel was six foot three inches tall, and this fish was larger than Mel and looked a lot more menacing in the morning light than one can imagine. The 'cuda was full of plainly visible teeth. The morning swim took on a whole new proportion of excitement as this large, toothy reef resident first moved ahead of Mel...and then did a slow turn to face him. It was a Mexican standoff.

As the chill began to work along the back of Mel's neck, he suddenly remembered the speargun clutched in his fist. It had been completely forgotten in this moment of sudden confrontation. Now the only worry Mel had was whether he could spear the fish safely, because a wounded large barracuda has very unpredictable moves. Some divers have been severely bitten by much smaller barracuda than the one now moving slowly towards him. He considered trying to just fend off the fish as it made a move to close in on him, but the barracuda made the decision for him. It began circling him, its jaws snapping, and each circle got smaller. Mel picked his best spot for a shot, just behind the gill plate, and as the fish passed within three feet of him, he fired. The result was instantaneous! A thrash of fury and savage whipping of the tail as the seven-foot barracuda took off on the end of the spear line. Mel had a seventy-foot parachute shroud line attached to the spear, and he let the fish thrash to the bottom where it rolled and fought the steel shaft. It stirred the bottom over a large area, but finally Mel was able to tow the fish back to the yacht, where he had quite a story to tell over a morning cup of coffee.

After a breakfast filled with a little barracuda excitement the Fisher group suited up, and with the camera equipment stowed aboard their eleven-foot skiff they headed for the wreck of the *Rhone*. It had turned into a beautiful day for diving. The ocean was flat calm and the water so clear you could count the queen conchs as they tracked across the flat, sandy bottom. Soon they were anchored over the stern section of the wreck forty feet below them. This part of the wreck was recognizable because about thirty feet of the stern was intact, with the huge propeller clearly visible. One of the propeller's blades was broken when the ship hit bottom with the engine turning at full speed. The drive shaft connected the stern section to a gear box that was barely recognizable because of the heavy coral growth.

Beyond the gear box lay the ship's engine, surrounded by debris that had once been the first-class cabin area marked by the numerous portholes. There were two boilers on the *Rhone*, one scattered towards shallow water, the other managed to remain near the engine and condenser tubes. What made the wreck interesting to Mel was the supports of the timber deck. The wood had long ago been eaten by teredo worms or scattered by storms, but the iron columns stood upright like a classical Greek ruin and now wore a colorful mantle of coral and sea growth. A small signaling cannon lay to one side of the columns.

As Mel, Doc Mathison, and the French captain swam the length of the wreck, the hull seemed like a huge warehouse out of place on the sea bed. Davits still swung out, empty of lifeboats. In later years this place would be the location of the filming of *The Deep*. As deeper water cast a blue shadow over the forward deck area they could make out the forward mast where it lay in the sand alongside the hull. Even the crow's nest, two-thirds the way up the mast, was still distinguishable. The anchors, normally stowed on the forward deck, were gone, lost in the savage hurricane that sank the *Rhone*. The rakish bow, still intact, lay in 84 feet of water, barely visible as the group turned back towards the stern.

The number of fish that made their home in and around the wreck was unbelievable! They were everywhere, swirling and flashing, or hanging as a cloud to be moved by larger predator fish that had their choice at mealtime. Somewhere near the center section of the site Doc Mathison grabbed Mel by the arm and pointed to a large spotted leopard ray that had emerged from deeper water and was now gliding along the sandy bottom near them. It had a wingspan of at least nine feet and a long whiplash tail. If he could ride the ray, it would make a great film sequence, and Mel decided to go for it.

The speargun still had the seventy feet of parachute cord attached, so Mel skinned down and planted the spear in the meaty part of the wing. With a thump and a billow of sand the ray was off for deeper water. Mel had time to just reach the surface before the parachute line was taut, and he found himself being towed through the water at breakneck speed. At first it was hard to keep his mask on, so he held it with one hand, the speargun with the other. Doc Mathison was filming the scene, but the scene soon left Doc far behind. Mel was being towed out to sea, and the only choice he had was either to let go of the speargun, or hang on for the ride. He hung on. It was a powerful leopard ray, and it wasn't about to tire easily. It was now out into deeper water, and Mel could not see bottom, but he was able to keep the ray from sounding by hauling in on the line which now seemed to bind this man-creature and sea-creature together. Mel began to wonder if he could make it back to the skiff once this sea ride was over.

In the meantime, Doc and the yacht captain had gotten into the skiff, hoping to catch up to the fast disappearing Mel Fisher. Trouble was the outboard engine wouldn't start. There is always that time when you need an engine to start and...nothing. They soon gave up and began rowing the boat in the direction they last saw Mel. In the meantime, the ray had decided to make a wide sweep and head back towards his home near the wreck site. Just as Doc had about given up, here came Mel waving his arm as the ray towed him by the skiff. Doc threw Mel a line, and they secured it to the speargun and the stern of the boat. Mel climbed aboard, happy to know he wouldn't be spending the night at sea, but his troubles were just beginning. The ray was towing the boat backwards towards the Rhone, and they were in danger of swamping. Finally the ray reached the sandy area alongside the wreck and settled to the bottom.

Mel pointing to leopard ray barb holes in his arm.
(1995 photo by Bob Weller)

A lot of the sizzle had gone out of the ray, so Mel felt it would be safe to take a ride holding on to the wing of the fish. He had Doc get the camera ready, and then dived down to where the ray had settled in the sand. Grabbing the leading edge of the ray's wing he braced himself, and just in time as the ray took off. As he did he whipped his tail over, and it was then that Mel realized that the ray had five large barbs near the base of his tail. They would be deadly if he got too close to them, so with one eye on the barbs and the other on the ray's eyes just a few inches away, he was able to steer the fish towards the surface and grab a lungful of air.

He shifted from one wing of the ray to the other, and as he did the fish whipped the tail over again, narrowly missing Mel with his barbs. In the meantime, Doc was getting some great film footage.

The ride lasted several minutes, and Mel seemed to be in control of the situation. It was when the ray did a sudden loop, twisting as it went, that Mel lost it. He didn't see the barbs until he felt them hit him in the upper right arm. It was numbing; it seemed that his arm was in a huge vise, and he couldn't scream out in pain. The ray was dragging him down into deep water, and the barbs had been driven right into the bone! It was the sudden impact of how serious the situation was that was bone chilling.

Mel was being pulled under water, and he could not pull loose from the barbs. Blood, green under water, was pouring from the two wounds, trailing behind as the ray dived deeper. Mel tried to brace his feet against the back of the ray and pull loose. The fins slipped, and he couldn't get his feet under himself. He was losing his breath, and he was now getting desperate. He had to do something, or he would drown. The ray had taken him over eighty feet deep, and it was a last desperate effort as Mel was able to brace his feet under him and push. The barbs did not come out of his arm, but instead broke off the ray's tail. He was free, and he wasted no time in racing to the surface. He just made it and gulped for air as he broke the surface. The skiff was nearby, and Doc Mathison was some distance away, swimming the camera back to the boat.

Fisher looked at his arm and saw two large four-inch-long barbs imbedded in the underside of his right arm. They were bleeding profusely, and he knew that as soon as the venom wore off...they would hurt! At that moment his arm was still numb, so as the French captain brought the skiff alongside, he asked if there was a pair of pliers in the boat. At least he tried to ask...but he did not know the French word for "pliers." He thought he could pull the barbs out before they became too painful. There wasn't a pair of pliers in the boat, and Mel gritted his teeth as Doc finally came up alongside and handed up the camera. "Some trip!" said Doc. Then he saw the blood streaming down Mel's arm. He quickly got in the boat, saw that the damage was severe, and said, "Let's head for the yacht pronto!"

Back on board the yacht Doc Mathison was able to surgically remove the two barbs, but as Deo later said, "It looked like a real mess." Doc and Deo were more than beside themselves, but Mel seemed to keep a cool head. He seemed in charge of the situation and accepted the fact that he paid for the risk he took. Doc's only regret was that he missed the last ride because the camera ran out of film. The captain quickly got underway, and late that day they were docked in Charlotte Amalie. At the local hospital they gave Mel a tetanus shot, morphine, some antibiotics, and cleaned out the two large holes in his upper right arm. After refusing a suggestion that he spend the night in the hospital, Mel got up off the emergency room operating bed, took two steps, and fainted.

That evening they had a big discussion on whether to wrap up the filming project and head back to California or take a few more days to complete the last section of the project. They had planned on finding "treasure" on this trip, and they had carried a small treasure chest as a prop for the occasion. Mel decided, as always, to finish the project in spite of the pain in his right arm.

Maegen Bay is a magnificent sandy beach that curves in a half moon. Surrounded by palm trees, it is considered one of the top beaches in the Caribbean. They decided to complete their filming there, and the weather cooperated. Within three days, and with the help of the local dive club, the Blue Mantas, they had wrapped their *Wings Over and Under Haiti* sequences and were on a 'plane heading back to California. The film was delivered to the editor, Homer Groening, and several weeks later came a telegram that made all the pain and anxiety worthwhile. It read, "Your film better than 'Beneath The Red Sea'."

6...PANAMA ADVENTURE

Mel's Aqua Shop was a success. Divers around southern California would spend their spare time just standing around talking to other divers as they visited the shop to get their tanks filled or to buy new equipment. It was a meeting place, and Mel enjoyed the companionship. Small talk always seemed to turn up more rumors of sunken treasure, and it really didn't take much to get the adrenaline flowing. Often Mel was asked the question, "When is the next treasure trip?"

For six years, whenever Mel came up with underwater projects, it meant chartering a boat, and the size depended upon the number of divers involved. The boats he had chartered never seemed to be equipped exactly the way he would like, and he never had total control of where they went nor how long they would stay. It was 1960, and somewhere along the way Mel had hoped that this was the year to buy a boat of his own. He and Deo decided that they would find a boat that would help their dive business, but also allow them to plan some long distance dreaming. And dreams of sunken galleons seemed to pervade their everyday lives.

Mel had hired some good people to help him run his business, people that he could rely on and who were as enthusiastic about diving as he was. It meant that he and Deo could take extended trips on treasure diving adventures without worrying about the business. Mel's father and mother took an active part in his Aqua Shop --it was a quiet retirement for them-- and they enjoyed listening to the bubbly excitement of divers recalling encounters with the underwater unknown. Deo's mother, and his Aunt Marion, were great with the growing Fisher clan. Dirk, Kim, and Kane were sprouting like stalks in a cornfield, and within a few months they would have a baby sister. In May, 1961, Mel and Deo had their first daughter. Taffi had red hair like her mother and the infectious smile that both of her parents were blessed with. She would complete the Fisher clan, all destined to become major players in the sunken treasure years that were about to begin.

Mel found a 65-foot boat with a white hull, twin diesel engines, and wide of beam, making an ideal diving platform. It was large enough to carry provisions, fuel, and a fair-size group of crew and divers on an extended operation. He named her *Golden Doubloon*, and although he had yet to find his first one, he hoped his luck would change with this new pride. With a boat this size Mel was now able to organize treasure hunting trips with more imagination and attention to detail. It also gave him the experience he would need in the years to come. Years later, both Mel and Deo would look back on these building years as the foundation that would carry them through some of the roughest times a couple could ever hope to endure.

The **Golden Doubloon** *in the Channel Islands.*

Records indicated that most of the treasure galleons which sank did so in the Caribbean. Stories of wrecked galleons on the Pedro Banks ninety miles from Jamaica soon held Mel's attention, and he began putting together his first major treasure hunting expedition in that direction. The hunt he had in mind would take the *Golden Doubloon* south along the coast of California and the

"Baja", across an open stretch of Pacific Ocean, and to the coast of Mexico. From there it was sight-of-land navigating to the Panama Canal. Once they were across the Panama Canal, they would be...in the Caribbean! What started out as a simple plan, flavored with the excitement of a treasure hunt, was about to spell near disaster for Mel and his crew.

The crowd around the Aqua Shop soon got word of the proposed Caribbean treasure hunt, and they wanted in! Before long Mel had twenty-five divers, each willing to throw a thousand dollars in the pot for a seat on the boat. The boat wouldn't hold that many, so a "names in a hat" selection process began. A date was set for shoving off, and from there planning moved rapidly. Supplies were ordered, and room on the after deck was cleared for a sixteen-foot Boston Whaler. Mel built additional bunk space to accommodate the divers, and he added a freezer, a new single sideband radio, and up-to-date charts of the Pedro Banks. Soon the supplies arrived and were loaded on board, fuel tanks were topped off, and loose ends at home were tied up. Mel found himself running down the dock just to do simple errands.

Eddie Tsukimura, captain of the **Golden Doubloon.**

The magic was contagious. Divers brought their wives or girlfriends to the dock to see the *Doubloon,* peer into the bunkrooms, or gaze down into cargo spaces. Some of the divers had work conflicts and decided to catch the *Doubloon* when it docked in Colón, Panama. Mel hired a captain to help him with the boat, and soon Captain Eddie Tsukimura was right at home storing supplies, running down tool lists, and checking out navigation equipment. Eddie brought his wife Masa along, and down the road the divers would praise her cooking. A nebulous mechanic by the name of Carl worked his way on board, rounding out the crew.

Then it was time. The day to shove off dawned with the promise of a journey full of sunshine and flat seas. Actually, the trip down the Baja peninsula went very quickly and smoothly. Fish, seals, and an occasional whale were common sights as the *Golden Doubloon* moved south along the coast. After several refueling stops, including the one that most of the divers looked forward to...Acapulco...they pulled into the port of Panama City on the Pacific side of the canal. Tailgating some large merchant vessels through the various locks, they eventually found themselves on the Colón side of the isthmus. They could almost smell the Caribbean breezes, and they just knew that sunken galleons, loaded with treasure, lay just beyond.

It was time to get "hyper", to feel the excitement that Mel had managed to generate back in Redondo Beach. The important thing was that they had a common goal, a common dream, a togetherness of determination. As they pulled alongside the dock at Colón, the rest of the group from California was already there waving. It was quite a reunion, and it took a while to tell the newcomers how much they had missed by not making the first leg of the journey. The number on board now totaled twenty-one, just enough to be cramped...but comfortable. The excitement of treasure makes cramped quarters a little more bearable.

While in Colón Mel had some last-minute shopping to do for fresh food and more supplies. His mechanic, Carl, decided to fly the coop. No one really saw him leave. As Mel stepped off the boat he asked John, a young teen-ager that was along on the trip, to change the oil. It was a simple task, and John jumped at the opportunity. He looked through the boat's lockers for cans of oil, but he found none labeled "oil". He did find some quart cans of liquid that certainly looked like oil, and he drained them into the engines.

The *Doubloon* left the dock early the next morning, heading out past the small islands that line the entrance to Panama. It was a pleasant day, sultry, so the Caribbean breeze was a welcome relief. Before long the open sea stretched out in all directions, and a feeling of anticipation had "all hands" topside. Mel was in the process of showing everyone the chart and where the Pedro Banks were located, when the first engine shut down. Without a mechanic on board, no one had any idea what the cause might be. Before they could tackle the problem, the other engine shut down. They were dead in the water, over thirty miles from land, and the current was taking them in the wrong direction, away from Colón.

Engines are always a mystery to people not mechanically inclined, but some situations can lead to an instant education. Diesel engines either run...or they don't run, so whatever was wrong had to be something basic. After some hesitation, John mentioned his oil change, and went to the storage locker where the cans of "oil" were stored. As it turned out, what John had poured into the crankcases was fiberglass resin! Oil and resin look the same, but resin has a rather binding effect on crankshafts. The engines had frozen up. After draining as much of the resin from the engines as was possible and refilling with oil, the engines were restarted. The group decided that it would be best to return to Colón and have the engines looked at by a mechanic. It temporarily put a damper on the air of excitement on board the *Golden Doubloon*, but with Mel's cheery attitude and Deo's smile things were soon back on course.

They arrived back at Colón late that afternoon, and Mel called a local machine shop that worked on boat engines. The owner had a look at the engines and said he would send a mechanic over first thing in the morning. Demostines Molinar, a young man with an infectious smile, was born and raised in Colón. In his twenty-five years he had never really traveled far from the docks of Colón. He had heard of, and read in the local newspapers about, the *"Gringos Locos"* that were on a treasure hunting expedition. Now his boss at the machine shop was sending him down to the docks to work on their boat.

"Mo", as he soon became known, stepped aboard the *Golden Doubloon* half expecting to see swarthy, "piratical" looking Americans covered in gold doubloons and pieces-of-eight. Instead, he was pleasantly surprised at the friendly greeting he received from everyone on board. These people were certainly down to earth, and the tall one they called "Mel" was careful to explain everything that had happened to the engines. They all offered to help in any way they could. The group seemed to like the way Mo worked...and certainly his pleasant nature.

Before he left that day, Mel asked Mo a few questions about family and his ties to the machine shop. Satisfied with the answers, Mel asked him if he would like to come to work for him. "I'll take you to Disneyland!" There may have been some discussion about treasure diving, but the salary Mel was offering him was more than twice what he was making then. He was single --and with no real strings attached-- so he accepted Mel's offer.

Mel needed a good diesel mechanic, and although Mo didn't know how to dive, he could swim like a fish. Mo would become a real asset to the expedition and in Mel's operation back in California. In order to keep from being delayed by customs and immigration people, Mel suggested that Mo stow away in the rope locker until they got offshore from Panama.

The *Golden Doubloon* left the Colón docks early the next morning, and by noontime they were well out of sight of land. What they were not aware of was a weather bureau announcement that a hurricane had just entered the Caribbean Basin. Their first real clue was the long, undulating ground swells without an accompanying wind to push them, that indicated a storm lay somewhere ahead. It was these swells, as well as the intense heat, that brought Mo out of the rope locker...to everyone's surprise except Mel's. The group wouldn't know until later just how happy they would be to have Mo on board.

It was late in the afternoon, and the ground swells had been building all day long. Now they reached twenty feet high, and the weather began to look pretty nasty. Black clouds filled the horizon to the southeast, and the wind seemed to come and go from different directions. When the wind began to blow steadily from the west, and much stronger, a sense of uneasiness crept over the group. Now they were hanging on to anything that didn't move...to keep from being thrown overboard. It became even more critical when the wind moved in the completely opposite direction of the ground swells. Now there were ten-foot-high breaking waves on top of the twenty-foot swells. Green water was coming down hard over the bow and forward cabin roof. To make matters even worse, as the boat slid down the back side of the swells, the stern began taking water over the side.

The sixteen-foot Boston Whaler, plywood, sacks of potatoes, and tools were weighting down the stern. The *Doubloon* began to sink lower in the water. Mel had Mo open up the hatch to the after lazaretto deck, and they found it full of water. Mel then opened the next hatch forward, and that space was full of water. About that time someone made the announcement, "The bilge pumps aren't working!" Suddenly, everyone realized that they were in danger of sinking. The reaction was spontaneous. Mel hollered, "Get some buckets!", and he had Mo climb down into the after lazaretto deck. The water came up to his chest. Someone climbed down into the next hatch and cleared away some floating debris. In moments a bucket brigade was started, as pails were filled with water and handed up to be thrown over the side.

It was too dangerous to try turning the boat around into the waves; the *Doubloon* would surely have capsized. All that could be done was to keep bailing. There were six watertight bulkheads in the *Golden Doubloon*; the engine room was in the fourth compartment. As long as the engine kept running they had a chance. They bailed feverishly. Now the Boston Whaler was gone, washed away by a large wave. Mel had the heavy items in the stern thrown overboard as well, trying to raise it up out of the water more. There was still a small dinghy stowed forward, and Mel turned to one of the women and told her to put some water and cans of food in that boat in case they needed it. It was an ominous order, one that turned some faint hearts stone cold.

The bucket brigade was making progress, until a large wave broke over the stern. The men scrambled out of the lower compartments as the water completely flooded the after deck. Mel opened the hatch to the rope locker and the third compartment, and that too was almost full of water. He turned to Eddie

Tsukimura and said, "Send an S.O.S.!" Eddie needed no prompting, and in seconds you could hear him above the howling wind calling, "Mayday, Mayday!!" Now the stern was under water, and the only thing keeping the *Doubloon* afloat was the remaining three watertight compartments. The engines were still running, but water had begun to leak into that compartment as well. It was time to do something dramatic, or they would soon sink.

Mel had an idea. There were still several sheets of 3/4-inch plywood on board, along with some two-by-four studs. "Let's build a cofferdam around the stern. It'll keep the water out while we bail!" There was at least three feet of water over the after deck, so Mel quickly slipped on a SCUBA tank, lashed a rope around his waist and attached it to a cleat to keep himself from washing overboard, and went to work. Grabbing a handful of sixteen-penny nails and a hammer he began nailing the plywood to the sides of the stern.

Mo had never put on a tank before, but in moments he had a mask and a tank on and was helping Mel nail down the plywood. Soon they had two sheets of plywood down each side, and two across the stern, effectively raising the sides above the level of the water. Everyone began bailing water, and just when they had the level down to the deck...a big wave smashed into the stern, knocking the plywood down. Mel and Mo never said a word; they put the tanks back on and began nailing the sides back up. This time they braced the sides with the two-by-fours, wedging them as solidly as they could. Once the walls were up, the bucket brigade resumed.

While they were bailing, they heard a ship answering Eddie on the radio. It was the *S. S. Olympia*, a Venezuelan freighter. The Venezuelans were about eighty miles away, and even though they were also taking a beating from the hurricane, they said that they were on their way to rescue them. There was a sense of relief just knowing that someone out there knew that they were close to sinking. It may have eased the tension somewhat, but the cofferdam was what turned things around for everyone. Now they bailed furiously, and gradually the stern came up out of the water.

The cofferdam held this time, and before long they had most of the water out of the after compartments.

The wind and the ground swells were as strong as ever, and the *Golden Doubloon* was still on a course that was taking them closer to the storm and farther away from land. They had to get the boat turned around and headed back to Colón. With the stern filled with water they would have capsized had they tried turning it against the wind. Now, they had a slim chance of making it. The waves and swells seemed to come in series, and somewhere Mel remembered that every seventh wave was the large one. It did not seem that there was a break between successive waves, and so they waited. If the boat was still sluggish, the chances were they would not get it turned before the next big wave hit them broadside. If that happened, the boat would capsize. It was a chance they were going to have to take. They waited, counting each wave, and when it seemed they had a slight lull, Eddie threw the wheel full starboard. The *Doubloon* began to respond, agonizingly slow at first, and then as the bow crested on a wave the stern swung around...and they were headed back to Colón!

Now they were taking waves head on, but the ground swells were pushing the boat ahead like a surfboard. Eddie jockeyed the engines, keeping the *Doubloon* from dropping down between swells, and they were no longer at the mercy of the hurricane. As soon as they had settled down, and everyone began breathing a sigh of relief, Eddie sent a message to the freighter *Olympia*, telling them that they were out of trouble. The *Olympia* responded by saying that that was a relief, because they were really taking a pounding. There was another call on the radio from Jamaica. As it turned out, Ann, one of the young ladies on board, had an older boyfriend in Jamaica that had picked up the distress call on his ham radio, and he had been frantically trying to raise someone on the *Golden Doubloon*. Love had its way, and once it was clear that the *Golden Doubloon* was out of danger, there were a few fond words spoken that brought a few smiles from the others on board.

The next morning they pulled up to the docks at Colón. The boat was a mess, but you could sense the relief on everyone's face as soon as they had good solid ground under their feet. For the next three days they all turned to, fixing up the boat and making it shipshape again. Ann decided that she would fly to Jamaica, and everyone wished her well. The first chance they all had to sit down together and kick things around, it was generally decided that they would give up the idea of going to the Pedro Banks off Jamaica. The *Doubloon* was never meant to take long trips across open water unless conditions were ideal.

In spite of the narrow escape, there was still some treasure hunting left in the group. The after effects of the hurricane were still hanging around, high waves and poor visibility, so they opted to go to the San Blas Islands. This was a small group of islands about sixty miles to the east of Panama, and also directly in the path of galleons sailing from Cartagena to Porto Bello. It seemed to be an ideal location to look for shipwrecks.

The sun was out, the skies seemed to have cleared, and spirits were up as the Fisher group left the harbor for the third time and turned eastward towards the San Blas Islands. Thirty miles down the coast was Porto Bello, the terminal of Spanish galleons, where each year the *feria* was held and European goods were traded for the precious gold and silver. It was the isthmus through which forty percent of the ships of trade passed on their way back to Spain. Until the Spanish fleet arrived each year, Porto Bello was a sleepy, mosquito infested harbor town. But once the fleet arrived, the fair began.

Merchants piled silver bars in stacks along the road, ignored by the local inhabitants. Prostitutes came to ply their trade with the sailors that had been away from home too long. Jugglers and magicians came to entertain, and proprietors set up temporary hotel rooms with fresh, hot water, a luxury to shipboard sailors and soldiers. The fair would keep the galleons in harbor for several months at a time, and over the years storms and hurricanes would take their toll. Scattered about the harbor and islands, as well as the reefs directly off shore, lie the ballast piles of many shipwrecks.

That night the *Golden Doubloon* was anchored inside the harbor, and most of the group went ashore in the small dinghy. There were few people living in Porto Bello; the ghost galleons had long ago disappeared, and the town had slipped back in time to the sleepy, mosquito-ridden town of legends. They were able to strike up a conversation with the more curious people who came to stare at the *Gringos Locos,* and soon they were trading canned goods for a few silver coins and a cane sword that one of the townspeople had found. Then they visited an old church near the center of town, one that had weathered the winds of time...and probably more hurricanes than anyone could remember. An older fisherman happened by, and Mel asked about local shipwrecks. The old man responded by waving his arm across the broad expanse of the harbor, and he smiled. Mel understood. The day had been a long one, and soon they were back aboard *Doubloon* in favor of an early morning start.

Cuna Indians in the San Blas Islands off Panama.

By sun-up the anchor was hauled, and *Doubloon* turned towards the harbor entrance. They had gone less than a half-mile when Mel peered over the side and exclaimed, "Look at the reef right below us!" It was a reef that rose high enough off the bottom to catch an unsuspecting, heavily-ballasted galleon. It was enough to send the anchor back to the bottom, and within minutes divers were over the side looking for the tell-tale scatter pattern of shipwrecks. And it didn't take long. Mo was the first to spot a shipwreck, and because it was the first time he had tried using a snorkel and face mask, he sort of gasped between mouthfuls of salt water, "Cannon, Cannon!" Soon he was surrounded by the other divers, all skinning down for a look at this iron beauty, covered in coral, but looking as menacing as the day it slid from the deck of a fighting ship. Other cannon were also discovered in the area, but not the elusive ballast pile. "It must have hit the reef and rolled over on its side. The wreck must be lying somewhere out there in deeper water." Mel's explanation seemed to satisfy everyone, and soon they were back on board *Doubloon*, heading eastward.

The following morning they reached the San Blas Islands. There were so many islands, they really had no idea where to start their search for Spanish galleon wrecks. The water was clear, and with one of the divers on the bow keeping a keen eye on the bottom, they began circling the area, Soon the bow watch called out, "Wreck below!" and the scramble for gear began again. It was probably an old English sailing vessel with pig iron for ballast. It did not seem to be old enough to hold anything of interest, at least not the gold doubloons and pieces-of-eight that were in the back of everyone's mind. As Mel and Deo swam around the perimeter of the wreck, Deo became conscious of a shadow that glided out of the deeper blue beyond the reef. It was a fifteen-foot tiger shark that had been attracted by the splashing of fins as the divers moved around the site. Common sense prevailed, and everyone eased out of the water as quickly as they could, leaving the striped tiger to browse the area by himself. They decided to check out the main island...and hauled anchor.

The island was a surprise. There were natives living there who had ancestors dating back hundreds of years. They wore gold decorations, breastplates, earrings, bracelets, and chains. Enough to really impress the Fisher group. And they were very friendly as well, answering the many questions the Americans were asking as best they could. They also had made some gold rings, which they now offered to sell. Mel suggested that the gold was possibly recovered from a nearby sunken galleon, but no amount of persuasion could induce the natives to divulge where they had recovered the gold. What impressed the Fisher group most was their way of life --the huts they lived in, the clothes they wore-- all seemed not to have changed over the past several hundred years. It was a side road to history they hadn't planned on.

When fish are few, bananas are plentiful.

Soon they were on their way again, the next stop being the Chagres River. The river had been the mode of transportation of the Peruvian gold and silver, from the Pacific side of the isthmus to the Atlantic side. It had been a faster means of carrying the gold and silver, rather than by *requas* of mules over the narrow thirty-five miles of mountain paths. The disadvantage was that corsairs of pirates, or English raiders, often lay waiting at the Atlantic mouth of the river, knowing that rafts carrying the treasure would be easy prey. For many years it had been a game of cat and mouse. The silty bottom of the Chagres River, as it emptied into the Atlantic, was the resting place of many ballast piles from vessels that were caught by the Spanish and sent to the bottom. No quarter was shown, nor asked. It was an accepted risk with high stakes.

It was a rough sea that evening, so *Golden Doubloon* was anchored near the head of the river. Mel and Deo sat on the stern of the boat that night, listening to the sounds of the wild animals and an occasional nearby crocodile. It was a rather idyllic setting, and a long way from their near sinking off Panama. It would give them a lot to remember in the years to come.

The following day they located three old shipwrecks with cannon scattered about. These were the first real old wrecks that Mel's group had a chance to pick around on. Each eyed the cannon, wishing they could take them back to California with them. Most of the divers had no idea what to look for, so anything that looked interesting found its way aboard *Doubloon*. Mel did locate a small cannon, one they could raise aboard the *Doubloon*, and securely lashed it to the stern. There may have been gold doubloons and pieces-of-eight just below the muddy bottom. This antagonized the divers, but there was little they could do about it. They just did not have the equipment it would take to do serious salvage. But they were close to what they had dreamed about. Here were old shipwrecks with promise, shipwrecks they could yarn ashore about when they got back to California.

Then it was time to head for home. They all knew it could not last forever, that time has a habit of catching up. There is always an emotional letdown when the end of a treasure hunt rears its ugly head. Yet somehow they all dealt with it, sitting on the bow or up on the cabin roof, watching the reefs slip beneath *Doubloon* as it headed back to Colón. Once there the artifacts were carefully crated up and shipped back to Los Angeles. About fifteen of the more odorous crates were left under the dock and are probably still there today.

The cannon had found a home on the stern of *Doubloon* as it passed through the locks and into the Pacific. A week later they were back home, with some valuable lessons that had been learned. The major one that would haunt Mel throughout his treasure career, was that financially the trip was a bust. He had started out with $25,000, and by the end of the expedition he had spent all of that, as well as another $25,000 that he didn't have. It took him a year to repay the debt. He vowed that on future expeditions he would make sure it was fully funded. It would never happen...

The growing Fisher family: Dirk, Kim, and Kane on Deo's lap.

7...CHALLENGE OF THE SILVER SHOALS

In the early 1960s Mel began putting together his treasure *finding* team. He may not have realized it at the time; it's just the way things happen sometimes. The first member of this illustrious group was Fay Feild. Fay was an electronics superstar who had won his underwater wings as a cave diver in Florida's underground springs. Then it was open ocean diving in search for his wife's favorite sea shell, the thorny oyster *Spondylus Americanus*. As it turns out, these shells are found primarily in old shipwrecks, so on weekends that's where you could find Fay...poking around the metal hulls of W.W.II vintage sites.

These were not always easy to locate, so being an electronics engineer he developed an underwater magnetometer. One that could pin-point old shipwrecks by detecting the change in the magnetic field on the floor of the ocean. The anomalies could be caused by iron hulls, but they could also indicate the presence of anchors, large ship's fittings, and even cannons. Fay designed the magnetometer so that he could tow it behind a boat, controlling its height above the sea floor by the speed of the boat. Along Florida's coastline it worked fine. There were shipwrecks every few hundred yards. Then he moved to California, settling in the Los Angeles area.

It wasn't long before Fay resumed his search for the thorny oyster, and the California coastline was loaded with shipwrecks just like Florida. The water was a bit deeper here, so he *had* to depend on his "mag" to locate them. It meant finding a good boat to tow it, something he had left behind in Florida. He looked up the 'phone numbers of local dive shops and found Mel's Aqua Shop. It was fortunate that Mel answered the 'phone when he called, and when Fay told Mel what he had in mind he got an instant invitation to bring his magnetometer down to the *Golden Doubloon*. When Fay stepped aboard the boat the following day, Mel had a cocktail waiting for him...and an offer of free dive trips if he brought his detector along. Mel determined that Fay really knew his beans about magnetometers, and that together they could locate old shipwrecks. It was the beginning of a relationship that would last over thirty years of serious treasure *finding*.

Fisher family breaking the waves.
Mel and Deo with Dirk, Kim, and Kane.

The promoter in Mel was evident when Fay arrived at the dock a week later for his first dive trip using the magnetometer. There was a large group of anticipating wreck divers sitting aboard the *Golden Doubloon* waiting for Feild to arrive. Mel had sold them all on a virgin wreck, one that they hadn't found as yet! Mel knew there were wrecks all over the channel around Catalina Island; he just needed Fay's magnetometer to find them. Fay just smiled at the prospects of having to produce a wreck site, and that day he did.

The next member to join Fisher's team was Rupe Gates. Rupe seemed to be a master of all trades; he was a mountain climber, cartographer, gold prospector, and he knew how to dive. His long-term contribution to the group --as a solid, serious diver-- was the capability of organizing an extended search and the intelligence to carry it out. He became involved in Mel's local operation through the gold dredging activities. But, like the others, he was soon caught up in the excitement of searching out old Spanish shipwrecks.

Walt Holzworth was a construction foreman in the Los Angeles area. His connection with the team was the interest he had in old Spanish colonial coins. Mel had several episodes on the local television channel about exploring old Spanish shipwrecks, always with the hope of recovering gold doubloons and pieces-of-eight. Walt looked at treasure diving as the only way he could collect Spanish colonial coins, and he could have fun in the bargain. He turned up at Mel's Aqua Shop one day, liked the people he met, and became a regular wreck diver.

Dick Williams had grown up in the oil fields of Texas. By trade he was a welder --a good one-- and somewhere along the way he learned to take diesel engines apart and put them back together. When he moved to the Los Angeles area the SCUBA craze was spreading throughout southern California. Dick was not a good underwater man, but good enough to get by. When shipwreck exploration became popular, Dick wanted in on the excitement. He became a regular on Mel's expeditions.

And of course there was Mo Molinar. Mo had made the trip back to Los Angeles aboard the *Golden Doubloon*. Sure to his promise, Mel let Mo live aboard the boat, which he kept clean as a pin and in great running condition. Mo got to know one of Mel's underwater instructors named Larry, who gave him SCUBA lessons in the pool...and later out in the ocean. Mo never forgot his first ocean dive. Larry had taken him down to a ledge seventy feet deep, and on the way down Mo had a great deal of difficulty equalizing the pressure on his ears. He couldn't communicate the fact to Larry until his nose began to bleed, turning the water green. Mo became a very experienced diver, going out on every *Golden Doubloon* dive charter. He rounded out the Fisher team of divers. It was a good group, but it was the magnetism of Mel Fisher that brought the group together, each lending his own asset to the team effort. They were ready to find out just how good they were.

It was time for the first assault on the Silver Shoals. The shoals had become a legend of treasure, even the name seemed to beckon treasure hunters. Quite a bit had been written about one particular wreck lying somewhere on the forty miles of dragon teeth. The Spanish galleon *Nuestra Señora de la Pura y Limpia Concepción* --the *"Concepción"*-- was part of the 1641 annual treasure fleet, the *Nueva España* or New Spain fleet that sailed to Vera Cruz by way of San Juan, Puerto Rico, and Santo Domingo on the south coast of Hispaniola. The fleet normally reached Vera Cruz by mid summer, but logistics were not what they are today.

As a result of the treasure not reaching the coast on time, the ships lay at anchor in Vera Cruz harbor for months while *requas* of mules struggled across the mountains with the shipments of silver. And then there were the Manila galleons with their cargoes of silks, spices, porcelain and gold, destined for the port of Acapulco. From there the mules again had to haul the shipments over hundreds of miles of mountain paths to reach the docks at Vera Cruz. Finally, when the treasure was safely stowed aboard, the New Spain galleons hauled anchor and set sail for Havana, sailing close to the rim of the Caribbean before turning south to reach Cuba. After docking in Havana, the *Nueva España* fleet had to wait until the *Tierra Firme* fleet arrived. For protection, the two fleets normally sailed back to Spain together.

The second annual fleet to leave Spain for the New World was the *Tierra Firme* fleet, whose destination was Cartagena on the coast of Colombia. From Cartagena the fleet traveled westward to Porto Bello, where they took on board the shipments of gold and silver from the Peruvian mines. It was the responsibility of the South Seas Armada to get the Peruvian treasure from the port of Callao to the port of Panama. From there it was transported over the isthmus by either mule train or rafting along the Chagres River to Porto Bello. In the meantime, the galleons lay at anchor in the harbor, waiting.

A common diversion was to send scouting vessels in search of ships involved in illegal trade. When the scouts were able to capture such a vessel, it was auctioned to the highest bidder. Both the king, and the captain capturing the vessel, received a share of the auction price. When the Peruvian treasure finally arrived, a fair was held, and the European cargo carried by the galleons was traded for the gold and silver. Once the precious goods were loaded on board, the Terra Firma fleet sailed back to Cartagena, where treasure from the Bogotá mint, as well as pearls from the island of Margarita, was logged aboard. Finally, passengers, luggage, and fresh supplies were taken alongside by tenders, and once the galleons were laden to their limits, the *Tierra Firme* fleet made sail for Havana. Bringing the two fleets together in Havana Harbor was a logistic nightmare, one that usually found both fleets well into hurricane season as they prepared for the long voyage back to Spain. That was the case in 1641, when both fleets made it to anchor in Havana on 27 August .

The *Concepción* was a majestic, high-sided galleon built in Havana as one of the king's armada. At the time it was considered a large ship of 650 tons capacity, with an overall length of 140 feet. She carried thirty-six bronze cannons and was a pride of ownership for Eugenio Delgado. Her captain was Admiral Don Juan de Villavicencio, a young 37-year-old nobleman who had become a very experienced seaman, working his way up to the post of admiral by merit, rather than by political appointment. The *Concepción* had made a number of trips across the Atlantic as part of the annual treasure fleet, and it was at a time when fortunes were made on a single trip. The silver mountain of Potosí was producing so much silver that Spain could hardly find enough vessels to bring the treasure home. Yet the more silver the mines produced, the more need the king of Spain had. It seemed at times that the flow of treasure would never cease. For this reason, ships badly in need of repair and overhaul were pressed into service. In 1641, *Concepción* was in that condition.

It had been eighteen months since the ship had been cleaned and caulked. Her bilges were constantly leaking, and the pumps were worked overtime, even in port. Villavicencio requested a further delay of the fleet's sailing while he made the necessary repairs. Captain-General de Campos, in charge of the fleet, denied the request, indicating that he could not risk delaying further because the hurricane season was upon them. The *Concepción* had been designated *almiranta* of the fleet and, as second in command, she was too important to be left behind. Two weeks after the fleets arrived in Havana, they were fully provisioned and standing out of the channel past *El Morro* fortress.

That first day the fleet encountered a brisk breeze and heavy ground swells. *Concepción* sprang a major leak in the stern, just under the turn of the bilge, and even though the crew quickly manned the pumps, it became evident that she couldn't make it. A cannon was fired to alert the *capitana* and the other ships of her plight, and reluctantly the *capitana* signaled for the fleet to return to Havana Harbor. Once there, wharf crews quickly unloaded the cargo from *Concepción* until she floated high enough out of the water to expose the leak. The seam was repaired, the cargo reloaded, and seven days later the fleet was back in the Bahama Channel sailing northward. The seven day delay was just enough to cause the disaster that followed.

Even before the fleet reached the center of the Gulf Stream the air turned muggy, and the wind seemed to have a mind of its own. As the galleons struggled to tack between the Florida reefs and the Bahama Islands, the hurricane struck them. The winds were strong from the south, forcing the fleet ahead of the mountainous waves. There was no turning back to the safety of Havana Harbor, and it became an individual fight for survival. The *Concepción*'s mortal struggle began within hours. New leaks appeared in the hull, and wet gunpowder sloshing in the bilges clogged up her pumps. Soon water rose to five feet in the holds, and the crew and passengers began bailing with buckets and bottles...anything to keep the water from rising further. But the heaving decks were continually awash as waves rolled across her. Cargo was jettisoned, as well as eight of her bronze cannon. Then the mainmast was cut down as the galleon turned broadside to the waves, unable to right herself. Without sails, and with water pouring into the hull from a dozen leaks, it appeared that *Concepción* was doomed.

By the third day the hurricane had moved elsewhere, leaving what was left of the fleet in shambles. Nine ships had been sunk, several others grounded, and the rest dismasted and hopelessly scattered. Only the *capitana*, the *San Pedro y San Pablo*, had managed to survive the hurricane and continue on to Spain. Although dismasted and leaking badly, *Concepción* miraculously remained afloat. The pilot was able to take a sun line and determine that they were somewhere north of the Bahamas. (On today's charts they were between Jacksonville, Florida, and Savannah, Georgia).

Somehow the crew got the pumps cleaned out and working again, and after plugging some of the leaks, with continual bailing they were able to keep the water from rising any further. A jury sail was rigged, and Villavicencio decided to attempt sailing back towards the Bahamas, possibly running his ship aground to save the treasure on board. Just as they made the decision, a south wind sprang up, preventing him from sailing in that direction. They were again at the mercy of the wind and currents...almost a floating derelict.

The only direction in which they could make headway was to the east, and then later to the southeast. Their only hope now was to make landfall somewhere near San Juan, where the ship could be repaired. For three weeks the galleon limped along, pretty much moving wherever the wind would take them, but always in the general direction of San Juan. Soon food and water became scarce, and then the ship was becalmed. Passengers and crew began to die. The situation had become desperate when finally the wind picked up. The chief pilot, Bartolomé Guillen, felt that the *Concepción* had sailed far enough to the east to be directly north of Puerto Rico. He suggested that the galleon be steered to the south, towards San Juan.

The admiral, backed by several experienced crewmen, argued that they could not be as far east as the pilot suggested. In fact, they were about 300 miles west of Puerto Rico and north of Hispaniola. Sixty miles east of Hispaniola lie the deadly reefs of the *Abrojos* (open your eyes). This bank of reefs is forty miles in length and lies just below the surface of the water. They are the dragon's teeth, and once a ship stumbles on these reefs there is no escape.

The pilot's decision overruled the captain's, and the ship was steered southward. Villavicencio was incensed. He produced a silver bowl on the poop deck, and before the assembled crew and passengers, "washed his hands" of the responsibility. The date was 23 October and for the next few days the galleon maintained a southerly course before indifferent winds. As night fell on 30 October, almost a month to the day that the ship had been struck by a hurricane, there was an uneasiness aboard *Concepción*. The seas did not "look right", and some debris floated on the surface. At 8:30 p.m. the ship struck the reef, lurching heavily on her side. The wind lifted the ship off that reef, pushing it ahead until it struck solidly upon another. This second reef tore away the rudder, but the hull remained intact. The crew and passengers were terrified. Throughout the night ocean swells rocked the hull against the sharp coral; the grinding sounds were agonizing.

By morning they were able to determine that their ship had settled on top of a large, flat reef. They were surrounded by a forest of coral heads rising some fifty feet from a white sandy ocean floor. There was a path clear of the reefs, if they could somehow winch the ship free of the reef that held her. The ship's anchors were too large to handle, so they lowered two of the smaller ship's cannon into the longboat, made fast a cable to them, and dropped them out beyond the reefs. Using them as an anchor, the crew began winching the *Concepción* off the reef and towards deeper water.

It was a slow process that took most of the day, and they would have made it, but just as the ship began to move off the reef a squall came up and drove *Concepción* back up on the reef. The squall swept across the shoals for two days, building seas that rocked the ship constantly. The anchor cables to the two cannon held for awhile, stretched over the sharp coral, but finally parted, and the galleon was driven further into the labyrinth of reefs where she became hopelessly impaled. The crew had fought hard to save her, but now they realized the battle was finished. They could now only try to save themselves. It was a tragic end for a gallant ship.

Now there was no thought of treasure. The longboat was loaded to the gunnels with thirty-three passengers, including Admiral Villavicencio, and they set sail to the south. A few days later they reached the shores of Hispaniola seventy miles from the *Abrojos*. There still remained 450 passengers and crew aboard *Concepción*, which was now rapidly disintegrating. Eight or ten rafts were constructed from what was left above water, and once filled with passengers and crew, the pilots directed them westward towards what they were sure was Puerto Rico. They were never heard from again. Seven days after *Concepción* grounded on the reefs, a final two rafts were built, and the pilots took their places on them. For some unknown reason, they directed these rafts to the south, where they were picked up by an English corsair a few days later. The treasure of *Concepción*, almost four million pesos, seemed lost forever.

There were seven salvage attempts made by the Spanish to locate and recover the treasure. They all failed, primarily because there were several major reef areas off Hispaniola, and the exact position of the wreck site was never known. Where the *Abrojos* are located in open water, the weather seemed always at its worse and salvage time limited. Large ground swells rolled across the reefs even during good weather. Then, in 1687, William Phips received financial support from several prominent English gentlemen to go on a salvaging expedition. With two vessels, the *Henry* and the *James and Mary*, they sailed for the Ambrosia Banks where the *Concepción* was thought to have sunk. Francis Rogers, in command of the *Henry*, was the first to arrive at the North Riff of the Banks. By luck, within a few days Rogers' crew of divers was able to locate the wreck site. Over the next sixty days they recovered almost thirty tons of silver, leaving twice that amount still encrusted in coral reefs.

After a hero's return to England, Phips put together another salvage fleet, and with utmost haste they sailed back to the North Riff. Upon arriving there they discovered a fleet of salvage vessels, over 25 in number, anchored on or near the submerged wreck site, each with its own divers probing the bottom for silver. The salvage boats were either chased away or contracted to dive for a share of what was recovered. Phips had a ten-gun frigate to back up his claim to the site, but this second salvage effort was doomed to failure.

The silver, what remained, was heavily overgrown with coral...or buried in the sand. Phips' divers used pick axes to break away some of the coral. Then he attempted to use gunpowder to blast away some of the coral, however, the bamboo pipe fuse he used ruptured before reaching the charge. The work was slow and tedious, with little reward in the end. After four months on the wreck site, provisions were running low, and the divers had become disenchanted. The fleet had not recovered enough to meet salvage expenses. They sailed back to England, ending the last major salvage expedition to what has been renamed "Silver Shoals".

By 1962 Mel had his "team" together, and he was ready to make a serious salvage effort on a major treasure site. He had taken the *Golden Doubloon* to a boatyard in San Pedro to have it hauled for repairs, and as luck would have it, the boatyard owner had seen some of the television episodes of Fisher on shipwreck sites. John Leeper asked Mel if he had a new expedition in mind, and Mel talked to him about the Silver Shoals. John had a 78-foot purse seiner, the *Don Pedro*, that he was using off the coast of Venezuela to look for new shrimp beds. He offered the use of the boat to Mel --and even offered $30,000 in expense money-- if Mel would organize the expedition. They had a deal.

Mel, Deo, Rupe Gates, Fay Feild, Mo Molinar, and John Leeper made that first trip to the Silver Shoals. John had the *Don Pedro* pick them up at the dock in San Juan, Puerto Rico. From there it was a full day's run out to the Silver Shoals, skirting the northern end to seaward and standing clear until they were somewhere close to the middle of the reef. Mel had read the book *The Hispaniola Treasure* which described Phips' expedition, and although it described the salvage, it did not identify on which part of the reef the wreck site lay. They would be starting from scratch in their search for *Concepción*, but Mel felt that with Feild's magnetometer anything was possible. The important thing was that they were actually there, that somewhere on the reefs that they were now looking at lay a fabulous sunken treasure. To be so near the site was a thrill, and to have a chance to locate the wreck where so many before them had failed was a challenge.

John Leeper's shrimp boat **Don Pedro. Credit: Deo Fisher.**

It was midday when they dropped anchor on the windward side of waves that were rolling across the reefs. Here and there the top of a reef caused "boilers", a description in the book that was quite accurate. For the most part the entire shallows remained just below the surface of the water, marked only by the dark change in color of the water. Looking across the forest of coral that stretched some forty miles to the west, and nearly double that from north to south, Mel suddenly realized how easily any wreck could disappear completely in such a remote area. In the accounts he had read it seemed obvious that *Concepción* had struck the reef somewhere on the east side of the banks. This was the side they were now anchored on, but the wreck could lie anywhere within the seventy-odd miles of reef exposed on that side. Leeper had anchored the *Don Pedro* as close to the reefs as he dared, and even then he felt that if a strong wind came up he could drag anchor. If that happened, *Don Pedro* would be added to the list of wreck sites on the Shoals.

The team went into a huddle, and Fay Feild suggested the first thing they did was to run a magnetometer survey along the front edge of the reefs. "Maybe we can pick up the cannons they used as an anchor." It was a good place to start, so Rupe Gates and Fay loaded the magnetometer in the small boat and were soon not much more than a dot, zigzagging around the columns of coral that extended into deeper water. Looking out over the shallow reefs Mel decided that the only way they could work inside was to build some kind of a raft, a raft large enough to hold the hookah rigs, suction dredge, and other equipment and still not have more than a few inches of draft.

The Fisher crew at Silver Shoals working off their "salvage raft". **Credit: Deo Fisher.**

Leeper had his crew break out some 55-gallon oil drums, and Mel began building a plywood deck. Before long they had a ten-foot by twelve-foot raft, supported by four oil drums and stable enough to hold all their gear. Then Rupe and Fay were back alongside. They had dropped a couple of buoys up the reef where they had gotten "hits", and they suggested it might be a good place to start the search. The adrenaline began to flow as John hauled anchor and moved *Don Pedro* the mile or so to where the floats were bobbing on the end of sixty feet of line. Mel and his team slid the raft over the side and loaded the gear on board.

Weather that day was reasonably good, the water was crystal clear, and the sun reflecting off the white sandy bottom gave the divers their first look at a pristine coral forest. What first impressed them was the immense size of the coral heads. They rose from the bottom as much as fifty feet, like standing columns of intricately carved ivory. Then there was the three dimensional wilderness of color that a virgin reef presents. Convoluted brain coral, with an unmatched green and yellow hue, was blended with the florist's artistry of racks of staghorn coral. Splashes of red gorgonias, yellow sponges, and purple sea urchins accented the undersea palette everywhere. The surge of ocean water created fields of undulating sea fans that seemed to be waving to the divers as they snorkeled on the surface. It was a mesmerizing experience, but it was time to go to work.

Soon the sound of gas-driven engines transformed the divers from "lookers" to "searchers" as they began scouring the bottom for signs of a wreck. The "hits" turned out to be ship's fittings, and as they moved into the shallower reef area they began finding pieces of pottery and more encrusted ship's fittings. It soon became obvious that the equipment that they brought along --gold dredges for working mountain streams-- was almost useless in moving the amount of sand they were faced with if they found a wreck. The depth they were working also was at the limit of the gas-driven air compressor they used to cause suction on the dredges. They were hardly making a dent in the bottom. This was going to be a trip that would build on their experience, but it would also bring the team that much closer together.

Once they gave up on the dredges, the divers fanned out and checked the bottom over for anything that looked man-made. They found vestiges of olive jars that every Spanish ship carried, more pottery shards and ship's fittings, copper sheathing, and then someone found a bronze spike! It had been worn by the abrasiveness of sand so that it was shiny. Up on deck they had a good look, and soon conversations revolved around contraband gold being carried back as spikes. Then the spike turned green...and the conversation turned to what was for dinner.

For three weeks the *Don Pedro* was moved from one location to another, along the edge of the reef. The logistics of keeping the raft close to the *Don Pedro* prevented them from exploring deeply into the shoals. But from what Mel had read, the *Concepción* couldn't have been pushed very far into the reef area, not unless mountainous waves had driven it there --and that didn't seem to be the case. So for the three weeks they had worked close to the reef's edge, the unsheltered side. And now the ground swells were building, causing pots and pans to rattle somewhere in the galley.

Then the marine radio broke into the daily routine with a terse message. A storm had developed to the east of their location and was expected to hit the Silver Shoals area within twelve hours. They barely had time to batten down the hatches, haul in the anchor, and head for deeper water before the first strong winds began to sweep across the bow. By nightfall the sea had become a field of whitecaps, and rain hammered at the pilot house windows as the *Pedro* bent into the oncoming storm.

If you can picture a rough storm at sea during the daytime when you can look out and see the size of the waves, the direction they're coming from, and feel the wind, then you realize how frail your vessel is. At night that feeling is tenfold. Not seeing allows the imagination to amplify the conditions, and it can be terrifying. With the sounds of the vessel working beneath your feet, the jarring as huge rollers strike the sides, or the bow as it shudders into green water head on, it becomes a "white knuckle" storm. Your knuckles turn white from hanging on hour after hour. No one sleeps, and if the storm is a rough one there isn't even a cup of hot coffee to steady the nerves.

Sometime during the night, when the waves were cresting over fifteen feet, *San Pedro*'s front cabin window was smashed by a wave breaking over the bow. Then water was pouring in, driven by the rain or waves, and everything was suddenly soaked. Deo quickly found a large piece of plywood and pushed it up against the broken window. By bracing her feet against the bulkhead she managed to keep the flood water out, while the others manned the only bilge pump on board. It was a rather antique, manual pump, but it worked. All night they pumped water, first in twenty-minute shifts, and then in shorter shifts as they all began to tire. Mel searched for something to make a more permanent patch on the window.

By daybreak they had the water in the bilge under control, and Mel found enough shoring to keep the plywood in place. The storm raged on throughout that next day, and it wasn't until the group neared the Turks and Caicos that they were out of the storm area. There was no thought of returning to the Silver Shoals and continuing the expedition. There would always be another day.

8...THE SHARKS OF SILVER SHOALS

When the Fisher team arrived back in California after their first trip to the Silver Shoals they were treated like professionals in the treasure salvage scene. Mel had taken quite a bit of underwater footage of the reefs, and in his local Los Angeles television show he was able to give a descriptive account of the expedition. When it came to riding out tropical storms at sea, he was becoming an expert. The entourage of divers to Mel's Aqua Shop seemed even more enthusiastic about sunken treasure than before, if that were possible. And treasure salvage was becoming a "buzz" word.

In the late 1950s, Teddy Tucker had recovered the "Bishop's Cross", a gold and emerald studded three-and-a-half-inch crucifix, from the wreck of the *San Antonio* in the waters of Bermuda. The cross made the cover of *Life* magazine. Art McKee was making history down in Florida waters. He had recovered three silver bars from a wreck off Gorda Cay in the Bahamas and enough coins and artifacts from the 1733 Spanish *capitana* off Tavernier Key to fill a museum. Then Tim Watkins and the crew of the *Buccaneer* began salvage work on the 1733 Spanish treasure fleet, making headline news in the *Miami Herald*. The icing on the cake was the success of the Real Eight group on the 1715 Spanish fleet.

Kip Wagner had located the wreck of one of the major galleons just south of the Sebastian Inlet on Florida's east coast. Compared to all other salvage operations, this one promised to be the chest of gold at the end of the rainbow. In the first few months of operation his group had recovered thousands of silver coins, gold coins, *K'ang Hsi* porcelain, and jewelry. According to reports, when the weather was kind, the coins lay exposed on a hard coquina bottom in twelve feet of crystal clear water. But when the weather was not on their side, winter storms would pile four to five feet of sand on top of the treasure. It put Kip's divers out of action until another storm came along and moved the sand somewhere else. Or else, they came up with an idea on how to move the sand themselves.

And so that was the case in the spring of 1962. Winter storms had dumped deep sand on top of the wreck site just south of the Sebastian Inlet, putting Wagner's group on hold until they found a way to move it. It was frustrating knowing that the treasure was so close...and yet so far away. One of Kip's key divers was Lou Ullian, a man looking for answers. Lou worked for the Air Force as one of the demolition people at Cape Canaveral. His job was involved with the "destruct" system of missiles, a job that sent him on several trips to California. While in the neighborhood of Los Angeles area he normally stayed near the ocean, at a motel in the Redondo Beach area, and he haunted the local dive shops for new ideas. The sand covering the Sebastian wreck site was his reason for stopping at Mel's Aqua Shop. Mel had been advertising his gold dredges in several national magazines, and Lou thought that possibly they could be used to move sand under water.

Lou stood in the doorway of the shop, looking for a friendly face. Mel was out on a dive trip, but Deo Fisher had the greatest smile anyone could possibly ask for. As they discussed gold dredges, Lou noticed the two small Spanish coins in one of the show cases. They were the coins Mel had purchased while in Porto Bello. "I see you have a couple of Spanish cobs." Deo looked at Lou quizzically, "We have what?" Lou pulled a silver piece-of-eight out of his pocket and dropped it on the counter.

"We're finding a lot of these down in Florida, where did yours come from?" After Deo told Lou about the Porto Bello trip, Lou gave her a run-down on why they called them cob coins. "They're cut from a silver bar that's been hammered to the right thickness. Each piece, about the right weight, is cut from the end of the bar. That's where the name came from, *cabo de barra*, or "end of the bar." When Deo found out that Ullian was part of the Real Eight group bringing up treasure, she made him promise that he would talk to Mel before he flew back to Florida.

When Mel returned from the diving trip that afternoon, Deo was pretty enthusiastic when she described the conversation she had with the Florida diver. Mel quickly gave the motel a call and invited Lou to have dinner with him. After dinner that evening Lou brought Mel up to date on the Real Eight activities, and as he talked about piles of silver coins lying on the bottom, he could see the fire in Mel's eyes. He ended his account with, "We don't count the coins anymore, we just weigh them!"

There was no doubt in Mel's mind that the treasure fires had been lit, and in his heart he knew that everything that he had been preparing for lay somewhere off the Florida coast. There was talk about a second trip Mel was planning for the Silver Shoals. Lou suggested that if Mel were flying into Miami, he should take a side trip to Sebastian and sit down with Kip Wagner. Wagner had an old chart of the Silver Shoals that might be of some help in locating the *Concepción*. It was the excuse that Mel needed to meet Wagner, one that was long overdue. It would be a meeting that was destined to change not only their own lives, but the entire salvage community as well.

Mel had become quite a celebrity in California with his television shows, training classes, and dive charters. After his recent trip to Silver Shoals the 'phone was ringing off the hook. People he had trained or who had been on previous expeditions were calling to find out when his next treasure hunt was going to get underway. Eric Schiff was one of those eager callers. He had set aside some mad money for making dreams come true, and salvaging treasure seemed to fit the bill. Walt Holzworth, already one of Mel's team divers, also had a few bucks from his contracting business that he was willing to risk on a treasure expedition. Before plans were complete for "Silver Shoals II" they had another investor. Arnold McLean, a physicist from Colorado, added his financial clout to the expedition. Suddenly Mel had over $30,000 in the pot, and so the project was underway. Mel drew up his first legal document, one that would indicate how the treasure would be divided if they found any. It would be a document that would haunt Mel in later years.

The one great thing about Silver Shoals II was the confidence that Mel had in the team. They now had the experience, good equipment, and together they could *think* a project through, make things happen. It was with this attitude that Mel flew to Miami ahead of the group and then made the 170 mile trip up the Florida coast to Sebastian for his first meeting with Kip Wagner. Kip lived with his wife Alice in a small house near the north end of

Sebastian, just off U. S. Highway #1. Not many of the local residents knew that Kip had recovered thousands of silver pieces-of-eight on the "cabin wreck" site he was working. And it was during the early days of treasure salvage when the state of Florida allowed the private sector to retain possession of what was salvaged until a division was effected. As it turned out, Kip had quite a pile of silver to show Mel when he stopped by on his first visit.

The treasure impressed Mel, and Kip spun stories of the eleven Spanish galleons that were driven ashore by a hurricane July 30, 1715. He told Mel about the wrecks he was sure of to date, of the silver wedges he had recovered from the wreck just north of the Fort Pierce inlet. He showed him some of the microfilm that his friend Kip Kelso had gotten from the *Archivo de Indias* in Seville, Spain. It was in an archaic Spanish called *procesal*, a style of cursive writing. Much of it had been translated, giving the Real Eight group strong confidence that the site they were working was either the *capitana* or the *almiranta* of the 1715 fleet. Both galleons were loaded with gold and silver, and the most important piece of information was the fact that quite a bit of the treasure still remained on the reefs or was buried in the sand just off shore. Kip's crew had a full-time jobs, so they only worked on weekends and on holidays. But even on a part-time basis they had been able to raise a considerable amount of treasure. Mel left Sebastian that night with a gnawing anticipation that he could find the treasure if given half a chance. He had a lot to think about on his way to the Silver Shoals.

The group met at the Miami International Airport. Mel, Deo, Rupe Gates, Dick Williams, Mo Molinar, Walt Holzworth, Fay Feild, Eric Schiff, Arnold McLean, and George Gillett were ready for the second assault on the Silver Shoals. It was quite an entourage of excited and enthusiastic treasure hunters. Mel briefly gave them a run-down on his meeting with Kip Wagner and passed along the visions of silver pieces-of-eight covering the sands off the beaches of south Florida.

Their next stop was San Juan, Puerto Rico. Here they were able to lease a fairly large eighty-foot sailboat, the *Karen*. As a safety back-up they leased *Namsos*, a smaller, rather derelict-looking sailboat that they dubbed, for lack of a better name, "Foul Bottom." The reason for that name was probably because the bottom was encrusted in barnacles. Before they could do much in the way of sailing they had to pitch in and give her a good bottom cleaning. The larger boat, on the other hand, had all the comforts you could ask for. Being a sailboat with a fairly tall mast meant that it was subject to rolling. For this reason the main dining table was on gimbals, so that even if the boat rolled...the table stayed level. Even the master cabin had a bathtub with dolphin handle fixtures, and it was also mounted on gimbals!

Salvage boat **Namsos** *on Silver Shoals.* **Credit: Deo Fisher.**

The major part of Mel's group made themselves comfortable aboard the *Karen*, along with the owner, Captain Swift. There was also an English navigator and his wife aboard. That comprised the permanent crew. Mo Molinar and Arnold McLean offered to sail with the owner of the *Namsos*, and the group got underway from San Juan Harbor, staying close to the northern coast until they cleared the headlands of Point Aguadilla. As they began the crossing of the Mona Passage, the weather turned gusty, and their sailboat began to roll. Large waves seemed to pick the *Karen* up and lay her on her side. On the back side of the wave the tall mast rolled her back the other way, only to catch the next wave. The eight feet of freeboard was reduced to inches at times. Before long everyone on board was seasick, except the helmsman, Captain Swift. Walt Holzworth tried taking him a cup of coffee, and after several hours...he made it. At one point the refrigerator door swung open, depositing eggs and a variety of breakables on the deck. What a mess!

Rupe Gates, Mel Fisher, Fay Feild, and Mo Molinar on the **Namsos. Credit: Deo Fisher.**

Once beyond the mouth of the Mona Passage the seas settled down, and the expedition took on a more cheerful atmosphere. The weather moderated, and the ocean took on that deep blue hue that seems to make everything worthwhile. It was as they were approaching the Silver Shoals that the *Namsos* caught fire. The flames were seen coming out near the base of the galley stack, accompanied by dark billowing smoke. It was serious enough at the time that McLean was on his hands and knees praying that they wouldn't sink. Finally, Mo Molinar was able to get the fire out --as a one-man fire brigade-- but somewhere along the way they lost the power to their refrigerator. The food went bad, and the crew would eat the rest of their meals aboard the *Karen*.

On the first trip to the Silver Shoals Mel's group had worked on the seaward side of the reef, where it dropped off into deep water rather quickly. There they had located the rudder and gudgeon of a vessel possibly of 1700s vintage. The major problem on that expedition was their inability to anchor in the shallow sections of the reef, the part with the greatest potential for wreckage.

Now, as they approached the shoals, Mel asked Captain Swift to maneuver in from the landward side. With Rupe Gates up in the mast to direct them around coral heads that rose from the bottom like minor mountains, they were able to make some progress through the maze of coral and anchor within the circle of reefs. It was a sandy bottom at forty feet. From the mast Gates said the scene below him was "awe-inspiring." It was everything the group of treasure hunters had ever dreamed of. Crystal clear water, reef colors beyond description, and fish! The fish were everywhere. Some of them defied description, with their colors and unusual characteristics. And, there were some big fish as well, the toothy kind.

As soon as their anchors were set, they had the small boat in the water and were ready to start the first look-see. Mel purposely had Swift anchor the *Karen* near where they had located the rudder on the first expedition. He was sure they could locate the main part of the wreck somewhere inside the reef. One of the first indications of a scatter pattern was the discovery of two large cooking pots. In fact, they were so big that George Gillett, who was over six feet tall, was able to lie down inside one of them and stretch out. These pots were obviously the primary cooking pots on board ship when meals to feed an entire crew were cooked up at one time. On board some of the major galleons carrying 300 or more passengers, the pots were absolutely huge.

Walt Holzworth and Mel Fisher explore reef at Silver Shoals.
Credit: Deo Fisher.

Cannon balls and ships' timbers mark an old wreck site at Silver Shoals. **Credit: Deo Fisher.**

The scatter pattern led the group along the inside of the reef for almost two miles. If it hadn't been for bits and pieces of pottery along the way, they may have missed the main pile of ballast stone. But, finally, there it was. The cannons scattered on top was the giveaway. Fay Feild's magnetometer was able to register the anomaly of a pile that seemed more like just another mound of coral, settled by several hundred years of storms and current. The *Karen* was moved to anchorage near the ballast pile, and the group went to work.

The divers used several large suction dredges that were "real bears" to move around the bottom. It was tough work as they bit into the pile of dead coral that had accumulated over the wreck. Live coral has a difficult time growing on a wreck because of the contaminate nature of the site. In fact, one of the ways of locating a ballast pile is spotting the break in the formation of the reef. Large coral formations will not grow on ballast stone; it's as simple as that! By the time the divers were able to reach ballast, the hole was several feet deep. Ship's fittings were welded to the ballast stone as the iron turned to oxides. Here and there were olive jars, the "jerry-cans" of the Spanish navy. Some of them were intact and sealed.

One day the crew opened the seal of a recovered olive jar on board the *Karen*. The jar contained fresh water, somewhat tainted after being submerged on the bottom for over 200 years, but quite possibly potable. Then there were the lead merchant seals. To identify their cargoes, merchants would tag each item to make sure that it reached its destination. Often, in a shipwreck that would be the artifact most helpful in identifying the ship and her cargo. The pile of cannon balls and musket balls grew by the day on board *Karen*. And then they found two copper coins. There were no dates, but they were copper coins, and the divers were sure that more coins --hopefully gold or silver-- were also in the cargo. But it wasn't to be.

Walt Holzworth and George Gillett were working near the side of the ballast pile one day. They had two large holes that they had cleared out by lunch time, when they took a break. As they swam back after lunch, they found that some visitors had up taken residence in their holes. In Walt's hole were two large eight-foot sharks. In George's hole a single, much larger shark reposed. For the next half-hour the two divers swam about, watching the sharks forty feet below them. The predators seemed to be in no hurry to leave the holes that Walt and George had worked on so hard all morning, and, finally, Walt swam back to the *Karen* and retrieved a steel prod. They had to be careful not to spear large fish like these. Sharks have a nasty habit of being unpredictable, and large sharks are hard to kill without the proper equipment. Mel would find out just how unpredictable sharks can be before this expedition was over. Walt swam down with the prod and rapped one of the sharks on the nose. It had the desired result. Both sharks made a hasty retreat from Walt's hole, along with the one in George's hole. Divers working near the end of the ballast mound said that the toothsome trio paid their respects as they swam through the site.

After almost three weeks of hard work Mel's group made a decision: the wreck they were working was certainly not the *Concepción* and was probably nothing more than a merchant *nao*, laden with cargo that had floated away when the ship hit the reefs. The next few days were spent exploring other scatter patterns, because there seemed to be wrecks everywhere they looked. Then they had anchor problems. One of the major problems with the Silver Shoals is the tendency to lose anchors and chains in the reefs. Storms come up quickly, and anchor lines pulled taut over the edges of sharp reefs soon part. Mel had planned on remaining in the Shoals area four weeks, but now their charter boat had run out of anchors and chain. In order to carry on with the expedition, they had to find something to anchor with.

Mel remembered the shapes of the reefs...and where they had lost one of their anchors during a storm. He decided that he had better retrieve it if he could find it. After searching the general area, he was able to spot the same reef where they had lost their first anchor. With the *Karen* standing by, Mel, Mo Molinar, and Gillett jumped into the small boat and headed for the edge of the reef. When they arrived there they had company. Several large sharks, their fins cutting the water, began to circle the boat -- really too close for comfort. Mel spotted the "hook" lying on the bottom in thirty feet of water, water so clear that it seemed he could reach down and pick up the anchor. He had never seen so many sharks before in his life, and he began to have some doubts about his own philosophy. He had always preached the fact that "sharks never bother you!" But now, with quite a gathering of black fins churning the surface within a few arm-lengths of their small boat, he had a small voice somewhere deep down telling him to be extra careful. Mel had his SCUBA gear on, and without taking time to change his mind, he rolled over the side and headed for the bottom and the anchor that now seemed within his grasp. The sharks followed him as if he were a piece of bait that had been tossed over the side just for them.

He had tucked a lifting bag under his arm, and now he busied himself attaching it to the anchor. It was hard to ignore the six-foot sharks that swished around him close enough that he could feel the water move as they passed. Now he had the lifting bag attached, and he fed air from his mouthpiece into the open end of the bag. It quickly filled, and the anchor began to move. One last shot of air, and the anchor was free of the bottom, standing straight up and starting to move towards the surface. Mel thought he had it made, then the anchor snagged on the edge of the reef and held fast! He couldn't budge it. Now the sharks made their move, and suddenly Mel realized that he had to defend himself. The sharks were brushing up against him, and with their jaws open, their intentions were not friendly. Mel began to kick at them furiously to fend them off. It seemed to agitate them even more. The situation had suddenly turned very nasty.

Mo Molinar had his SCUBA gear on and had just rolled over the side of the boat. When he looked down and saw the situation Mel was in, the hair on the back of his neck began to tingle. He had a shark "juke" stick, one that Mel had made for just an occasion like this. He had welded a large washer about three inches up the shaft of the spear so that the shark couldn't take it away if it were stuck in him. Mo headed for the bottom, the juke stick straight out in front of him. On the bottom he began to jab at the sharks, the sharp point making an impression on the sensitive snouts of these hungry fish. Mo and Mel were now back to back, Mel kicking at them with his fins, and Mo juking at them with his spear. They circled, giving the divers a little more room on the bottom. Mel motioned for Mo to give him a hand freeing the anchor, and in a few minutes they worked it out from under the reef edge and sent it bubbling towards the surface. Now the two divers had the shark frenzy to deal with as they headed for the surface themselves. The sharks were rolling for dinner, and Mel and Mo just managed to roll up on the boat rail ahead of them.

Mel was whipped, the strength drained from him as he hauled himself out of the water. He managed to get seated on the edge of the boat, his legs still in the water, when one of the sharks made a lunge for his knee. As Mel jerked his leg out of the way...he lost his balance and fell back into the water! Mo saw what happened and jumped back in as well. For the next few minutes it was kicking and juking the sharks all over again. They both finally rolled back into the boat, their legs free of the water, and heaved big sighs of relief.

This day wasn't over yet. George Gillett was a photographer and as yet hadn't gotten an underwater shot of the sharks. With all the action going on around him, he completely forgot the camera. With the divers now resting in the bottom of the boat, he made the statement, "I'm going down and get some shark shots!" Mel warned him, "Better not, they're hungry today." George said something silly like, "Who's afraid of the big bad shark!" and disappeared over the side. In a few moments Mel could clearly see him on the bottom with lots of finny company. In fact, it was difficult to see George because of all the sharks! Then they noticed that he had backed himself into a crevice in the reef to keep the sharks from getting behind him. Mel knew George was having a bad time of it; he only hoped the photos would be worth the risk...if the camera ever made it back to the surface. It wasn't long before Gillett broke the surface alongside the boat, and in one flash of energy he was in the boat without touching the sides. Mel never did figure out how he did that. Afterwards, the photographer freely admitted, "*Now* I'm afraid of sharks!"

One day the group discovered a section of the wreck protruding from under a massive coral head. This section of the wreck looked promising, and so they decided to finally use a bit of the dynamite they had brought along for just such an occasion. The divers placed a few one-pound charges under the coral head...and tamped it in good. It produced quite a boil when it went off, spreading white coral sediment over the entire area. The bottom visibility went to zero, so they decided to wait awhile and let it settle.

It was the next morning when Mo had a look. As he swam down over the rubble pile he almost bumped into the big shark, sleeping at the bottom of their newly dug hole. In a moment he was back on the surface, "Mel, there's a big shark in our hole!" Mel had his gear on, and as he slipped over the side he picked up a seven-pound sledge hammer. As he swam down towards the hole, Mo pointed out the dark shape just beginning to move around the bottom. Mel thought he had scared the shark out of the hole, because as he swam in, the shark disappeared. It wasn't over.

As Mel checked the sections of wreck that now were uncovered, he felt the rush of water behind him. It was just a glance, but it was enough to let him know the shark was back. In fact, the shark had settled in the hole right behind Mel, and the fish was a bit bigger than Mel. Mel had about decided to let sleeping sharks lie, but suddenly remembered he had a sledge hammer in his hand. Sledge hammers are dead weight under water, and as Mel swung it over his head it almost threw him backwards. But somehow he hit the shark on the head. For a second it was a Mexican standoff: the shark looked at Mel; Mel looked at the shark. Then it was over. With a whip of his tail the shark was out of the hole and heading down the reef, looking for parts safer for a shark with a hangover.

Rupe Gates hadn't seen the sledge hammer episode, and actually he hadn't seen a shark during the entire Silver Shoals expedition. It seems that everyone else had sighted sharks, either close up or circling while they worked the bottom. It occurred to everyone that Rupe was just too damn serious about digging up treasure that he wasn't aware of what was going on around him.

The wreck that the group was working had struck the edge of the reef where the bottom dropped off into very deep water. Just inside the reef was a hole possibly seventy feet deep. They had located the galleon's rudder in this hole, and Fay Feild had taken a personal interest in moving the debris out of the hole while he searched for treasure with his metal detector. The top of the reef was no more than knee deep. Connecting the hole with deep water was a channel four feet wide and six or eight feet deep. Everyone had a feeling that the galleon had dug the channel as it washed over the reef. Because of the shallow reef and wave action, the best way to get into deep water was to swim the channel. This day Mel decided to check the outside edge of the reef, but halfway through the channel he was blocked by a fairly large shark that had settled there, possibly waiting for dinner to come along.

Mel thought that this might be a good time to show Rupe a shark up close. He back-paddled out of the channel and then went up to the boat to get Rupe. "If you want to see a shark come on in, and bring a shark billy with you!" Rupe couldn't find a billy club, but he did grab a miner's pick they had been using to break up the coral. Following Mel on the surface, he was soon at the entrance of the channel out to deep water. Mel motioned for him to go ahead, and he followed close behind as they worked their way along the channel. As they made one of the sharp bends, Rupe finally got to see his first shark. It was a good sized one, and it was now facing Rupe, about eight feet away. He decided a little aggressiveness would probably scare the shark away, so he made a lunge towards it. He was wrong. The shark must have had the same thing in mind, because it lunged at about the same time. Suddenly they were no more than two feet apart, and Rupe could remember that the shark's eyes were kind of small for such a big head! Instinctively he made a swipe at the shark's head with the miner's pick...and missed! But it was enough to spook the big fish, and he took off with a rush, right over the top of Rupe. Enjoying a ringside seat to the episode up to that point, Mel was almost bowled over as well by the departing predator. The last they saw of the shark it was at the bottom of the seventy-foot hole, circling Fay --who was completely unaware that he had company. Later, they both had a laugh about it, and Rupe never once complained after that about not seeing sharks on the Silver Shoals.

In fact, it was just a day or so later that Mo and Rupe were working the air lift near the hole and making the water very murky. The current was moving the fallout down the reef, where a huge tiger shark was on the prowl for breakfast. When Mo first saw the monster it had just begun circling near the top of their twenty-foot air lift; the shark was almost as long as the air lift. Rupe didn't see the shark on its first pass, and Mo tried to point it out. Rupe just kept working the mouth of the air lift around the edge of the hole they were digging. Mo moved up so close to Rupe and the air lift that Rupe must have known something was up. Then, on the next pass, Rupe saw the big tiger shark as well! It was an instantaneous decision on both their parts to head for the surface...very slowly, so as not to give this striped monster an incentive to roll for breakfast. Once in the boat, they sat there for the longest time discussing politics, women, anything to pass the time away. It was the biggest shark that Mo had ever seen in all his diving days.

The next few days went by very quickly; they always do when you're having fun. There was so much to see and explore within the reefs of the Silver Shoals that there would never seem to be enough time. But there were some major decisions to be made, ones that would affect all of their lives. And of course, the money had run out. It was time to gather in the boats and gear and head back to Puerto Rico.

Almost as the sun set on the boilers that marked the shoals as they disappeared astern, Mel was huddling with his team. The fire had been lit in Mel to explore the Florida potential of the 1715 fleet of Spanish shipwrecks. He spoke to the group in terms of following the dream on a full-time basis. There would be risks -- the possibility of not finding anything at all and winding up broke. But the opportunity to dive warm, crystal clear water --and the chance of finding Spanish pieces-of-eight and gold doubloons in the bargain-- was indeed tempting. The fever was setting in on the group, and by the time the plane landed in Miami, they were all, each and every one, ready to plant their own personal anchors in Florida.

Rupe Gates and Fay Feild had obligations they had to attend to, so they booked flights back to California. Mel and Deo, Mo, Dick, and Walt rented a car and, after a few 'phone calls, were on their way to see Kip Wagner. Kip wanted another Real Eight member to hear what the Fisher group had to say, so he called Lou Ullian to sit in on the meeting. Before long they were all gathered in the front room of Wagner's house in Sebastian, and Alice Wagner put the coffee pot on.

Then Kip opened a box with the *K'ang Hsi* porcelain cups that they had recently uncovered. They were dainty teacups without handles. Very fragile! Some were white with blue designs, others were green or a terra-cotta brown, and each had a Chinese symbol at the very bottom of the bowl. Wagner then explained how they were found, "Lou Ullian and Dan Thompson were fanning away at the sand, a patch that looked sort of reddish-brown, when all of a sudden the water turned red! Here were these cups, packed in a sort of clay and straw, with cochineal dye. We think that the Spaniards used the dye to keep people from stealing the cups. That way they would be caught *red-handed*!" Someone made a comment that the banks today must have gotten that idea from the Spanish.

Kip's group had recovered over 24,000 silver coins by this time, and when he pulled the wash tub of coins out from under the bed there was a sudden gasp of disbelief. Kip reached into the tub and handed Mo a silver coin. "Here, Mo, have one. This is what they look like." There were some gold coins as well, and a gold chain or two, enough to get the adrenaline flowing. It gave Mel the incentive to make his future plans.

Kip and Mel finally got down to brass tacks. Mel offered Kip to "bring my entire team to Florida and work your wreck sites on a fifty-fifty basis...after the state of Florida takes its twenty-five percent. If we find nothing, we get nothing. It won't cost your group a cent; we'll pay all expenses." He explained to Kip that he had a professional group that knew what it was doing. And Kip really needed help. Working only on weekends, it would take a lifetime to explore all the wreck sites he had leases on. Kip and Lou agreed that it sounded like a good idea. They wanted to bring it up for a vote to their entire Real Eight group at their next board meeting. That was the way they left it when the meeting broke up, a meeting that was destined to change the name of the coast of Florida between Sebastian and Fort Pierce to "The Treasure Coast."

9...FLORIDA SUNSHINE AND SHIPWRECKS

Mel had reached an agreement with Kip Wagner that he would bring his team to Florida --along with all their equipment-- and work his wreck sites for fifty percent of whatever came up off the bottom. They would work one year, paying all their own expenses...and without salary. If they hadn't found anything within the year, Mel would give his team the option of throwing in the towel and going back to California. But he was optimistic, and he had the confidence that if the treasure was there, he would find it.

When Mel and Deo got back to Mel's Aqua Shop in Redondo Beach it was quite a change from the promise of Florida treasure. Mel was running a small mail order catalog business on diving equipment. He advertised that divers could buy any diving equipment made in the U.S.A. --and some of the international gear as well-- through his store. This meant parts too, and some of the European parts were either impossible to get or had long lead times. He stocked most of them in his storeroom. While Mel and Deo were on the Silver Shoals Mel's mother and father ran the business.

When they opened the front door after nearly two months of playing hooky in Florida and the Silver Shoals, the first thing that caught their eyes was the pile of mail. They had set up a Ping-Pong table to put the mail on, and the table was covered in packages and letters! There was also a pile of letters and packages around the table on the floor. This pile was nearly two feet high, and in it were checks, orders, bills, and inquiries. It represented several weeks of hard work to catch up on. After allowing the shop to air out and checking to make sure everything was as they left it, Mel turned to Deo and asked, "Would you rather open up all this mail, pay all the bills, fill out the orders, bank the checks and hope there's something left over...or would you rather sell out and go treasure hunting?" Deo hardly skipped a beat, "Let's go!"

Richard Pasker had always shown an interest in owning part of Mel's business. Now Mel made him a proposal. "How would you like to buy all the mail on the table and floor and the key to the front door for $40,000?" It didn't take Richard long to accept the offer, which included paying Mel $400 a month rent on the building. Now Mel had to sell all the diving gear in the store.

There was quite a number of SCUBA stores in the L. A. area, and each month the owners held a meeting. It was at the next meeting that Mel announced he was selling out. It was a devastating blow to everyone; they looked at Mel as their leader. His television series had been a tremendous influence in bringing divers into their stores. Sales of gear had been going up year after year. Now he was moving, and although everyone wished him well, they would miss him. He said that he would hold a ninety-day sale of all the equipment in his store, including his dive boat *Golden Doubloon*.

The rush was on, and each day found his supplies disappearing. Eddie Tsukimura quickly bought the *Golden Doubloon* for $29,000. Mel gave him ten years to pay it off; Eddie had been a good friend. In fact, Eddie ran the *Golden Doubloon* out of Los Angeles harbor until he sold it in 1994, telling stories of the trips he took with Mel Fisher, King of Divers.

At the end of ninety days the store was bare. Richard was already busy ordering a new inventory of dive gear. All that was left to do was pack up...and move. Mel had an old Cadillac, and he had hitched a trailer on the back. It was now loaded with clothes, furniture, and equipment. Mo got to drive the Cadillac; Mel drove a Buick station wagon with Deo and the four Fisher youngsters aboard, and pulling Fay Feild's small "mag" boat *Reef Comber* behind. By the time Rupe Gates, Dick Williams, and Walt Holzworth filled out the convoy there were six cars heading east.

It was an exciting time for everyone. It was leaving the old behind, starting a fresh, new career in a land full of sunshine and promise. Who wouldn't have been excited, and Mel was like the Pied Piper leading the pack! There was a lot of singing, joking, smiling...until they reached the Arizona desert. Then the heat began to take its toll, first on the cars and then on the enthusiasm. The cars were breaking down. They would drive fifty miles and then sit, waiting for the cars to cool down so they could add water to the gurgling radiators. It was half luck, half miracle that they made it across Texas. It was the biggest state they ever had to cross under those circumstances.

It was when they reached Louisiana that they had discrimination problems. At first it was a restaurant that wouldn't serve them because Mo was "colored". He quickly offered to wait out in the car, and after a few words from Mel one of the waiters carried out Mo's dinner on a big silver platter covered by a silver dome. Mo had an easy smile and laugh, but this brought out the best in him. He never stopped smiling until they reached Alabama. Then, when it was late at night and the Fisher convoy was whipped, they stopped at a motel. The owner refused to rent them rooms because Mo was "colored". Mo offered to sleep in the car to prevent a big argument between Mel and the motel owner. In 1963, discrimination along the Gulf Coast still persisted, but it was changing. No one slept much that night.

Finally, crossing the Florida state line seemed magical. There were cheers from the dust-covered entourage --they had made it! The palm trees and orange groves were definitely Florida. The warm sunshine and a slight tropical freshness seemed to make the nine days of non-stop roadwork seem all worthwhile. It was July, and the rest was all downhill from there.

The next stop was Vero Beach, and following Route 60 right to the Atlantic Ocean seemed the natural thing to do. They dusted themselves off and decided that lunch would be great at the Driftwood Inn. The view out over the ocean was what they had traveled so far to see, and it was worth it. While the group was deciding on what to order for lunch, Mel stepped outside to a nearby lifeguard stand. There was a muscular, suntanned guard by the name of Charlie Gaulnick sitting there, watching the swimmers splash around the water's edge. Mel opened the conversation with, "I just drove all the way here from California to dive on Spanish galleons. Are there any around here?" Mel wasn't quite sure if this lifeguard knew about Spanish galleons, but he was pleasantly surprised when Charlie beamed. "Yeah. There's one right over there." He was pointing just to the south, where a small point of land marked the first green of the Rio Mar Golf Course.

"Does it have any cannons on it?" Charlie hesitated. He didn't know this newcomer from California, but there was a certain enthusiasm in his voice that made Charlie want to share what he knew about the wreck site. "Yes. Last time a northeast storm stirred up the bottom sand I counted nineteen. They're big ones. There are a couple of big anchors sitting upright near the ballast pile...have to be at least sixteen feet long. The cannons and anchors make a great underwater photo when the water is clear."

Mel looked south along the beach where Charlie had pointed out the site. A point of land seemed prominent, about six city blocks from where they stood on the boardwalk outside the Driftwood Inn. "How far off shore is it?"

"About 900 feet. That point of land is the first green of the Rio Mar Golf Course. I swim out from there. The water is about nineteen feet deep, usually pretty clear. There's another wreck right out there." Charlie pointed to a rounded boiler that was just becoming exposed as the tide changed. "We call that the 'Boiler Wreck'. It's the *Breckenshire*, sank there about sixty years ago. I pick up a few lobsters around it, then sell them to the local restaurants."

Mel thanked Charlie for the information and asked him if he would show him the wreck someday. Charlie said that he would be glad to. Fisher would explore it himself years later.

When Mel finally returned to the group, they were finishing up lunch at the Driftwood Inn. He was beaming, "Well, let's buy a house right here by this old Spanish galleon. It looks like a real nice place." After he told them what the lifeguard had said, they all agreed that Vero Beach was the place to live. Rupe Gates was soon able to rent a small apartment. Dick Williams and Walt Holzworth found trailers they could rent on Route 1 between Vero Beach and Fort Pierce. Mo was able to rent a small house on the west side of Fort Pierce. Mel and Deo found a nice motel with a pool that gave them a decent family rate; after a month or so they found a home on Greytwig Road. But the base of treasure salvage operations moved to 628 Banyan Road when Mel and Deo decided their growing family needed roots. They bought the house for $17,000 --a lot of money in 1963-- but it was in a quiet, tree-lined neighborhood. The ocean was only a few blocks away, a short walk to check to see if it was a good day for diving.

Dirk Fisher (r.) with members of the Shark Club.

It was here that the Fisher children began to grow into the dream of treasure salvage. Each morning the divers would gather around the breakfast table for hot coffee and doughnuts while Mel outlined the plan of the day. Dirk and Kim were old enough to feel the excitement generated in these morning get-togethers. In fact, it wasn't long before Dirk started a local Vero Beach diving club called the Shark Hunters. It must have been a reflection on Mel's Silver Shoals escapades. When the surf was up and the only swimmers off the sandy beaches were paddling surfboards, Dirk and Kim were right among them. It would be a few years before Taffi and Kane were old enough to join their brothers.

Those first few weeks moved slowly for this treasure group from California. It was evident that the California pace of doing things was much faster than the Floridians were used to. Their first trip to the "Cabin Wreck" site found a caravan of six cars winding down a narrow sandy road that would one day be replaced by Route A1A. With mangrove trees and orange groves on each side of the road, it wasn't long before it was taking more pushing and shoving than horsepower to move the cars through the brush. Although they had the fire of enthusiasm to see the Cabin Wreck site, they never made it that first trip.

It would be days later when they stood in front of Kip's beach cabin looking seaward at the second reef less than 300 feet away. Kip had told them that it was here that a pile of cannon lay, and it was here that they were picking up silver coins by the thousands. It was enough to whet the appetite of every land-locked sailor, and these sailors were about to spring out into the world of serious treasure salvage. It was an hour or so of standing there, or walking a few steps north or south, and then back in front of the cabin. They seemed to talk in voices barely above a whisper, and they didn't understand why at the time. Yet, after traveling thousands of miles, and many dreams later, here they were standing in front of treasure. It was still out there. They could sense it, feel it, almost reach out and touch it. It would change all their lives, and they were ready for the challenge.

The wreck site that lay in front of Kip's cabin was either the *almiranta* or the *capitana* of Captain-General Ubilla's 1715 fleet. It had been loaded with almost 3,000,000 pesos in silver coins packed in 990 chests. Also carried on board was over 36,000 pesos in gold that had been salvaged from the *almiranta* of Barlovento, which wrecked near Havana in 1711. And then there was the passengers' baggage, scattered along the beach for miles and filled with the fortunes of Spaniards that had struck it rich and were returning to Spain. The galleon had struck the third reef about 1,000 feet offshore, sinking to the bottom in three-and-a-half *brazas* (twenty-three feet) of water between the second and third reefs. The topdecks separated and came ashore, dropping eleven cannon just inside the second reef before disintegrating along the beach. It was little wonder that Kip Wagner's group had recovered so much treasure up against the second reef. The Spanish had been able to salvage only 736 boxes of coins and none of the gold. Over 760,000 pesos in silver remained scattered over the reefs, enough to get excited about...and Mel's group was excited.

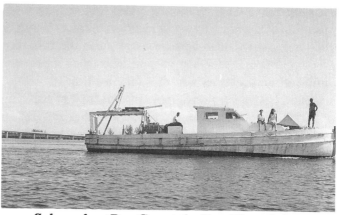

Salvage boat **Dee-Gee** *at the Fort Pierce inlet.*

Getting a work boat was the first order of business. There was a forty-foot, diesel engine work boat advertised in the paper for $2,000. They checked it out and found that it was a suitable salvage boat, wide of beam with a cabin forward to stow gear. They bought it, named it the *Dee-Gee*, and went to work overhauling the engine and scraping her bottom. After a few days of tender loving care it was ready to go salvaging. After Mel and Kip signed an agreement, the first wreck that Kip put Mel on was the "Wedge Wreck", just north of the Fort Pierce inlet.

As it turned out, the wreck was the *Urca de Lima*, and it was Ubilla's *refuerzo* or storeship. The *urca* had not been sunk by the hurricane, and after the storm passed she was the only ship afloat...at least for the next twenty-four hours she was. The *urca* had managed to drop her anchors and ride out the storm just inside the second reef. But the hurricane had sprung her mainmast, and the seamen aboard were unable to cut down the rigging. The waves rolled the *urca* from side to side during the day, finally opening up her hull. She sank on the spot in sixteen feet of water. There was only one-and-a-half *codos* (twenty-three inches) of water over her main cargo hatch, so all of her treasure was salvaged. In fact, the *urca* was able to victualize (provide with food) the other survivors until help arrived from Havana.

Kip had worked this site in 1960 and had recovered about a dozen silver wedges from under the ballast pile. As a result they nicknamed her the "Wedge Wreck". Their recovery was lost in the flood of silver coins from the Cabin Wreck site the following year. So when Mel took his group out to the site, they found a well-rounded ballast mound thirty-five feet wide by ninety feet long, with about twelve feet of water over the top of the pile. The sandy bottom stretched to the beach, and seaward lay the reefs. Mel had Arnold McLean's discriminating metal detector, one that could tell ferrous from non-ferrous metal. Not long after they began to work the pile Mel got a good solid "hit" on what appeared to be an irregular ballast stone. He brought it to the surface and handed it to Rupe Gates. "This thing has to be silver or something. I got a good reading on it." Rupe hit it with a five-pound sledge hammer, and the black crust broke away revealing...a silver wedge! It was the first treasure that the group had recovered in Florida and, although it had no markings, it was beautiful!! It was like a silver cake, or better yet, the icing on the cake. The cake they already had --they were treasure-finding!!! They worked the Wedge Wreck for about a month, finding a few silver coins but not much else.

The next wreck site that Kip put Mel on was the wreck off Sandy Point. If you were to stand in front of the Driftwood Inn at Route 60 and the ocean and look to the south, you would see a point of land about five miles away. That is Sandy Point. The *almiranta* of Echeverz' 1715 *flota* came ashore here. She was the *Rosario*, an English-built galleon that was sold to the Spanish in July, 1713. She was ballasted at over 350 tons and carried fifty-four cannons. The galleon struck the outer reefs about 2,000 feet offshore, and at one time forty-two cannon marked her path into the first reef. Salvagers during W.W.II had picked up most of her guns for scrap, but three still remained about 700 feet from the beach, on top of the first reef. The wreck site seemed to disappear after that, carrying with her 700 cannon balls weighing ten pounds each and at least another twelve cannon. The *Rosario* has not been located even today, but some day it will be. It was carrying a number of gold bars and about 50,000 pesos in registered treasure. Again, the passengers baggage would have contained a considerable treasure. Echeverz' son Pedro was the commanding officer of the *Rosario* and, along with a number of very important passengers, he did not survive the sinking.

Kip went with Mel that first day to point out the wreck site. They anchored the *Dee-Gee* about 200 feet offshore, just seaward of the first line of reefs. "The wreck is right about here," exclaimed Kip, pointing along the purple line of reef where it met the white sandy bottom leading to the beach. Mel went over the side and in a few minutes came up holding a ballast stone. Kip smiled and said, "The wreck is here, it's just scattered."

It was a flat calm day, and the water was clear. Mel and the others went on a scouting trip, checking over the sand pockets and the tops of the reefs. Before long, Mel spotted what he thought was the cascabel of a bronze cannon. He excitedly began fanning away the sand. Suddenly, that was all there was, and Mel thought to himself, "That sure is a short cannon." It turned out to be a bronze bell weighing close to fifty pounds. That was almost as good as a bronze cannon, except that the bell had no markings. He swam it back to the boat, but halfway there he had to drop the metal detector. It was a struggle to leap from the bottom to the boarding ladder, but he made it before the bell took him back to the bottom. Then, he couldn't find his metal detector. After some circle-searching he finally found it, some distance from where he had dropped it. The current was strong over the Sandy Point site.

They worked Sandy Point for the rest of the summer, recovering almost 2,000 silver coins that had been badly eroded by the sea. And along the cannon trail they recovered their first gold...two gold Bogotá two-*escudos*. Mel had a large gold ring made up with one of the gold coins. It was a badge of office for his new profession as "treasure-finder." The treasure lay scattered in the reef, and they were beginning to find it. The salvage season off Sandy Point ended there on a blustery September day. It hadn't been as successful as they had first imagined, but they were gaining experience every day, and they had the patience to see this first year through.

After some discussion it was decided to start an operation in the Florida Keys, where the water was clear and a whole lot warmer during the winter. Paying all expenses out of pocket meant that they had to keep diving, weather or not. They applied to William Kidd, head of the Florida Archaeological Division in Tallahassee, for a lease in Monroe County, and they were pleasantly surprised when Kidd granted them a salvage lease covering the entire county. They chose the name Armada Research as the Keys subsidiary of Treasure Salvors, the principal operating name for their group. They put Dick Williams in charge as operating manager in the Keys. They went to work with Fay Feild's magnetometer and before long had plotted twenty-five wreck sites. It would be a long winter.

William Kidd was the figurehead of the newly-formed state archaeological group, and he was easy to get along with. With a name like Kidd, he had to have a good sense of humor. The guidelines he set were easy to follow and had very few restrictions. "Gold fever" had yet to hit the State Department.

That first winter in the Keys, Armada Research rented a house large enough to hold the divers and their gear. Then it was endless days dragging the magnetometer along the reef line facing the deep blue Gulf Stream. The first wreck sites they located were in the Delta Shoal area off Marathon. One had a particularly large ballast mound, with ten-foot cannons scattered across the top of it. It was located in Coffins Patch and would later be identified as the *San Ignacio*, one of the missing 1733 Spanish galleons sunk by a hurricane. This site proved interesting enough that they spent the winter months picking through it.

There seemed to be wrecks everywhere, both old and fairly modern. They would pick out a prominent reef near the edge of the Gulf Stream, where the deep blue came up to meet the emerald green shallow water. Here they ran a magnetometer search in the shallow flats behind the reef, and here they located scatter patterns of wreck material...and more often a trail of ballast stones.

Without a way of moving the deeper sand, they were content to pick over the ballast mounds. There were iron cannons, mast rings, and more than a few huge anchors to mark on charts for future inspection.

The water was chilly, and when winter storms swept the outer reefs from the northeast the visibility left a lot to be desired. But they were in Florida, doing what they had always dreamed of doing, hunting for old Spanish galleons. They were a happy bunch of campers, spending every possible hour out on the reefs and gaining experience that would stand up well in the coming months.

Fisher family complete. Taffi, Kane, Kim, and Dirk.

10...THE GOLD WRECK

O ne evening Kip Wagner received a knock on his door. When he opened it, there stood three men who would be partly responsible for changing the name of a section of the Florida coastline to the "Treasure Coast". Bruce Ward, Don Nieman, and Frank Allen had come to Kip with a few gold coins they had recovered. They were dated in the 1714 period and were obviously from one of the wreck sites that Kip had an interest in. The trio had come to make a deal.

Kip Wagner checking out a silver plate concreted to a cannon found south of Sebastian Inlet. **Photo by: Dan Wagner.**

This was 1963, a time when sunken treasure was just beginning to rear its golden head. Finding coins along the beach meant certainly there was an important shipwreck just offshore. These three men were not treasure divers, although they did buy a small fourteen-foot boat and tried finding the source of coins they were picking up. They hadn't found what they were looking for, in fact, they were not quite sure what they were looking for. It was frustrating knowing that a golden galleon lay somewhere just offshore and not having the knowledge or the equipment to locate and salvage it. So they had come to Kip's doorstep to see if they could work something out.

They had the location --or close to it-- and they wanted a percentage for the information. Kip invited them in, and they sat around for awhile getting acquainted. Kip looked at the coins they had brought, showed them a few he had found, and noted that they seemed to be from the same time period. Kip was interested, but only if it was from a site he did not already know about. There were plenty of beachcombers scouring the beach after a bad storm, and some of them were picking up coins. The three men that sat facing Kip said that they had recovered the coins "out in the water." Frank Allen, a school teacher from the Orlando area, was their spokesman and soon got around to the reason they were there. "Can we make a deal if we show you where we found the coins?" Kip was interested, but firm, "Not if it's a site I already know about. Is it north or south of the Fort Pierce inlet?" Allen answered simply, "South."

The five sites that Kip was aware of were all located *north* of the Fort Pierce inlet; this had to be a new site. They discussed a percentage if the group could put Kip right on the site. They reached an agreement of forty percent, shook on it, and Kip later drew up a written agreement to that effect.

Mel had returned from his winter in the Keys, and after a few telephone calls Kip met with Mel near the Fort Pierce inlet. Together they drove to Frederick Douglass Park located two-and-a-half miles south of the inlet. The park was referred to as "Colored Beach" because during W.W.II it was used primarily by black people. There were a couple of changing rooms, an outdoor shower, and a few makeshift barbecues near a dirt parking lot. Kip led Mel along the beach, explaining that "some beachcombers have been picking up gold coins along this beach." He gestured towards an old tree, stripped of foliage and white with age. It had taken a dead hit by lightning several years before and was now leaning precariously seaward. "They found a few of the gold coins near the tree; the rest of them were scattered to the north from here."

Mel and Kip stopped to look at the line of reefs that lay only a stone's throw from where they were standing. The water was a dirty brown color, and only the surge over the tops of the reefs gave any indication that it would be a dangerous place to anchor a salvage boat. "Any idea where the ballast pile might be?" Kip shook his head, "It can be anywhere. The coins seem to have scattered a long way up the beach." They stood there awhile, trying to visualize a galleon breaking up in the surf line 250 years before. "Gold coins are too heavy to move around much; the pile has to be pretty close in. I'll get started on it right away." There was an eagerness in Mel's voice. It was almost as if he could sense a certain destiny waiting for him. He was about to become a legend.

Mel gathered his diving crew together and mapped out the area they would be working next. They called it the "Colored Beach Wreck" site. There was anticipation as they began operations that spring. They had six more months before the year was up, and they knew that their funds would possibly be vaporized before then. It had to be there; if only they could find the big pile of treasure before money and enthusiasm gave out.

That first trip to the site found the water still frigid and murky. All they could do was string out the magnetometer and drag a control buoy search over the area with the most potential. There were "hits", and after dropping a buoy near the anomaly, it was followed by a groping search over a reef or a sandy bottom. Visibility on the bottom was almost an inky blackness, and most of the hits were never located. The buoys were left in place until the water was clearer, but none of the hits was of a size to indicate a cannon or an anchor. The weeks began to drag on without success. In April, the water began to clear up, and the previous hits were investigated, but nothing was found to get excited about.

Mel Fisher and Fay Feild "magging" on the **Dee-Gee**
south of Fort Pierce Inlet.

One of the frustrating things for a salvage diver is to have clear water on top, but as he nears the bottom it is like being shut in a broom closet. The lights go out. Mel was intrigued with the idea that somehow he could "push" the clear water from the surface down to the bottom. He built a heavy plywood deflector on the stern of the *Dee-Gee*, and it worked...but not very well. Fay Feild was a genius about things like this, so Mel called him at his home in California. After explaining his problem over the 'phone, and what he had tried to do with the plywood, the two of them came up with a design to vector the propwash of the boat downward. Between the two of them they sketched the design out over the 'phone. What they came up with would later be known as a "mailbox". That's because it looked just like a mailbox, straight on four sides, with a ninety-degree curve at the top. Designed to swing down over the boat's propeller, it looked cumbersome.

Mel started building the deflector at Law's Fish House on Taylor creek, using the welding class techniques he had been taught at Purdue. About midnight Dick Williams stopped by, attracted by the electrical display. "Whatever you're building, you're keeping the neighborhood awake!" Mel told him about Fay and his idea on a deflector to get the clear water down to the bottom so they could see. Dick would be one of the benefactors, and being a master welder in the oil fields, he took over the project. With Mel cutting and Dick welding, they finally got the job done about daybreak. The end product was probably a little heavier than they had anticipated, and it *did* look like a mailbox!

The Fort Pierce inlet is home to a number of cargo vessels working the Bahama Island routes of supply. Some fairly large vessels use the inlet, so the U. S. Army Corps of Engineers keeps the inlet depth dredged to thirty-eight feet. The tidal sweep of the water through the opening carries the outfall of river and creek waters from miles away. Water hyacinths growing in the shallows turn the water into something resembling a weak cup of tea. When the tide takes the outfall seaward, the surface of the ocean takes on a brown blanket that rapidly spreads to the north and south along the coast. By the time the tide change halts the advance, the water has lost its visibility for as much as three miles. Working the bottom on the Colored Beach Wreck site, two-and-a-half miles south of the inlet, the divers' underwater visibility changes from several feet to several inches in a matter of minutes.

Mel decided that the best place to try out the new deflector was directly seaward of the inlet. They anchored the *Dee-Gee* in fifty feet of water about an hour after high tide. The flood of brown water had already begun its run to sea, and although there was still about fifteen feet of clear water on the surface, the bottom had about three feet of mud from years of run-off, and the visibility was already an inky black. The spot they had selected was over an old sunken barge. A hairy buoy marked the location. The deflector was dropped down over the *Dee-Gee*'s propeller and locked in place. In a moment they began to rev up the engine, slowly at first to see if the welding job would hold together. Once they were sure the deflector wouldn't come apart on them, they inched up on the throttle.

Mel was in the water, watching as a shaft of clear water funneled down to the bottom. He followed it, hovering just above where the blackness and the green water swirled. He watched as the layers of mud seemed to peel away and vanish into the perimeter of a maelstrom that surrounded him. Suddenly he could see the decking of the old barge. It was not only pushing clear water down to the bottom, the propwash was also uncovering whatever was there. Mel was surprised at the results, as surprised as the several large jewfish that had made their home in the wreckage. They could see this man-fish, just as Mel could see them. The "blower", as it was to be called later, would become the primary tool of the treasure salvager. It was the beginning of a new era in treasure salvage.

The winds of winter churned the waters off Fort Pierce, Florida, making any thoughts of salvage cold and uninviting. Treasure Salvors' boat ran course after course parallel to the beach, searching for the ballast pile they knew had to be somewhere close by. In the pile there would be anchors and cannon that would give them an anomaly. But day after day the magnetometer, trailing one hundred feet behind the *Dee-Gee*, remained silent. They had decided to cover 1,000 yards in all directions seaward of the Frederick Douglass Park, pacing fifty feet between sweeps and keeping beach markers aligned to keep them on course.

That winter of 1963, the weather never seemed to cooperate. Many days found ten-foot waves rolling in across the Bahama Channel. Afterwards, for a week or so, the water would be a milky white. When it seemed to clear up, the rain would come down in torrents. Then the flow of rainwater out of the Fort Pierce inlet would spread to the south like a dark underwater cloud. Even if the magnetometer got a "hit", the divers could not tell what the anomaly was. They would mark it with a buoy and check it out another day.

Christmas, 1963, had come and gone, the ornaments put away, and the Fishers' first New Year's celebration in Florida was history. They hadn't found their treasure yet, and so the celebration was of past expeditions to Panama and the Silver Shoals. But on everyone's mind was the treasure of the 1715 fleet. Records from Spain indicated that a substantial amount of treasure remained after the Spanish completed their salvage efforts in June, 1716. Over 1, 200,000 pesos in registered treasure remained somewhere on the bottom, scattered over the reefs close to shore. But why were they having such a difficult time finding it?

They had been working their magnetometer in search patterns over the area north of Frederick Douglass Park for almost three months and had found no trace of the wreck site. There was less than six months left of their one-year commitment to work Florida. Something had to be done to keep from wasting any more time. Ward, Nieman, and Allen had agreed to help them locate the wreck site, but now it seemed that every excuse possible was given why they could not come to Fort Pierce. It was obvious that the trio had recovered their gold coins on the beach and not out in the water. Mel called Kip and asked for a meeting.

"It's just not worth it! We've looked for that ghost galleon for over three months...and it just isn't where those guys said it was." Not only was he wasting time and money, but his share of any recovered treasure was even less than what Kip had agreed to give the three beachcombers. Mel figured it out that with the state of Florida taking twenty-five percent, and then Ward, Nieman, and Allen taking forty percent, the final split between Kip and Mel would get them only twenty-two and one-half percent apiece. With Mel paying all the bills and doing all the work, it was time for a re-shuffle. Mel advised Kip he no longer had a deal. The percentages had to change, or he was pulling his crew off the Colored Beach site.

Kip could see that it was a bad deal for Mel. In fact, he was a little surprised that Mel hadn't complained about it earlier. He offered to try a re-negotiation with the beachcombers for a smaller share. It was also evident to Kip that Ward, Nieman, and Allen had found the coins on the beach, not in the water. They had not known the exact location of the wreck site, only a general area where the coins had washed up on the beach. Part of the deal that

Kip had with them was that they would put Mel on the ballast pile, something they couldn't do. Mel agreed to go back to work while Kip set up a meeting with the beachcombers.

Within days, Ward, Nieman, and Allen sat across the table from Kip Wagner. The three sensed what was in the wind, but said nothing. Kip simply stated the facts. "Mel and his crew have been magging the area you put us on for the past three-and-a-half months, and so far...nothing! You promised to put them right on the ballast pile, and you haven't done that. Quite frankly, you haven't lived up to your end of the deal, and unless we make a new deal, Mel is going to pull his crew off the site." Ward seemed to be the spokesman, and he asked what Kip had in mind. "You can chip in and help pay expenses, take a lower percentage, or we can drop the whole project." Ward asked, "What kind of percentage are you talking about?" Kip looked at the three of them across the table, then turned to Ward and said, "We get ninety percent, you get ten percent."

It took less than a heartbeat before Ward exploded, "Ten percent, not on your life!" Kip was patient, and after waiting for the initial shock to settle, he stated again that, "Ten percent is better than nothing at all. And besides, if there is as much gold on the site as you think there is, ten percent could amount to quite a bit." The three stared at Kip from across the table, and it was obvious that they would have to think about this. Ward stood up and said, "No deal! Let's go guys." With that they stomped out of the house.

In the time it took them to drive around the block, they were back. Kip wasn't surprised. Without sitting down, Ward said, "We've agreed to fifteen percent." Kip shook his head, "Sorry guys, it's ten percent or nothing." Another few moments of silence, and then, "Okay, we agree to ten percent." Kip simply said, "It's a deal." They shook on it. Later the entire group --Real Eight and Mel's team-- confirmed the deal formally with the beachcombers. It was a gentleman's agreement, and they all shook on it. "No need to draw up new papers, as long as we all agree." Kip would regret those words later.

Mel went back to work magging the area north of Frederick Douglass Park. The blower worked better than Mel had hoped.

On days when the bottom was a limpid green, clear water from the surface gave them at least a few feet of visibility. The first week of April, 1964, saw a change in the weather. Winds from the west flattened out the ocean's surface, and the Gulf Stream moved closer to shore, bringing with it clean, blue water. Towards the end of the month they made their first hit. Rupe Gates checked out a rather large anomaly and surfaced shouting, "Cannon!" It lay against a reef, and within minutes of using the blower to dust off the sand in the area, about one hundred silver coins were uncovered near the edge of the reef.

The area was further north than the original area they had searched off Douglass Beach, about 1,500 yards from the park road. It was almost five hundred yards further north than the dead, bent tree they had been using for a landmark as the north boundary of their original survey. This new area now became ground zero. As they widened the search area they found more Spanish cannons and a pair of old anchors. They knew that they were getting close. They could feel it. Every day on the site they had a new enthusiasm, a sense of urgency. Everyone volunteered to be the first one in the water. There was no longer talk of a "ghost" galleon. Then they found the ballast pile!

The ballast pile lay little more than eight hundred feet from shore, between two limestone reef formations. The water was twelve feet deep above the formations and sixteen feet between. A coral reef extended to the north, sand to the south. Shoreward were two more lines of reefs, rugged and shallow. It would be a difficult area to work. After the coin find, it was like waiting for the second shoe to drop. It dropped on May eighth.

Mo Molinar was working the bottom by himself, about fifteen feet seaward of the blower activity. He saw that rare glint of gold in the sand, and with heart-thumping excitement, he picked up an eight-pound disk. Before he could head for the surface with his prize, he spotted another glint of gold. He could hardly believe his eyes, but there was a second gold disk! With both hands full of gold he bolted for the surface. He had to ask, "Mel, is this brass, or is it...?" Before he could finish, Mel finished for him, "Gold!" It brought instantaneous chaos on board the *Dee-Gee*. Rupe

Gates nearly stepped on Mo's head as he headed for the bottom himself.

It seemed that everyone had a chance to mount up and ride off in all directions as they scoured the bottom. But there was no more gold to be found that day. Only the ominous waterspout that was steering their way could cause them to call it quits and head for the dock...and a long overdue celebration.

♐

Fay Feild, inventor, electronics "wizard", treasure salvor, and Fisher family friend. He was instrumental in the development of the early propwash deflector known as a "mailbox".

11...A CARPET OF GOLD

"You are invited to a birthday party!" It was Taffi Fisher's birthday, a young, bubbly three year old with red hair like her mother. Mel used the party as an excuse to bring the salvage divers together and share in the excitement of Mo's gold find. Only his Treasure Salvors group was aware of the two gold disks that Mel now kept hidden in his closet at 628 Banyan Road in Vero Beach. Mel wanted to make the announcement with the entire Real Eight group together, and what better excuse than a birthday party! And so, on May eleventh, the salvage divers gathered. Kip Wagner, Lou Ullian, Dan Thompson, Harry Cannon, Del Long, and Doc Kelso, all members of the Real Eight group, were in for a surprise.

It was difficult for the Treasure Salvors divers to keep a lid on the excitement that each felt as the salvagers gathered in Mel's living room. Mel, Deo, Mo Molinar, Rupe Gates, Dick Williams, and Walt Holzworth were the new kids on the block. Kip's group had been diving on the 1715 wreck sites for four years, each year bringing up some great treasures. But the gold had escaped them. Now, in their first year, the "amateurs" had hit it big. Trying to keep a straight face, act casual, and not grin too much, was an extremely difficult task, but Mel and the rest pulled it off.

After wishing Taffi a happy birthday, the two groups sat around for an hour snacking, having Mel's favorite double rum and coke, and talking shipwrecks. Kip was actively working the Cabin Wreck site, and it was producing quite a bit of silver coins and some great artifacts. Mel had been frustrated because he had spent almost four months chasing the elusive "ghost galleon" off Colored Beach and had finally located a few of her cannon and the ballast pile. In many ways, the Real Eight divers were a little hesitant to discuss their successes for fear of upsetting this new group. And so it went for about an hour.

Mel had hidden the two gold disks under a sofa cushion, and for that first hour Lou Ullian sat perched over fifteen pounds of gold. When he finally moved into the kitchen to fix another double rum and coke, Mel slipped the heavy disks from under the cushion and put them in Mo's hands. At the time no one seemed to notice. Lou came back into the room, and there was a pause in the buzz of conversation. Mo took that opportunity to walk to the center of the room and announce, "This is what you are looking for!", and he held up the two disks.

***Diver Walt Holzworth holding two gold disks
moments after recovery.***

At first there was shocked silence; the Real Eight group could hardly believe what they were looking at. It was only after they looked around the room and saw the ear to ear grins on the Treasure Salvors divers that they realized the gold disks were the real thing. Then pandemonium broke out, and everyone was talking at the same time. Each Salvors diver had his own version to tell of the day the disks came up, and each story got better than the one before it. But it really didn't matter which version was the best, the real thing was lying there on the coffee table. The change in both groups was almost instantaneous. They were laughing and grinning, slapping one another on the back, and suddenly they were one. The Salvors group had become veterans over night, and the two groups stood on equal ground. They were accepted by their peers as treasure *finders*, and in the treasure salvage community, that is as good as it gets.

The disks remained the center of attraction until almost midnight. Taffi, the birthday girl, had long since drifted off into slumberland. When the divers went their separate ways that night, surely more than one had dreams of gold disks scattered over the ocean floor. It would be a night they would never forget.

Mel Fisher surfacing with a 20-pound copper disk.

The next morning, May twelfth, 1964, Mel woke up to a strong wind out of the east. As the day wore on it seemed the wind increased to near gale proportions. There would be no diving that day. A few of the divers met, and together they walked the beach where they could see the buoy about 700 feet offshore, marking the gold spot. The waves were rolling in, curling across the reef into a white froth and thundering to the beach. There was some concern that the buoy would walk the bottom and the gold spot would be lost. The buoy stayed in place for the next eighteen days as the wind continued to howl from the wrong direction. It is more than frustrating to watch the seas churn your salvage site into an opaque watery mess, but knowing that more gold could be only a few yards from shore compounds the frustration.

For the next three weeks the *Dee-Gee* got special attention. Oil was changed and the transmission checked, compressor spark plugs were cleaned, anchor lines were inspected for reef damage, and the marine radio was turned on and off a dozen times. The team was ready to go the moment the weather let up. And then it was the morning of June first. The wind had shifted around to the west during the night, flattening out the seas a bit. The word by 'phone was "Let's go!", and daybreak saw the gear being stowed aboard *Dee-Gee*. By the time the sun had a chance to dry the dew off the windshield, they were out of the Fort Pierce inlet and heading south towards the wreck site two-and-a-half miles away.

Patience and perseverance are the two primary traits salvage divers must learn, and the Treasure Salvors group had already been initiated. For the next few days they diligently worked the gold spot, moving the *Dee-Gee* only a few feet at a time as they excavated the sand around the ballast pile with the blower mounted on the stern. They found nothing, no trace of shipwreck material, not even a pottery shard. It was as if the site had given them just a nibble --enough to keep them excited-- then stood back and smiled as the divers worked each day through empty holes in the bottom of the seabed.

It was lunch time, and Mel pointed to an area about seventy feet north of the gold spot. "I think we ought to look over there; I feel lucky." Anchors were reset and the *Dee-Gee* winched over to the new location. Then the divers settled back on the engine cover for a hot cup of coffee and a sandwich. There was some talk about working the ballast pile the next day, and everyone kept his fingers crossed for the good weather to hang around. Mel had kept the engines of the *Dee-Gee* idling during lunch to move the sand off the bottom. Mo was the first to finish his sandwich, and he slipped into a SCUBA tank, pulled on his fins and face mask, and waved as he rolled over the side.

Visibility that day under water was at least twenty feet, and as soon as Mo was in the water and looked down, he couldn't believe his eyes! The bottom of the ocean looked like a carpet of gold!! There were coins lying everywhere. He let the weight of his tank and gear carry him to the bottom; he could hardly breathe. Once there Mo began gathering up coins in both hands. When he couldn't hold any more, he headed for the surface. "Gold! Gold!!" he shouted, and leaning over the stern he opened his clenched fists and let the other divers see the coins. It was bedlam as the divers scrambled for the water. Now everyone was on the bottom, picking up gold coins which seemed to be lying everywhere.

Gold doubloons the size of a silver dollar, gold four-*escudos* about as large as a fifty-cent piece, and it seemed hundreds of one- and two-*escudo* gold coins littered the sandy bottom. It was an elevator, up to the boat with a handful of coins, then back down again to scoop up more. It went on for most of the day, and when the last had been picked up the count was 1,033 gold coins, a small fortune in 1964 when the average gold shipwreck coin was worth at least $500. They were an exhausted, but exuberant group of divers who tied up to the dock at sunset. The 'phones buzzed long into the night as Kip's group was brought up to speed on what Mel's group had found. The divers were too exhausted to do much in the way of celebrating, but they were back on the site at daybreak.

The blanket of gold coins had been recovered in a narrow area between a limestone reef on the seaward side and a more rugged reef shoreward. Now they anchored the salvage boat within a few feet of the rugged reef and dropped the blower down over the boat's propeller. That first dusting of the reef was everything they had hoped for; there were gold coins in almost every pothole. They were scattered all over the reef, and after the ones lying on top were picked up, the divers went after the others that ...d managed to squirrel their way into cracks and fissures. By the end of the day they had added 900 more gold coins to the "pot of gold." It was a dream come true, one they hoped wouldn't end.

Bringing up the gold! Rupe Gates, Walt Holzworth, Dick Williams, Mel Fisher, and Mo Molinar.

The coins were mostly Mexican "cob" type coins, irregularly cut from a planchet of gold, clipped to the right weight of twenty-seven grams to an eight-*escudo*, and then struck with dies. Dates on the coins ranged from 1699 to 1715, but more often than not, the date was missing because the planchet was not large enough to contain the entire shield and its inscription. There is something about gold coins that creates a "gold fever" with everyone that holds one in his hand. It is said that if you close your eyes and squeeze the coin, it will become hot. And, if you make a wish, the wish will come true. As the divers fondled the coins, unable to believe that this was actually happening to them, they surely made many wishes. It *was* a dream come true.

Mel Fisher on* Dee-Gee *deck with a wet suit of gold coins.

By the end of the week over 2,500 gold coins had been recovered. This presented a problem to both salvage groups. If word leaked out that literally "millions" of dollars in gold lay exposed on the bottom of the ocean, the area would soon be swarming with pirate divers. It was necessary to keep a lid on the recoveries until they were sure that they had cleaned out the gold hole. They also realized that they had to report their finds to the state of Florida in a timely manner. It was a dilemma that would soon begin to rock their boat.

***Mel Fisher and Kip Wagner with treasure recovered
2-1/2 miles south of Fort Pierce Inlet.***

Mel's group had help from the Real Eight divers as Ullian, Long, and Thompson helped in the recoveries. As the gold coins dwindled in numbers, the excitement and enthusiasm did not. The salvagers had their celebration, and it was a humdinger! But there seems to be a cloud in every silver lining, and the treasure clouds were quick in forming. It was during the following week that Mel noticed a low-flying airplane buzzing their salvage site. One of his divers noticed someone in a white shirt and tie peering out of the 'plane with a pair of binoculars. The state of Florida had arrived.

12...THE TREASURE WAR BEGINS

I t is amazing what effect gold has on the lives of people; the
people on the street, the salvage divers, the state officials, and
bureaucrats as well. In 1849, Sutter's Mill in northern
California became the mecca for thousands of prospectors from
all over the United States. They traveled to the west coast by ship,
mule train, horse and wagon, and many on foot. There was hope -
-that one chance in thousands-- that they would find a pocket full
gold nuggets and be set for life. And life was pretty rugged in
northern California in 1849. Home was usually a sailcloth tent. It
was cold at night, hot during the day, a back-breaking struggle to
pan the streams for gold, and an even harder struggle to keep
what was found. There wasn't much to look forward to other than
the next pan full of gravel.

In many ways the same thing happened in Florida that summer
in 1964. National publicity was suddenly bestowed upon the
small, quiet community of Fort Pierce. Until that time, the only
interest anyone had in Fort Pierce was the inlet it provided from
the Intracoastal Waterway to the Atlantic Ocean, the only inlet
along forty-six miles of the east coast of Florida. But in 1715 the
Spanish treasure fleet would have a hand in changing that image.
One of its galleons was destroyed close to shore --during a savage
storm-- less than three miles south of the inlet, spilling thousands
of gold and silver coins among the reefs. Soon after Mel Fisher's
group Treasure Salvors recovered the golden bonanza the story
was carried in every newspaper and on every television station
across the country.

The value of the find was estimated in the millions. *National
Geographic* published the story in January, 1965, and the color
photographs of coins and jewelry, as well as the intriguing story
of treasure found, aroused the treasure fever in every reader.
Thousands of people drove, flew, even hitch-hiked their way to
the Florida "Treasure Coast" as it was now being called. Many
actually expected to pick up enough gold coins along the beach to
make them rich. More metal detectors and phony treasure maps
were sold in stores and on street corners in three months than
were sold in the entire United States in a year. The beach opposite

the site where Mel's boats were salvaging became a grandstand with often a hundred or more people swinging metal detectors, wading in the surf, or just sitting as spectators. And at night the sand dunes became a habitat of sleeping bags, stuffed with people drawn by the ineradicable desire to be close to treasure, to riches beyond the imagination.

The Treasure Salvors Team.
Mo Molinar, Dick Williams, Walt Holzworth,
Mel and Deo Fisher, Fay Feild, and Rupe Gates.

Then, suddenly, the sleeping giant of bureaucratic control was awakened. Until that time the arrangement between treasure salvagers and the state of Florida had been what has to be considered a "gentlemen's agreement." Art McKee had received the first treasure salvaging lease in 1951. The state officials never visited him in the Florida Keys where he was actively salvaging

Spanish galleons from the 1733 fleet. He opened a museum on Plantation Key and stocked it with coins and artifacts he recovered, and he gave the state twenty-five percent of what came up from the bottom. Here was a mutual relationship which was entirely satisfactory until it was discovered that the state could not protect McKee's leases from outside intruders. Even then, the relationship continued at arm's length.

In 1960, Kip Wagner worked out a lease arrangement with the state that gave him exploratory rights which covered fifty miles of coastline, from Sebastian Inlet to St. Lucie Inlet. At that time Florida had the Internal Improvement Fund, an agency that was given the responsibility to monitor salvage rights. Van H. Ferguson was the director, certainly a gentleman in his own right. Realizing that salvaging shipwrecks along the coast would produce some potentially valuable contributions to the Florida State Museum in Gainesville, he appointed Dr. William H. Sears and Dr. John M. Goggin of the museum to work with the salvagers.

The relationship became a very informal, first name arrangement, one that satisfied both parties. At that time the state received a twenty-five percent share. It was a free gift from the private sector, one that did not cost the taxpayers a cent. In 1962 this was the *only* state program to monitor treasure salvage. At an official meeting of the Internal Improvement Board in 1962, the arrangement between the state and the salvors was recorded in the minutes. Not a great deal of treasure was coming up off the bottom, but enough for Sears and Goggin to see that somewhere down the road a large museum would be required to exhibit it. Before Goggin died in late 1962 he wrote a number of articles on Spanish fleet recoveries that are highly regarded even today. After 1962 Wagner had an even closer relationship with Dr. Sears, with quarterly reports and 'phone calls to circumvent rumors that surround all treasure projects.

In 1963, Van Ferguson retired. Governor Farris Bryant appointed William Kidd to succeed him, and Dr. Sears continued to act as the liaison between the state and the treasure salvagers. The Improvement Fund was an important agency; treasure hunting was only a small part of its responsibilities. So as it turned out, "Billy the Kidd" was in the saddle when Mel Fisher struck gold. Kip Wagner had called Dr. Sears and advised him personally that Fisher had recovered a number of gold coins, and that they were being placed in a local bank for safekeeping until a division could be effected. Sears said that that was satisfactory.

At the time, it is possible that Sears did not inform Kidd of the recovery immediately. When rumor that Spanish gold had been recovered from a wreck site near Fort Pierce reached Kidd, he was levitated from his chair. Rather than consult Sears, he decided to check on the rumors himself. He called into his office Florida Highway Patrol Captain Ed Reddick and Paul Baldwin, manager of the Internal Improvement Fund and employee of the state for twenty-nine years. He asked them to go to Fort Pierce and see if they could get a lead on the movement of Spanish gold in the area. James Bond --Double-O-Seven himself-- would have blushed at the antics which followed.

First it was the airplane flyovers, binoculars trained on the salvage boats. Then, rather than openly approaching the treasure salvors and getting straight answers, the state's "investigators" went to several prominent business men in the area to ask if they had seen anything in the way of Spanish gold. Next they went to the local photographers to ask if they had taken pictures of any gold recently. Finally on the list were the express companies, who were quizzed to determine if they had received any gold for recent shipment. In the meantime, Reddick did some "sand snooping." Hidden in the thick palmetto bushes that stood behind the dune line, he watched for hours --through high-powered binoculars-- as the Fisher boat *Dee-Gee* worked just offshore.

The boat was less than 600 feet from the shoreline, so Reddick missed nothing. The divers had nothing to hide; they were too elated with what was being recovered to hide much of anything. Then Reddick rented a boat, a beard, and a fishing pole. The next day he was near the *Dee-Gee* fishing. Before long he was able to strike up a conversation with the divers, who promptly invited him aboard the boat. The entire operation was discussed freely, and Reddick went back to his own rented boat...probably disappointed.

It seemed to Reddick and Baldwin that they had run into a blank everywhere they looked. As a last resort, Baldwin and Reddick decided to check out local banks. In two banks in Vero Beach and one in Melbourne, they found that gold had been deposited in safety storage areas --part under the name Cobb Coin Company and part under Real Eight Company. One box in Melbourne had the label "State", and several bags in the two Vero Beach banks were similarly labeled. To them this meant the salvors had planned to split with the state.

Three weeks of investigation completed, Reddick and Baldwin reported back to Kidd on what they had uncovered. Kidd's first reaction was to arrest Fisher as a "poacher" on the treasure site. Rather than a 'phone call, Wagner was astonished to suddenly have a group of state officials at his doorstep. He politely explained that Cobb Coin Company was part of the Mel Fisher group, and that Mel worked for him. Fisher was called in, and both salvors were very cooperative. At Wagner's home were a number of larger artifacts, and Wagner pointed out ones that had been labeled for the state. The end result was that Kidd had a clearer picture of the relationship between salvors and the state of Florida. Both sides agreed that controls and better accounting procedures were needed in view of the treasure that was being recovered. But in Tallahassee...trouble was brewing.

Carl Clausen was hired as the Internal Improvement Fund underwater archaeologist. His job was to begin monitoring the day to day dive operations of the salvors and making sure that the state received its fair share. Carl set about doing more than that. He began a systematic study of the wreck site that Fisher's group was working, two-and-a-half miles south of the Fort Pierce inlet. This wreck was soon identified --to the best of everyone's knowledge-- as the *patache* of the 1715 fleet *Nuestra Señora de las Nieves* (Our Lady of the Snows). On a bottom survey chart the locations of recovered artifacts, cannon, anchors...and anything else of importance...was drawn in. Soon the semblance of a scatter pattern began to emerge. His work began creating an interest in the state's efforts to grab a larger share of the booty that was now estimated at over $1 million.

Kidd made the mistake of writing a letter to Col. Kirkman of the Department of Public Safety, in which he indicated that Reddick's investigative work had "located sizable recoveries of gold and silver, which have been removed from state-owned property. They are now in the process of inventorying and collecting all of this material and storing it in a safe location. Let me say that through the efforts of Ed I believe the state of Florida will recover two or three hundred thousand dollars that otherwise would have been lost". This letter fell into the hands of members of the board of the Improvement Fund. Suddenly both Kidd and Governor Bryant came under a blistering attack in their handling of treasure leases.

The *Miami Herald*, always on the lookout for a controversy, jumped on the issue like a chicken on a June bug. On the front page of the Thursday, December 17, 1964, *Herald* was the headline, "Is $1Million in Spanish Gold Lost?" It was reported by Robert Sherrill that treasure hunters had gone out of their state-granted leases to recover more than a million in Spanish gold, and that state officials did not find out about it until investigated by a Florida Highway Patrol captain. This story was followed up on almost a daily basis, highly critical of the way Kidd and Bryant ran the treasure program.

Dr. Charles Fairbanks, chairman of the Department of Anthropology at the University of Florida, and also chairman of a special advisory committee to the Improvement Fund, jumped on the bandwagon. He let the *Herald* know that "Since our meeting in March, and at every meeting since, we have advised the trustees of the Improvement Fund that the state should take over 100 percent of the treasure salvaging operation." The *Herald* headlined this, "State Lost Treasure Because It Wouldn't Listen To Us." The article went on to say that the state leasing policy of offshore treasure hunting and salvaging is inconsistent and chaotic, and that the state's effort to protect its ocean treasure has been virtually non-existent. Shortly afterwards, Kidd resigned.

Before Kidd left, he stated for the records, "Although Real Eight's records were not as good as they might be, they were as good as you could expect. Gold fever is gold fever, a man's hands will shake when he holds the stuff. If the state is not too strict on commercial salvagers, it is only right, because the companies invest a great deal of time and money in the treasure hunt." To Kidd must go the credit for the re-opening of Florida's coasts to treasure hunting. Kidd must also be credited for the fact that treasure hunting is done with a minimum of violence and claim-jumping. Thousands of people have died for Spanish treasure. What was taken by force in the days of Jolly Roger today is taken by lease.

Governor Bryant, throughout the controversy, sided with the treasure salvors. He believed that private enterprise, for a seventy-five percent cut, could do a better job. But because of the pressure of the press --and members of his cabinet-- he made some changes. In 1965, at the suggestion of Secretary of State Adams, the responsibility of the treasure program was transferred to the Antiquities Board. Paul Selle was placed in charge of the program that was headquartered at the museum in Gainesville. In the face of a series of articles in the *Miami Herald* on "possible piracy" of recovered treasure, a moratorium was called on salvage work until new leases and guidelines could be written.

The *Miami Herald* articles, true to their controversial nature, were full of innuendoes. In one article by Sherrill, it stated that, "Most of the recent rich discoveries have been made by one company which, for reasons best known to itself, staked out claims under a variety of names 'Armada Research', 'Treasure Salvors', and 'Universal Salvage'. By whatever name it operates, the company feeds all its treasure to another group 'Real Eight Co., Inc.' " The *Herald* knew that Real Eight was the contractor of record on the treasure sites, that all recoveries would go through that company.

Wagner explained that Fisher's group was Universal Salvage when it moved from California to Florida as a sub-contractor. Once in Florida, they adopted the name Treasure Salvors and set up Armada Research to work treasure sites in the Florida Keys. A simple explanation such as this was ignored by the *Herald*, which opted for controversy at the expense of the treasure groups. Other newspapers picked up on the story, and as an end result the public suddenly had an image change of salvage divers. Rather than the "dream come true" visualization of sunken treasure, Fisher's group was pictured as a band of thieves, stealing from the state.

Mel Fisher may have seemed calm on the outside; inside he was seething at the lack of good press reporting.

As it turned out, all the publicity had generated a number of other treasure salvage groups, all wanting to get a piece of the action. They flooded the switchboards to the office of Robert Parker, the new director of the Antiquities Board, in an attempt to have leases assigned. Several of the groups had prominent politicians supporting them, putting pressure on Parker's office to open up the fifty miles of coast that Wagner had under his agreement with the state. In order to relieve the tension building between his group and state officials, Kip Wagner gave up the fifty-mile exclusive, but was able to negotiate a deal with Parker giving him exclusive leases to the eight sites he believed to be of the 1715 Spanish treasure fleet. The remainder of the fifty miles was opened to other salvors. The rush was on.

13...THE TREASURE COAST

In 1965, the east coast of Florida --from Sebastian Inlet south to Fort Pierce Inlet-- entered the history books as the "Treasure Coast". Mel Fisher had hit it big...what many historians estimated at over $5 million in Spanish treasure, recovered from the salvage site just south of the inlet at Fort Pierce. For awhile it seemed that the treasure would never stop. The Real Eight group brought their salvage boat *Derelict* to the Fort Pierce site to help in the recoveries, trying out a new type of propwash mounted on the side of the boat and driven by a deck-mounted engine.

Mel holding up a treasure coin.

In May, they were dusting an area a few hundred feet north of Mel's boat when they also hit it big. Over 1,000 gold coins were recovered, some still stacked in piles on the bottom. In the meantime, Mel's group continued to recover gold and silver coins, as well as jewelry and artifacts, from the wreck that had scattered northward along the reef for over a mile. It had become an unbelievable wreck site.

As the news of the treasure spread across the United States, an old nemesis appeared unexpectedly. Eric Schiff, from California, heard of Mel's good fortune, and being one of the early days' investors in the Silver Shoals expedition, he was sure that his contract with Mel still held water. He sued for some of the treasure as a partner in the old company, Universal Salvage. The case was dismissed, so he filed again. Three years later it moved to arbitration in California, where it died. But the time and the aggravation --as well as the attorney fees-- put a heavy load on Mel. He began to wonder if any more unknowns would come out of the woodwork.

In the Florida Keys, Mel put Dick Williams in charge of Armada Research, and using Fay Feild's magnetometer they soon began locating a number of wreck sites. The Florida Keys seemed to be a magnet for wrecks. Almost every reef had signs of debris...some modern, some fairly ancient. Marathon became a base of operations, because most of the wreck sites with potential were located within an hour or so of boat travel. A ballast pile in Coffins Patch, a few miles northeast of Marathon, soon became the target of a full-scale operation. Here was a fairly large shipwreck, sporting a number of ten-foot cannons sitting atop ballast stones that were piled six feet high over an area 130 feet by fifty feet. Conglomerates of cannon balls and barshot were everywhere. Ship's fittings seemed to weld the ballast stones together.

As each significant "hit" was discovered around the site, a red buoy was dropped. When they ran out of red buoys, they used green buoys. One day, as Williams looked out over the several acres of red and green buoys he remarked, "Looks like a Christmas tree, loaded with ornaments!" Thereafter the site became known as the "Christmas Tree Wreck". It produced many silver coins and artifacts for Armada Research along the scatter pattern that stretched from an old abandoned beacon foundation towards Key Colony Beach several miles away. In later years the scatter trail became the "sleeper" of the 1733 fleet when a bonanza of treasure was recovered.

As the winter months of 1965 approached, Mel moved his Fort Pierce crew south where the water remained clearer...and warmer. In that way he could stay actively salvaging throughout the year. It had been a very successful season overall; they had recovered more gold and silver than in any previous year. By the end of '65, Treasure Salvors and Real Eight had salvaged over 37,000 silver coins; a 250-pound packing chest of silver coins; 1,782 gold coins; forty-one disks of copper; twenty-nine silver wedges; twelve silver "cup cakes"; an assortment of rings, earrings, brooches, and miscellaneous jewelry; and thousands of historical artifacts.

One of the problems that Mel would continually face in his salvaging career he now encountered as 1965 came to a close. In the salvaging game there is an inherent financial crunch that faces the salvager. Although Mel and his group had recovered an amazing amount of gold and silver coins worth millions, it was many months from the time of recovery until a division with the state of Florida was made. Then a division with the Real Eight group had to be made, followed by a division with the partners of Treasure Salvors. The next major hurdle was one of marketing the coins. The dilemma was...if a large number of coins hit the market at once, the value of each would drop considerably. There was a growing demand for 1715 era coins because few, if any, existed in collections before the recovery. At the same time, flooding the market with gold and silver coins simultaneously just wasn't feasible.

Mel had formed a company, Cobb Coin Company, exclusively for the purpose of marketing the coins, but sales were slow. In the meantime the day to day operations had long since eaten up the initial cash that the California group had started with. Mel found some relief at the local banks. His reputation along the east coast was golden, and by using some of the coins as collateral he was able to secure a loan from each of two local banks for $100,000.

Later he had to secure an additional loan from a Fort Lauderdale bank for $60,000, but the Treasure Salvors ship remained afloat. When he desperately needed transportation, Mel put a few gold doubloons in his pocket and visited the local Cadillac dealer; he was able to drive home in a new Cadillac.

Bad press relations continued to fester, seeded by the academic community as well as state officials. Dr. Hale Smith, another University of Florida anthropology professor, made a press statement, "Employing ordinary recovery procedures, we could have found the Fort Pierce wreck. The locations along the east coast are well known to scholars. The state can salvage the wrecks cheaper than can private salvaging companies." It suddenly appeared as though locating and salvaging old Spanish galleons was a "piece of cake." This was quickly followed with another attempt by state officials to take over this seemingly lucrative salvaging business.

Attorney General Earl Faircloth asked the state legislature to "put Florida into the treasure salvaging business." He said the state of Florida should send its own divers to the bottom of the sea to bring up valuable gold, silver, and jewelry --as well as the historical artifacts which sank with Spanish treasure ships over 200 years ago. "That way the state could keep *all* the booty, estimated to be in the hundreds of millions of dollars." Faircloth further stated that others on the state Antiquities Commission were not so sure that the state had gotten the full amount of its twenty-five percent of everything brought to the surface. "There has been some pirating." He added, "I do not think it would cost the state a lot of money to do the job. Besides, commercial divers do not have the time, nor do they care, to save historical items like a 'ship's log' and cannon balls."

The salvage community was shocked at the numbers that the state officials were bouncing around. It was obvious that most of the people attacking the treasure salvage community had little or no knowledge in this area. But they were also aware that state-hired archaeologists had little enthusiasm or desire to dive for treasure among the reefs where visibility was usually a matter of inches, and daily encounters with fairly large sharks could raise the hair on the back of your neck.

In 1966, Haydon Burns was elected governor of Florida. It soon became clear that he was strenuously opposed to the idea of the state becoming involved in the business of hunting treasure. Two members of his cabinet, however, continued to oppose him in favor of the state taking over the treasure hunting business. Siding with Attorney-General Faircloth was the re-elected Secretary of State, Tom Adams. Together they proposed setting aside three large sections of the Florida coastline that would be off limits to the salvage community. This area would be designated for state-financed historic salvage. The proposal was voted down in a cabinet meeting --four to two!

What Burns did see down the road was the Treasure Coast as a valid tourist attraction. The state's board of tourism began highlighting the treasure recoveries in brochures that were being mailed not only in the United States, but overseas as well. The name "Treasure Coast Mall" became a favorite among the communities and cities near the ocean. You could now buy an automobile at "Treasure Coast Motors". Before long signs along U. S. Highway 1 were displaying "Treasure Coast Boating Center", "Treasure Coast Carpets and Interiors", "Treasure Coast Irrigation", and "Treasure Coast Plating and Polishing". The traveling public had now become aware of what Wagner and Fisher had found. It was something you could hang your hat on, something that visitors were eager to hear all about. In the barber shop chairs the first question asked was, "Did you hear if anything came up today?" It was a reputation that salvage divers would manage to keep alive for many years to come.

And Mel Fisher continued to help make it happen. He devised the "Gold Digger", a barge with three prop washes on board. Art Hartman, a fellow treasure salvor, helped build the barge with junkyard parts to keep the costs low. By using airplane propellers instead of the usual boat propellers, the diameter of the propwash was increased significantly. From the first moment the barge was put into use it was a huge success. The barge began uncovering large areas of the bottom without moving the four anchors which positioned the blowers. And they began finding treasure. The crew was so ecstatic that they dumped a box of laundry soap on the tilted canvas roof over the barge, watered it down, and spent the day sliding off the roof into the ocean.

*A jubilant group of salvage divers celebrating
the launching of the "Gold Digger".*

As artifacts from the wreck site south of the Fort Pierce inlet began to thin out, he moved his barge to a new site opposite the first green of the Rio Mar Golf Course in Vero Beach. It was here that the *capitana* of General Echeverz' 1715 fleet had come ashore. The *Nuestra Señora del Carmen* at 1,072 tons was the largest galleon of the eleven ships sunk in the 1715 hurricane. Armed with fifty-two iron cannon, she carried in registered treasure 79,967 pesos in gold bars and coins, 309 *castellanos* of gold dust, 1,175 pesos in *plata doble*, three gold chains, and other general cargo. The galleon had passed through the outer reefs intact but was rolled over on her starboard side by the huge waves when it reached shallow water. Much of her treasure was not recovered by the Spanish salvagers because the ballast stones had covered the treasure when it sank.

As Fisher's crew began dusting the wreck site 900 feet from the beach, he found two large anchors and nineteen cannon still atop the ballast pile. In eighteen feet of water he began uncovering handfuls of silver coins, then two beautiful gold crosses studded with pearls, gold rings with emeralds, then several gold bars, and finally 149 gold coins. It was a great wreck site. The Treasure Coast was still living up to its name.

14...HUNT FOR THE BIG "A" BEGINS

"I'm buying a house with the biggest pool and the biggest sand box in the world!" The children of Mel Fisher sat on his armchair and on the floor at his feet with mixed emotions about moving to the Florida Keys. They had a lot of friends in Vero Beach, and they thought the school they were attending was great. Their house on Banyan Road was close to the ocean, but the thought of having a big swimming pool and sand box made it a bit easier to accept the change. Once the move was made --to a house on the ocean-- Mel made a sweeping gesture and said, "See, I told you it was a big swimming pool. And the beach is probably the biggest and best sand box anyone could ever ask for!" Dirk, Kim, Kane, and Taffi already knew what to expect from their ebullient father.

Several reasons caused Mel to move to the Keys. Treasure Salvors had run its course with the 1715 fleet of treasure galleons. The state of Florida, as well as the press, had given Mel a hard time, and to top it off Real Eight had asked the courts to clarify their contract with Treasure Salvors. Behind the scenes there had been some problems with Real Eight giving contradictory statements to the IRS regarding Treasure Salvors, and in turn Real Eight felt that Mel's group hadn't given them some credit where credit was due in the recoveries.

Another reason for the decision to move south had been the state's new restrictive policies on treasure salvage. Once the state took control of the treasure hunting business they imposed bonds on the salvors and required daily logs and tagging of each item brought to the surface. State agents were assigned to the salvage vessels to make sure that the state received its fair share of the recoveries. The vessels were required to remain at the dock until the agents arrived, and often that was hours into the diving day. Outside the three-mile limit the state was not involved, and the wrecks along the outer reefs of the Keys came under federal law which was much less restrictive.

But the crux of the matter was that the drive that Fisher's group had was taking them beyond the circle of Real Eight salvage. Mel was considerably more dynamic, but some inner drive...something that all the previous experience had been leading up to...now led him south. He never knew exactly what it was; all he felt was that something bigger in life was waiting for him. He could only follow his hunches, and those hunches led him to the Florida Keys. Here the waters were warm and clear all year, and wrecks were scattered across just about every reef on the charts.

Mel Fisher at his Vero Beach office.

So in 1968, Mel moved his family to Islamorada on Upper Matecumbe Key. The fraternity of salvagers was already well established when Mel dropped his anchor among them. There was some envy regarding the rich 1715 recoveries, but in general they quickly accepted Mel because he seemed to know what he was doing. Salvage diving in the Keys was more of a hobby on weekends; only a few of the divers actively made a living from the old wreck sites, and only then as a charter for visiting divers.

Mel soon found out that the 1733 fleet of Spanish galleons had been picked clean by the Spanish salvors. The 1733 hurricane was not a devastating one, and it left the fleet sitting on the bottom pretty much intact. Other than the *San José*, most of the fleet's bones had been picked clean. The *San José* was there on the old Spanish chart of the 1733 wreck sites, about a mile inshore and a bit west of the *El Infante* site, but no one had been able to find her. Bobby Klein, Craig Hamilton, Bob Weller, and Marty Meylach had searched the area since 1961, dragging swimmers behind their boats while looking for a tell-tale smudge of gray or the few scattered ballast stones that indicate a wreck site. But the area seemed to be nothing but flat sand with waving eel grass, gradually deepening into Hawk Channel towards shore.

Tom Gurr and his crew on the salvage vessel *Parker* were full-time salvagers, and they needed a potentially good wreck to satisfy their investors. He had moved his salvage operations to the *El Infante*, but not with any hopes of a lot of treasure. For a percentage, Mel loaned him the use of Feild's magnetometer to locate the *San José*. During the month of July, Gurr *did* locate the *"José"*, under deep sand in thirty feet of water at the edge of Hawk Channel. The wreck lay just outside the state's three-mile limit, so Gurr's group began salvage work without a state lease.

As treasure began to come up from the bottom, the state moved in. Through state legislation they were able to claim that in the Florida Keys the Florida state boundaries lay three miles beyond the outer reefs, and that put the *San José* under their jurisdiction. They confiscated all treasures recovered by Gurr, creating one of the darkest days of the relationship between the state and salvage divers. Gurr made international news when he dumped barrels full of artifacts back in the ocean while television cameras recorded the event. It seemed that the state of Florida had beaten the salvage divers, that sunken treasure was *not* what dreams were made of.

To bolster spirits, Mel threw a party and invited all the divers to his house. It was during this get-together that someone brought out a copy of Potter's *The Treasure Diver's Guide*. Turning to the section of wrecks in Florida waters, they began looking at the "two star" and "three star" wrecks that Potter pointed out. The *Atocha* was a "four star" wreck site, and it had never been located. On board was over a "million pesos" of registered treasure. The exciting part of Potter's story was that the *Atocha* was supposedly sunk very close to where Mel had settled down with his family: *Cabeza de los Mártires en los Cayos de Matecumbe*; "the head of the keys in the keys of Matecumbe." Islamorada was located on Upper Matecumbe, and it was the general consensus that this is the key Potter was referring to.

Suddenly a light turned on inside Mel Fisher. For some reason it seemed the "Big A" was the wreck he had been looking for all his life. This was a fabulous galleon. Thirty-five tons of silver, almost 200,000 silver coins, and at least 500 pounds of gold was the beacon. Because the ship had sunk in deeper water, the chances were that everything would be intact, in a pile rather than scattered for miles over the reefs. The records had the *Atocha* sinking in ten brazas of water (fifty-five feet), and the only water that deep in the Middle Keys was just outside the outer reef. That is where Mel Fisher began his search for the *Atocha*.

Alligator Light sits on the edge of the Gulf Stream roughly five miles offshore. From Mel's rented house on Upper Matecumbe he could see the singular flashing light at night as it swept the reefs to seaward. He outlined the areas he felt had potential, those areas showing fifty-five feet of water, and he laid out a grid pattern. The search began there, on the northeast side of Alligator, and swept northward along the edge of the blue that kept the fathometer pegged at fifty-five feet, the magnetometer creating a spume of water as it worked at the end of a hundred-foot electronic cable.

Skirting Crocker Reef and Davis Reef there were anomalies leading into shallow water. On Crocker, four cannons lay scattered towards the back edge of the reef, the scatter pattern disappearing into Hawk Channel. But Hawk Channel had only thirty-five foot depths --too shallow for what he was looking for-- so Mel moved on. Little Conch Reef had a number of salvage boats working the *El Infante* wreck site, a 1733 galleon that had been producing small amounts of treasure for years. But it was up on top of the reef, in sixteen feet of water...much too shallow for any sign of *Atocha*.

Pickles had several wrecks, some sitting in shallow water and more modern than what Mel was looking for. Another wreck contained large bronze pins, standing like soldiers three feet above the bottom and tracing the outline of a ship's hull buried beneath the white sand. As the mag survey moved further north, the reef outside Molasses Light had a number of hits, each taking several days to examine. The survey dragged, and the days and weeks turned into months...without a solid lead to a 1622 galleon.

Back on Islamorada the Fisher family was having fun. Kane and Taffi sank a rowboat in the middle of the canal behind their house and practiced "salvaging" it. Before long they got pretty good at it. The house on Islamorada had no grass in the front yard, only sand. Somehow Dirk had talked his father into letting him bring an alligator home. Some thought of making a pet --or a future belt-- was the reasoning. The alligator grew to be three feet long, so Dirk built a sand moat complete with a sand castle in the yard, filled the moat with water...and turned the alligator loose in the moat. It wasn't long before the alligator disappeared, and Dirk was looking for something else of interest.

Dirk was a pretty good diver by this time, and with Kim and Kane in tow they located a Portuguese Man-O-War. Here is a pretty significant sea creature, with a beautiful plume and almost transparent tentacles hanging below. They managed to pick it up in a bucket, carry it to the house, and put it in the sink. They cleaned it thoroughly of all the sand, and it was there that they learned the lesson of the stinging tentacles. Somehow they got it back into the bucket and into the canal behind the house. The memory of those stinging tentacles was a lesson they never forgot.

Mel had taken a break from the mag routine and anchored his boat, *Buccaneer*, over the site of the 1733 *nao, Tres Puentes*. The wreck had been worked by other salvagers, and quite a bit of treasure had been recovered, but Mel was happy just looking for leftovers. Dirk and Kane decided to take the auxiliary Boston Whaler over to another 1733 wreck site, the *Herrera*, in Hawk Channel about one-and-a-half miles from where the *Buccaneer* was anchored. The *Herrera* lay in eighteen feet of water, so without tanks the boys were holding their breaths and diving down to fan the bottom with their hands. Working off the edge of the ballast --in the sand flats towards shore-- they recovered some wooden dead-eyes, pottery, and some great artifacts. When they came back aboard the *Buccaneer* and showed their father what they had recovered, he was really proud. These boys were real "chips off the old block."

Deo Fisher helps son Dirk with SCUBA tank.

As the magnetometer survey of the reefs extended beyond Molasses Reef Light, Mel had to move dockage of the *Buccaneer* to Ocean Reef at the north end of Key Largo. This was a rather plush yacht club, and the battle-scarred salvage boat attracted a lot of attention from the northern visitors. So much in fact that when Mel located a large twenty-two-foot galleon anchor in the sand near Dixie Shoal, the owner of the Ocean Reef Club gave Mel $1,500 in fuel and dockage credit to bring the anchor in and set it on his dock. The anchor is still at the club today. The large anchor had given the group some excitement, and at the end of several unsuccessful days of magging the area, they decided that some galleon had simply lost one of its anchors.

After nearly one hundred days of magnetometer work they had covered the sixty-odd miles from Alligator Light to Fowey Rocks Light with no sign of the *Atocha*. Considering the possibility that the depth had been recorded wrong, or that the bottom had changed over the past 350 years, Mel decided to begin a search on the inside, in shallower water. Inside the dragons teeth, the reefs are numerous, lying often just under the surface. On cloudy days the water takes on a blue-steel color that often hides the reefs until an unsuspecting boat finds itself impaled. Maneuvering around the reef heads while dragging a magnetometer is a job for only the most experienced. The survey slowed to the crawl of a snail.

Before long they came across the wreck of another 1733 vessel, the *El Populo*, in thirty-two feet of water two miles southwest of Pacific Reef Light. The wreck had been located two years earlier by Carl Ward, Carl Frederick, Bob McKay, and Lee Harding, but the group had left the cannon on the site, working the ballast pile with a suction dredge. This wreck was the *patache* of the fleet and carried no treasure, but it still contained some great artifacts. Other than a cursory examination, the group continued with the survey.

Time in the salvage business is money. Every day the fuel bills and expenses mount up, and Mel knew that spending even a single day on a shipwreck that obviously was not the *Atocha* --or any other non-producing site-- was adding to the hole in the bottom of his money bag. They did, however, spend a few days on the "Pillar Dollar Wreck" site off the north end of Key Largo. The wreck had initially been located and worked in the early 1960s by Art Sapp and Bobby Savage, and later by Bob Weller and Ray Manieri. The deep sand inside the moon-shaped reef had yielded quite a number of pillar dollars dated 1770 to 1778, boarding cutlasses, muskets, flintlock pistols, pewter plates, and a pair of silver candelabras. With blowers on the back of the *Buccaneer*, Mel was able to dust the sand from the edge of the reef and add a few more pillar dollars to his growing collection of Spanish coins.

The magnetometer survey to the north of Alligator Light did not turn up a single clue to the wreck of the *Atocha*; it was time for a major shift in the search pattern. Mel moved his family to Islamorada, to a concrete house across U. S. Highway 1 from the old movie theater. A new element had been added to the search for *Atocha*. Competition was something Mel never had to deal with before, but when the word spread that he was looking for the Atocha, it generated interest in several other professional salvage teams.

Now, on any given day, another salvage vessel, the 136-foot *Revenge*, could be seen just beyond the outer reef with its own magnetometer streamed behind a chase boat. Burt Webber headed up a group called Continental Explorations, one with adequate funding and the most advanced electronic gear a salvage outfit could ask for. But even more important were the researchers that Burt had working on his side. Jack "Blackjack" Haskins and Art McKee, two of the more renown translators of archival Spanish, had joined Burt in the search. It would only be a matter of time before one of the two groups would discover this rich galleon.

To speed up the search, Mel hired Harold Williams, a Fort Pierce helicopter pilot, to bring his autogyro to the Marathon area. It seemed a much faster method to mag the edge of the reefs from the air, and a much better vantage point to see the outline of wreck sites. With Fay Feild working the electronics, Williams was able to drag the magnetometer along the edge of the reefs not only much faster, but with better accuracy. Any change in the bottom that was unusual was checked out. Each anomaly was marked with a Clorox bottle on the end of a weighted line and later checked out by the *Buccaneer*.

The search began on the south side of Alligator Light, and before it was completed it had stretched southeastward to American Shoal Light, a distance of fifty-two miles. It had been an expensive survey, and still there was no sign of *Atocha*. It was an area that, closer inshore, Mel's group Armada Research had been working shipwrecks since 1965. There were numerous shipwrecks in the area covered, many of them late 1600s and early 1700s, but not a trace of *Atocha*. Although frustrations ran high, the Fisher family was as solid as a rock in its support of Mel's search. Finally, Mel got his big break.

Several years earlier, while still living in Vero Beach, Mel and Deo joined a new Methodist church which was then under construction. Meetings were held in the gymnasium of the local high school, while Bible classes were held in one of the school rooms. Mel and Deo were attending Bible study classes, and the teacher was a tall, friendly Eugene Lyon. Gene had previously been a city manager, then taught history in the local community college. His wife Dot worked in the Fort Pierce library. Both Gene and Dot had casually met the Fishers on other occasions, but through the church they became close friends. Gene had decided to go back into the educational system for his graduate work in Latin American history. At the University of Florida he had learned to read the older Spanish archaic script, something he did very well. Years before, Mel and Deo had traveled to Madrid, Spain, where he had purchased a few old Spanish books about shipwrecks. Because he couldn't translate the Spanish, they sat on his bookshelf gathering dust.

One day, after Bible class, Mel and Gene were having coffee and doughnuts when Gene mentioned the fact that he could translate old Spanish. Within minutes Mel had Gene sitting in the front room of his house and had stacked the old Spanish shipwreck books in front of him. There was a glint in Gene's eyes as he picked them up and...very easily began reading some of the pages to Mel. The more he read, the more he became interested. "My gosh, I can't believe how many tons of gold and silver and everything was on these ships!" The night wore on, and it was apparent that Gene knew his old Spanish. Page after page was filled with old accounts of shipwrecks, sunken in many parts of the Spanish overseas empire. Gene mentioned to Mel that he would be traveling to Seville for research on his doctorate thesis in the near future.

When Mel began his search for *Atocha*, he contacted Gene, offering him $10,000 and one percent of any treasure recovered if he would research the *Atocha* while in Spain and help him locate the wreck site. The 1969 salvage season came to a close, and neither Mel nor his competitors were any closer to locating the *Atocha*. February 1970 produced cold weather, even in the Florida Keys, and the Fishers decided to take a vacation to Majorca, and then to Seville, and see how Gene was making out. It was a pleasant surprise for Gene, and he appreciated any visitors from the States. He introduced Mel to Angeles Flores Rodrigues, a skilled translator who had sent numerous documents on shipwrecks not only to Mel, but to just about every salvager that was willing to pay for the information.

The Fishers had the opportunity to see the inside of the archives, a cold, thick-walled stone structure sitting near the Guadalquivir River. The records in the Spanish archives are unbelievable, going back four hundred years into the colonization of the New World: forty thousand bundles of carefully preserved and guarded documents --an amazing fifty million pages of history! Being able to decipher even a single page of the scrolling *procesal* style handwriting requires an incredible amount of patience. The Fishers wished Gene well and flew back to Florida as the 1970 salvage season got underway.

It was ten days later, as Gene scanned Menendez' Florida expense account among the colonial accounting papers, that he saw the entry, "1622, accounts of Francisco Nuñez Melían, of what he salvaged from the galleon Margarita". He quickly called for the salvage account: *Contaduria* 1, 112. Shortly the bundle lay on the table in front of him, and although worms had eaten holes through many of the last pages, he was able to pick out a familiar phrase, "*Cayos del Marques*". To Gene that translated, "in the keys of the Marquis". Retracing through the pages he was able to find the phrase four more times. This was something new, but where were the "keys of the Marquis"? In the archives is a greater collection of maps of the overseas empire, and on one of the maps including the Florida peninsula was the "Tortugas". The next island group towards the tip of the Florida Keys was the island group named "Marquez". Another chart was more specific, "Cayos del Marquez". That was it!

It made sense to Gene that at the time of the 1622 hurricane the term "Matecumbe" meant all the island group of the Florida Keys, except the Tortuga group. Mel was searching way too far up the Florida Keys. The *Atocha* and *Margarita* lay west of Key West. He wrote Mel a letter and advised him that he was sure the *Atocha* and *Margarita* lay forty miles west of Key West, in the vicinity of the island of Marquesa.

As soon as Mel received the letter, he and Deo were on a 'plane to New York and then to Spain. By 9:00 a.m. the following morning they were sitting on the steps of the archives, waiting for Gene to show up. It was cold and a bit windy when Gene showed up wearing a heavy G.I. coat, stocking cap, long underwear, and mittens. He beamed when he saw the Fishers, and in minutes they were sitting across the street from the archives having a hot cup of coffee. Gene mentioned that he had found an additional document since he had written the letter. When the archives opened, they crossed the street and climbed the wide, pink-marble staircase to the lobby.

The Fishers were not cleared to enter the working areas, so Gene brought the document down to show them. It was hard to read the flourishing handwriting; Mel only shook his head, accepting what Gene had translated. Mel pumped Gene's hand, "This is the break we've been waiting for! If you can pin-point the exact location...there's a bonus in it for you." The same day, Mel and Deo were on their way back to Florida...on the new trail of the *Atocha*!

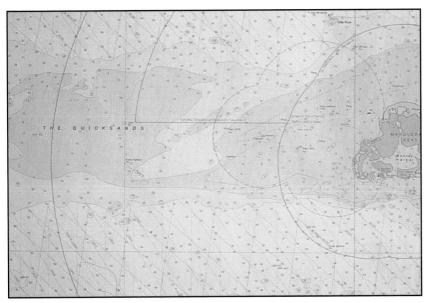

TOP: Hydrographic chart of the area between Marquesa Key and the "Quicksands". BOTTOM: Aerial view of Marquesa Key, Mooney Harbor entrance to the left. **Credits: Pat Clyne.**

TOP: Using an air lift and metal detectors, Mel Fisher's divers work the **Atocha** *site.* **Credit: Pat Clyne.**

BOTTOM: Sketch of the mailbox, or duster, lowered over boat's propellers. **Credit: Treasure Salvors.**

TOP: Friendly 6-foot barracuda keeps vigil over salvage efforts.
Credit: Pat Clyne.

BOTTOM: Don Kincaid holding first **Atocha** *gold recovered near the anchor in 1971.*
Credit:Treasure Salvors.

TOP: Former "Bouy" Tender **Arbutus,** *used as on-site base for divers. Mel Fisher and Chuck Sotzin watch dredge outfall. BOTTOM:* **Arbutus** *sunk at anchorage near the "Quicksands". She remains there yet today.*
Credits: Pat Clyne.

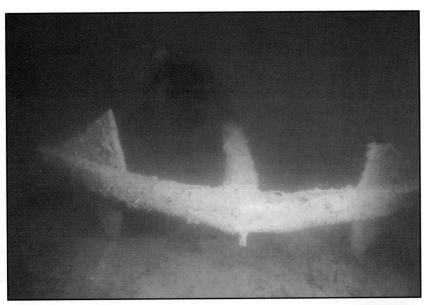

TOP: Anchor of the **Atocha,** *located near the "Quicksands".*
BOTTOM: **Atocha** *anchor being hoisted alongside the recovery vessel.*

TOP: Salvage vessels **Dauntless, Swordfish,** *and* **Virgalona** *nested together over* **Atocha** *the week of the discovery. BOTTOM: A* **Santa Margarita** *bronze cannon stands vigil as salvage efforts begin in 1980.* **Credits: Pat Clyne.**

TOP: A diver checks out hull timbers of the **Santa Margarita.** *BOTTOM: A gold chain is recovered as divers erect a grid system to control archaelogical recoveries.* **Credits: Pat Clyne.**

TOP: The "Mother Lode" ballast mound. A silver bar and ship's timbers lie in foreground. BOTTOM: A "reef" of silver bars on the **Atocha** *ballast pile.* **Credits: K. T. Budde-Jones.**

Scattered seventy-pound loaves of silver litter the timbers of **Nuestra Señora de Atocha** *55 feet below the surface of the Straits of Florida. Silver coins, spilled out of a nearby crate, are also visible.*   **Credit: K. T. Budde-Jones.**

TOP: A chest of silver coins spills its contents onto the ballast mound.
Credit: K. T. Budde-Jones.

BOTTOM: Beautiful, intact Spanish "olive jar" emerges as sand is dusted off the main ballast pile of **Atocha.**
Credit: Pat Clyne.

TOP: A diver recovers a silver ewer on **Atocha**.
Credit: Pat Clyne.

BOTTOM: Mel Fisher catches emeralds as they fall from the air lift near the **Atocha** *ballast pile.* **Credit: Pat Clyne.**

TOP: The moment of discovery. Gold bars and gold disks being discovered along the **Atocha** *scatter pattern.* **Credit: Pat Clyne.**

BOTTOM: An encrusted gold crucifix with pearl pendants, recovered from the **Atocha** *site.* **Credit: Pat Clyne.**

TOP: Red cedarwood shipping box full of silver coins moments after discovery on the Atocha *site.*
Credit: Pat Clyne.

BOTTOM: Silver bars being hoisted aboard the salvage vessel in a shopping cart basket. **Credit: Damian Lin.**

TOP: Diver recovering a silver plate on the **Atocha** *site using a 6-inch air lift. BOTTOM: Mel Fisher, with sons Kim and Kane, holding gold bars and gold chains recovered from the* **Atocha.** **Credits: Pat Clyne.**

TOP: Unique gold crucifix with pearl pendants from the **Atocha** *recovery.*
Credit: Pat Clyne.

BOTTOM: Eight-inch gold salver recovered from the **Santa Margarita.**
Credit: Pat Clyne.

TOP: Gold "Poison Cup". Note the bezoar stone holder located in the center. **Credit: Pat Clyne.** *BOTTOM: Diver K. T. Budde-Jones handles the air lift as a silver chest is uncovered on* **Atocha** *"main pile".* **Credit: Syd Jones.**

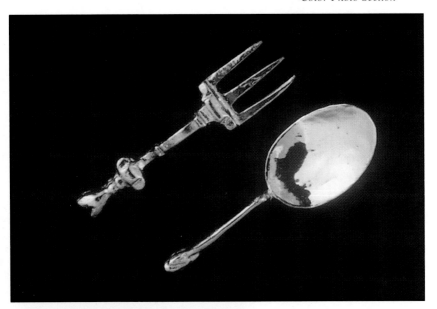

TOP: Gold fork and gold spoon from the Atocha *site.*
Credit: Pat Clyne.

BOTTOM: **Atocha** *gold and green: Muzo emeralds and gold chains make* **Atocha** *one of the richest prizes ever recovered.*
Credit: Pat Clyne.

TOP: What dreams are made of: **Atocha** *gold bars and chains. BOTTOM: Emerald crosses recovered from the* **Atocha** *scatter pattern near the "Bank of Spain".*

184

TOP: Bleth McHaley and David Horan planning strategy for a Supreme Court appearance. **Credit:Pat Clyne.**

BOTTOM: John Brandon displays the intricately carved gold belt with jeweled insets he and his crew found on **Atocha.** *Possibly the greatest artifact ever found on a Spanish galleon!*
Credit: Pat Clyne.

TOP: Gold and emerald jewelry recovered by the crew of the **Saba Rock** *on May 27, 1985.* **Credit: Pat Clyne.**

BOTTOM: Deo Fisher holding **Atocha** *gold rosary with ebony beads.*
Credits: Pat Clyne.

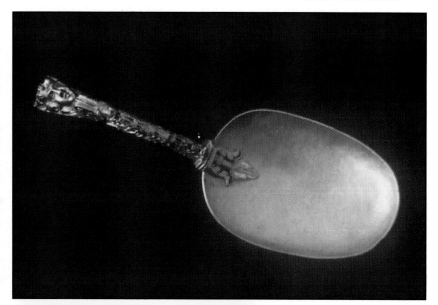

TOP: Gold spoon recovered in 1985 from Atocha.
Credit: Pat Clyne.

BOTTOM: Handle of gold spoon (above) with unique engraving. **Credit: Pat Clyne.**

TOP: Silver coins of the Atocha, with dates 1608-1622.
BOTTOM: Gold and coral rosary recovered by Bouncy John near the "Bank of Spain" in 1973.

TOP: Portuguese cast bronze mariner's astrolabe recovered from the "pilot's chest" in 1985.

BOTTOM: A silver wine pitcher lined with gold and used for communion services. **Credits: Pat Clyne.**

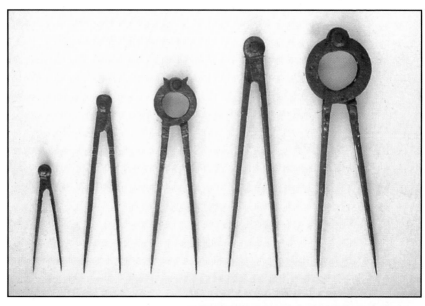

TOP: Bronze navigational dividers recovered from the **Atocha** *and* **Santa Margarita.**

BOTTOM: Gold rosary cross with nine emeralds. **Atocha 1985.** **Credits: Pat Clyne.**

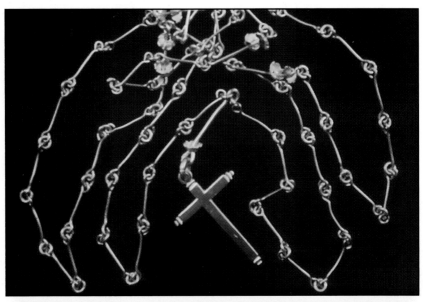

TOP: *Gold cross and chain.* **Atocha 1985.**
BOTTOM: *Golden emerald parrot, recovered by the* **Golden Venture, 1983,**
near the "Quicksands".   **Credits: Pat Clyne.**

191

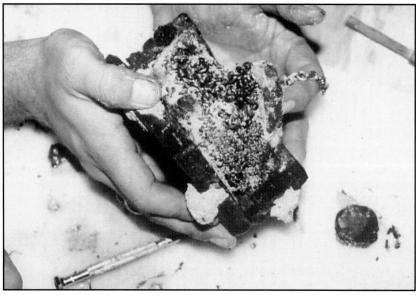

TOP: Cliff Robertson, actor, and Mel Fisher with a box of treasure about to be opened for TV. BOTTOM: Box contained two gold chains and twelve silver coins. **Credits: Pat Clyne.**

TOP: Gold filigree hinged frame and a gold venera. Frame recovered by Andy Matroci, medallion by Berrier and Long on 1715 fleet. BOTTOM: Gold bonanza from **Nieves** *site (1715), Fort Pierce, FL.* **Credits: Scott Nierling.**

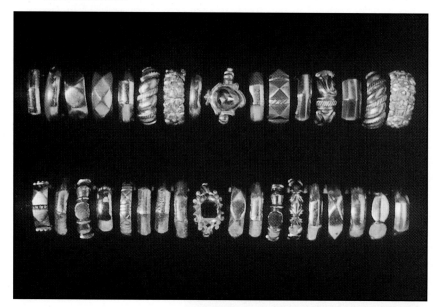

TOP: *Rings of* **Nuestra Senora de las Nieves,** *1715 Spanish treasure fleet.* **Credit: Scott Nierling.**

BOTTOM: *A unique golden enameled brooch recovered from the* **Nieves** *site by John Brandon's crew.* **Credit: Pat Clyne.**

TOP: "TODAY'S THE DAY!" Mel Fisher in radio contact with son Kane on **Dauntless** *the day* **Atocha** *mother lode was found. BOTTOM: Mel and daughter Taffi celebrating finding* **Atocha** *mother lode.* **Credits: Pat Clyne.**

TOP: Deo and Mel Fisher, with Eugene Lyon, weighing the gold bars which were recovered from **Margarita.** *BOTTOM: The Treasure Salvors crew and their "end of the rainbow".* **Credits: Pat Clyne.**

TOP: Deo Fisher with actress Loretta Swit on movie set during filming of "Dreams of Gold"

BOTTOM: Mel Fisher holding a jar of emeralds. More than 3,000 were recovered from the Atocha site.
Credit: Pat Clyne.

TOP: Mel Fisher and Johnny Carson on one of the Atocha *salvage vessels.*
Credit: Pat Clyne.

BOTTOM: Mel holds one of the largest emeralds recovered from Atocha.

15...MARQUESA

The search for the *Atocha* was taking on a new, serious intensity. Over the past year the Fisher team had been operating solely on the words from Potter's *The Treasure Diver's Guide*. It described the *Santa Margarita* as being "lost on a sand bank which is located on the west side of the last of the Matecumbe keys, next to the head of the Martires off the Florida coast. At 7:00 a.m. of that day the captain of the Margarita saw, one *legua* (league) to the east the galleon *Nuestra Señora de Atocha*, *almiranta* of the fleet, without rigging or sails, and as he watched he saw it go down and sink to the bottom." Even Mel's competitors had searched the area offshore from Matecumbe for the past year...and continued to do so.

But Gene Lyon had given Mel the break he needed. The word "Marquesa" shifted his entire search a hundred miles further to the west. The Marquesa Keys lay 25-30 miles west of Key West-- beyond the end of the islands which offered daily logistic support, warm meals, and a hot shower every night. That one word closed the substantial gap between casual research and dedicated research, and it gave Mel his first legitimate key to the *Atocha* treasure. In retrospect, if Mel could have looked down the road that faced him and seen the almost insurmountable problems in a zealous bureaucratic grab for sunken treasure, a circle of jealousy and greed even within the salvage community, and finally the personal tragedy in the *Atocha* quest, there is absolutely no doubt that he would have pulled up stakes and called it quits.

The problem was that Mel had never been a quitter. What he could not control --or influence-- always had a habit of working out. And now he was faced with the biggest challenge of his life. The strength that was to carry him through the next fifteen years would be his belief in himself...and his belief in *Atocha*.

The *Virgalona* had shut down its engines, and the drift had carried her over a sand bar less than fifteen feet deep. The Marquesa Key was out of sight, some ten miles to the east, and yet seemingly --in the middle of nowhere-- was this large sand bank. "Hey, way out here the water is only fifteen feet deep? The *Atocha* could have hit right here!" Mel stood on the bow to scan the sudden rise in the bottom from a depth of forty feet, and Mo Molinar agreed as he looked over the side at the sand rising abruptly below them. "Let's anchor up and have a look." Within minutes *Virgalona* settled with her bow into the tide that was now beginning to move at freight-train speed over the sand flats.

They spent the afternoon in circle searches, but the bottom gave up nothing but rolling sand dunes and sea fans bent over with the current. It was Mel's first look at the area where he was to spend the next fifteen years in his search for sunken treasure. It was also the first time he was faced with an underwater search completely out of sight of land. The ocean is a vast expanse that seems endless when there are no landmarks. At the time, his group had nothing in the way of sophisticated navigational equipment. Del Norte, Loran, and GPS would come years later, but Mel was navigating by the seat of his pants.

They anchored that evening in Mooney Harbor, inside the protection of the Marquesa Keys which form a natural circular barrier of coral and mangroves. It was from the western key, less than a thousand yards from where the *Virgalona* lay at anchor, that in 1622 the Marquis de Cadereita directed the salvage effort to locate *Atocha*. If only the keys could talk, they might have given Mel some encouragement. Mel realized that if he hoped to locate *Atocha*, he had to come up with some means to run a controlled search pattern. He was already aware that with the wind blowing in one direction, and the tide running in another direction as it was on the sand bank that day, it would be difficult to run a steady course with the mag boat.

Fay Feild's proton magnetometer had the capability of detecting cannons and anchors within fifty feet of either side of the "fish" they were dragging behind the boat --even in fifty-five feet of water depth. But somehow he had to control the pattern or they would easily miss something "out there", and his gaze swept the vast expanse of open ocean. The *Atocha* was out there somewhere, possibly just a few miles away, but it was even worse than looking for the proverbial needle in a haystack. In this case the elements were against him; the wind, the tide, and the weather could turn a flat calm sea into raging, foam-filled six-foot waves in a matter of minutes. He had a lot to think about that night.

His fruitless searching of the Upper Keys over the past year had been valuable to some extent; his group was developing into a professional "Mag Team", one that could react quickly to anomalies --or magnetic responses-- on the magnetometer. The "A-Team" he had first started with in Vero Beach had thinned somewhat. Dick Williams and Walt Holzworth had both decided to retire and sold their stock to an outside group. His saddest day was when Rupe Gates decided to sell his stock to Mel, retire, and move to Idaho where he could build a ranch and spend time with his family. Mel's reaction was, "Man, I won't be able to keep going without him." Rupe had been the stabilizing force in a treasure operation which had, at times, seemed to mount up and ride off in all directions. Mo Molinar and Fay Feild remained as a nucleus for the new team that was now becoming very proficient in search techniques.

Mel felt he was very near treasure, but finding it would pose his greatest challenge. As he pondered the future, the sand bank he searched that day would remain undisturbed for two more years before it gave up its treasure of gold, silver, and bronze. Mel was closer than he thought.

When Mel returned to Key West, he called an old friend of his, Jim Odom, who owned Odom Offshore Oil Company. Jim had purchased Fay Feild's magnetometer patent, and their relationship had been cemented by numerous exchanges of information. Mel asked him what the best navigation system was for his type of operation. When advised that a "good system" would cost upwards of $70,000, Mel replied that he didn't have the money. Odom offered to come down and look at the Marquesa area.

He flew in one day from his office in Baton Rouge, and after a look-see at the open ocean Mel had to deal with --and with a lack of funds-- he suggested using theodolites to track the search pattern. Theodolites are instruments that are usually used in surveying, utilizing a telescopic attachment to measure angles. They would cost only $1,500 each, an amount that Mel could dig up. He bought a pair of them.

The area that Gene Lyon had pinpointed as potentially being the "best shot" covered over 150 square miles of ocean bottom. Somehow Mel had to set up a theodolite near the edge of this area to control the search pattern. Looking over a chart of the area, he spotted the Coast Guard symbol of a wreck on the edge of Half Moon Shoal. Something welled up inside Mel; the symbol indicated the location of the *Valbanera*, the same wreck site that Mel and Deo spent their honeymoon on seventeen years before. There had to be some inner direction guiding him to this spot. He decided to set up the first theodolite on the overturned hull of the *Valbanera*. It was an easy decision to make, and he was sure that the *Atocha* had to be close by.

As they approached the *Valbanera*, Mel had warm memories of evenings with Deo, sitting on the stern of Ciesinski's charter boat and listening to the night sounds over the water. Rebecca Shoals lighthouse still stood as a sentinel, the only break in a vast expanse of ocean. The hull was still there, a little less intact than it was in 1953, but large jewfish still called her home. As Mel slipped over the side of the *Virgalona* and swam to the hull, the fish seemed like old friends. He almost recognized some of the larger jewfish.

The job was how to mount a four-legged tower to the hull, then build a platform that would be sturdy enough to stand up under wind and wave. The hull was pretty rusty but still had enough metal in it to support a platform. Welding angle iron to a rusty hull didn't seem to fill the bill. Mel had a better idea.

Taking a seven-pound sledge hammer, he marked four points on the hull, then he banged on the marks until he had clean metal showing. He wrapped some iron wire around a slim core of magnesium and stuffed the slug into a piece of half-inch conduit. After attaching a high-pressure hose from a tank of pure oxygen to the conduit, he opened the valve, flooding the pipe with oxygen. Next he took a blowtorch and held the flame on the end of the conduit until the magnesium caught fire. Then, due to the intense temperature of the burning magnesium, the entire tube of iron wire and filings also caught fire in a blinding ball of heat.

Grasping the other end of the conduit, Mel slipped over the side and dived to the hull of the *Valbanera*. Touching the burning end of the tube to the bare metal, it began burning a hole through the hull. This worked, and soon he had a hole big enough to pass a bolt through. He then burned holes at his three other marks. When had finished, he came back to the *Virgalona* and found four bolts long enough to go through the hull.

With another diver remaining on the outside, Mel swam down underneath the hull and then up inside. "It was kinda spooky, because there were some pretty big jewfish still living in the hull. They would swim down the companionway ahead of me, thumping their tails. Then we got to the engine room, and I could the see the pencils of daylight coming through the four holes I had burned." He pushed the bolts, backed by large flat washers, through the holes. The diver on the outside guided the bolts through holes in the angle iron legs and bolted them in place.

It wasn't long before the angle iron framework came together fifteen feet above water, and several days later a platform was completed. It was large enough for a single diver to stand, bent over a theodolite telescope, and guide the mag boat on a straight course by radio communication. It had a small guard rail for the diver to rest against, and this soon became a nesting place for errant seagulls and pelicans. And it wasn't long before the standing room was whitewashed with bird excrement.

There were other problems as well. The tower was not a work of art. It leaned to one side and was promptly dubbed the "leaning tower of pizza." It also was not as steady as Mel would have liked it to be; the waves breaking over the hull of the *Valbanera* --as well as high winds-- moved the tower from side to side. This threw the crosshairs of the theodolite off considerably, making it impossible to keep the mag boat on course. Mel had his divers rig cables between hull and the tower, much like a tall TV antenna. Now it was steady...and probably a source of wonder to anyone passing along the edge of Hawk Channel.

It was the first day of the survey, and Mel was on the platform giving Mo Molinar on the *Virgalona* course corrections over the hand-held radio. The tower was the *hub* of a wheel, but the *rim* was seven miles out. He found that the *Virgalona*'s blue hull disappeared from sight over the horizon, three miles from the tower. So that first day the runs were short. As *Virgalona*'s hull slipped from view, Mel would have Mo turn the boat about and head back towards the tower. As the day began to wear on, rain squalls began to sweep in over the horizon.

At first Mel's only concern was that when the rain passed between the tower and the mag boat, he would temporarily lose sight and contact with Mo. He would have the *Virgalona* stop and hold steady until the squall moved away. When the wind began to pick up, Mel found himself holding onto the small guard rail around the tower as he peered through the telescopic sight. Then the *Virgalona* was engulfed in a fairly large squall that passed within a mile of the tower, and over the radio Mo said that it was like a miniature tornado that was blowing things off the boat!

After the squall passed they continued the search, but now the squalls were becoming more ominous. Suddenly Mel looked up from the 'scope, and he was surrounded by rain storms in all directions. He had never seen so many squalls at one time in his entire life. It was frightening, and now he had a large waterspout heading right for him. His first thought was "Is this tower going to hold up if the waterspout hits me?" He was glad they had put up the four supporting cables; at least he had a chance. He was more than relieved when the liquid tornado passed by the tower a few hundred feet away, but now the winds were up to gale force, over fifty miles per hour.

The squalls were thicker and moving past with lightning speed, and with them came the rain. Mel was drenched, and he had to shut down the radio and just hang on. He couldn't see *Virgalona*, and he knew that Mo couldn't see him. The waves were now over ten feet high, and whipping froth across the tops reduced visibility to less than one hundred feet. The waves were rolling just below the bottom of the platform and Mel, for some unknown reason, conjured up the picture of five seamen hanging onto the *Atocha* foremast in 1622 as the ship sank to the bottom in a raging hurricane. They must have had similar thoughts, as Mel hung on out there.

Just when Mel began to wonder if *Virgalona* was going to make it through the storm, it appeared alongside the tower, bouncing up and down like a cork in a tempest. Somehow Mel managed to leap from the tower to the bow of the boat, and they pulled safely away. By compass, they steered back to the Marquesas and, once anchored inside Mooney Harbor, white knuckles relaxed their hold on anything solid that they had to hold on to. Mel breathed a sigh of relief, "That was a real blow! I think it was probably the beginning of a hurricane!" It was Mel's first day off the Marquesas...one that he would never forget.

When the *Virgalona* had begun to disappear over the horizon only three miles from the tower, Mel realized that he had a problem. He had to extend the range of sight if he wanted to use the tower. It didn't take long to figure out the solution. Mel bought the longest fishing pole in Key West --about thirty feet. To the top of it the crew tied a large plastic bag, painted with a brilliant, fluorescent orange paint and filled with wadded newspapers. With this mounted alongside *Virgalona*'s cabin, the theodolite operator could see the mag boat long after it disappeared over the horizon. The survey moved along slowly, too slowly to suit Mel. The crew was as eager to find the *Atocha* as Mel, and when Mel suggested working at night using a strobe light, he got an instant "Yeah!"

They now divided up into three crews, each taking a shift, and the survey went forward at a fast pace. Each pass along the grid was within fifty feet of the one before. When a "hit" was registered on the magnetometer, a buoy was dropped over the side to mark the spot. During the day the boat would stop its run while a diver went over the side to check out the hit. Then it was back on course, being careful not to drift too far off the line of sight. At night the buoys were left in place until they could be checked out in daylight.

And there were a lot of hits to check out. When the hits were deep and out of sight, checking them out meant lowering the *Virgalona*'s blower and dusting off five to ten feet of sand over the target. It was necessary, even though hit after hit turned up nothing but modern debris. Barrels, metal fish traps, winches, and anchors seemed to litter the bottom of the ocean. The survey had to stop each time the search boat got a signal. There had to be a better way.

Bob Holloway had met Mel on the dock one day, and the two of them hit it off immediately. Bob had retired from his contractor's job in Indiana and had traveled to Key West because he loved to fish. He bought a 34-foot Chris Craft and named it *Holly's Folly*, a boat he felt comfortable in out of sight of land where billfish swam in the blue Gulf Stream. Mel offered him the biggest fish of all: Treasure, when they found the *Atocha*. He chartered *Holly's Folly* to run supplies out to the survey crew, and before long Bob Holloway became a stockholder in Treasure Salvors. He became one of the most dedicated members of Mel's crew.

Soon Mel designated Bob's boat as the mag boat, freeing up the *Virgalona* to dig up the hits while *Holly's Folly* continued the search pattern. Teamwork was everything, and the Holloway crew had it all. Bob's sister, Marjorie "T.T." Hargreaves, and Kay Finley completed the crew, and each knew how to read the anomalies from the magnetometer. They never complained about working well into the night...or when wind and waves made keeping a compass course exasperating. The crew rotated jobs, sometimes to keep awake, sometimes just to keep from getting bored. The survey went on day after day, and the days stretched into months.

The survey crew completed the area designated by Lyon as the "best shot" at locating the *Atocha*. Without moving from the platform above the *Valbanera* hull, Mel traced out a triangular area to the west which included Rebecca Shoal and Isaac Shoal, an area that covered about half the territory of the first survey. He applied for state search lease for this new sector, but rather than wait for state approval, he began magging the area immediately. Within a few weeks this new survey was completed without any positive results. If anything, Fisher became aware that his team was now becoming very proficient in the operation.

Mel then decided to search the area immediately to the east, towards Cosgrove Shoal. Again he requested a search contract from the state of Florida for this new area, and again, rather than waiting for approval, he began looking for a location to set up his theodolite station. He recognized that state reaction to his search requests would be slow in coming, and time was not on his side. It did not appear that the state had an interest in supervising the survey crew as it worked some fifty miles west of Key West. In a way he was right, but the state officials were becoming agitated because they knew that Mel was working without their approvals of the search requests.

There is a lighthouse atop Cosgrove Shoal. It was unattended for years, but the upkeep was still the responsibility of the U. S. Coast Guard. When Mel observed that the lighthouse was locked up and there was apparently no one living there, he had the survey crew mount the theodolite on the upper platform, and the crew set up to survey an area that overlapped and extended the first survey four miles to the east.

Cosgrove Shoals lighthouse was about twenty miles east of the *Valbanera*. To the south, the water dropped off abruptly into the deep blue depths of the Gulf Stream. Here the ability to see the mag boat as it worked its way northwestward was much easier. The platform of the lighthouse was about sixty feet above sea level, giving the crew a sweeping view of not only the Marquesas Keys, but of the islands to the northeast towards Key West as well.

As Mel stood on the platform he could see the shallow reef a short distance away. The reef was called Marquesa Rock, and the person in command of the 1622 Spanish treasure fleet was the Marqués de Cadereita. Captain Gaspar de Vargas, in charge of the salvage operations in 1622, had called the islets on which they had set up operations "Marquesa Keys" in honor of the Marqués. Mel thought that there was a good chance that the *Atocha* had first struck this shallow reef before it sank in fifty-five feet of water closer to the Marquesa Keys. He was eager to get the survey started, and his enthusiasm rubbed off on the entire crew.

Here again the bottom of the search area was filled with modern debris, as well as some old shipwrecks, but none as old as what Mel was looking for. Then the Coast Guard found out that Fisher had a theodolite crew up on Cosgrove Lighthouse. They dispatched a cutter to the site and ordered the divers off the lighthouse. Fortunately they had just completed the survey, so now it was a case of "where to move to next?"

What became more important was the frustration at finding nothing of importance. The crew members were becoming worn out and probably a little sloppy in running the survey. With their eyes glued to the theodolite telescope they would guide the mag boat along its course. Sometimes the boat would drift ten or twenty feet off to the east or west, and the divers would monotone, "Ten west, nine, eight, seven, west, five, four, three, two, on course!" Then, when the boat reached the end of the run, the operator would move the theodolite over a couple of seconds and bring them back to the lighthouse.

Mel had the theodolite crew trade off with the divers on the boats. One day they would work the tower, the next day they would help dive up the hits that were detected the day before. Holloway had already put thousands of miles over the bottom with *Holly's Folly*. The engines in the boat needed constant attention as valves were ground down time and time again. Before the search ended he would have to replace both engines. The team was hanging together, but only because of the optimistic attitude of Mel and his pronouncement, "Today's the day!"

Without their knowing it, as they finished the Cosgrove search area, they had come within a shadow of the *Atocha* ballast pile. Forty-one tons of silver would have to wait a while longer to see the light of day.

16...*CAYO HUESO*

The Overseas Highway seems to skip along the Keys over short spans of concrete, each equipped with bridge fishermen tending lines strung out in the clear tidewater. As the highway curves westward, and each key seems to get smaller as the bridges stretch to reach the next island of mangroves, one is suddenly aware of the beauty of the water surrounding the Florida Keys. Gradually one sees more water than land, and the colors reflecting the corals and sea grass are as if a famous painter had spent his lifetime creating something that could be enjoyed by every passerby. The water is crystal clear, and the colors come through in all their variegated pastel hues. Although it is 130 miles from Florida City to Key West, it's a drive many wish would never end. Even before reaching the last bridge into Key West a visitor senses a different atmosphere...remoteness. It makes one feel he is "leaving his troubles behind."

Cayo Hueso is a "conch" town. It got its nickname from a time when strange boats coming into port in the early 1800s always brought an instant fear of raiding pirates. Pirates were roaming rampant throughout the Keys and Florida straits, preying on merchant sailing vessels trading between the young United States and the islands of the Caribbean. When the strange new boat would raise a conch to its foremast, instead of a "jolly roger", it meant that these were friendly sailors. The townspeople then knew it was safe to go back about their business. Key West stands alone, almost unprotected, against the ravages of weather and time. Survival seems to best describe the ways of these hardy "conchs" who made their living from the sea. The coral soil was fit only for building weather-beaten wooden homes that leaned into the wind and for burying their ancestors --marked by stones that humorously read, "I told you I was sick!" From the sea they harvested shrimp, fish, and lobster. And from the many shipwrecks that bilged their bottoms on the local reefs, they salvaged timbers to build their stores and homes. The cargoes often provided a change in diet or other items which made the shout "Ship ashore!" a welcome change in their daily routine.

Over the years the pirates disappeared, but the town retained its remoteness, and friendliness. Everyone knew everyone else, and there were few secrets not known by everyone in town. Change was slow in coming, even when the U. S. Navy established a base on the waterfront, and white uniforms provided a new source of income. Tourists began to admire Key West as the "end of the line", and fishing boats became charter boats. Northern visitors found a small town, with beaches of coral and sand and a wondrous ocean view. Quaint stores graced streets lined with pale pink frangipani, and the aroma of Cuban tobacco leaves being rolled into cigars drifted down the lanes marked "Pirate Alley". Hungry customers were drawn to lamp-lighted carts by the sizzle of conch fritters and *bollos* being dropped into a deep fryer. As the sun set, one of the remarkable treasures of the old town emerged from the shadows. Beyond garden walls of yellow allamanda were secluded patios with old iron tables, half hidden with green table cloths. Crimson hibiscus floating in a crystal bowl on each table, a candle flickering under a hurricane shade, and the fragrance of *galán de noche* drifting from the pathway was an invitation that dinner was being prepared in one of the many gourmet restaurants.

When Mel and his salvage team arrived in Key West the town's character had begun to change, and they were accepted as part of the change. It was a Mel Fisher kind of town. He had become a sort of celebrity, and when the buzzword "*Atocha*" began to permeate the everyday conversation, townspeople began to remember that their town was, after all, built on a history of shipwrecks. It was a time of change for the Fisher family as well. The children were no longer children; they were young people who had matured very quickly. And they loved their new environment. Surrounded by water, it was a town where you could go anywhere by boat. Their first home was a small two bedroom house behind the Keywester Motel...too small for Mel, Deo, Taffi and Kane. Dirk and Kim had remained in Vero Beach to finish school and would rejoin the family later.

Bob Moran had come into Mel's life as a result of his spending a month in a Cuban jail. He was a treasure diver, but his treasure was somewhere off the coast of the Dominican Republic. He was running his boat there from Florida when it capsized and sank off the coast of Cuba. No amount of persuasion could convince the Cubans that he was not running drugs, and he spent more than a month in jail before being freed by the American Consul. While languishing in a concrete cell he kept his mind occupied by mentally building a Spanish galleon and stocking it with sunken treasure. What a great tourist attraction that would make! When finally freed, he no longer had a boat, nor much of anything else, so he settled back in Florida.

When Mel struck it rich off Ft. Pierce, Bob became a close associate. Once all the gold was up off the bottom, Mel had enough business sense to know that once you sold it...it was gone forever. But, if he could display it and charge admission, he would have his cake and eat it too. Mel and Bob thought alike, and they formed a new company called Treasure Ship, Inc. There were investors that believed in the idea as well, and before long Mel and Bob flew to Sweden where they purchased an old lumber ship, a wooden-hulled sailing vessel. Rupe Gates was the seaman in the group, and it was his responsibility to sail it back to Florida. Once it arrived in Fort Pierce, Bob set about to reconstruct it into a 16th-century Spanish treasure galleon; the name "Golden Doubloon" seemed appropriate. By 1967 the project was completed and was an obvious success. When it was opened to the public, the lines formed early and lasted most of the day. In 1967 Mel didn't know much about the destructiveness of teredo worms, although he had read about them in the old Spanish accounts. He was to learn firsthand.

When Mel moved his operation to the Keys, Bob moved the *Golden Doubloon* to a dock in Fort Lauderdale. It wasn't long before the first of a series of misfortunes befell the converted galleon. There was a holdup, and the thieves made off with about $70,000 in Spanish gold and silver coins. There was some consolation in the unexpected. As the thieves ran across the parking lot to their getaway car, one of the bags broke, spilling silver coins across the lot. Without the time to scoop them up, they left the coins lying there. As it turned out, many of the gold coins they had taken were reproductions, and the real treasure lay in the parking lot, to be recovered by Moran as the thieves disappeared down the highway. It created a lot of publicity, and for a short time the museum was busy. But it was downhill from there.

Bob then decided to move the galleon to North Miami Beach. At first it seemed like a good idea; it was the wealthy end of Miami Beach, full of condominiums and tourists. It possibly would have attracted its share of tourist dollars, except one night it sank alongside the dock. Much of the display was ruined, and the investors were unwilling to put more money into getting the museum back in shape. Mel was able to trade the investors' stock in his company Treasure Salvors for their interests in the *Golden Doubloon*.

Cayo Hueso...*Key West.* Credit: Ernie Richards.

He had the galleon towed to Key West, where it was moored at the gasoline docks. It was to serve a twofold purpose from that point on. It was restocked with treasure and again opened as a museum. Key West was a tourist town, and sunken treasure was part of the local vernacular. The museum was a hit. The galleon also became Mel's office, a place where he could keep in radio contact with his salvage boats and administrate the never-ending search for investors. At the same time he could maintain a visible appearance for the tourists that came aboard to see the treasure Mel had recovered from the 1715 and 1733 Spanish treasure fleets.

Mel was happy. He sat for hours, the 'phone cradled between his ear and shoulder, talking to investors about the $400 million in treasure aboard the *Atocha*. He was sure he would find it in a matter of days. But money was slow in coming. There were days when the only money for boat fuel and food for the crew was what had been taken in as admission on board the *Golden Doubloon*. The system was breaking down unless a financial infusion was forthcoming. Mel had purchased a gold-colored Cadillac from a car dealer in Vero Beach several years earlier with gold coins. Even that was now running on thin tires. He tried forming several companies in the hopes of stimulating investors. Man Key, Inc., Woman Key, Inc., Margarita, Inc. --all in the background of the search for *Atocha*.

Taffi Fisher off Marquesa Keys.

At one time Mel invited all the investors to a cook-out on Boca Grande Key. Over 200 showed up and were ferried by boat from the dock in Key West. They were given metal detectors and told that it was possible that pirates had buried their loot on the island. To make it more interesting, he buried a few numbered tags, and those finding the tags were rewarded with silver "pieces-of-eight". That night, around a bonfire, Mel brought the investors up to date on the search. He spoke of the $400 million in gold and silver on board, and assured everyone it was "just a matter of days before we find the 'Big A' ". They all went away happy, except Gene Lyon, whose blood was the objective of the many mosquitoes that breed in the island's mangroves.

The surveys continued, and the next theodolite tower was a natural. On Marquesa Key was a Navy range spotter's tower. From there they could control the search to the southwest, south, and southeast. It seemed that this had been the area chosen by the Navy to make their torpedo runs and practice low-altitude bombing. The search crew began logging hits on almost every run. Often the torpedoes were lying fully exposed on the hard marl bottom, while other times they were buried under a few feet of sand. When his crew began to locate them, Mel called the Navy and asked if they were of any value, if so he would be willing to recover and return them to the experimental station in Key West. He was advised just to "mark" them with a buoy, and the Navy would be sent to recover them.

Once Fay Feild detected a row of what he thought were cannon. When he and Mel dived down to investigate, they found rounded lumps on the bottom, covered over with sand. They were about to bang away with a sledge hammer when something made them stop. Dusting with the *Virgalona* blower suddenly made them realize just how precarious an area they were searching in. The lumps were mines. They had stumbled onto a minefield that had been laid by the Navy during W.W.II, and the mines were still active! They quickly moved out of the area.

The magnetometer search was full of highs and lows. The bombs at first were exciting, and Mel even brought a few in to the dock. But after awhile it seemed the ocean floor was littered with them, and the search began to slow to a standstill. It was decided to "read" the anomalies --once they became familiar with bomb and torpedo hits-- and those anomalies were merely plotted on the chart and left undug. It may have been this decision that allowed the *Santa Margarita* to slip through the search pattern undetected. If the salvage crew had any idea just how close they were to both the *Atocha* and the *Santa Margarita* they would have uncovered every possible hit.

In any event, they searched the area to the west and southwest of Marquesa Key without a trace of the two missing galleons. It was September 1970 when Mel received a packet of information from his contact in Spain. Señora Angela Flores Rodriguez had uncovered some information in a *legajo* marked *Santo Domingo 132*. Her transcription of the deciphered scribblings stated, from an eyewitness account, "dragging her cables the *Margarita* was lost upon a bank of sand which is to the east of the last key of the Matecumbes." She had sent the document, written in Spanish, to Gene Lyon to translate into English, and when this was read over the phone there was a stunned silence. Based on this new information Mel had been searching for months on the wrong side of the Marquesa Keys.

Mel and Gene both agreed that based on the Rodriguez translations, the *Margarita* --and the *Atocha*-- had to lie somewhere between the Marquesa Keys and Key West. Even though this gave Mel a new incentive, it also left him frustrated. He was short of funds, and now he had to begin all over again in an area that was twenty-five miles long and at least five miles wide. Another 125 square miles!! One thing that bothered him more than anything else, was the fact that within this 125-square-mile area there was not a single location where the water was fifty-five feet deep. Gaspar de Vargas, the diver in charge of the Spanish salvage operation in 1622, had stated that the *Atocha* was located in fifty-five feet of water.

Mel was in a quandary. He had believed Señora Rodriguez when she originally sent him information that the *Atocha* was "off the Matecumbes". He had searched the Upper Keys for a year and had found nothing. He had searched the area Gene Lyon had pinpointed "off the Marquesas" and had found nothing. Now it was back to square one, but should he believe Gaspar de Vargas, or Angela Rodriguez? He decided to extend the search to the east towards Key West. His crew set about building a theodolite tower on Boca Grande Key. It was a labor of love, because the crew felt just as confident as Mel did that this must be where the *Atocha* ballast pile lay. When the tower was completed, the survey moved forward. It was in this area that they soon got large anomalies, ones that "pegged" the needle on the magnetometer. The *Virgalona* was brought in and began dusting the sand off the hit. The deeper the hole, the stronger the signal, but they couldn't dig a hole deep enough to uncover whatever it was. It was finally determined they had meteorite hits that were imbedded deeply in the sand.

There were other hits as well. The divers were surprised when a large anomaly south-southwest of Boca Grande Key turned out to be an Avenger, a W.W.II-vintage Navy aircraft trainer that had "turned up missing" from its Fort Lauderdale base. The hatch was gone, an indication that the pilot was able to bail out. The Navy was notified and a buoy left to mark the spot. For four months they searched the area to the east of Marquesa without success. The fact that there wasn't a depth of fifty-five feet in the area bugged Mel. One of Mel's associates, Norman Johnson, suggested they send to Seville and obtain a copy of the microfilm that Angela Rodriguez had translated. Possibly she had made a mistake.

Gene Lyon wrote to Angela and soon had a copy of the *legajos*. Upon deciphering the sketchy document, Gene discovered that Angela had made a mistake in translating "*ueste del ultimo cayo*", which meant west of the last key, not east! It was easy to miss the translation; "*este*" and "*ueste*" can be misinterpreted by the way the scribe wrote his "*e*" and "*u*". The mistake had cost Mel four months, and his funds were down to near zero. The search now shifted back to the west side of Marquesa Key, and a search for financial backers or sale of 1715 treasure took top priority. The greatest problem with raising new investors was the fact that not a single trace of either the *Atocha* nor the *Margarita* had been discovered thus far.

The only place Mel had yet to search was south of Marquesa, near the sand bank. There was a ready-made theodolite tower near the bank. The *Patricia*, a decommissioned Navy destroyer had been sunk and used as a bombing target. As Mel made arrangements to sell some of the last of the 1715 treasure, the crew set up station on the *Patricia*. They were about to make their first *Atocha* find.

17...THE GALLEON ANCHOR

The state of Florida had made some bureaucratic changes in the Division of History, Archives, and Records Management. The new head of the department was a former state senator, Robert Williams, a person who distrusted all salvage divers. The state archaeologist, Carl "Tony" Clausen may have been hired for the position in 1965 because of his total distaste for salvage divers. His feeling was that all ancient shipwrecks should be salvaged by marine archaeologists, even though there were over 4,000 such sites along the east coast of Florida alone and less than a dozen active marine archaeologists in the entire United States. Together they would present Mel with his greatest headaches.

Early on, Mel thought he could easily find the *Atocha*. It would be in 55 feet of water and near the Marquesa Keys. Normally the water is fairly clear there, and SCUBA diving would have made it simple to find the pile of ballast. It would be in one big mound, not scattered over several miles of bottom like the 1715 fleet wreck sites. With her cannons nearby it would have made quite a magnetometer target. But now, after two years of searching the Upper Keys and around the Marquesas, Mel still did not have a single clue that he was on the right track.

His greatest priorities were fuel for the boats, food for the crew, and staying three jumps ahead of his creditors. The value of his 1715 treasure was rising as the public demand for treasure coins increased. He was able to raise some cash by moving the Fort Pierce treasure from one bank to another, borrowing more than enough to pay off the first loan. But with expenses some days running over $1,000, the new cash would not last long. Something had to happen, and soon.

The *Patricia* had been sunk about four miles west of the Marquesas. The Navy had used the derelict destroyer as target practice for years, and unfortunately for Mel's salvage crews, they still did. The salvage crew was able to mount the theodolite station fairly high above water on the upper decks of the *Patricia*. From their vantage point they could easily see the Marquesas to the east, and to the southwest –some eight miles– were the "Quicksands", named for the rolling bank of sand and coral that seemed to move on the slightest provocation.

As the survey got underway, they quickly found the area surrounded by bombs and bomb fragments. The depth of water was only twenty feet, and once they were used to the bomb anomalies, they dismissed them. If they had decided to dig up every "hit", the job would have taken ten years or more. What the survey crew did find out was that bombs exploding in the water kill fish. As a result, swarms of bull sharks and barracudas remained in the area, waiting for the next bomb to fetch up dinner. When a swimmer would enter the water he was immediately surrounded by literally hundreds of barracuda. They were never physically bothered by the big fish, because they were more curious than hungry. But it gave the crew some experience with "denizens of the deep" that they could write home about.

The survey moved out to deeper water, and then it was Saturday, June 12, 1971. Bob Holloway and his all-girl crew had been crisscrossing the edge of the Quicksands, where the water was only eighteen to 25 feet deep. The *Patricia* was eight miles away, at the very limit of visibility by the diver peering through the telescope crosshairs of the theodolite. It was a flat calm day, a day without too many signals from the magnetometer being towed 100 feet astern. The sea bed was a continuous rolling sand dome, uninterrupted by coral or bottom growth. It was a day of boredom, of watching the compass and keeping a straight course. Bob was about to put *Holly's Folly* into a turn and bring it back on a course towards the *Patricia* when Marjorie Hargreaves shouted, "Anomaly!" She had been watching the needle on the magnetometer amplifier when it did a "peg reading", indicating a very large iron object on the bottom. Marjorie picked up a buoy with a concrete block anchor and let it drop over the side. Bob circled and throttled back as he approached the buoy marking the hit. The diver on the theodolite watched as the spot on the horizon stopped and dropped an anchor. It would take awhile for the search boat to check out the hit, so he was able to relax for a few minutes until told to "put me back on course."

Holloway suited up, and slipping into a SCUBA tank harness he dropped over the side to check out the anomaly. The water was crystal clear, with visibility almost unlimited, and swimming along the bottom to where the buoy marked the area, he spotted a large iron ring partially buried in the sand. As he fanned off the sand covering the ring it became apparent that the ring —almost three-and-a-half feet in diameter— was at the end of an anchor shank that lay buried deeper in the sand. The anchor had to be huge, and it was old. Holloway had found a galleon anchor.

Back on board his boat he called the *Virgalona* on his marine radio. Rick Vaughan was Captain of the "*Virge*" that day; Molinar had the week off and was back in Fort Pierce with his family. "*Virgalona*, this is *Holly's Folly*. I have a large anchor, possibly a galleon anchor, on this last hit. I suggest that Mel come over and check it out." The *Virgalona* was closer to the Marquesas checking out the previous days hits, but within minutes they had covered the several miles and were anchored alongside the buoy *Holly's Folly* had dropped. It was decided to dust the sand off the anchor with the *Virgalona* blowers, and they were lowered over the props.

Soon a hole six feet wide and several feet deep partially uncovered the huge anchor. The divers went over the side to take a closer look. Interestingly enough, the wooden crossarm was missing, and the anchor's flukes lay flat along the bottom. Lyon had determined from the Spanish archives that the *Atocha* was carrying six anchors. The largest of the anchors was a sheet anchor, fourteen to sixteen feet in length, carried in the hold in the event of an emergency. For ease of stowing, the crossarm had been removed and stored alongside. The *Santa Margarita* carried the same number and type of anchors. There was a strong possibility that this could be one of their anchors.

As Mel circled around the bottom near the anchor he spotted two small dark objects and picked them up. Back on the surface he held them in his hand. "This is it! Today's the day!" He held two lead musket balls up for everyone to see. He was convinced (possibly the only one on board) of the significance of his find, there were some smiles, and someone asked, "This is what?" Still smiling, Mel dropped back over the side and continued searching the bottom as *Virgalona* moved and blew another hole. This time he picked up more musket balls and the neck of an olive jar, the sealed plug still in place. He knew from previous experience that one of the best indications that the shipwreck is Spanish is from all the olive jar shards. The Spanish galleons carried hundreds of them, for water, oil, wine, all types of fluids. This time on the boarding ladder he shouted, "Today is the day! I've found it; I'm so close I can taste it!" The excitement was building when a few minutes later Rick Vaughan came to the boarding ladder and handed up two pieces of a broken olive jar. As he climbed aboard he slipped off a glove and shook out a small black encrusted object. It was a coin, a sulfided, silver piece-of-eight! Mel rubbed off some of the blackened sulfide and was able to read part of the inscription around the edge of the coin.: PHILIPPVS IIII. "That's about right for 1622."

It was time for a celebration. All the pent-up emotion of two years of fruitless searching seemed suddenly behind them. There was hugging and back-slapping, and the silver coin passed from hand to hand, each being careful not to drop it. It was, indeed, a significant find. It was the first visible evidence that the *Atocha*, or the *Margarita*, could be nearby. The *Virgalona* remained at anchor while *Holly's Folly* continued the search. The theodolite operator, fully excited over this latest find, now directed the search boat unerringly along the next range. More holes were dusted near the anchor, and other artifacts began to uncover...a barrel hoop, more pottery shards, but the most important recovery came the following day.

Don Kincaid was a photographer who had been invited out to take underwater photos of the galleon anchor. It was noontime, and 'most everyone was in the forward cabin having lunch. *Virgalona* had just finished opening up a large hole with her two blowers, and Kincaid dropped over the side with a SCUBA tank to take the photographs. As he swam down through the settling maelstrom of sand, he spotted what appeared to be a fistful of brass chain links along the side of the crater that had been dug. As they began to disappear in the sliding sand he grabbed them in his fist, waved them at Rick Vaughan, who was in the bottom of the hole, and headed for the surface.

As Don reached the surface, his "brass" links took on a gold look and were heavy enough to be the real thing. On the bottom he wasn't that impressed, he had never found gold before, in fact he had never had the chance to dive a treasure wreck before. But standing on the boarding platform with the gold links balled in his fist, he suddenly had the hairs on the back of his neck standing at attention. He shouted, and after a moment Fay Feild looked out the cabin door. When he spotted the gold chain in Don's hand he uttered a few cheerful curse words and bounded out of the cabin, quickly followed by everyone else on board.

There was no doubt that this was the most excitement the Fisher crew had experienced in several years. In many ways it was a reward for perseverance, for the hours, days, months of constant magging and digging up worthless modern iron in the junkyard of the Keys. Searching in six to eight foot seas, when the wind and rain made safety in Mooney Harbor seem like the comforts of home, because the entire crew believed in the *Atocha* almost as strongly as Mel Fisher did.

They laid the gold chain out on the engine hatch cover, the three sections measured eight-and-a-half feet of butter-yellow links, each link about three-eighths inches in diameter. Needless to say, there was a celebration. Mel could see *Holly's Folly* magging some distance away and he got on the marine radio. "*Holly's Folly*, this is *Virgalona*. Come in please." In a moment..., "This is *Holly's Folly*, go ahead, Mel". "Bob, this is Mel. Come on over for lunch. You got that?...Come over for lunch." It took Bob Holloway a few seconds to remember that "come over for lunch" were the code words he and Mel had worked out for when they found gold. "I'm on my way!" And with that, he swung the helm over and pushed the throttle full open. In minutes he had settled alongside *Virgalona*.

Mel called Bob Moran in Key West, and several hours later a boat with Bob, Chet Alexander, and Ingrid Nilsen tied up alongside. Someone located a bottle of champagne, a single bottle, but it was enough for everyone to have a sip. It was better than any New Year's celebration. It was a giddy time for everyone; it made each one want to sing and shout for no reason at all. Someone did a little jig on the fantail; others dived over the side to see if they could find more gold...forgetting to put on face mask and fins. Joytime lasted until dark when the boats settled behind the mangroves in Mooney Harbor. A buoy floated over the anchor nine miles away, a symbol of treasure found.

As quickly as possible, Mel filed a salvage claim with the state of Florida for the area adjacent to the Quicksands. To protect himself he also filed a salvage claim to the area between the Quicksands and the Marquesa Keys. The state indicated that they would study the request, and in the meantime assigned a state agent aboard the *Virgalona* to make sure that exploration-digging only was conducted. An exploration lease meant that nothing could be recovered, so when the *Virgalona* uncovered an encrusted matchlock musket, iron barrel hoops, cannon balls, an encrusted sword, and a broken piece of silverware, the state agent made them leave the artifacts on the bottom. Not to be dismayed, the divers swam them over to the anchor, and individually tied them to the shank with monofilament line.

As part of granting a salvage contract, the state of Florida had to make an on-site inspection. To this end they sent their marine archaeologist Carl Clausen, accompanied by Arthur Ergle and Allen Saltus, in a sixteen-foot outboard boat from Key West. *Virgalona* was anchored near the anchor buoy when Clausen's boat pulled up and anchored nearby. The state had to take charge of any artifacts recovered, so Mel had some of his divers swim down and retrieve the items they had tied to the anchor. When Clausen had all the artifacts safely in his boat, Mel called over to him and asked if he would sign a receipt for the items. Carl contemptuously raised his middle finger as he started up his engine and gunned back towards Key West. Mel made a note of the proceedings in his log.

18...THE BANK OF SPAIN

Neither Mel nor Gene Lyon had any idea whether the artifacts were from the *Atocha* or the *Santa Margarita*. They were certainly the right period, and the feeling was that it had to be the *Margarita*. She had sunk in only twenty feet of water, about the right depth for the Quicksands. And the records indicated she had dragged her cables until she struck a bank of sand. But somewhere in the back of Mel's mind he was sure he had the *Atocha*...wishful thinking more than fact. Now he needed a theodolite tower on the Quicksands to control and intensify the search there.

While sitting at the Pier House one day he looked out at the row of derelict boats and spotted an old tug, the *Bon Vent*. After some inquiries, he discovered it was sitting there because it had no engine. It was 125 feet long, large enough to make a great theodolite platform, so he bought it for $2,500 and had it towed out to the Quicksands. There he opened the sea valves, and it sunk on the spot. It was there to stay, unless a hefty hurricane came along and moved it.

The survey of the area was now better controlled, and each course run was kept at fifty feet from the next. The one problem with the magnetometer was that it could not pick up the smaller artifacts, these anomalies would show as possibly nothing more than a ripple on the meter. It would be necessary to dust the sand away to recover anything. With the sand as deep as twenty feet in some places, the *Virgalona* began blowing a series of holes, and these were logged on a chart of the area to make sure the holes overlapped and that each gridded area was completely covered. The digging went on enthusiastically, each hole with the potential for more treasure. The problem arose again that nothing could be recovered under a "search" lease from the state, unless they had a specific agreement with the state's marine archaeologist, Carl Clausen. They were reminded of this constantly by the state agent who now rode to the site every day aboard *Virgalona*.

During one period of time the divers did bring to the surface some musket balls, silver spoons, coins, and rudder pintles which attached the rudder to the ship's stern. The state agent instructed

Mel to throw the items back into the ocean to satisfy the contract regulations. The pintles could have later helped identify the location where the ship was built, and possibly what ship they came from. They were never recovered again.

Late in June one of the divers surfaced with a stack of nineteen sulfided silver coins. After some communication with Tallahassee, Fisher was allowed to keep them for a later division with the state. When Don Kincaid projected a slide of the coins on a screen, Gene Lyon was able to pick out a date, 1619, as well as the "P" Potosí mint mark on several of them. He also found a rare "RN" mint mark standing for Nuevo Reino de Granada, the Bogotá mint. It was rare because no coins were known to exist from the mint before 1630! The importance of this find was that it nailed down the approximate date when the galleon carrying these coins sank. It had to be after 1619, and the mint mark indicated it was part of the *Tierra Firme* fleet. During the 1622 hurricane eight vessels had been lost, but only three of them had been carrying any quantity of silver coins. The *Rosario*, lost on Loggerhead Key in the Tortugas, had been completely salvaged by Gaspar de Vargas. This left only the *Atocha* and *Margarita* carrying the silver coins being recovered near the Quicksands. Which one was it? It would take another two years to find out.

After weeks of delay, the salvage contract was approved by the state, but only for the area adjacent to the Quicksands. Mel spoke to Senator Williams about the second salvage lease between the Quicksands and Marquesa Keys. Williams assured Mel that he would not give a lease to any other salvage group, that only one lease per wreck site would be approved. This conversation was routinely taped for the record. For a time the relationship between Fisher's group and the state of Florida seemed to improve. Mel now had three boats working the site. *Holly's Folly* was the "mag" boat; the *Virgalona* and Chet Alexander's *Aquanaut* were used as salvage boats with blowers to dust the sand on the bottom.

Under the salvage contract, Florida required that a state agent be present on each boat when it was on the site. Furthermore, the state agents would work only forty hours a week! The Quicksands lay 35 miles west of Key West, and Mel's boats all anchored each night in Mooney Harbor in the Marquesas nine miles away. They normally left anchorage at 7:00 a.m. and never returned until dark...about 6:30 p.m. Unless the weather kept the boats at anchor, that was the schedule the boats had followed since they began searching for the "Big A". The state made it clear; they could afford only a single agent for each shipwreck contract. Mel finally made an agreement with state. He would meet the state payroll for two more agents, buy their equipment, teach them to dive, and feed them on the boat. The state still balked on the forty hour work-week, and Mel had to agree to hire a total of six agents in order that his boats could keep working. When his funds were already running low, this was a cruncher, but Mel seriously believed he would find the *Atocha* in a matter of days. After all, he already had the anchor and a gold chain, so he knew he must be close. He agreed to the state terms, and the boats went back to work.

The year 1971 held another great day for the salvage crews. Rick Vaughan and Scott Barron each recovered a six-inch gold bar while working under the *Virgalona*'s blowers. The recovery had a far-reaching effect. The *Miami Herald*, usually not friendly to Fisher's salvage efforts, printed the story of the recovery in a favorable light. The wire services picked up on it, and Paul Harvey, a staunch supporter of Mel's, broadcast the news nationally on his radio show. When asked by newspaper reporters what he thought of the recovery, Carl Clausen implied that there was "something funny" about the bars, particularly if they came from the seventeenth century. Another treasure salvor, Bob Marx, flatly stated that the anchor Mel had found had been taken from one of his sites, and that the gold bars were "phonies". Even Art McKee on Plantation Key, suggested that Mel was "just trying to sell stock". He knew how hard it was to raise capital for a salvage operation.

Because of Mel's need for financial help, and his hucksterism, the rumors spread like wildfire. But within the Fisher team it was business as usual. They knew the bars had not been "planted" and that publicity would not always be favorable. Mel quietly told them, "As long as we know the truth, that's what matters." He refused to rebuff his detractors. The gold bars brought a more serious threat to Mel's operation. It provided the incentive for his competitors to abandon their search for the *Atocha* in the Upper Keys. Before long Burt Webber moved his 135-foot salvage boat *Revenge* to Key West. Jack "Blackjack" Haskins, one of the better historians as well as a good salvager, and John Berrier teamed up in their search of the archives in Seville for more clues. The year ended with storms and windy weather shutting down all diving operations.

The following year began with Carl Clausen warning Fisher that he was violating his contract in a number of areas. The allegations that a number of accidents had occurred, as well as poor working conditions, brought a suggestion that Mel's operation be shut down. A written report recommended that an in-depth investigation be made unless Fisher vastly improved the physical condition of his work boats, machinery, and equipment that he used to conduct the contract with. Shortly afterwards Clausen resigned, and a new marine archaeologist, Wilburn "Sonny" Cockrell, was made his replacement. Some would say later, "Out of the frying pan, into the fire."

Mel was able to gain a few investors, and he also sold his Vero Beach homesite. Sale of some of the 1715 treasure was completed, giving Mel a bit of financial breathing room. From Seville Gene Lyon obtained a complete copy of the *Atocha* and *Margarita* manifests. The *Atocha* carried 901 registered silver bars, 161 gold pieces, and over 250,000 silver coins. The gold pieces were not itemized as bars, discs, or other bullion. It was suspected that the unregistered treasure on board *Atocha* would be considerable. With manifest in hand, and the two gold bars, Mel's ability to raise investors became a bit easier. His desire to find treasure seemed to rub off on people that had a great deal of money. Mel was genuinely believable, and as a result he came back from money-raising trips with his pockets full of checks from people who wanted to see him succeed and who wanted to own some of the treasure when he did.

It was houseboat time. Mel couldn't find someone willing to trade him a nice home in Key West for stock in Treasure Salvors, but Chet Alexander had the use of a large 20-foot by 40-foot houseboat that was tied up behind the power plant. He said the

Fishers could use it. The houseboat had been sitting behind the plant for several years, and it showed. It was pretty dirty, and not in the greatest of shape. The entire Treasure Salvors crew turned out, and together they cleaned, scrubbed, painted, and vacuumed the houseboat until it shined. What a group! Mel moved it to a dock adjacent to Roosevelt Boulevard on the south side of Key West. That would be home for Mel, Deo, Kane and Taffi for the next few years. Mel found another houseboat, not quite as large as the first, tied up to the yacht basin with a "for sale" sign on it. Before long he had traded some stock in Treasure Salvors for the boat and towed it to Mooney Harbor, the inner lagoon of the Marquesa Keys. This would be home for the boat crews during their hunt for *Atocha*.

The Fisher houseboat, moored alongside Roosevelt Boulevard, Key West.

A third houseboat turned up at the Vero Beach Yacht Club. The owner wanted to sell it badly, but wouldn't trade for stock. He finally did trade for a couple of 1715 gold bars, and Mel had it towed to Key West where he moored it outboard of his own. When Dirk and Kim completed school in Vero Beach that year, they moved into this smaller houseboat. As it turned out, Mel's houseboat had leaks in her bottom, and only by having strong ropes between her and the dock kept it from rolling on its side and sinking into the adjacent channel.

And as the summer wore on, Don Kincaid was caught alone on the Marquesa houseboat with a hurricane approaching. He put as many anchors out as he had aboard, tied the bow to some mangroves, and waited it out. When the hurricane passed, he was still there. One day when the supply boat pulled into Mooney Harbor, they noticed a number of bullet holes in the side of the houseboat. Kenneth "Ding-A-Ling" Lingle was the only person aboard at the time, and before unloading supplies they wanted to know "What happened". His reply, "I got bored and was killing time." He had shot the clock on the wall full of holes! They finished unloading supplies and quickly left.

The search of the Quicksands area was going slowly because of the deep sand. At times the *Virgalona* blowers just could not reach bottom, which in some places was almost twenty feet deep. Mel had a couple of boats still working on the 1715 fleet. One of these was the "Gold Digger", a barge with three blowers in a row that ran its entire length and were all run by Volkswagen engines. The one thing about the Gold Digger, it could move sand! Mel had it towed to Key West, and before long it was moored over the galleon anchor. Within minutes the entire anchor was exposed for the first time! It measured fifteen feet in length. For awhile it seemed they had the answer to the deep sand, until the engines began shutting down with sand and shells being caught up in the water intake. Then one day a sudden storm, with ten-foot waves, broke the barge from its moorings and sent it winging towards Half Moon Shoals. The *Virgalona* was able to catch up with it before it became another wreck site, and towed it back to the Quicksands. Before long Mel termed it a liability and it was towed back to Fort Pierce.

Art Hempstead had an 84-foot barge located on the Miami River. He had raised cannon up and down the coast, and when he suggested giving Mel a hand, Mel said "C'mon down." Art had large airlifts on board that normally move a lot of sand, but it wasn't long before he found that the swirling currents around the Quicksands made controlling the airlifts too difficult. He went back to the Miami river.

The more Mel looked at the deep sand on the site, the more he felt that unless he could move it, he would never find *Atocha*. His thoughts were on *big* boats with *big* props, then Lou Tilley called. He had a couple of Mississippi river tugs, the 54-foot *Northwind*, and the 59-foot *Southwind*. "They have *big* props for small boats; do you think they will work?" Mel traded Lou stock in the company for both of them and sent a crew, including his son Kim, to bring the boats from New Orleans to Key West. The tug boats were never designed to work in the open ocean. They sat low in the water with the main deck just a few feet above the water. In the open ocean the deck seemed constantly awash, and the pilot house was built so high that she rolled like a bowling ball in high seas.

When they arrived in New Orleans they found the *Northwind* not in running condition. It was decided to tow the *Northwind* to Key West and work on it there. No sooner had they cleared New Orleans and the delta, when a bad storm struck. The waves were soon ten feet tall, and the *Northwind* began to sink on the end of her towline. The *Southwind* had bilge pump problems and had taken on so much water that she listed heavily to port until her engine on that side was completely underwater. There was an overwhelming fear on board *Southwind* that if her sister ship sank, the water was deep enough to drag both ships to the bottom. Someone stood by the towing hawser with an ax, while Kim got on the marine radio and asked the Coast Guard for help. Soon a Coast Guard cutter was alongside, and they were able to get hoses aboard both vessels and pump them dry. The cutter then towed both tugs back to New Orleans. Another day, a calmer day, both tugs made it to Key West. It was an inauspicious start for the tugs, one that would end in tragedy.

Dirk Fisher, at age 19, was made captain of the *Northwind*, and Kim Fisher, at 17, became captain of the *Southwind*. The *Northwind* would need some extensive work, and while this was underway Dirk worked off his brother's tug. Kane Fisher, at age

13, also worked with his brothers on board the tug. By age 11 Kane had already recovered his first gold. While working the "Rio Mar Wreck" of Echeverz' 1715 *capitana,* he had located many small gold nuggets in the cracks that typify the hard bottom around the site. By flattening out the end of a coat hanger he was able to work the nuggets out of the cracks until he had quite a pile. When the state man aboard the salvage boat said he was "taking custody of them", Kane made him count each one and give him a receipt. The Fisher boys made quite a team.

There was a cloud of gloom over the Fisher camp when Fay Feild said he had to leave. Treasure hunting had given him an ulcer and had contributed to his divorce. He would return some years later, but it left only Mel, Deo, and Mo Molinar from the original "A-Team". With the Fisher boys growing up fast they kept the momentum going.

Bleth McHaley joined their team about that time. She had met Mel while he had his shop in Redondo Beach, and she worked for *Skin Diver* magazine. Her husband had been recently killed in an automobile accident, and when she found herself in Key West she looked Mel up. First she became a small investor, and then Mel asked her if she would like to work for him. She jumped at the opportunity and became one of the team's shining stars. At first she ran the supply boat out to the Marquesas, and then she took over the public relations department, something she did very well. It was a time when the new state marine archaeologist Sonny Cockrell was shaking his chains. His first letter to Mel admonished him for not turning over some coins promptly to the state. Next he ordered Treasure Salvors not to make any statements about the history of any shipwrecks unless a state representative was present to prevent any errors. Bleth had her work cut out for her.

One day Otis Imboden, a *National Geographic* photographer, and Dennis Kane, chief of the Society's television division, dropped by to see Mel. Mel had worked with the National Geographic Society in 1965 on the Kip Wagner story, and as the *Atocha* story began to develop they felt there would be a great story here. After listening to Mel and seeing the artifacts that had been recovered, they signed two contracts for $10,000 each. One contract was for an exclusive story if they did find the *Atocha*, and the other was for a television documentary on the find. It was a shot in the arm that Mel really needed. It helped him financially, but it also helped stifle the rumors that he was "salting" the wreck site to gain investors. When *National Geographic* puts their stamp of approval on a project, you can bank on it being legitimate.

Mel and Deo Fisher at Fort Taylor, Key West.

Bob Holloway had turned his attention to an area west of the Quicksands, an area called "New Ground". While magging in this area he discovered a completely intact, old shipwreck. *National Geographic*'s timing was perfect, and a filming crew was sent out to the site. The wreck was wedged into a break in the reef where it dropped from twelve feet to deeper water. Here were cannons, anchors, ivory tusks, stacks of pewter plates, tankards, and piles of slave shackles. Although it was dubbed the "H.M.S. Woolworth", they knew it was an African slaver that sank much later than the *Atocha*. At first it was a coin, and then a silver spoon, that dated the wreck in the late 1600's. Finally, the ship's bell was recovered, identifying it as the *Henrietta Marie*. Attention was back again on the Quicksands.

Other than the anchor, a gold chain, and two gold bars, the findings of treasure had not been significant as 1972 became history. Winter storms kept the boats at their docks as the 1973 salvage season began. As May weather approached, the seas flattened, and the boats again began their systematic search for treasure near the Quicksands. Kim Fisher had been able to train his crew on the *Southwind*, and they found that with the tug's huge 43-inch props they could dig a ten-foot hole in a matter of a few minutes. It appeared that Mel had been right in his gamble to use the tugs. But it was the old faithful salvage boat *Virgalona* that struck paydirt first.

They found a trail of the scatter pattern early in May and began to recover muskets, swords and daggers, a pair of scissors, lock and key, and a barshot. Then, on May 19th, they began to pick up silver coins --36 that first day-- and then 244 pieces-of-eight two days later. Then they hit it! On May 25th, the *Virgalona* was at anchor. With John Brandon and Steve and Spencer Wickens on the bottom, Molinar turned up the engines. Soon the maelstrom of sand reduced the visibility to zero. The divers were used to being bounced around the bottom of the hole by the thrust of the boats' propellers, but as Mo throttled back they were unprepared for what had been uncovered. On the sides of the hole, the bottom, everywhere, there were blackened silver coins.

One of the divers broke the surface and shouted for Mo to shut off the engines, "We've hit it!" Suddenly everyone in the boat was over the side, helping to recover the coins that were coming up almost by the bucketful. By the end of the day they had recovered 1,460 pieces-of-four and -eight. Mo called Key West on the marine radio to let the office know, and Bleth McHaley promptly called the *National Geographic* people in Washington to tell them the news. They were excited and said they would send a film crew down immediately. With that thought in mind, Bleth called Mo back on the marine radio and asked him to wait for the *National Geographic* film crew before he blew another hole. Her message was clear, "The 'Bank of Spain' is closed!"

♤

19...SILVER BARS

The Bank of Spain adventure was the beginning of a great year of treasure recoveries. The year 1973 will long be remembered as the first year when each new day held the potential for great discoveries in the area of the Quicksands. On June third the *Southwind* relieved *Virgalona* on the site, a few days before the National Geographic Society people arrived. They would not be disappointed. The *Virgalona* had opened the door of the bank, and now the *Southwind* was about to make a withdrawal. As the sand was dusted away silver coins tumbled out of the sides of the crater by the hundreds. Even as the hard marl bottom was reached under fifteen feet of sand, they found coins cemented to the floor of the ocean.

As they dusted the sand away in an even wider circle the coins never seemed to stop. They were everywhere, even in clumps, sliding down the side of the crater as it was being dug. At first the divers were carrying the coins to the surface by the handfuls, then in bags. After awhile, they just piled them in the middle of the hole until they had a bucketful, and then tied a line and let the crew on the surface haul them up. Nearly 5,000 silver coins were recovered before the Bank of Spain closed its doors. Mel figured it probably was the contents of two boxes of coins that had been carried in the sterncastle. Each box normally carried 3,000 coins, made up in three burlap bags (*talegas*) of 1,000 coins each. But if the wreck were the *Atocha*, there would be 81 more boxes of coins nearby. The ship carried a total of 250,000 pesos in coins, enough to stir the imagination.

The scatter pattern was taking on a definite direction, and a fairly narrow one at that. From the galleon anchor the trail led to the southeast, towards a patch reef that lay seventeen feet below the surface. About 3,600 feet separated the anchor from the edge of the patch reef. The water gradually deepened from seventeen feet to fifty feet as it reached the reef, and it was on everyone's mind that this could possibly be the reef that the *Atocha* struck, "and sunk shortly thereafter." As Kim Fisher moved the *Southwind* along the scatter pattern he expected to uncover the mother lode at any moment.

Dirk and Angel Fisher with the **Atocha** *astrolabe.*

On 17 June the log of *Southwind* recorded the recoveries of cannon balls, three rapiers, two swords, a dagger and a flintlock musket, and a total of 180 silver pieces of eight. About noontime Dirk Fisher was on the bottom checking out the side of the last hole when he spotted a circular bronze artifact that had begun a slow slide towards the bottom of the hole. When he picked it up it seemed heavy, and a bit encrusted. By the time he got it to the surface he realized what it was. It was a mariner's astrolabe, an extremely valuable recovery. When Kim reported the find over the marine radio, Key West was ecstatic. There were less than two dozen known astrolabes in the world, and if it had markings it could lead to the identification of the shipwreck.

In 1622 the only real navigational aids the pilots had were the compass, a sand timer to determine the speed through the water by timing a block of wood floating from one end of the ship to the other, and the astrolabe to measure the height of the sun above the horizon at its azimuth. At noon there are about three minutes that the sun neither rises nor lowers, and this is called its azimuth. The elevation at that point is the latitude the ship is in, and when spending weeks at sea, out of sight of land, it gives the pilot some assurance that his dead reckoning plot is close. An astrolabe is a very personal part of a pilot's tools, much like his bronze dividers, so often they inscribed their names on the instrument. As Dirk held this one in his hand he, wondered who the pilot was, and if it might have significant markings.

The *Southwind* props were doing a fantastic job of moving sand. In sand ten feet deep the hole opened up almost ten feet across. If treasure were there they would find it. At the same time, with divers working under the blower, none of the more fragile artifacts were damaged. A majolica bowl was recovered intact, as were gold links to a chain. Even a small gold button was recovered directly under the blower. Kim maneuvered the *Southwind* close to the northwest corner of the Bank of Spain and began dusting a new series of holes. He was in the water to watch the hole develop when he uncovered a long gold bar, bent double. The gold rod was without any markings, probably contraband. It was a gold hole because in minutes a four-and-a-half-pound gold disk appeared, with markings of the mint and a stamp indicating fifteen-and-a-quarter carats purity. The first gold coins to be recovered were next, two gold 1-*escudo* coins about the size of a nickel, minted in Seville. The passengers would have carried a few gold coins as pocket change to purchase gifts or tobacco in Havana for the trip back to Spain.

Then it was the Fourth of July, a day of fireworks and celebration, "Bouncy" John, a converted hippie who would become one of Fisher's best divers, provided the fireworks. He had transferred aboard the *Southwind* as engineer and bilge cleaner and was making one of his first dives. In fact, this was the first hole of the day for *Southwind* and Bouncy John volunteered to be the first diver of the day. He was on the bottom as the blowers dusted the sand from around him, kicking furiously to stay in the hole as the thrust of water moved him around at will. As the hole gradually deepened and hard bottom appeared, there were a number of ballast stones scattered about, but the sudden flash of pink and gold made his heart begin to beat like a full dress band.

The propwash was at full fury, and it was difficult just to stay on the bottom, let alone try to pick up what appeared to be a gold chain that was stuck to the coral. He cupped his hand over the artifact and just hung on for what seemed like an eternity, until the engine finally shut down. For a few minutes the settling sand blotted out visibility, but soon it cleared and he was able to raise his hand. It was a beautiful gold rosary of gold with pink coral beads. The gold cross and chain measured about 12" long, possibly meant as a gift for a small child. When Bouncy John hit the surface he shouted "Beads!" and swam to the ladder, his outstretched hand holding it up for someone on board to take it. It was his first real artifact, certainly his first gold from the site, and he wore a grin for the next several days.

The day wasn't over yet. Sometime after lunch Kane Fisher, now 14 years old, and Mike Schnaedelbach were working under the blower. Everybody on board was excited, this had been a terrific week of treasure, it seemed everyone was bringing it up. There were some ballast stones in almost every hole, an indication that the hull of the ship had opened up and was spilling her cargo and treasure as it bounced along the bottom. Kane and Mike hung motionless above the blowers as they dug towards the bottom. Around the outside of the hole the sand created a maelstrom, almost like watching a dust storm rush across the desert, reducing visibility to zero. But dead center between the blowers the water was clear, and the divers were able to watch the hole develop.

As the hard bottom became visible, and the ring of clear water spread, Kane spotted something unusual on the bottom. "It looked like a black loaf of bread", and before the sand had settled there were two more loaves lying in the bottom of the hole. Kane tried picking one up, but it wouldn't move. It was not only heavy, but cemented to the bottom. He came up to the boarding ladder and suddenly had everyone's attention. "I think I've got a silver bar down there. Someone hand me a rope and I'll tie it off....it's too heavy to swim up." Back on the bottom Kane and Mike tied off the first bar, and an eager topside crew hauled it up.

Mike Schnaedelbach was able to pry the second bar off the bottom and, picking it up in his arms, he tried to swim it to the surface. He was able to just barely get his head out of the water before the weight of the silver bar began to drag him under. He grasped the anchor rope with his legs and hollered for a line. When the line came close he grabbed for it...and promptly sank the twenty feet back to the bottom. Before long the other two bars were aboard the *Southwind* and the excitement began to mount. The reason was that under the encrustation you could see markings, lots of markings. It meant that finally...they were close to unlocking the secret as to which galleon they had. The *Atocha*...or the *Santa Margarita*.

Bleth McHaley happened to be on board the *Southwind* that day, and she radioed ahead to the Key West office with the news. It started a chain reaction. Mel was aboard another tug that had left the site earlier in the day. When he heard the news over the radio he turned the tug around and headed back to the Quicksands. Bates Littlehales, a National Geographic Society photographer, was in Key West and when alerted that silver bars had been recovered he hopped a ride on Treasure Salvors fast Mako supply boat with Don Kincaid. It took them less than two hours to reach the site, about the same time as Mel arrived. Bob

Holloway got underway with *Holly's Folly*, and a large group of well-wishers, and they also headed for *Southwind*.

The afternoon wind had picked up, pushing waves ahead of it that soon were breaking over the *Southwind*'s railing leaving the deck awash. Preston Shoup, a Treasure Salvors executive, had telephoned Gene Lyon at his rental cottage on Big Pine Key. "You'd better head on down, they found a mess of silver bars out there!!" Gene made the thirty-mile trip in record time, pulling up near the *Golden Doubloon*. Preston had his fast, small outboard boat already full of television people and their gear, and it was low in the water. There were some misgivings as they pulled away from the dock and headed over the flats at breakneck speed. By the time they covered the forty miles everything was wet. Gene was never happier to see the three story yellow superstructure of the *Southwind* as it came into view over the tops of the waves.

The three bars lay in a fiber glass tank covered by six inches of water. The markings were fairly clear, even through the heavy silver sulfide that covered the bars. They were heavy, somewhere between seventy and ninety pounds each, and it took a little manhandling to get them out on the deck where everyone could get a better look. Lyon was able to brush away some of the sulfide from the surface and read the Roman numerals on each bar indicating its mint tally number. They were numbered 569, 794, and 4584. Also on each bar were a series of Roman numerals indicating the purity. The bars were struck with the numbers II U CCCLXXX (2380) against a silver purity of 2400. The bars were almost pure silver! There were round seals indicating the tax had been paid, as well as other symbols possibly representing the shipping marks of the owner and the person the bars were consigned to. Those marks could be the best identifying marks on the bars.

Mel was in the center of a huge celebration. There were now over forty people gathered on the *Southwind* decks as more boats filled with well-wishers arrived. With that many enthusiastic people, Mel had to move the celebration back to Key West. There was an underlying feeling of emotion for Mel. The state agents on board the salvage vessels had not been kind in their reports to Tallahassee, and it festered a feeling among the bureaucrats that

Mel was a con artist. Senator Williams had awarded Burt Webber, as well as Dick MacAllaster and Jack Haskins, search contracts in the Marquesa area. Although he had promised Mel he would not give more than one contract on each wreck site, he was not honoring that commitment. Even within the salvage community Mel had problems with his competitors believing that he had found any part of the 1622 fleet. Mel had been spending quite a bit of time trying to find investors to keep the operation going. A salvage operation "feasts" on money for food, fuel, repairs, lawyers, salaries and office expenses. With each recovery the word was passed to the news media that whatever had been recovered was "planted" or "salted" in order to get investor interest and their money. The problems had been building for months, but now, suddenly there were three silver bars that would positively identify which wreck site Mel's group was working.

Gene Lyon quickly returned to Key West, and when the library opened on Thursday morning he was there with three rolls of microfilm that held the manifests of the *Santa Margarita* and the *Atocha*. He first felt that because of the depth at which the bars were recovered, it was probably the *Santa Margarita*. The *procesal* writing was slow to decipher, and each frame had to be carefully studied. There were literally thousands of items making up each manifest, and it was slow going for Gene. After three days he had finished the *Santa Margarita* manifest, and he had not found any of the bars with the same descriptive marks. There was a Sunday break when the library remained closed, but on Monday morning Gene was there when they opened the doors. As he threaded the *Atocha* manifest microfilm onto the reader there was a bit of skepticism that possibly the bars were from another galleon altogether. That would be a heart breaking letdown. The first silver bars on the manifest had been loaded in Havana harbor, and the markings were not familiar. The next group of bars had been loaded on board *Atocha* in Cartagena. The scrollwork of the scribe, and the notary seals of each bar, were ornately written across a somewhat worm-eaten page. Then...there it was, bar number *quatro mil quinientos e ochenta e quatro*: 4584. The silver fineness of the bar was also the same 2380, and the weight in Spanish was 125 marks, 3 ounces. Gene was able to translate that to 63.58 pounds. When Lyons boarded the *Golden Doubloon* the celebration was still in full swing. Almost a week had not dampened everyone's enthusiasm. Gene was able to show Bleth McHaley the *Atocha* manifest, and the matching marks. That seemed to be the fuse that ignited an even more hilarious outcry. She picked up the radio and quickly called Kim Fisher on the *Southwind*. "We've got it, the 'Big A'. We've found the *Atocha*!!" Gene tried to temper the enthusiasm by telling her that the bar should be weighed first to make sure it matched the manifest. To everyone within earshot that would merely be the frosting on the cake. As far as they were concerned...it was the *Atocha*! It was enough incentive for Kim to pull his anchors and head *Southwind* for Key West. On board *Southwind* both Kim and Kane Fisher felt the growing excitement. Their father had been searching for the *Atocha* for five long years, and had been under fire most of that time. If they actually had the *Atocha* it would satisfy all their dreams. To be able to find the galleon for their father was a dream come true. They stood on the bridge as the tug approached the dock near the *Golden Doubloon*. They had expected a crowd on the dock, but it was hard to believe that so many people had gathered to watch them bring the silver bars ashore. What they didn't know was the growing tension of hope that the bars would match the weight on the manifest. Mel had borrowed a freight scale and it was sitting on the deck of the *Golden Doubloon*, along with a crowd of onlookers. Kim brought the tug up smartly alongside the *Golden Doubloon* and soon the lines were made fast, and a transfer of treasure began. The young crew passed over a bag containing 700 silver pieces of eight, the small gold rosary that Bouncy John had found, muskets, swords, barrel hoops, cannon balls, and finally...the three silver bars. Considering the silver sulfide covering the bar #4584, the scale was preset at 63.60 pounds. When the silver bar was finally placed on the scale you could hear a pin drop. The balance arm of the scale wavered a bit, but finally settled down...dead center! The bar weight matched the manifest, and the cheers were instantaneous. It was celebration time all over again.

241

20...TREASURE FEVER

Treasure is a magnet for publicity. The greatest problem lies in that a magnet has a negative pole, as well as a positive pole. The discovery of the three silver bars, and the publicity that followed, gave Mel the unbelievable swings in emotion one can expect from treasure found. When the wave of publicity spread like ripples on a pond, the world suddenly awakened to the fact that this treasure salvor in Key West could momentarily unlock the mystery of an extremely rich treasure galleon. It was like waiting for the next shoe to drop. The story was carried as front page news throughout the states, in Spain, and in Germany as well. The 'phones in the *Golden Doubloon* office began ringing off the hook; reporters and television crews wanted a piece of the action. Treasure makes news.

Mel and his three boys, Dirk, Kim, and Kane all expected to find the mother lode on their next dive. It almost became a competition within the family as to which one would discover the big pile. It was on all their minds that the great bulk of *Atocha* gold and silver could not be far away. At the end of each week it was frustrating for them to raise anchor and head for Key West, relieved by one of the other salvage vessels. But the search along the narrow corridor southeast of the Quicksands continued to produce great artifacts, and the competition between boats in bringing in the most significant treasures became a jovial point of contention whenever the weather allowed the crews to spend some time together at the local brewhouse.

Outside the Key West treasure community, the war clouds of treasure were gathering. Bob Marx was having an ego problem at the time, finding it difficult to admit that Mel had finally recovered something significant enough to indicate that the wreck was the *Atocha*. In an article published by the *Orlando Sentinel* he still contested the location of the *Atocha*. His research still placed the *Atocha* off the Matecumbes, "thirteen miles from the Holiday Inn at Islamorada". He did not give an explanation as to why he never salvaged the shipwreck, as valuable as it was, if he knew the exact location. It may have been his evaluation of the treasure on board which he said was estimated at $10 million, rather than the $400 million Fisher had suggested. In a rare burst of exasperation he stated that "Fisher damaged his credibility as a historian by claiming that he had found the *Atocha* off the Marquesas".

Burt Webber also had a problem with the silver bars. He had been searching for the *Atocha* for several years off the Matecumbes and had cost his investors thousands of dollars in chasing information supplied by Angela Rodriguez. He wrote a letter to Tallahassee, addressed to Senator Williams, advising him that Fisher's identification of the silver bars having come from the *Atocha* was "all wrong. The bar markings did not match the manifest markings." He wrote that it was premature to identify the wreck site as the *Atocha*. This statement was made in spite of the fact that Gene Lyon had actually matched the shippers' marks of the bars in the margin of the manifest of the *Atocha*. Although Burt would later recant his statements to Williams, the initial damage was done.

Criticism within the salvage community usually stems from the high value salvors place on their "expected recoveries" in order to attract investors. Mel had to raise money to keep the operation going; he was so close to the "big pile" he could taste it. Somehow he tried to relate that to potential investors, and as a result he was accused of "hucksterism". The recourse of other salvagers --not able to raise money so easily-- is criticism. Mel, again, refused to rebuff his critics. Raising money to continue the operation was foremost in his mind and at the top of his priority list. If it made the job any easier he was prone to exaggerate the amount of treasure he expected to find. But in the salvage of treasure, all bets are off when trying to be factual about unrecovered treasure. When a shipwreck is scattered about the bottom, the amount that was on the ship and the amount that can be recovered may vary considerably. But investors want to know "How much treasure was the *Atocha* carrying?" Translating the pesos to "artifactual" dollars is where the greatest discrepancy arises.

A stern-faced Senator Robert Williams strode up the gangway of the *Golden Doubloon* with not much of a handshake when Mel greeted him as he stepped aboard. Behind him were the Florida Marine Patrol, fully armed. The greeting was cordial but brief. Lined up for his inventory were several white Styrofoam coolers filled with treasure. The state had come to claim custody of Fisher's recoveries. As soon as the state received official word that the silver bars had been brought ashore, Senator Williams decided it was time to take custody of all the treasure. He phoned Mel that he would be flying down to Key West shortly and to have the booty ready for his inventory. The artifacts were impressive, but Williams tried not to show much in the way of emotion as they packed the astrolabe, 2,000 silver coins, a bronze mortar, Bouncy John's pink coral rosary, a pair of dividers, three silver candelabras, the silver bars, and hundreds of other artifacts in the Styrofoam coolers. There was a brief hostile encounter when, as he was leaving, Williams spotted a lead sounding weight in the museum's gift shop. He demanded to know "why it was not included in the treasure he was taking back." Mel was able to show him that it was an artifact recovered from the 1715 fleet, and that it had been divided with the state some nine years previously. Williams was escorted back to the airport by the Marine Patrol, leaving Mel with an empty feeling. For a time it was nice having the treasure close at hand; it certainly had cost Mel five years of hard work and every cent he could put together.

No sooner had Williams returned to Tallahassee when he announced that he would have to cancel Mel's salvage contract. Someone had advised him that Mel hadn't filed the corporation reports, nor had he paid the corporate tax. The news media picked up on this juicy news, fueling the running battle with the *Miami Herald*, who believed in controversy as the cutting edge of news. Deo quickly found the receipts and copies of the reports, flew them to Tallahassee herself, and presented them to Senator Williams. Before leaving, she received a written apology from the state attorney's office, but again, the damage had already been done.

When it rains, it pours. A customs service official appeared one day in Mel's office with a complaint that his tug boats were not licensed and lacked the proper papers. When he was presented with them he could only apologize, saying he had to check out all complaints. Then Taffi, coming home from school one day, saw the houseboat had a heavy list to one side. It was in danger of sinking and sliding off into the middle of the channel. She rushed aboard, gathered up all her photo albums --and her dog-- and stacked them up on the dock. She then called her father to let him know that their home was about to become another *Atocha*. He had some of his crew rush over in the company truck and put a sump pump on board to bring the houseboat back on an even keel. They couldn't detect the leak from the inside, so they took a wet cloth, and swimming around the side of the boat with the cloth pressed against the hull, they were finally able to locate the leak when it was suddenly sucked into the hole. They patched it with hydraulic cement, making it safe for awhile at least.

Mel had some good news as well. First, he had finally hired an archaeologist, one that he hoped could ride the fence between the state and the salvage crews. Duncan Mathewson would fill those shoes very adequately over the next twelve years. He arrived the day the *Southwind* brought the silver bars ashore, and he was overwhelmed with the excitement and enthusiasm of the entire Fisher team. He settled in and very quickly began to assimilate data that would determine the direction of the scatter pattern. It wasn't long before the entire organization realized that he would be doing a very important job...documenting and identifying the priceless artifacts. His biggest task would be to convince the divers of the importance of archaeology on the site. Logging the location of holes dug is crucial, because where treasure was *not* located is sometimes as important as where artifacts *are* recovered.

Some of the clouds hanging over the Fisher family had a silver lining. On July 28, Dirk and Angel Curry were married on board the *Golden Doubloon.* Angel and Jo Arden Stuart had become part of the team on board *Northwind,* first as the cooks, and then Angel as records keeper and Jo as an artist, sketching artifacts as they came up off the bottom. The entire crew aboard the *Northwind* was living a dream come true. Wages were somewhere between terrible and non-existent, but it didn't matter. They were doing what they wanted to do more than anything else in the world, dive for treasure. If someone wanted to pay them for having the time of their lives, that was great. As long as the supply boat brought food out once a week --or when it didn't the divers could fill the evening menu with fish or lobster-- life was full of sunshine and roses. It was natural then for Dirk and Angel to fall in love, and it wasn't long before Kim and Jo had stardust in their eyes as well. They would marry at a later date.

The wedding of Dirk and Angel was one out of a storybook. Mel and Deo decked out the *Golden Doubloon* with a Hawaiian theme. Angel wore a white satin sarong with a white satin top, a lei of orchids, and a circle of orchids in her hair. Her bridesmaids, including Taffi and Jo, wore pink and yellow flower-printed sarongs with similar tops. Each wore a lei of Hibiscus around her neck and in her hair. Dirk wore white slacks with a Hawaiian shirt, as did Kim, his best man, and the other groomsmen. Pastor Arville Renner, who had baptized Dirk as a young boy in his church in Vero Beach, had traveled to Key West to perform the ceremony. They stood on the poop deck of the *Golden Doubloon,* facing the Marquesas to the west, as the sun was just setting. The timing was perfect, Pastor Renner read the service, and the "I do's" were said just as the red glow of sunset haloed the entire ceremony.

Afterwards there was a party, with over 200 celebrants overflowing the decks of the *Golden Doubloon* onto the docks. A fountain of champagne would run dry before the night was over. Dirk and Angel decided to take a trip across country, to California, as a honeymoon. They were able to visit Mel's existing "Aqua Shop" under new management, and they spent some time with his Aunt Marion and Uncle Merle Unger, the couple partially responsible for raising the Fisher children when Mel and Deo were off on treasure hunting expeditions. Meanwhile, the search for *Atocha* went on.

Wedding Day for Dirk and Angel.

At first it looked like a conglomerate of shells, not much larger than the size of his palm, and Kim almost missed it as he hung over the hole being dusted by the *Southwind*. He was in a four point anchorage that morning to the east side of the Bank of Spain, a hundred feet or so from the pile of silver coins they had found a few weeks earlier, and here the water was a bit deeper. The sand was still billowing away from the center of the hole, and the marl bottom was now visible. The clump of shells didn't move, even with the thrust of water cascading down from the surface.

Then Kim spotted the glint of a small patch of gold somewhere among the shells, and until the engine throttled back, his eyes never left that spot on the bottom. When he was able to finally dive down and pick up the clump it seemed heavier than usual, and turning it over he could see that it was more gold than shells. Hanging on the boarding ladder he could see that it was a cup of some kind, crushed somehow when the wreck scattered over the area. The outside of the cup had fine etchings of what appeared to be dolphins, and the handles were golden dolphins. Inside the rim appeared to be settings for precious stones, and although the cup was crushed flat, Kim could see a single emerald still encased in one of the settings. Later, when the cup was restored it was found to have a cage-type holder in the bowl to hold a bezoar stone. This stone was supposedly able to absorb arsenic poison, thus protecting the drinker from being poisoned, and the golden chalice was labeled "The Poison Cup". It was undoubtedly the most significant gold artifact recovered to date. It was cause for a lot of hooting and hollering on the *Southwind*.

In that same area they also recovered seventeen silver candelabras, each bearing a religious motif, a lamb, cross, or a sacred heart. It was a time when the crew of *Southwind* began to wonder what would come up from the bottom next.

The excitement was short-lived. Just when everything seemed to be going well, tragedy struck. It was August eighth and the *National Geographic* film crew was aboard. After the silver bars, it seemed that a major story would break at any time. There were guests on board as well. Bates Littlehales, one of the *National Geographic* photographers assigned to the *Atocha* story, had been in Key West since May when the major recoveries began. He was a veteran photographer who found himself away from home and his family on many occasions. When he could, he would take his eleven year old son Nicholas with him.

"Nikko", as the crew of the *Southwind* nicknamed him, was a strong swimmer and already an experienced SCUBA diver. On this day he had his own gear along when he and his father boarded *Southwind*. The *Southwind* was not equipped with "mailboxes" like the *Virgalona*. Instead it had a wide deflector mounted on its stern, like the scoop of a snowplow, which when lowered below the tug's keel deflected the propwash downward. The *Virgalona* had a cage built on the blower that surrounded the propeller, the *Southwind's* 43-inch propeller had no such protection. It was not unusual for guests to swim off the stern of the salvage boats, watching the divers work in twenty feet of clear water. But they were always instructed to enter the water off the stern.

The engines of the *Southwind* had just been revved up to start dusting when Nikko, unnoticed, dropped over the side. He had in mind to swim towards the stern, but instead the suction of the huge prop pulled him under. It was over in a moment. The boy suffered huge gashes that would prove fatal. Kim Fisher and the crew quickly brought him back aboard and called the Coast Guard to send a helicopter. A nurse on board, Mrs. Chalmers, tried to help, but she could tell that Nikko was gravely injured. The accident happened about 4:30 p.m., but it was nearly two hours later when the helicopter arrived, having to fly from Miami. They rushed Nikko and his father to Key West, but he died before they reached the hospital. Mel was on board *Southwind* at the time and he was visibly shaken. It was a nightmare that would haunt him for years.

Mel's problems were suddenly multiplying. Within days of Nicholas Littlehales' death, on August twelfth, the *Golden Doubloon* sank at dockside. Teredo worms had had a feast and the museums bilge pumps had been working overtime to keep the ship dry. During the night the pumps failed, and by morning the decks were awash. The Key West fire department responded and was able to pump it dry and get it afloat again, but the exhibits had some severe seawater damage that would shut the museum down until it was completely refurbished. Mel moved his office ashore, no doubt wondering what could happen next. He didn't have to wait long.

The phone rang ominously. "Mel, you have to stop selling stock in your company right now! The SEC is launching a full scale investigation into your stock sales...seems someone lodged a complaint." It was Mel's lawyer on the other end, and the news couldn't have come at a worse time. His records were still pretty soggy from the *Golden Doubloon* sinking, but he felt confident everything would work out fine. He had nothing to hide. Almost before he was off the phone the Securities Exchange Commission auditors moved into Mel's soggy office. The complaint they had gotten concerned Mel selling unregistered stock. Their attention was focused on the records of Treasure Salvors, the parent company, and Armada Research, Mel's salvage group operating in the Florida Keys, 45 miles east of Key West. The records were a mess. Mel had never been a great keeper of books, and he couldn't afford a book-keeper. In his drive to finance the search for *Atocha* he had often written contracts on the back of paper napkins, or whatever else was available. But he always honored the contracts, often giving the investors some silver pieces-of-eight up front, telling them that "You can hold these as a sort of collateral. If we don't find a lot of treasure, you can keep them." Very few people realized just how difficult it was to finance a treasure salvage operation, particularly when you don't have a proven wreck site.

Mel was remarkable in his fanatical belief that he would find the mother lode, and he made others believe as well. As a result, the investors were never worried that a complicated contract was never signed, sealed, and delivered. Over a period of time Mel had sold, or traded, shares in the parent company Treasure Salvors for big bucks or equipment he needed to continue the search. He sold a small percentage of stock, in the order of $1,000 for .01% of treasure recovered during a one year period only. There was never an intent to deceive or defraud the investors. That did not satisfy the SEC auditors. After a lengthy investigation they agreed that Mel did not have any criminal intent, but they warned him against future sales of unregistered stock. The publicity that emanated from the investigation seriously hurt Mel's relationship with the financial world. It temporarily shut off stock sales, his main resource to finance the search. He was dead in the water, and without a division of treasure from the state of Florida, he soon found the money barrel dry. He shut down the operation, let the crew go, and tied the salvage boats to the dock.

As the end of the 1973 salvage season approached, the state of Florida again reared its ugly head. Because of the adverse publicity Senator Williams threatened to not renew the salvage contract. Previously, when a re-enactment of the finding of the astrolabe for *National Geographic* had been conducted near the Quicksands, Williams was infuriated to the point that he threatened cancellation of Mel's salvage contract that day. Mel's lawyer was able to intervene and save the day. Now, Sonny

Cockrell, the marine archaeologist, insisted that the charts of the salvage area were not adequate, and that the proper forms and reports were always late. Even the speed that the salvage boats were dusting the sand away from artifacts was criticized as "not the proper speed for recovery of priceless artifacts." The state had never used a blower to excavate a shipwreck site. In fact, it had never excavated any shipwreck site in its own waters. Although the charges were mindless, the heat was on Mel to get his act together. To that extent Bleth McHaley and Duncan Mathewson became invaluable assets to Treasure Salvors.

Bleth became the front office V.P. in charge of publicity, and she was able to start a more favorable campaign of news releases to get the monkey off Mel's back. Duncan approached his job with a great deal of enthusiasm, in spite of the archaeological community's display of disgust that he had joined a "treasure salvage group that sold historical artifacts." He began to map out the location of various recoveries and quickly determined that a scatter pattern was evident, leading to deeper water. By this time a substantial amount of treasure had been recovered. As he put together the list, it seemed impressive. There were three gold bars, a gold disk, eleven gold coins, Bouncy John's coral bead rosary, Kim's gold cup, a gold religious medallion, two gold rings, and ten gold chains. On the list were the more than 6,000 silver coins, three silver ingots, seventeen candelabras, a silver ewer, silver spoons, a silver inkwell, and a silver plate.

The *Atocha* was an armed galleon, so it was natural to expect to recover military artifacts. To date they had brought up 24 swords and daggers, nineteen muskets or arquebuses, about 100 iron cannon balls and four stone balls. And then there were hundreds of encrusted objects, including the astrolabe, four pairs of bronze dividers, a sounding lead, and many other unidentifiable objects. This had all been recovered along a fairly narrow path near the Quicksands, and Duncan saw that the corridor of artifacts either led to deeper water, or over the shallow sand bank. He was bothered by the lack of ballast; only a few hundred pounds had been discovered so far, and the *Atocha* had to be carrying sixty tons or more. Based on what had been recovered so far, he believed that part of the sterncastle had broken up in that area and that the primary ballast pile, as well as most of the silver, lay somewhere to the east in deeper water.

In November, the state approved Mel's salvage contract, but not without a hassle involving Senator Williams. Mel also asked for a search lease nearer the Marquesas so that he might search for the *Santa Margarita* as well. The state approved leases for Jack Haskins, John Berrier, Burt Webber, and Richard MacAllaster to search off the Matecumbes for the *Atocha*, something that stunned everyone in the room considering the proof that Mel had located the *Atocha* near the Marquesas. As the year ended the financial situation at Treasure Salvors was a disaster. The divers, crew, and the guides in the museum had been laid off. The electric power was cut off to the *Golden Doubloon*, and then the phone company discontinued service. With recovered treasure worth several million in state hands, Mel was frustrated. Without a division with the state he had nothing from the *Atocha* to sell, nothing to show for his four years of effort and the hundreds of thousands of dollars he had already poured into the search. A year that had started out with so much promise was ending on an emotional low. That was the trouble with treasure fever.

21...CANNONS OF THE ATOCHA

In a sea-girt kind of town like Key West, the Fishers quickly became a part of the local scene. Surrounded by water, it seemed natural living on a houseboat. By 1974 there were three Fisher houseboats...docked together alongside Roosevelt Road. Dirk and Angel lived on one. Kim and Jo Stuart were married in April, and when they returned from a Michigan wedding, they moved into the other. Mel, Deo, Kane, and Taffi remained on the original houseboat moored in the middle. It seemed natural that Taffi and Kane would commute from the houseboat to the *Golden Doubloon* office by Boston Whaler. Other than bicycles, that was the only transportation they had. Besides, the boat was faster. And of course, they all slept on water beds which, when combined with a rocking, rolling houseboat that moved with the wind and passing craft, was at times like surf-boarding.

Deo spent much of her time at the *Golden Doubloon* office. She was the force that held the staff together, always with time to listen and the positive attitude that it took to keep things "copasetic" when, financially, they were about to collapse. Mel had the challenge of keeping the operation fiscally stable, and that had become more than a full-time job. When he wasn't on the road talking to potential out-of-state investors, he was on board the *Golden Doubloon* reaching investors by phone, or meeting tourists visiting the museum. Having a photo taken with Mel and his large gold chain draped around everyone is a souvenir cherished by a great many visitors to Key West. Dirk now had the *Northwind* running well, and he rotated with Kim and the *Southwind* out on the Quicksands. But most of the time the two tugs remained tied up to the dock, out of fuel and out of food.

By mid-August, Mel was finally able to sell half of the remaining 1715 treasure. Mel Joseph, a Delaware contractor, purchased the treasure for $315,000, enough for Mel to pay off the loan to the Tampa bank that held the treasure as collateral, pay his crew back wages, and fuel up the salvage boats. The weather was still good, and both Dirk and Kim headed their tugs towards the Quicksands. And they found gold! Hank Spinney, while diving off the *Southwind*, recovered a rather unique gold bar with 21-carat marks, five round royal seals that indicated it was legal tender, an assayer's bite near the middle of the bar, and "En Rada" in a small square box near one end. For over eighteen years that mark would puzzle the numismatic world, until John deBry, a researcher from Florida, would determine that it was the mark of the Peña-Renda family mint in Peru.

Pat Clyne recovered a large gold chain almost seven feet long, and in the same area several other gold chains were recovered. Silver coins continued to be uncovered, along with a number of arquebuses, swords, and other personal armament. What became more frustrating to Mel was the fact that they were rich in artifacts, several million dollars worth in fact, but could not realize a single cent from what was recovered until they had a division with the state of Florida.

Investor Mel Joseph with Deo and Mel Fisher.

Competition from other professional salvagers now began to give Mel cause for concern. Jack Haskins, one of the better translators of the Spanish archives, had found the "Marquesas" information in the *legajos* in Seville. He returned to Florida where he was joined by John Berrier and Richard MacAllaster, two good professional salvagers, in applying for leases just to the east of Mel's active lease. Burt Webber also finally decided that Mel had actually recovered part of the *Atocha*, and he moved his operation into the area. They all were able to receive leases to the area adjoining Mel's, with a good possibility that the *Atocha* mother lode lay within their lease.

Although Senator Williams had promised not to issue other leases to the same wreck site, he changed his mind. He had other problems with treasure salvage to deal with. His office soon became concerned that the United States Supreme Court would overturn the 1968 Florida Constitutional sea boundaries. In that state document the sea boundaries extended beyond the outer reefs, and the reefs within the state jurisdiction included the Dry Tortugas. This meant that if the constitution was upheld, the *Atocha* lay within Florida state waters. But the Washington rumblings indicated that the Supreme Court was about to over- rule this decision. If it did, the *Atocha* would lie outside the State jurisdiction, and Fisher would no longer have to divide with the state. Rather than lose it all, Senator Williams called for an early division.

A date of March, 1975, was tentatively set, and the Fisher staff set about the laborious job of "pointing up" the artifacts that had been recovered to date. This was no easy matter. Some of the artifacts were priceless, and attempting to place an estimate on their value was impossible. In pointing each artifact they had to be compared to other artifacts, some with known sales value, in order to determine an equitable number of points. Somewhere down the road the state had hopes of establishing a museum of sunken treasure in Tallahassee. Towards that goal they privately desired the more unique artifacts that gave an insight into Spanish life aboard ship. On the other hand, Mel wanted a selection of coins and gold bars to divide with his investors, and that could be sold to further his search for the mother lode.

The treasure that Senator Williams had picked up in Key West had been stored in the basement of the Leon County jail. It was decided that the division would be held there. March fifth found the entire Treasure Salvors crew decked out in day-glo orange sweatshirts emblazoned with "Atocha" and gathered in the basement of the jail, along with a number of visitors, the press, and TV personnel. Steel bars separated them from a fabulous array of gold and silver coins, gold disks, gold and silver bars, gold chains, a coral and gold rosary, silver candelabras, a rare astrolabe, and encrusted swords, muskets, and other armament.

The new secretary of state, Bruce Smathers, was there, along with Senator Williams. Mel Fisher was pointedly ignored as he sat at a table with Smathers while Williams gave a short speech of acceptance of the state's share of treasure. Smathers also gave a short speech, at the end of which one of the spectators stood up and asked, "Is Mel Fisher here?" Mel stood up and introduced himself. Smathers was a bit embarrassed when Mel then presented him with an encrusted sword from the *Atocha* site. He recouped with a generous "Thank you, this is the realization of everyone's dream, to find a sunken shipwreck." Williams was not given a memento from the *Atocha*. From the division Treasure Salvors received 1,073 cleaned and 3,420 uncleaned silver coins, the three silver bars that had been recovered to date, four gold bars and two bits of gold bars, all except one of the gold coins, the gold chains, the coral rosary that Bouncy John had recovered, most of the silver candelabras, and enough swords, muskets, daggers, and cannon balls to make their investors happy. The gold cup that Kim Fisher had recovered near the Quicksands had been crushed during the 1622 hurricane, but inside could be seen an emerald, held by a setting. When the cup was brought out for the division, the emerald was missing. After some heated conversation with state officials, Mel had to accept that the stone had been "lost in cleaning".

The division gave Mel's group a boost. It meant that Mel could finally begin to reward his investors, people who believed as he did in the *Atocha* and who had the patience to see him through his first five years of searching. The remaining coins and artifacts were to be sold to keep the operation going. It appeared as though the financial clouds were finally dissipating. Two weeks after the division the United States Supreme Court handed down its decision on the question of Florida state territorial waters. It had been decided that Florida could not claim jurisdiction based on their 1968 Constitution which included ocean bottom well beyond the outer reefs. Boundaries suggested by a masters report ordered by the court should prevail, putting the *Atocha* outside the state's control and in federal waters. It was a huge victory for Treasure Salvors.

When the decision was announced, Treasure Salvors called Senator Williams at his office in Tallahassee, asking him what, in his opinion, should be done next? His reply, "business as usual". After the phone call there was a sense of uneasiness in the Treasure Salvors office. Williams had been too crisp, too short, as if he were about to explode. The state of Florida had been literally slapped on the wrist by the Supreme Court, and Mel

Fisher was to blame. Unknown to the salvagers, Senator Williams was already in the process of applying to the federal government for the lease on the *Atocha*, in the name of the state of Florida.

Dirk Fisher had completed deep sea diving school in Fort Lauderdale, and by March, 1975, good diving weather had settled over the Marquesas. He put his diving crew together, and with fuel and provisions on board the *Northwind* they headed out of Key West Harbor. For some time he had been convinced that the mother lode lay "somewhere" out there in deep water. An opinion shared by their archaeologist, Duncan Mathewson, who had been studying the scatter pattern of recovered artifacts. As the salvage got underway, the golden artifacts began to emerge from the sandy bottom.

Joe Spangler, working from the *Southwind*, came up with one of the more unusual artifacts, a golden bos'n whistle. It was hung from a double strand of gold chain and contained an earwax spoon as well as a manicure set. It became Mel's favorite artifact, wearing it to speaking engagements, or piping meetings to order. It even brought smiles along the streets of Key West when Mel would pipe on it to show that it worked even after resting on the bottom of the ocean for over 350 years. It was the "spirit" of salvage diving, something from the bottom that gave the entire salvage crew a boost.

And there were other gold discoveries. Tom Ford, a red-headed newcomer to the salvage crew, added more gold fever when he came up with the largest gold bar recovered so far...an ornate 24 ounces of butter-yellow gold with eight royal seals, four purity marks of XXI, or twenty one carats, and the mint seal GDRS. This was the seventh gold bar to come up off the Quicksands, and along with the gold disk, thirty gold chains, the gold cup and whistle --as well as other gold artifacts-- it seemed that the bottom of the ocean was strewn with gold.

Just when hopes were high and the salvage operation seemed to be going well, cooperation with the state of Florida officials seemed to have reached the impossible stage. In a phone call to Senator Williams, Mel advised him that although the *Atocha* lay outside state jurisdiction, he was still willing to donate 25% of the recoveries to the state. He reminded Williams that the proposal he had drafted and sent several months earlier to his office had not been accepted nor returned. Williams brushed him aside.

For months Mel had been putting up with the vagaries of the state agents who were assigned to his salvage vessels. Often they would not show up until noon-time, and the boat could not leave without them. On June 2 the situation reached the breaking point. With gold being recovered almost daily on site, the captain of one of the salvage boats called Mel and asked if he could leave without the state agent on board. It was 10:00 o'clock in the morning, and they had been ready to go since early sunrise. Mel said, "Go!!" At 3:00 o'clock that afternoon the state agent arrived at the dock only to find the salvage boat gone. He called Tallahassee and notified Senator Williams, who had left word that if such an instance occurred he was to be called immediately. An enraged Williams called Mel's lawyer, Dave Horan, and accused Mel of breaking his "unofficial" contract. He threatened to "close Mel down immediately". He advised that he would be sending one of the state attorneys to Key West within a week to get things straightened out.

The following week Williams and attorney Jack Shreve flew into Key West and met with Mel and Dave to try reaching a mutual agreement of cooperation. When the negotiations ended, it was agreed that neither party would contact the federal government. Horan had heard rumors that Williams was secretly negotiating with the government and wanted something in writing to protect Mel's salvage operation. Within days the federal government did assert authority over the *Atocha* site #8M0141 under the Antiquities Act of 1906 which claimed shipwrecks on the outer continental shelf. The die was cast, as David prepared to battle Goliath.

The scatter of artifacts seemed to lie in a very narrow corridor northwest to southeast and no more than 150 feet wide. To the southeast lay deep water and the patch reef, an area with a hard clay bottom and poor visibility. To the northwest lay the Quicksands and shallow water. There was certainly the possibility that the *Atocha* struck the patch reef and scattered to the northwest. If that were the case the ballast pile and mother lode would lie somewhere in deep sand. But the declaration of salvager Gaspar de Vargas that the *Atocha* lay in 55 feet of water with only her foremast above the surface after the hurricane contradicted that theory. Could the area around the Quicksands have been much deeper at one time? In 350 years it was entirely possible that thirty feet of sand had settled over the hard marl bottom.

Dirk Fisher didn't believe that. Some inner feeling pointed him towards the deeper water. Saturday evening, June 12, Dirk dropped the *Northwind* anchors just to the northwest of the patch reef in forty feet of water. He had tried repeatedly before to break through the hard clay bottom with a jet hose, but to no avail. If the mother lode lay under the clay, it would be extremely difficult to uncover it. Dirk was ready to try again.

Kim & Lee Fisher with gold bars & chain. **Credit: Pat Clyne.**

During the night a thunderstorm had ghosted in off the Atlantic, causing the *Northwind* anchor to drag over the hard clay bottom some distance from the patch reef. The following morning, with a cup of coffee in hand, Dirk stood on the bow of his salvage vessel and tested the anchor line with his foot. It was slack. Even though the sea was flat calm he would have to reset the anchor. The superstructure of *Northwind* was so high that it would act as a signboard if any wind came up, dragging the anchor even further. Finishing his morning coffee he slipped over the side and swam out along the anchor line until it angled for the bottom. Beyond floated the anchor buoy and, swimming over to it, he pulled himself hand over hand to the bottom forty feet below.

The water on the surface was clear, but as he neared the bottom it turned a milky green. Visibility was only a few feet, enough to see that his anchor hadn't dug in. He reset it and swam back to the surface. Even though the visibility was poor, for some unknown reason he decided to scout the bottom a bit before swimming back to the *Northwind*. As he kicked along the smooth bottom, he suddenly stopped short. He had almost run into a pile of green objects. It took him a few seconds to realize it...he was looking at a pile of bronze cannon!! He touched them to make sure he wasn't dreaming, then burst to the surface shouting, "Cannons, bring a buoy!"

Dirk was over 150 feet from the *Northwind* when he broke surface. At first Angel thought he was being attacked by a shark, his shout sounded urgent. The *Northwind* crew quickly determined that he wanted a buoy, and that he wasn't leaving the spot until they brought one. While waiting for the marker, he dived down again, to count them. There were five cannon, and even though Dirk had never seen a bronze cannon underwater, he knew instantly what they were. Soon the entire *Northwind* crew was diving to the sea bed, rubbing their hands along the sides of the cannon and tracing the dolphins that were the lifting rings. By mid-morning Key West was alerted to the discovery, and near pandemonium erupted. If they thought silver bars had started a frenzy, the cannons were an explosion of activity.

Duncan Mathewson, Don Kincaid, Pat Clyne, and a Channel 4 television newsman from Miami were soon on their way in a fast boat, arriving close to noontime. It was an awesome sight, five large cannons had been lying there for 350 years, and for the past four years the salvage vessels had been working so close it was almost impossible that they had missed them. Yet there they were, more bronze cannon than had ever been recovered before from a shipwreck in U.S. waters. Mathewson's first instructions were that they could not be moved until photos were taken of them *in situ*. He had brought with him a platform to set up the camera and a tape to measure distances and the azimuth for bearing. A search was conducted in the area for possible parts of the gun carriages, or other obvious artifacts. Duncan then allowed the *Northwind* to lightly dust the bottom with its blowers to clear the sediment that covered the clay bottom. Afterwards an inspection of the bottom turned up a copper ingot and three gold "bits".

It wasn't until the following morning that Mel, Deo, and the office staff were on the site. By this time Dirk had the *Northwind* dusting the bottom with its blowers, working his way to the northwest. About four moves, and thirty feet away, Pat Clyne surfaced shouting, "Hey, we've got four more bronze cannon over here!!" It seemed as though it couldn't get any better than that. Bronze cannon, a trail of gold, the mother lode had to be close by. The cannon were the most important find they could have made other than a pile of 1000 silver bars. It called for a celebration. Overnight it was worldwide news. The other shoe had dropped.

On July seventeenth a bronze cannon from each group was raised to the *Northwind's* deck. The numbers inscribed on the bronze surface matched those on the *Atocha* gun inventory. There was absolutely no doubt now that Mel was tracking the *Atocha*. It was decided to bring the two cannons into Key West, and *Northwind* left early the following morning. The trip back to Key West was a triumphant one. The bronze cannon resting securely on the stern deck gave the crew a feeling they were transporting the crown jewels. Dirk was normally at the con when *Northwind* was underway, but on this trip he left the driving to one of his divers. He and Angel remained on the stern near the cannon, almost like parents with their first-born. A crowd had gathered as the *Northwind* eased up to the dock behind the *Golden Doubloon*; all of Key West sensed history in the making.

Even as the bronze cannons were being transferred to the deck of the *Golden Doubloon*, lawyer Jack Shreve was arriving from Tallahassee. Dave Horan sat behind his desk as Shreve made his point. "The situation between Mel and Tallahassee has unfortunately deteriorated. The best the state can do is allow Treasure Salvors to salvage the *Atocha* site under the state's permit on a month-to-month basis." Horan leaned forward, "What kind of a percentage is the state willing to give Treasure

Salvors?" Shreve wasn't sure what that would be as yet, that it would have to be negotiated with the federal government, and Treasure Salvors would have to accept whatever percentage the state provided. Horan peered at Shreve over the rim of his glasses, "Is that the state's last word?" Shreve answered, "That's all you're going to get, and if you don't take it you're making a big mistake. It's that...or nothing!" He offered to return to David's office at 1:30 to get Treasure Salvors' answer.

When Shreve left, Dave was angry. The state had broken every promise they had made, and now, after five years and several million dollars of expense in searching out *Atocha*, the state bureaucracy was about to step in and take it away from Mel. It would leave him with nothing except an arrangement with the state that could be canceled on a moment's notice. David and Goliath were about to collide. The week before Dave had determined that the rumor was true, that the state of Florida had filed for a federal antiquities permit on the site. In fact, the permit was ready to be signed at any moment. He called the dean of his law school, Joshua Morse, an expert in Admiralty law. After three hours on the phone Dean Morse not only understood the problem, he was willing to work up a rough draft of an Admiralty claim that Dave could file in Federal court. It arrived by mailgram the following morning, and Dave had spent the rest of the day completing the lawsuit. It basically was a lawsuit that "arrested" the wreck site, placing it under the custody of the finder. As soon as Shreve left his office Dave put together the final draft of the lawsuit, called Mel, and received his permission to file the Admiralty claim. He had just enough time to drive to the Key West airport and catch the next flight to Miami where he could file the lawsuit.

When Shreve returned at 1:30 and learned that Horan was flying to Miami to file the lawsuit, he was incensed. "He is making the biggest mistake of his life!", and he stormed out of the office. Mel Fisher and David Horan were about to take on two great adversaries, the state of Florida and the U.S. Government.

261

22...TRAGEDY AT SEA

T he first two *Atocha* bronze cannons were safely stowed in water-filled boxes on the deck of the *Golden Doubloon* museum. The entire Fisher crew was ecstatic. It seemed as though some ethereal spirit had been hovering over their shoulders. When the treasure hunt seemed to have reached its darkest hour, the sea had given them hope, had given them a new burst of enthusiasm. The mother lode had to be near the cannon pile, and they would soon find it. There was an air of excitement in everything they did, in the plans to return to the deep water and continue the search.

Stories of the recovery were headline news across the country, and soon the parking lot next to the dock was full. A line of visitors was huddled over the cannon, with hands in the water tracing the curve of the dolphins that were the lifting rings and the strange markings near the touchhole that indicated cannon weight. Mel found himself stopping to gaze at the cannons every time he left his office in the stern of the *Golden Doubloon*. In fact, he found excuses to leave his office so he could make sure he wasn't dreaming. He had searched for bronze cannons most of his salvaging career and had never found one. Now, he had more bronze cannons than anyone had ever found on a wreck site in North America.

There wasn't a lot of cash left in the Treasure Salvors bank account, but regardless Mel was quick to hand out bonuses to every member of the *Northwind* crew. To his son Dirk, he gave a $10,000 bonus and suggested he take a few days vacation and have some fun. Dirk had always wanted a Peugeot, a French automobile, and with the bonus he and Angel drove to Miami and promptly bought one. Rather than take a short vacation Dirk was eager to get back on the site. Besides, if the mother lode were close to the cannon pile, Mo Molinar could find it first with the *Virgalona*. The drive back to Key West took only 2-1/2 hours.

When *National Geographic* received word of the bronze cannon find, they asked Mel not to salvage them until they could get a crew down to Key West to film the event. The crew arrived on Saturday, July 19, 1975, and stacked their gear on the *Virgalona*. By 2:00 o'clock that afternoon the *Virgalona* had been provisioned and was heading out of the channel at Key West for the Marquesas. *Northwind* left the dock shortly afterwards and kept *Virgalona* in sight as they made their way down the chain of islands. It was possibly 5:00 p.m. when Mo anchored the *Virgalona* about a mile offshore, near "Tower Island", just to the west of Mooney Harbor. Mo had decided to anchor here, rather than in Mooney Harbor, because of the mosquitoes. In the summer time they were fierce, and without air conditioning below decks it meant the portholes and doors were left open, an invitation to the night flyers unless you anchored offshore where the ocean breeze kept them near the mangroves.

Shortly afterwards the *Northwind* anchored about a mile further offshore. Molinar raised Dirk Fisher on the marine radio and suggested he anchor closer to the *Virgalona*, but Dirk declined. It was Angel's birthday and they were having a celebration, he suggested that Mo and his crew come over for some birthday cake and champagne. Mo declined, but John Brandon, Spencer Wickens, and one of the *National Geographic* film crew decided they would run over in the anchor boat and help with the celebration.

The whole Fisher crew was on a high. Every single one of them expected to locate the mother lode of the *Atocha* the next day. It had to be close to the pile of bronze cannon. It made sense. They had followed the trail from the galleon anchor and the Bank of Spain in twenty feet of water, and now they were working in forty-foot depths. The Spanish records indicated that the galleon sank in 55 feet of water. They had to be getting close. That evening the birthday celebration seemed to be much more than that, it was as if six years of methodical magging and dusting holes in the ocean's bottom was about to pay off. There must have been visions of boxes of silver pieces-of-eight and piles of silver bars on everyone's mind as they celebrated.

That evening Dirk asked Brandon and Wickens if they would spend the night on the *Northwind*, the three of them had been pretty close during the years of searching the Quicksands area. But in a radio call to Molinar on the *Virgalona*, Mo said he wanted the divers back aboard so they could get an early start in the morning. By 10:00 p.m. Brandon, Wickens, and the *National Geographic* photographer were on their way back to the "Virge". It was a glassy night, not much in the way of a sea breeze, so they hoped for a good night's sleep. But there was little sleep for any of them as they tossed and turned, eager for daylight and the thought that they would soon find the mother lode. Lights were turned off on the *Northwind* about 11:00 p.m. as Dirk told his crew they had "a big day coming up tomorrow!"

That morning, while *Northwind* was tied up at the dock in Key West, a rubber hose connection to the toilet came loose and the 80-p.s.i. water pump that supplied the flushing water system had begun filling the bilge with sea water. When Dirk and Bouncy John drove up to the dock they saw that their salvage vessel had taken on a list to starboard, and on closer inspection below deck they found the problem. Dirk had Bouncy go to the marine hardware store and buy a complete new fitting, and with it in place they were able to pump the bilge dry. The problem seemed to be resolved. Somehow, some way, possibly with the clattering of the air conditioner nearby, the hose fitting worked itself loose. About 3:00 a.m., while the boat-full of divers slept, the hose came loose again, and water ominously spurted from the open hose under 80 pounds of pressure.

"Hey, look out up there!!" The words were clear, clear enough to wake up Don Kincaid asleep on the deck near the pilot house. He raised up and looked aft, near the stern where he had heard the voice. It must have been close to 5:00 a.m., the stars were still out, and there was enough light to see the winches and gear stacked near the rail. He thought he saw something else, something that was unfamiliar, like the figure of someone sitting on the stern railing. He rubbed his eyes and reached into the pilot house to get his glasses, and as he did he heard the voice again, this time much clearer. "Hey, look out up there!!"

Putting on his glasses he looked back at the stern again, but the figure, or apparition, was gone. As he shook his head to make sure he wasn't dreaming, he noticed the *Northwind* had quite a list to her. He climbed down the ladder to the main deck and shook Donny Jonas awake. Jonas was the engineer in charge of pumps, and together they opened the door to the engine room. They were surprised to find the water above the deck in the engine room compartment. In an instant they both realized it was a critical situation that called for immediate action.

Donny shut off the water pump and began opening valves to the fuel tanks to transfer fuel from one side of the *Northwind* to the other to balance the now very steep angle the boat had taken. Kincaid started down the passageway, banging on doors to wake the divers. Almost as he did, the *Northwind* began to roll over. He was able to make it to the open door and step out on the deck, and as he did he kept walking up the side as the salvage vessel turned turtle.

Up in the pilot house Bouncy John woke up as he was sliding across the deck, coming up abruptly against the railing. He looked down as the water came up to meet him and had no choice but to drop off the deck into the ocean. As he fell, the cabin wall gave him a good thump on the back as it rolled over on him. He scrambled up on the now overturned hull about the same time as Kincaid did. Soon other heads began bobbing in the water near the edge of the hull. Young Kane Fisher, Keith Curry, Angel Fisher's young twelve-year-old brother, Peter Westering, and Bob Reeves, a photographer.

In the crew's compartment Rick Gage and Jim Solanick had been sleeping in the bunk beds against the starboard hull. Gage had the topside bunk, next to the porthole, and Solanick had the lower bunk. As the *Northwind* rolled on her side Solanick suddenly found himself on the deck, which actually was now the starboard side. Water was pouring through the porthole in front of him, and somehow he realized what was happening. The hatch leading to the corridor that ran the length of *Northwind* had swung open. Jim fumbled through the hatch and crawled along the corridor until he came opposite the crew's head. In the head was another porthole, and this one was on the port side. Jim could see open sky through this porthole and scrambled for it.

Solanick had a pretty good body build and that, combined with the small opening of the porthole, almost cost him his life. He first tried squeezing through, but his shoulders just wouldn't let him. As the water rushed up behind him, filling the head, he made a desperate attempt to squeeze through, arms first. He popped out of the porthole, held for an instant by his hips, and then as the water pressure in the compartment behind him increased he was pushed free.

When Solanick popped to the surface for air the hull loomed above him and he could see the figures of six other survivors. They helped him up the barnacled bottom, unconscious of the shells cutting his bare feet. As they sat huddled on the hull, numbed by the realization of what had happened, they were suddenly aware of the sounds coming from the hull directly beneath them. They were screams and cries for help. They were coming from Donny Jonas, now trapped in the engine room compartment with the water steadily rising.

Bouncy John was the first to react. "We've got to help him!" He began hammering on the hull and shouting, "Go to the door!" Then Bouncy slipped over the side and swam down under the taffrail to the door leading down to the engine room. He banged as hard as he could on the door, until he had no breath left, and then surged back to the surface. It was still very dark, and tangled lines hung down from the foreboding shape that but a few minutes before had been their salvage vessel. It was unreal, almost a nightmare in slow motion that you hoped would soon shake you awake.

Back on the hull the sounds of Jonas could still be heard, pleading for help. Again Bouncy John hammered on the hull, shouting for Jonas to go to the door. And again he slipped over the side, making the now longer swim down the taffrail to the engine compartment door, where he banged on it as long as he could. Choking for air, he made his way back to the hull. Suddenly, the sounds beneath them stopped.

Donny Jonas felt the *Northwind* roll beneath his feet. He had no time to climb over the engine and get out the now disappearing hatch. Suddenly he was in total darkness. He was confused and disoriented, and the oil in the bilges had suddenly covered his eyes, ears, his nose, even his mouth. He had his head in a pocket of air, a pocket in which only his head and shoulders were above the rising water. He shouted for help, but could hear only the sounds of the *Northwind* sinking around him. In desperation he screamed, causing a clammy helplessness in the survivors that sat only a few inches above him.

The air pocket was now to his chin when he felt something bump him. He couldn't see, but as he grabbed it he knew it was a flashlight. It was one of those unexplainable happenings, a one in a million shot in the dark. He wasn't sure if it was a waterproof flashlight or not, but when he turned it on, the light flooded the small air space he was trapped in. He was an eighteen-year-old with but a few moments to make the right decisions. He realized that he was upside down, that the deck was directly over his head. If he wanted to swim out he would have to swim down to the hatch, and then up. He got a grip on himself, saw the bulkhead where the hatch was located, took a deep breath, and pulled himself down. The hatch wasn't there.

There wasn't much air left in the small space, and he had to think clearly. Then he realized, upside down...the starboard side was now the port side. The hatch was on the other side of the stack. Moving over, he sucked in some more air and pulled himself down several feet. There it was, the hatch that he somehow had to get open. But as he pulled at it, it wouldn't open. The air pressure on the inside was holding it. Bracing himself, he was able to finally get it to move before he was gasping for air. With diesel oil burning his throat he was able to take one last lungful of air, then ducking down he pulled open the hatch and swam through. It was a long swim down the corridor and up the ladder to the hatch leading to the outside deck. He made it, and swimming as hard as he could he swam from the salvage vessel that now hung head down, her pilot house touching bottom nearly forty feet deep.

When Jonas surfaced fifty feet behind the overturned hull he began waving his flashlight frantically. He could hardly see, his eyes burning from the diesel oil. Bouncy John dived in and swam to him, grasping his arm and pulling him back to the safety of the hull. Almost as he climbed up the side, the hull settled, sinking beneath the surface. The explosion of air from the hull as it disappeared sent a number of articles into the water. One of these was a small yellow life raft, the blow-up, one-man size. Someone swam over and retrieved it, and after it was inflated they put young Keith Curry in it while the rest of the survivors clung to the sides.

The survivors now numbered eight. Missing were Dirk, his wife Angel, and Rick Gage. They could only wait for daylight now and hope that the currents would not take them too far from the area. Their fate lay in the possibility that someone on the *Virgalona* would spot them at daylight. Numbed and fatigued, thunderstruck at the sudden tragic turn of events, they had another hour to wait before sunrise.

The sun had just come up, but the morning was still hazy as the crew of the *Virgalona* came to life. Mo Molinar was always awake at the crack of dawn, but he wasn't alone this morning. Seems as though everyone was eager to get started. Mo was the first to look out where the *Northwind* had been anchored and commented when he didn't see it, "Hey guys, looks like Dirk headed for the site ahead of us. Let's go!" They hauled anchor as the diesel engine came to life, and Mo set a course to the west towards the Bank of Spain. At first no one gave much thought to the *Northwind* not being in sight, even though Dirk usually got a later start than Molinar. They assumed he was as pumped up as the rest of them, that the magnetic attraction of the mother lode was enough to jump-start any crew.

Something drew Mo's attention off to the south a mile or so. At first it was a dark speck on the water. He turned to Brandon, "What do you think?" Brandon shook his head. There was a sixth sense that made Mo put the wheel over and head for the object, and soon they could make out that it was a raft of some sort. Now everyone was crowded up in the wheelhouse. "It looks like some Cuban or Haitian rafters." Mo said he would pick them up and call the Coast Guard, but as they drew closer they realized it was young Keith Curry standing up in the small yellow raft waving a life jacket. Even as Mo cut back on the engine to come alongside the raft, he could see the diesel oil slick. He suddenly knew what had happened. Turning to Brandon and Wickens he said, "Get your gear on!" As they drew alongside the raft Mo was almost afraid to ask, "What happened?" "The *Northwind* sank", was Kincaid's response.

The eight survivors clambered aboard the *Virgalona*, and Kincaid broke the news that Dirk, Angel, and Rick Gage were missing. The oil slick had spread to the east about two miles by this time, and pieces of flotsam could be seen drifting with the current. Molinar kicked the throttle forward and headed down the slick to see if possibly any of the missing three had managed to hold on to something afloat. Reaching the end of the slick and finding nothing, he circled back to where the anchor float of the *Northwind* bobbed on the surface.

John Brandon jumped in the water and guided the *Virgalona* alongside the *Northwind* where she lay on her starboard side. Back on board Mo turned to Spencer Wickens and Brandon, knowing they were close to Dirk and Angel, and solemnly said, "Looks like you have to go down and bring them up" Both divers nodded, and saying nothing dropped over the side. Tim Marsh, Don Kincaid, and Tom Ford also suited up and in minutes were ready to go. Jim Solanick let Kincaid know where he thought Rick Gage should be, and he and Marsh headed for the bow section.

It was daylight now, possibly 9:00 a.m., as Brandon and Wickens swam down to the superstructure. Everything seemed surreal, from an absolute high of excitement, to a sudden tragedy that was incomprehensible. The *Northwind* lying on the bottom wasn't supposed to happen. This was a bad dream. They knew exactly where Dirk's cabin was, directly behind the wheelhouse, and hoping against hope that Dirk and Angel may have been able to stay in an air pocket, they peered in through the porthole. There was Dirk's hand, and they recognized the coin ring on his finger. He was still in his bunk, with sheets floating about.

Swimming down to the door leading into the cabin they opened it, and Angel's body was right at the door. Spencer went to look for a sheet to wrap her body in before taking her to the surface. With her younger brother there to see her, the shock would be too much. Before they could find a sheet, Tom Ford was suddenly there with them, and he took Angel in his arms and swam her up to the surface. Brandon and Wickens went after Dirk. They had to swim down the ladder and into the room, and Spencer motioned that he would go in and bring Dirk out. Both divers were crying in their masks, this was a heart breaker.

As Spencer tried to get through the tangle of bedsheets and blankets that floated about the room, they snagged on his regulator, and he was having trouble. He ducked back out of the room, and Brandon went in. John was able to bring Dirk's body out the door, and Spencer found a red, white, and blue sheet to wrap his body in. They brought Dirk to the surface. Kincaid and Marsh soon had Gage's body to the side of the boat. The three bodies were placed in the stern and wrapped in sheets. Don Kincaid had called the Coast Guard on the marine radio and advised them of the *Northwind* sinking, that they had three bodies on board. Asking if they should wait for a Coast Guard vessel to arrive, they were advised to "bring the bodies in." Mo opened the throttle on the *Virgalona* and headed for Key West. Don then tried to reach Mel without success.

In the early hours of Sunday morning, Bob Hall answered the radio call. Bob owned a restaurant near the *Golden Doubloon* office and offered to try and reach someone by phone. He was able to raise Bleth McHaley. Mel and Deo had decided to spend the night at the Pier House. The celebration of the bronze cannon recovery had sapped their energy and they needed to get away by themselves. It was after daybreak when their room phone rang. It was Bleth McHaley. "There has been an accident on the *Northwind*. I suggest you both come on over to the galleon office." Mel understood that the Coast Guard had been notified, and instead of driving to the office, Mel and Deo drove over to the Coast Guard station. It was still early in the morning, and the station wasn't open yet. Soon a uniformed sailor let them in, and they were told the tragic news, the *Northwind* had sunk and Dirk, Angel, and Rick Gage had drowned.

The Fishers were thunderstruck; it couldn't be happening. They clutched each other in disbelief. They kept waiting for the officer to tell them there still was some mistake, there was still hope. They were told that the *Virgalona* was on its way to Key West with the bodies on board and would dock behind the galleon office.

By early afternoon a small group of close friends and well-wishers had gathered at the dock. There were no words that could describe the immense depth of emotion that had overwhelmed them all. As *Virgalona* slowly made its way towards them, Mel could only offer, "It's a powerful ocean. It takes men and ships."

Salvaging treasure had taken its greatest toll.

23...TREASURE OF THE *SANTA MARGARITA*

The winds of winter moved northward from the Marquesas earlier than usual. It was February, 1980, and the seas surrounding the Quicksands and the island chain leading to Key West lay flat and calm. It gave the Fisher divers an unexpected jump on the salvage season, and they took advantage of it. However, there was a new intensity in their search, a new mission. Their target was the *Santa Margarita*.

Like Indians circling the wagon train, Mel's competitors were closing in on the hunting grounds of the *Santa Margarita*. Olin Frick was well known for his raids on Art McKee's "Capitana" of the 1733 fleet in the Upper Keys. He had engineered a standoff, including the flourishing of rifles, when his salvage vessel *Buccaneer* and McKee's *Jolly Roger* came face to face over the "Capitana" ballast pile near Tavernier Island. Now he was on the hunt again, this time in Hawk Channel off the Marquesas. He and a partner, John Gasque, had managed to contract with Fisher to raise the *Atocha* cannons in 1976, and this had whet their appetites for sunken treasure. With the help of investors they had outfitted two salvage vessels, the *Juniper* and the *Seeker*, and now they had pushed their search pattern into the area leased to Treasure Salvors.

In a display of muscle they fired rifle shots at nothing in particular. It did get the attention of the divers on the *Swordfish*, one of Mel's salvage vessels that was nearby. Then, in March, Mo Molinar had taken the *Virgalona* to the edge of the *Atocha*-adjudicated lease area to monitor Frick and Gasque. It was evident that Frick was crossing over into Mel's area. As they swept their magnetometer ever closer to them, Frick suddenly turned the *Juniper* and headed directly for the port side of the *Virgalona*. Mo pushed full forward on both throttles, but the *Virgalona* was a slow boat to begin with. For a few moments it seemed that his crew might have a long swim back to the Marquesas, but as Mo watched, the *Juniper* barely missed the stern of *Virgalona* and their anchor boat by a few feet.

Mel took the matter to the federal court in Miami, and Judge Mehrtens issued a restraining order against Frick and Gasque. They would later be sentenced to five months in jail for violating Mel's leased area. But the die was cast. Something had to be done in locating the wreck site of the *Margarita*. Mel already had been appointed custodian of the *Atocha* wreck site by raising the bronze cannon and the three silver bars. This was definite proof he had located a part of *Atocha*, and by admiralty law he had custody of the wreck site no matter where it might lead.

Shortly after the *Northwind* sinking, the state of Florida decided not to enter the Treasure Salvors lawsuit filed by Horan in Miami. The resulting admiralty lease gave Mel full possession of the *Atocha* and her treasures. The state attorneys, including Jack Shreve, decided that their rights to the *Atocha*, if any, were marginal. Instead, they did join with federal authorities to request the Coast Guard to seize the wreck site. Only a public relations campaign by Treasure Salvors' Bleth McHaley prevented that from happening. At that point the salvors' attorneys tried to negotiate jointly with the state of Florida and the federal government, whereby the salvors would continue to give Florida 25% of all recovered treasure and allowing them to keep the treasure which they received in the March division.

On August 10, 1975, a meeting was held in Washington, D. C., with all parties present to determine if a working relationship could be reached. It was doomed to failure. Senator Williams was obstinate in his assertion that Treasure Salvors was destroying the wreck site, that only state archaeologists could "save the *Atocha* for future generations." The federal spokesman stated that the government owned 100% of all recoveries, and Treasure Salvors' only compensation would have to come from a congressional appropriation for efforts. The matter would have to be heard in a federal court.

After a flurry of activities on both sides, the final decision was handed down on August 21, 1978, by Judge William O. Mehrtens, U.S. District Court for the Southern District of Florida. The decision was in favor of Treasure Salvors! Within the ruling Judge Mehrtens made the following comments:

"The finding of a great treasure from the days of the Spanish Main is not the cherished dream of only the United States and Florida citizens; countless people from other lands have shared such thoughts. It would amaze and surprise most citizens of this country, when their dream, at the greatest of costs, was realized, that agents of respective governments would, on the most flimsy grounds, lay claim to the treasure."

Mel and the treasure salvage community had won, thanks to their attorney David Horan! For the time being, the state of Florida ceased its relentless attacks against Mel. David had defeated Goliath.

But the *Santa Margarita* was a different matter. This wreck site had not been awarded to Fisher. Even though they had combed a wide area of the sea bottom in search of a trace of the galleon, it had been to no avail. With treasure being recovered along the *Atocha* scatter pattern, the *Margarita* had been put on a back burner. Gene Lyon had identified the area that the *Margarita* probably struck a sand bar and sank, but it was now ten years down the road, and Mel had not located a single trace of the ship. It was fair game for his competitors.

One thing Mel had going for him throughout his salvage career was the people who joined him in his quest for treasure. These people were not only knowledgeable, but dedicated to the hunt as well. Now Mel had called a brainstorming session of those close to him in an effort to find the *Margarita*. They met at retired Navy Commander John Cryer's house on Riviera Drive in Key West. All the boat captains, as well as the Treasure Salvors principals gathered together. Gene Lyon gave a briefing on all the best archival information he had relating to eye-witness accounts of the vessel sinking and an indication of what she was carrying at the time. Cryer, a former U. S. Navy meteorologist, attempted to reconstruct the storm and wind pattern that sank the *Atocha* and *Margarita*. In the end they all offered the "best bet" spot on the chart where the *Margarita* may have sunk.

The *Santa Margarita* was a large galleon of 630 tons, built of oak in Viscaya, Spain. When she left the harbor in Havana she was carrying 13,000 pounds of tobacco; chests of indigo; five tons of Cuban copper in slabs; 419 registered silver ingots; 118,000 silver coins in boxes; 1,488 ounces of gold in fourteen bars and disks; silverware; eighteen bronze cannon; sixty extra muskets, pikes, and lances; and at least fourteen passengers and 73 soldiers. The contraband on board was substantial, including many gold chains and gold coins.

In 1626-28 the site was partially salvaged by Francisco Nuñez Melián. By dragging an inverted copper bell over the area --with a diver seated inside-- he had located the ballast pile. Before the Dutch chased him from the salvage site, he had recovered 392 of the silver bars --67 of which were contraband-- 68,622 silver coins, 75 pieces of worked silver, five silver lamps, four silver vases, one silver cup, one silver salt cellar, one silver bowl, 143 copper slabs, twelve muskets, four swords, five pieces of artillery, eight bronze cannon, and other silver artifacts. The indication was that the site still held substantial treasure.

Mel wanted all the help he could get in locating the galleon before his competitors found it. He had a salvage captain, Bobby Jordan, attend the meeting. Bobby had worked for Mel previously under Armada Research in the Middle Keys. He was a good salvager, one who knew his business, and he had one of the better salvage boats, the *Castilian*, an aluminum crew boat formerly used in the oil fields. Mel offered Bobby 5% of anything salvaged from the *Margarita* if he found her, and a 2% piece of the *Atocha* treasure. Bobby was to receive fuel and food for his salvage boat, and $100 per day for expenses. He also had the loan of one of Fay Feilds' proton magnetometers and a VHF radio in order to communicate with the other salvage vessels.

There were conflicting documents that indicated the *Margarita* could be either east or west of the Quicksands area. Mel asked Jordan to search to the west first, and if nothing were found, then shift his search to the east. Mel directed Syd Jones, captain of the *Swordfish*, to search to the west as well. Kane would take the *Virgalona* to the east. The hunt was on.

There is a dynamic ridge of sand separating the Atlantic Ocean from the Gulf of Mexico, sand that is moved around by storms and the strong current flowing between the two bodies of water. On the coral plateau, beyond where the nine bronze cannons of the *Atocha* were recovered, were several known wreck sites and ranges that the salvage boats had used to guide them in their magnetometer surveys. There was the range ship *Patricia*, a Navy destroyer that had been sunk and used for bombing practice by the Navy Air Force. Mel had used it for a short period of time as a theodolite tower. It had a circle of range posts around it that the planes used in their bombing runs. There was also a range called "Two Posts" that Mel had used as Del Norte towers in the early days.

To the north was a drug boat, the *Bon Vent*, and at one time Mel had also used it as a theodolite tower. To the west was what remained of the *Arbutus*, the engineless, 187-foot Coast Guard ex-buoy tender that Mel had purchased as a divers platform. It had sunk several years earlier, and now all that remained above water were her masts. In the flats towards Marquesa Keys lay the *Eagle*, a 188-ton motor vessel that had sunk in 1945.

The area seemed to be a graveyard of sunken ships, a graveyard scattered with modern debris as well. This is what had confused the magnetometer runs for ten years, the contamination of anomalies. Syd Jones extended the *Swordfish* search pattern to the west where he did locate another wreck site, but it was not the *Margarita*. Bobby Jordan worked the *Castilian* to the west as well, but after only a few fruitless days' searching, he followed a hunch and moved eastward. According to Lyon, the *Margarita* had struck a sand bar in 22 feet of water and sank shortly afterwards. There is a definitive four fathom depth that is recorded as a line on the hydrographic charts by the U. S. Coast and Geodetic Survey group. Bobby found himself following this line as he began his magnetometer survey towards Marquesa Key.

Treasure Salvors had asked Bobby to use his Loran to plot the position of the search pattern, but Jordan wasn't comfortable using Loran. He was an ex-Navy man and had been hunting treasure for too many years. He did it his way, using visual bearings on the many wrecks and markers that surrounded the area. He kept his fathometer pegged on the 24-foot depth as he swept the sandy bottom. About six miles west of Marquesa Key he got a large hit, one that made him drop a buoy and circle back over the area.

The sand was dusted away with the *Castilian* blowers, uncovering a section of what appeared to be wrought-irons rods, banded together and weighing about eighty pounds. They were not modern, but at the time it was difficult to tell just how old they were. Getting underway, Jordan suddenly had a much larger anomaly. When diver Craig Boyd went over the side to check it out, it was rounded and green with verdigris. Dusting the sand away revealed a large, six-foot-in-diameter copper pot. This definitely was old! The pot was turned upside down, and at first it was difficult to tell what it had been used for, cooking or possibly even a diving bell. Syd Jones had determined by this time that the wreck he had located was probably an 1800s site, and when he heard the news about the copper pot on the marine radio, he brought *Swordfish* over to give Bobby a hand. Kane also brought *Virgalona* to the area.

Soon *Swordfish* located another set of the wrought-iron rods, almost at the same time that Jordan discovered two small six-foot bower anchors nearby. Then the *Swordfish* found a third small bower anchor. Another kedge-type anchor with chain, possibly more modern, was located by Kane from the *Virgalona*. As news spread about the anchors and the pot, there was a sudden realization by everyone that they may have located the area where Melián and his salvagers, in 1626, had been chased from the *Margarita* site by the Dutch, leaving their anchors behind in a haste to keep from being captured. The wrought-iron rods, banded together, could have been used as anchors as well.

The trail led to the northwest, towards the shallows between the Atlantic and the Gulf of Mexico, and now the current over the shallows made the search more challenging. It was difficult to stream a magnetometer behind the salvage boats and maintain a course. Now the search became more visual. The bottom was hard and with little sand cover. Suddenly there were a few ballast stones and pottery shards, definite signs of a Spanish galleon. Before the end of the day they recovered a few blackened, sulfided clumps of coins. To say the least, the salvagers were exhilarated.

That night the three salvage boats anchored near the Marquesas, and the crews gathered together to talk about what they had found. The clumps of coins were cleaned and found to have been minted in Potosí during the period of Philip III. It was the right period for the *Margarita*. It was an exciting time; they were sure that they were on the right trail. The following days the trail led northwestward towards what was later called the "Gorgonia Plateau", eighteen feet deep and covered with sponges and gorgonias. Beyond the plateau the water deepened, and here the bottom was covered with sand. The strong current had built mounds of sand, deposited by water rushing by at six to eight knots.

As Bobby Jordan steered the *Castilian* along the interface of the plateau and the deep sand, Craig Boyd standing on the bow of the boat spied a glitter on the bottom and promptly dived over the side. He came up holding...a bar of gold! Jordan dropped anchor and joined him, and together they located two more bars of gold, one of them over five pounds and measuring eleven inches long.

When the *Castilian* arrived in Key West Harbor with the three gold bars there was a champagne party. They knew they were close to the main pile, and it would just be a matter of time. For a moment Mel wondered how his previous crews had missed the scatter pattern. They had magged through that area before, but the numerous bomb cases and modern debris had thrown them off.

He promptly filed an admiralty claim on the area, arresting it as the *Santa Margarita*. The date was April 4, 1980. The finding of gold was the shot in the arm that Mel and his crews needed, but it also heralded the beginning of a more serious situation between Mel and Bobby Jordan. Jordan felt he should have a better contract, one that would give him a bigger share of what was coming up off the bottom. Mel took Bobby's request before the executive committee of Treasure Salvors, where a re-negotiated contract was denied. It seemed like only a matter of hours before the salvage vessels were refueled and heading back to the Marquesas.

The *Swordfish* and the *Virgalona* converged on the trail of artifacts that led over the Gorgonia Plateau and into the sand beyond. Within a week two more gold bars were recovered, and then there were silver coins everywhere. Where the *Margarita* had struck the reef there still remained a large gash, with ballast stone scattered towards the ridge of sand separating the Gulf and the Atlantic. Now the divers were bringing up swords and arquebuses, typical of a major galleon.

Then it was May twelfth, a day the divers will never forget. One of the other boats was having some problems, and Syd Jones had taken the *Swordfish* over to lend a hand. The *Virgalona* was short of divers, so Don Durant volunteered to swim over from the *Swordfish* just before it left. The *Virgalona* was having compressor problems; it just didn't work, so hookah-rig diving was out. They relied on tanks, and when they were out of air it meant returning to Key West and having them refilled. Kane had anchored the *Virgalona* near the area where three days earlier Bobby Jordan had recovered an eleven-pound ship's bell, silver plates, a sword, hundreds of silver coins, and a section of an astrolabe.

The current was strong in this area, so strong that the *Virgalona* blowers were not effective in moving the sand from the bottom. Don Durant was a strong swimmer, and near slack tide he decided to swim the area and check it out. Several hundred feet away he looked down and could hardly believe what he was seeing. Here was an intact part of the hull, and it appeared as though it were covered in artifacts. "Hey you guys, come over here!!" he shouted. Kane was able to get the *Virgalona* anchored over the spot, but the current had picked up again and the blowers were useless. When Kane dropped over the side, the first thing he spotted was six silver bars, appearing as if they had been in two boxes at one time. In the initial excitement at least two more silver bars were recovered...and a large gold bar. They raised the *Swordfish* on the radio and suggested that they "Come on over, it's all here!"

Bronze cannon recovered from the **Santa Margarita**

Before long Syd Jones had backed the stern of his salvage boat up close to the stern of the *Virgalona*. The blowers on the *Swordfish* were powerful enough to move the sand, and they were about to begin when Ted Miguel suggested they not use the blowers until the site had been mapped and photographed. He recognized that they were looking at an historic section of an ancient galleon which could be lost forever if the blowers disturbed the wooden structure. Instead, they kept the engines on both salvage boats in idle as the divers, sucking on the last of the remaining air in their tanks, recovered hundreds of silver coins that lay about the sandy bottom. Late that afternoon the salvage boats headed back to Key West, with a tired, but elated, diving crew.

The hull structure lay between where the bower anchors and copper pot had been recovered earlier, and the three gold bars that Jordan had found. Mel decided to do a complete photo mosaic of the hull structure, and Pat Clyne began to assemble a camera track. It would enable him to take photos that overlapped, providing one of the best archaeological studies of a 1622 galleon *in situ*. In the preceding days it became apparent that the scatter pattern of the *Santa Margarita* followed a fairly narrow pathway to the north.

Kim and Mel Fisher with gold chains from the
Santa Margarita

First a bronze cannon was located some 300 yards away from the hull, and a bullfrog leap beyond was another bronze cannon. Near the ridge where the current of the Gulf made diving more difficult they discovered one of *Margarita*'s huge anchors. The path was a hard bottom filled with monkey holes, small holes, and large holes, that were the result of prehistoric trees whose roots left their mark when the seas covered the land. Archaeologists would call them "solution holes". The holes were filled with artifacts, coins, and chains, almost like a Christmas stocking.

Just when the picture seemed so bright, gold fever struck. And it struck one of the toughest old treasure hunters in the business. It was 23 May when Jordan pulled away from the fuel docks in Key West. By noon time he was anchored over the *Margarita* scatter pattern, about 200 feet north of the reef where he had first located the three gold bars. Once the anchors were set and the blowers had dusted the sand away exposing a hard coquina bottom, the *Castilian* divers went over the side to be greeted by a glitz of gold. It was a golden bonanza. Within hours they had recovered fifteen gold bars and a large gold disk. More than 50 pounds of gold, and there was more!

That day they recovered five gold coins, six silver bars, two copper ingots, and 581 silver coins. Unknown to the two Fisher agents aboard the *Castilian*, Jordan had prepared for just such a situation. He strapped on a .22 caliber pistol, loaded an M-1 carbine rifle and rested it on the control bridge console, and then using a pre-arranged signal, called his wife on the marine radio. "I found the fish. Should I turn it over to the fish farm?" His wife understood the message and must have suggested that the fish farm was out. When R. D. LeClair requested permission to use the radio to call Fisher and tell him of the good news, he was refused permission. Jordan hauled anchor and headed for Key West.

When the *Castilian* entered Key West Harbor the Mariel Boat Lift was in full progress. Dock space was non-existent, but Jordan had no plans to dock. Don Kincaid was watching with binoculars from the Pier House at the end of Duval Street as *Castilian* briefly dropped anchor in the harbor. Just as quickly the anchor was hoisted, and *Castilian* headed north, up the Keys. Don wondered "what Bobby had in mind" at the time, but the impact of gold fever didn't surface until two days later.

Bobby took *Castilian* up the coast twenty miles to Summerland Key. Here was the home of his financial backer, Finley Riccard. Jordan's attorneys soon arrived at the home, and the following day Peter Craig, a Deputy United States Marshal joined them. The treasure that Jordan had on board was "arrested" as Jordan placed an admiralty claim on the wreck site. The Marshall had no idea it was the site of the *Margarita*.

R. D. LeClair and Frank Moody, the Fisher representatives on board *Castilian*, were then allowed to call Mel and advise him what was happening. As it turned out, Jordan's attorneys had already filed an admiralty claim the week before, on 21 May. It was Bobby's contention that Mel had not originally located the wreck, and that because he found it...he deserved a larger share than the 5%. Suddenly the air was filled with legal litigation. Dave Horan, Mel's attorney, filed a motion in federal court restraining Jordan. On 2 June an order temporarily restraining Jordan from further salvage on the site was issued, and later the treasure Bobby had recovered was ordered returned to Treasure Salvors. A later injunction made the order permanent, and Bobby Jordan was off the site of the *Margarita* permanently. He also lost his 5% of the treasure that was recovered from the *Margarita*, a treasure that later amounted to more than twenty million dollars. In the end he also had to pay legal fees and court costs --the cost of gold fever.

As the summer wore on, *National Geographic* photographers and writers came to the site to document the treasure being recovered. Divers were in the process of re-enacting the recovery of one of the bronze cannon when they stumbled onto the "cannon ball clump." Later, near the clump, they excitedly located a stack of silver bars. In the same area, when they turned the blowers on to dust the sand from the monkey holes, the holes were filled with coins. They brought them to the surface in buckets. In front of the main pile, where the bottom began to rise towards shallow water, it looked like a lead factory. Lead bottom sheathing was all wadded up where the galleon had first struck. There was lead everywhere. Syd Jones, and his wife K. T., were magging to the northeast of the main pile, towards the outer reef, when they got a good hit. Diving down they located a small bower anchor just inside the first reef. The shank was pointing directly towards the main pile. Following the lead they soon located three large anchors, each pointing in the same direction.

The anchors of the *Margarita* had been located. One of the anchors had the date 1618 struck at the crown. Then in August the weather had turned funky; the winds and current caused some rough weather over the bar. Kane, with the *Virgalona*, had completed his tour on the site, and was about to head back to Key

West when Jones brought the *Swordfish* in to relieve him. It was a good potential area, Kane had recovered some nice artifacts, and Syd wanted to continue where *Virgalona* had left off. By the time the *Virgalona* had hauled anchors and was heading back to Key West, the current had moved the *Swordfish* away from the spot. It was difficult for the *Swordfish* divers to relocate the last hole dug, so Syd went in the water to help.

Deo and Taffi Fisher examine gold bars and chains recovered from the Santa Margarita *site*.

Once the salvage boat was winched over the area and the props began to dust the bottom, Syd hung from the mailbox watching the sand roll away from under the thrust of the prop wash. As he watched he noticed a faint "square" appear as the last of the sand cover disappeared. Once the engine was cut back to idle he dived down for a closer look and knew instantly what he was looking at. It was a box of gold bars and gold chains. He scooped up what amounted to nine gold bars and eight gold chains, about 25 pounds of gold, and did the best he could to swim to the surface with it. He made it, just long enough to get the crew's attention on deck, and then the weight and the current sent him plunging to the bottom again. It was knee-jerking to hold that many gold bars and chains. He was able to make it to the boarding ladder on his next try, it was the most exciting day of his salvage career. About fifteen feet away they later recovered an ivory box with silver hinges and a silver bar. It seemed that the bottom was full of such surprises.

By the end of the summer the gold from the *Santa Margarita* totaled 54 bars, bits, and disks weighing 106 pounds. There were 43 gold chains, 53 gold coins, close to 12,000 silver coins, and eighteen silver bars. It was an exhilarating experience for everyone aboard the salvage boats, as well as those back in Treasure Salvors' offices. They shared in the excitement together. It seemed for a while that it couldn't get any better than this.

24...TRAIL OF FRUSTRATION

With the recovery of the *Santa Margarita* treasure it suddenly seemed like a whole new ball game to Mel. His job was easier somehow, but it also felt at times like a high-speed train barreling down the tracks at ninety miles an hour. In one respect, for a while, his financial problems seemed to evaporate. The initial recoveries from the *Margarita* were estimated at $20 million, a mind-boggling sum to have been "picked up" from the floor of the ocean. But it wasn't so much the dollar value, it was the glitz of gold chains, gold bars, a beautifully ornate gold plate, gold coins, silver bars and coins, and artifacts that played on the fantasies of everyone that saw them.

Salvage vessel **Dauntless** *underway for the Marquesas.*

He was invited to participate in an investment seminar being held in Montreal, Canada. It was a "rush" sort of participation with only a few days for planning, and Mel was able to reserve two rooms where the seminar was being held. In one room he laid out a display of gold and silver from the *Margarita*, one that would have dazzled anyone entering the room. In the other room he set up a video of the salvage boats working on the *Santa Margarita* recovering treasure. Mel found a secretarial service nearby and had an old *Margarita* contract re-worded to reflect the recoveries and what might still be on the bottom. The new contract was on a one year, limited partnership basis, with an offering of thirty units at $20,000 per unit. The interest in the display and video was overwhelming. By the end of the seminar he had sold all thirty units and had $600,000 in his pocket ready to go treasure hunting.

The Treasure Salvors group began to congeal with a singleness of purpose. It was time to concentrate on finding the *Atocha* mother lode. With new financial support the crews were paid, the boats fueled and provisioned, and they could now stay on site longer. The crews were excited. Each day they expected to find the ballast pile, or at least the scatter pattern leading to the pile of silver bars. They began earlier in the morning, and worked until sunset, yet it wasn't a tired crew that recounted treasure stories on the fantail of the salvage boats long after working hours.

Back in Key West the staff was documenting the *Margarita* recoveries. As usual, the phones were ringing off the hook, and Deo Fisher became the link between Mel and the outside world. As the executive secretary of Treasure Salvors she fielded hundreds of phone calls from well-wishers and "wannabes". The news media had a great story to tell, and they all wanted to "hear it from Mel". But Mel had a more important job to do, he had to direct the salvage boats in the final search for the mother lode. Like everyone else, he felt that it had to be close.

He put Bob Moran in charge of the on-site operations, and Bob handled the job from his 42-foot Chris Craft. The chart room in Key West became the "buzz room", with direct communications with the salvage boats as each hole was dusted on the ocean floor and as each artifact was recorded as it came to the surface. Ed Little composed a mosaic of the previous "hits" they had recorded on the magnetometer surveys. It gave everyone a clearer picture of the areas that no longer had potential, and they were eliminated from "hot" zones. It narrowed the search pattern considerably, and it gave everyone expectations that finding the big pile was only days away.

The scatter pattern of major artifacts that had been discovered to date lay along a narrow corridor less than 150 feet wide and stretching from the patch reef in water forty feet deep, to the northwest towards shallow water and the Quicksands. Mel set up a checkerboard grid pattern along the corridor, and the salvage boats began dusting each ten-foot square.

As the summer doldrums of 1982 settled over the Marquesas, John Brandon had his crew visually looking for traces of the *Atocha*. A swimmer was dragged behind the salvage boat at the end of a line, scanning the bottom for anything that may have been missed by the magnetometer sweeps. There were still eleven bronze cannon missing, and a magnetometer would not pick up bronze. They were not finding treasure, and so John would anchor his salvage boat over the "Coral Plateau", an area between the bronze cannon area and the Quicksands. This was an area in which John had previously found a number of silver pieces-of-eight visually, not using a metal detector. Now, with metal detectors on board, he thought at least they could pick up a few silver coins. The water was 22 to 24 feet deep, and the plateau was covered with small monkey holes, six to twelve inches in diameter and filled with mud and sand.

John, and Danny Porter, were in the water that first day, and within thirty minutes they each had picked up about 100 silver coins. They were everywhere. John then rigged up some small buoys with fishing weights on the end and told the rest of his crew that Danny and he would drop buoys on the "hits" they got, "and the rest of you can dig up the treasure!" Chuck Sotzin, Mel's nephew, Laney Southerly, and Clay Cordary were soon in the water following behind the two metal detectors. For the first hour they were all kept pretty busy, then John heard a banging on the metal boarding ladder. When he and Danny swam to the back of the boat his crew was beaming. They held up a piece of gold with a ruby in the center. At first they thought it was a religious medallion, except there were loops at both ends. They jumped back in the water, this time searching with even more intensity.

Before long more gold pieces were located, along with an eight-foot, heavy, twisted link gold chain. The following day they continued the search, all thoughts of dragging a swimmer behind the boat forgotten. Before the day ended they had a total of thirteen gold pieces, each mounted with a different precious stone or pearl, and all pieces seeming to fit together to form a belt. Another smaller five-foot, ten-inch gold chain was recovered, along with three gold bars and twelve two-escudo gold coins, each dated 1621-22. All except one were Old World Seville mint, but one had the "NR" for Nuevo Reino, the New World mint at Bogotá.

When Mel heard the news about the finds on the marine radio, he asked John to bring them quickly into Key West, or he would be willing to run out in a boat and pick them up. An exhibit of treasure was being shown at the Key West Martello Museum, and Mel wanted to have this new find shown for the first time. John wanted to bring the pieces in himself, so reluctantly he hauled anchor and headed for Key West. No sooner did he hand the gold buckle pieces over to Mel, than he was headed back to the Coral Plateau. For the next ten days his crew conducted a methodical search of a 100-foot radius around the first thirteen gold pieces. When the search ended they had recovered a total of 23 gold belt pieces and over 400 silver coins.

Bob Moran helped determine that the gold pieces were part of a belt. In a book he happened to have on board his boat was a painting of King Philip II's daughter. Around her waist, and around her neck, hung a belt almost identical to the pieces that John and his crew had found. It helped to date the jewelry being recovered from the *Atocha* site. Today the belt is still considered the greatest artifact to have been recovered from a shipwreck.

Salvage vessel **Golden Venture** *on the "Bank of Spain".*

Ian Koblick brought another large 105-foot salvage tug, the *Golden Venture*, into the hunt. It's huge propeller was able to move the deep sands near the edge of the Quicksands, and in July, 1982, they recovered one of the most breathtaking jeweled artifact from the *Atocha* to date. The water depth was only twenty feet, and the sand almost fifteen feet deep where the *Golden Venture* was anchored near the Quicksands. The huge tug's propeller was able to move the sand into a mound that surrounded a hole almost forty feet in diameter, exposing the hard marl bottom. There was considerable excitement when twenty gold finger bars were recovered in a small area. Then, it was a small gold chain with finely-wrought links. But the day stood still when a small, kippered herring kind of box was uncovered.

Silver box containing emerald pectoral cross and 10-carat emerald ring recovered by divers on the Golden Venture.

K. T. Budde-Jones and Frederick Ingerson were in the water and, after a five-minute dusting with the boat's prop, they settled to the bottom with metal detectors to check for artifacts. Rico first spotted the small oblong box that resembled a discarded sardine can. It looked modern, and he swam over and showed it to K. T.

It deserved a closer look, so K. T. swam it to the surface. Sitting on the boarding platform she also thought it looked recent, and rather than be embarrassed by bringing up a modern piece of junk...she shook it. It rattled. Knowing that sardines didn't rattle, K. T. stripped off her SCUBA gear and carried the encrusted box topside, where she and Dick Klaudt gently cleaned and opened it. It was unbelievable. Inside lay a large gold cross with seven large emeralds, the largest would later be measured at 65 carats. Alongside was a gold ring with a ten-carat emerald stone, a match for the pectoral cross. It took their breath away.

Emerald pectoral cross and 10-carat emerald ring recovered on the "Bank of Spain". **Credit: Scott Nierling.**

Not long after, Ian was on the marine radio to Key West, advising them that they had recovered "something substantial". Mel said he would come out and pick it up. Ian suggested that he bring it into Key West himself and said he would leave as soon as he could get his anchors up. "Bring the *Golden Venture* to the Pier House dock, I'll have the TV and news people there to meet you." By late that afternoon the salvage vessel entered Key West Harbor, and as it neared the Pier House dock Ian could see the crowd gathered expectantly. To add to the excitement of the moment, Ian had spread a velvet cloth out on the table in his cabin and placed the small gold chain on the cloth. At the end of the table he had a small towel folded over, and under the towel was the gold cross, ring, and the silver box.

As lines were made fast to the dock, Mel asked the news media to wait for a few minutes while he and Deo stepped aboard to look at the treasure. Ian led them up to his cabin and waved them to the table. As Mel saw the small gold chain you could almost sense the disappointment. The *Margarita* had given up 43 gold chains, many of them over five feet long. This chain was small in comparison, and although any gold chain was a great recovery, Mel was having second thoughts about the crowd of news media waiting on the dock. It was Deo's curiosity that made her lift the edge of the towel at the end of the table. Mel heard her gasp, "Mel...look at this!!" Mel looked at Ian and saw the broad grin on his face. He knew he'd been had.

The gold and emerald cross made big news. It was undoubtedly intended to be worn by a bishop or even someone higher in the church. On the back of the cross were etched two religious figures. One of them was Nuestra Señora de la Leche, the Virgin suckling the infant Jesus. The other figure was a saint and the Madonna holding the Christ Child. It was an impressive church talisman.

Mel needed something to dust large areas of the bottom, but portable enough to be carried on any one of his salvage boats. He heard of a device called a "Hydro-Flow". It was a big pipe, about twenty feet high and four feet in diameter. Inside were three vanes, like huge turbo-props with a close tolerance near the sides. Two two-inch hydraulic hoses connected the five tons of metal to a water pump, one leading the water into the driving housing, the other returning the water back to the pump.

When Mel took it to the site and had the crew of one of the salvage boats rig it alongside, they were all amazed at how easily it was controlled. By varying the amount of hydraulic fluid being pumped into the hydro-motor, the height of the Hydro-Flow above the ocean bottom could be controlled. And it dug a huge hole in the sand, a hole that measured forty feet across at the top and twenty feet in diameter where the hard bottom became exposed. Mel had picked an area about one-third of a mile southeast of the bronze cannon recoveries, quite a distance from the scatter zone. He chose this area because of the sand and hard clay bottom.

Something was needed to separate the clay from the bottom, one of the problems that had been a bug-a-boo for the blowers on the salvage boats.

As he swam around the hole checking to see how well his new invention worked, he found a ballast stone halfway up the edge of the hole. Surfacing with it in his hand he said to himself, "My God, how did that get way out here!" The spar buoys marking the bronze cannon area, and other buoys that stretched towards the Quicksands, seemed a long way off. He was convinced that *Atocha* "had to have passed right over this spot. Ballast stones do not float!" He put his son Kane on this new trail, a trail that would eventually lead to...the mother lode.

Kane followed the trail out into deeper water. He had always believed, as did Dirk and Duncan Mathewson, that the *Atocha* lay somewhere out in Hawk Channel. It was a trail of frustration, of finding a few iron spikes, a ballast stone, or an encrusted object. It certainly wasn't the thrill of finding silver and gold near the Quicksands, but it was the first concrete evidence of *Atocha* material out in Hawk Channel. For a while the *Swordfish* and *Virgalona* helped Kane search the deep water, and spirits rose and fell each time something was recovered, regardless of how insignificant. Eventually the other salvage boats went back to the Quicksands area where they continued to find gold and silver. Kane persisted, a nagging frustration that lasted for two and a half years.

Back in Key West the office on the *Golden Doubloon* was in danger of being flooded. Over the years the ship had sprung leaks, had almost sunk on numerous occasions. A rubber diaper had been placed under the hull when teredos had made a feast of the exposed wooden planking. Now Mel had fourteen sump pumps at work, each spouting one-inch streams of water from the hull, and it was barely staying ahead of the rising level of water inside the hull. A decision had to be made, either haul the *Golden Doubloon* and have extensive repairs made to the hull, or let it settle alongside the dock once and for all. The decision was made to let it settle when the pumps began to fail. The museum and most of the office papers were moved ashore before the galleon hit bottom. It remained upright, with the main deck and most of the office above water, and for awhile the staff was able to continue using the office. But then one night a storm came up out of the southeast, and by morning the galleon had been blown over on her side --away from the dock-- splitting amidships as well. Papers that had been left in the office were soaked, and desk equipment became unsalvageable. It was time for a move.

A new office was set up on Simonton Street, where a bank of fans were used to dry out the papers, stock certificates, and documents. Otherwise, it was business as usual. Over the next two years the office would move several times, first to the Conch House on Caroline Street, then to the Admiral's office and Administration Building. Their final move was to Warehouse Building 48 on the old Navy base, the location that they are in today. Their current headquarters at 200 Greene Street is an old brick structure, six stories high with an antiquated service elevator that gives you a thrill every time it negotiates the 55-foot, noisy climb to the top floor.

The first level is six feet above the street, and it is on this floor that a museum of major proportions --and international acclaim-- began to emerge. There was room for a gift shop near the entrance, and Bleth McHaley was placed in charge of getting it off the ground and running. At the rear of the first floor, the office staff arranged files and desks, as well as a chart room, and for the first time there seemed to be room for everyone.

Golden Doubloon *sunk alongside the dock at Key West.*

292

Taffi Fisher was now a beautiful young lady, as effervescent as her father, and as stable as her mother. Good looks ran in the family. She had graduated from Catholic High School in 1979, about the same time that the Fisher family moved off the houseboats. A nice home had come up for auction on Raccoon Key near Stock Island, after the owner had tried his hand at drug running. Mel was able to buy it at $100 above the value of the bank mortgage. It was the first "real" house that Deo had since moving south from Vero Beach. It was a happy time for the Fishers. Kane introduced Taffi to José Quesada, a house painter who would try his hand at selling in the gift shop. He was soon making more in sales commissions than he was painting, so it became his full-time job. He also was having palpitations of the heart beat when Taffi was in sight. A romance bloomed, and in 1981 the two of them were married. In 1982 Joshua was born. Two years later Nicole, Mel's first grand-daughter, was born. The Fisher family was growing.

A legal milestone was reached in 1982 when Mel's lawyer, Dave Horan, argued successfully against the state of Florida in the highest court in the land. This highlighted seven years of state appeals that covered 141 hearings in which the state argued over ownership of *Atocha*. The Supreme Court affirmed the principle of admiralty law, halting the attempted take-over of the *Atocha* site by the state of Florida. Even as they left the court house in Washington, state of Florida lawyers were trying to determine how they could write new legislation which could override the constitutional admiralty guarantees. The greatest of all political challenges that treasure salvors would ever face still lay ahead.

Mel Fisher's greatest challenge, however, came from a different direction. Because of a bladder infection, the resulting medical examination revealed polyps within the bladder. As Mel lay on the operating table, the doctor let him watch on a TV monitor as he removed the polyps. "It was like an air lift. The doctor used some kind of wire to snip off the polyps, then the air lift would come behind and scoop up all the parts." Mel could relate to this, but not to the results. The polyps were malignant. He accepted the fact that as we age, these kinds of medical problems begin to rear their ugly heads, but in many ways it signaled the mortality in all of us. When the Treasure Salvors staff, and Mel's family, heard the news they were shocked. To them Mel had always seemed indestructible, someone who had fought so many battles and had always won. As Mel began chemotherapy treatments, they were sure he would win this one as well. So was Mel.

25...MOTHER LODE!!!

It's a big ocean. You never begin to appreciate just how big it is until you try to return to a spot no larger than the car parked in your garage. Without stationary bearings of any kind on land to guide you, or a visible reef nearby, it's an impossible task. In 1982 Mel had used theodolite towers stationed on the various surrounding islands or modern shipwrecks to guide the magnetometer sweeps. Considering that the days were hot and the theodolite operators had to sight for hours at a time through a telescope with crosshairs in guiding the sweep boats on their controlled runs, there was certainly room for error. When they did get a "hit" on the magnetometer, a buoy was dropped and divers from another salvage boat would check it out. Sometimes the buoys drifted or were blown away by storms that came up out of nowhere, so it wasn't a perfect salvage situation. The area in Hawk Channel where the mother lode should have been was criss-crossed time and again with magnetometer surveys. It just didn't seem to be there.

As the final push got underway to locate the mother lode, Mel made a fairly expensive decision to install a Del Norte navigational system in the Marquesas. This system consisted of two transmitting towers, and the receiving station located on the salvage boat indicated the exact distance from each tower. Plotted on a chart it gave the boat a location accuracy of three to five feet, the kind of accuracy it took to return to the magnetometer "hits" and check them out. From that point on the Fisher floor was covered with charts, spread out to locate old anomalies that they may have missed. The *Atocha* ballast pile and silver bars had to be there. It became a game, one that every visitor had a chance to play. "Where do you think the mother lode is? Put your mark on the chart!"

One day Rose Chibbaro, Mel's accountant, stopped by the office on Caroline Street to visit. She owned several Pomeranian dogs as pets, and this day she had three of them with her. As usual, the floor was covered with charts, and Mel was sitting cross-legged in the middle of them with Ed Little, his cartographer, transferring overlays from other charts. Mel waved "hello" when Deo opened the door for Rose, and as the dogs pranced in one of them had a call to nature...right on one of the charts! Rose was thoroughly embarrassed, and she stammered out, "Oh Mel, I'm so sorry!!" Instead of being upset, Mel broke out in a big grin..."That's it, that's where the big pile is!! Get the coordinates off that chart quick."

Out in the middle of Hawk Channel Kane Fisher was doing the best he could to follow a sparse trail of ships' artifacts. He had been made captain of the 56-foot salvage tug *Dauntless*, and along with his crew he started at the point where Mel had located a single ballast stone with the Hydro-Flow. It was about 1500 feet southeast of the bronze cannon location, and the trail had led Kane into deeper water, towards the center of Hawk Channel. It was the area that both Kane and Duncan Mathewson believed the mother lode would be located. For a time the *Virgalona* and the *Swordfish*, both salvage boats, would join in the hunt. They had systematically salvaged the *Santa Margarita* site for eighteen months, but now the target was the silver bars of *Atocha*.

They would leap-frog down the projected trail, each covering several hundred feet of ocean floor, dusting the bottom with the blowers and diving on every magnetometer hit. As a result, hundreds of hits were checked out by the divers, all mostly modern. There was excitement, of sorts, when they would recover an artifact such as an encrusted spike or a ballast stone. But soon the other boats became disenchanted. Gold and silver coins and artifacts were still being recovered near the Quicksands. These paid the bills, put fuel in the salvage vessels, and put food on the table for the divers. Kane was again left to himself, moving the *Dauntless* down the trail further to the southeast.

Then, in late summer of 1984, something happened that would change the entire complexion of the search. Bob Moran, the on-site project manager, was towing Fay Feild behind his boat *Plus Ultra* while setting up a remote sensing survey of the area to the northwest of the Bank of Spain. As they traveled over the bottom towards the Quicksands, Fay spotted another bronze cannon on the bottom. It was one of the missing eleven cannons *Atocha* carried. With news of the find, Mel sent one of the salvage vessels out to dust the bottom around the cannon, and a number of artifacts were recovered. While searching 1-1/2 miles further to the northwest two more large galleon anchors were discovered. Suddenly it seemed that those believing the *Atocha* had been driven into the deep Quicksands were right. The focus of attention now shifted from the deep water theory and Hawk Channel. Kane seemed a lonely figure as he continued to the southeast.

It was in one of Treasure Salvors "head hunting" sessions, with everyone pouring over the charts now dotted with circles indicating the holes that had been dusted on the ocean floor, when either Duncan Mathewson or Mel noticed something different. The scatter pattern that included the cannon and anchors had "bent" to the north. "It's almost as if the sterncastle of the *Atocha* was swept away on the backside of the hurricane, there is a definite curve to the trail of artifacts." After some serious consideration, the curve was applied to the scatter pattern that Kane was following into Hawk Channel. He was searching too far to the south. Kane's trail had completely dried up, and that would explain it.

Salvage Vessel **Dauntless** *over the* **Atocha** *scatter pattern.*

A new plot was laid out, this time it curved gently more to the east. Again Kane and the crew of the *Dauntless* felt they would find the ballast pile any day as they set off on a new direction. They were joined by the 167-foot salvage vessel *Saba Rock*. This new vessel had a seven-foot-diameter blower on the stern that could easily move the deep sand in Hawk Channel where the water was now over fifty feet deep. Captain of the *Saba Rock* was

Ed Stevens, and on board with him was his fiancée Susan Nelson. Susan was about to make the find of her lifetime...

It was Memorial Day weekend, 1985, almost five years since the *Margarita* had been located. After finding the *Margarita* the entire Treasure Salvors crew had felt that they would find the *Atocha* mother lode in a matter of days, certainly within weeks. But after thousands of hours scouring the bottom, and mile after mile of new magnetometer sweeps, they had come up empty. Where could it be? The *Dauntless* and the *Saba Rock* were now approaching the path that *Margarita* took as it was swept onto the shallow sand bank three miles to the north. It was a calm, clear day, and the *Saba* had just completed dusting the bottom fifty feet below. Susan had dropped over the side and swam down to join Andy Matroci on the bottom.

Before she could locate him she spotted something on the bottom, "It looked like a piece of yellow plastic." Suddenly it struck her, it was a gold bar! Even as her skin began to tingle with excitement, she spotted another...and another. She waved Andy over, and together they gathered up all the bars they could see and rushed to the surface. The excitement was contagious, and soon they had a lot of help searching the bottom. Before the day was over they would bring to the surface thirteen gold bars. Mel heard the news and rushed out to the site on one of the company's fast boats. As they stood on the deck the following morning getting ready to dive, Mel suggested they "keep an eye out for emeralds. The *Atocha* was carrying some."

Almost on the first dive, Syd Jones, and his wife K. T., surfaced with four beautiful pieces of gold jewelry, studded with a total of sixteen emeralds. Other divers began to bring up silver coins, and soon they had over 400. Susan still had an eye for gold, and before the day was over she uncovered an exquisite gold chain. It had been a real glory hole, and again everyone felt the mother lode had to be close by. The trail dissipated, then nothing.

When nothing was found for some distance beyond the glory hole, someone suggested that the glory hole was a bounce spot of the *Margarita*. After all, the *Margarita* had given up quite a number of gold bars and chains. Some serious consideration was given that possibly the *Atocha* lay well beyond the Quicksands, and that the search should be re-directed there. Kane went to his father and said, "Dad, I still think it's in Hawk Channel, and I'm going after it." He had his father's blessing.

Kane laid out a line of buoys that extended two miles to the east-southeast from the glory hole and went to work. He was joined by *Swordfish* and *Virgalona* as they all concentrated together along the range of bobbing buoys. Kane would dust the bottom, send a diver down to check it out, and if nothing were found move *Dauntless* 100 feet further along the range. The other vessels did the same, leap-frogging each other as they covered more of the ocean floor. The *Saba Rock* had an engine casualty and soon hung by an anchor, helpless as the other vessels worked to the southeast.

Now it was July first, and Kane reached the end of his two mile line of buoys. They hadn't found the ballast pile, and they had run out of any trace of a scatter pattern. Kane decided to lay out another mile of buoys and keep going. It seemed that the glory hole was in fact part of the *Margarita* bounce spot, but Kane was determined to see this through, even if he wound up in Biscayne Bay. The channel had now deepened to 54 feet of water. Another fact seemed to come together, that Captain de Lugo, on the *Margarita*, saw the *Atocha* sink "one league east" of the *Margarita*. The *Dauntless* was closing in on that location, a location that had been magged many times. Could they have missed the *Atocha* ballast pile?

The Fisher family had always been close to their church. Mel and Deo were founding members of the Methodist Church By The Sea in Vero Beach. When the family moved to Key West, the Fisher children were enrolled in the Catholic school there. Taffi Fisher graduated from Mary Immaculate Catholic High School located on Truman Avenue in Key West. When she married José she joined the Protestant Episcopal church, a church that provided a retreat and Taffi's own personal logbook. It was a logbook in which she made promises to God, such as "I will make an altar visit once a month." She kept that promise for years, making the visit to her favorite church, St. Mary, Star of the Sea.

It was the morning of 19 July, and she was late for work. She had been given the job as curator at Treasure Salvors, in charge of all the artifacts being recovered. She had stopped for a traffic light on Truman Avenue, and across the street was her favorite church, St. Mary's. She suddenly realized she hadn't kept her promise in almost two months. Looking at the traffic light and waiting for it to change, she was torn between getting to work late or going to church. As the light changed, suddenly the church bells began to chime. At 9:30 in the morning Taffi had no idea why the bells would be ringing, but in any event it was enough to make up her mind. She made a quick left turn and pulled into the church parking lot.

There was no one in the church at that hour on a Friday morning as she knelt to pray a few pews from the front. She had a lot that was troubling her. There was a problem with her marriage, her brothers had other problems as well, and what bothered her most was that her father had recently been diagnosed with cancer. She closed her eyes and the feelings seemed to pour out. "It's not fair that Dad might die before he finds the mother lode. He's spent all this time and money, you can't leave us with his legacy to fulfill. We have to find the *Atocha*. Please give me some sign." There were tears in Taffi's eyes as she crossed herself. Something made her look up. Over the altar was a large stained-glass window. It had always been there, but somehow Taffi had never really "looked" at it. What made her look up was this strong shaft of sunlight coming through the center of the window, and for the first time...she saw it. In the center of the window was the stained-glass image of a galleon in a storm, and the sun shone directly through it. She couldn't believe it; it had to be the sign she was looking for.

Out on the *Dauntless* it was late in the afternoon. Kane and Steve Swindell were making the last dive of the day when they found a ballast stone, olive jar neck, and a barrel hoop. Back on the deck of *Dauntless* the crew agreed that the barrel and the olive jar could have floated for quite a distance, but the ballast stone was the clincher. The *Atocha* had to have passed over this area. As they discussed it, Andy Matroci reached down and picked up a blackened sulfide coin, a four *reales*, lying on the deck. "Kane, did you bring this up?" Kane shook his head, as did Steve Swindell. Wondering where the coin had come from, they then examined the barrel hoop more closely, and there, stuck to the encrustation, were three more sulfided coins.

Without hesitation, Kane said, "Let's winch the stern over where we found the hoop." In minutes the *Dauntless* was being winched over the thirty feet or more to the edge of the last hole. The engines were revved up one more time as the sun began to slip below the horizon. Within minutes Kane went over the side, and when he reached the bottom he was greeted by a sight that every diver dreams of. The hole was scattered with coins, hundreds of them.

That night it was difficult to sleep. About 3:00 a.m. Andy Matroci got up and went to the galley to get some cookies and a glass of milk. He bumped into Kane there. "What are you doing up?" Kane nodded, "I can't sleep, same as you." Together they stepped out on the stern of *Dauntless* and found two more of the crew there working on warmed over cups of coffee. Before the sun was up all six members of the crew were on the stern, drinking coffee and trying to guess how close they were to the *Atocha* ballast pile. The general guess was within 100 meters. They didn't know it, but they were less than forty feet. There was a tension in the air, a desire to get started. One of the crew members shouted, "Come on sun, let's rise and shine!" As the sun's first rays scattered light behind the cloudy horizon the engines burst into life, and the day began.

In 54 feet of water each diver-pair was able to check out two holes before running out of air or going into decompression time. It was 6:00 a.m. when Bill Barron and Del Scruggs went over the side to check out the first hole. It was still fairly dark on the bottom, but against the pure white sand they could see objects they recognized as shipwreck artifacts. There were coins, two fifty-pound copper ingots, and two encrusted square spikes. The *Atocha* contract called for square spikes. The *Dauntless* was moved ten feet and another hole dusted. The second hole produced 22 more coins, twelve copper ingots, and more pottery shards.

As the morning shadows began to disappear from the bottom, *Dauntless* was moved again and the propwash deflected downward as sand swirled from the third hole. The next diver-pair in the water, Bill Moore and Steve Swindell, looked down on a hole "full of coins". It took some time to gather them all up; there were hundreds. Excitement up on deck was mounting, each trip to the surface by the divers had the rest of the crew hanging over the rail to see what was coming up next. The fourth hole of the morning was a windfall in artifacts. The *Dauntless* log read, "Hundreds of artifacts." Artifacts meant silver plates, forks, spoons, candelabras, more copper ingots, and pottery shards.

By now the *Dauntless* had been moved forty feet from the first hole of the morning. It was after 9:00 a.m. and Andy Matroci, the lead diver on the *Dauntless*, and Greg Wareham were chomping at the bit to get into the water. The engine was revved up for five minutes, and as it idled down both divers dropped over the side.

The first thing they saw when reaching the bottom was a hole full of silver coins. Rather than gathering them up at once, they decided to take a look around. The visibility was a blurred fifteen feet as Andy flippered off in one direction, and Greg in another. Within minutes, Andy was back in the hole and had already picked up over a hundred silver coins and put them in his net bag, when he felt his buddy tap him on the shoulder.

When Andy turned around, he knew that Greg had found something great. With eyes big as saucers, he beckoned Andy with his finger to follow. The coins in Andy's bag suddenly seemed insignificant. He dropped the bag and followed Greg out of the hole. Greg hesitated for a moment, trying to get his bearings, then spotted what he was looking for and flippered off with Andy in hot pursuit. Soon a low, gray reef, no more than two feet high but several yards long, materialized among the strands of sea grass and sponges. Behind it rose a pile of ballast stone. As the two approached the reef it took on the shape of a stack of dark, grayish loaves of bread. The hairs on the back of Matroci's neck bristled, he wanted to shout. Only gurgles and bubbles escaped his mouthpiece, but something like "Silver bars, silver bars!" seemed to rumble from his throat. The two divers locked arms and rolled and tumbled about the bottom. The *Atocha*, the greatest sunken treasure of all times, had been found!!

When Andy and Greg broke the surface shouting "Mother lode, mother lode!!" the scene on board *Dauntless* was bedlam. Divers on deck were jumping and shouting "*Atocha, Atocha...we got it!*" Somehow, in all this insanity, Kane found a moment to climb up into the wheelhouse and flip on the marine radio. He was able to reach home base in Key West, and Bleth McHaley answered his call. "We've found it. We've got the mother lode!"

If there was bedlam on the deck of *Dauntless*, the radio message started a riot in the offices of Treasure Salvors. Suddenly people were dancing on the desks, rushing about to spread the news. The phones began ringing, adding to the inability to think clearly, other than the sixteen-year hunt was over. Someone shouted "Where's Mel?" McHaley called the house, and Taffi and Deo were told of the *Dauntless*' radio message. Over the phone Bleth was almost unintelligible, she was choked, the words just couldn't come out right. Deo had to call back to make sure she had understood what Bleth was trying to tell her, that they had found the mother lode. She asked, "Does that mean that mother has to go out and sit on it?" At first it was hard to believe, there had been so many false alarms. Gradually it dawned on them, and they were soon speeding to the office.

Mel had gone out, and Deo had no idea where. Phone calls were made to all of Mel's old haunts without finding him. Things got frantic. The local Key West radio station was called and soon an announcement was being made every five minutes, "Will Mel Fisher please call his office, you've found the *Atocha*!" Everyone in Key West knew of Mel's good fortune before he did. An hour passed and still no word from Mel. Bleth next called the Key West police station and asked that they put out an APB on Mel. They would find him one way or the other.

Mel had just stepped out of a local dive shop on Duval Street after buying a pair of fins, a face mask, and a snorkel. It was pouring down rain. As he stood there thinking about making a run for the office a few blocks away, a passerby recognized Mel. "Hi, Mel, you better get over to your office right away. You found the *Atocha*!" That was the first news he had heard about Kane's find, and he wasn't quite sure he understood exactly what the man meant. It did convince him to make a run for the office. Ed Little saw Mel coming across Greene Street and ran out to meet him with an umbrella. As soon as he was inside he realized "Today *was* the day!" The office staff was still dancing on the desks, and someone was popping champagne corks. Everyone was shaking his hand and slapping him on the back. He kept saying, over and over again, the only words which could describe how he felt, "Fantabulous, absolutely fantabulous!"

There was, a lull in the celebration, and Mel got on the marine radio and raised his son Kane on the *Dauntless*. He tried to keep a calm voice as he asked "What's going on out there?" He had to "shush" the noisy crowd behind him so he could hear. Kane replied, "Put the charts away, I've found it!" Mel grinned from ear to ear, "What's it look like?" Even for his young years, Kane sounded much like his father. "Silver bars are stacked like cordwood. Coins everywhere." After a pause, "What do I do next?" Mel replied, "I've waited a long time for someone to ask me that."

That first night Mel Fisher sat in his living room with John Brandon, one of his divers. John had driven all the way from Fort Pierce when he heard the news. He looked across the room at Mel and saw the tears running down his smiling face. John, knowingly, said nothing, and Mel offered only, "I guess I'm just happy."

26...SALVAGING THE ATOCHA

It was Saturday, July 20, 1985, when the *Dauntless* crew discovered the *Atocha* mother lode. The excitement it caused in the Key West office of Treasure Salvors was indescribable. Pent-up emotions ranging back seventeen years seemed to explode into a wild release of happiness. It was deserving. Almost before the dancing atop their desks stopped, the office staff asked Mel, "Can we go out to the site and see for ourselves?" Mel was just as eager as the rest, but he said, "The *Dauntless* found it, let them have their day alone. Tomorrow's the day!!" With that, he ordered cases of champagne and cases of glasses to be delivered aboard the *Magruder* moored at the dock behind the office. The other salvage boats, *Virgalona* and *Swordfish* were already on the site, alerted by the *Dauntless* as wreck material was uncovered. The lights burned late into the night as investors and the news media around the country were advised that "Today WAS the day!!"

Out on the *Dauntless* the emotions were just as evident, but the crew became a lot more somber as they realized their part in history in the making. It is hard to imagine the excitement in salvaging a treasure galleon wreck site. To be the first to see the *Atocha* mound of ballast stones 75 feet long, thirty feet wide, and rising four feet above the bottom. To swim alongside 1,041 silver bars, most of them seventy to eighty pounds each, stacked like cordwood four feet high and nearly twenty feet long. Here, also, are boxes of silver coins, 3,000 in each box, the wood long gone, but the shape of the box unmistakable.

Where the boxes had broken, the coins were spilled across the bottom and into the ballast like shells along a sandy beach. Huge timbers were just under the ballast stones, the ends eroded away by time and teredo worms. Artifacts, time capsules of a life at sea, lie scattered about the site covered by a veil of sand and sediment. Around the edge of the ballast were twenty-pound copper disks, poured into a sand mold 363 years before and destined for the cannon foundries in Spain. Aboard *Atocha* were wealthy passengers. They had traveled to the New World to make their fortunes, and in 1622 they were on their way back to Spain with personal possessions that would have been fit for a King.

Although the sterncastle of *Atocha* carrying most of this wealth had scattered almost nine miles to the west by a second hurricane, there were still signs of opulence everywhere. At first Kane wanted to bring up as many bars of silver as he could, so that his father would realize the rewards of so many fruitless years along the search trail. Andy Matroci reminded him that Mel had an exclusive contract with *National Geographic* to film the recovery. Maybe he should wait. The treasure diver in Kane won out, and a few eighty-pound bars of silver greeted Mel the following morning as the first contingent of celebrants arrived. Soon the *Virgalona, Swordfish, Dauntless* and *Magruder* were nested side by side, and the celebration began in earnest.

Jimmy Buffet and Mel Fisher sit atop a pile of Atocha silver bars. Credit: Wendy Tucker.

By noon, when Mel glanced across the stern of his salvage boats, he could see nearly fifty small boats tied one to the other like chicks around a mother hen, as well-wishers and news media joined in. At one point Mel had to ask many of the revelers to move over to the *Magruder*, the *Dauntless* being dangerously overloaded and in danger of capsizing. Jimmy Buffet, a friend of Mel's, was doing a photo shoot near Marquesa Key for the cover of his latest album, *Margaritaville*. He learned of the *Dauntless* finding the mother lode over his marine radio, and before the sun settled he had covered the six miles of open ocean between Marquesa Key and the pinwheel of small boats clustered about Fisher's navy. On board *Dauntless* he was greeted by a celebrating crew that was already rolling. After a lot of backslapping and hand-wringing, Mel exclaimed, "Do you think anyone here has a guitar?" There was a mixture of shouts and laughter as Jimmy answered, "I think I can find one."

It took Buffet several minutes to clamber over the boats separating his boat and the *Dauntless*. In the meantime Mel suggested, "Maybe we should build Jimmy a throne of silver bars!!" There was an immediate "Yeaaah!", and within minutes a dozen or more silver bars were stacked on the stern. Before Jimmy arrived back on board, someone hollered, "How about a throne for Mel??" In an instant a second throne of silver bars was raised alongside the first, and soon Mel and Jimmy, smiling like Cheshire cats, were the center of one of the greatest hoe-downs the Keys had ever heard. Songs like, *A Pirate Looks at Forty*, and *Margaritaville* rolled across the waters long after sundown. It was an aurora of companionship that ended so many years of frustration, the humility of a job well done.

Now it was time to salvage the treasure. Duncan Mathewson soon gathered about him a group of renown archaeological experts who helped coordinate the location and preservation of artifacts. Duncan made it evident that "blowers", deflecting the salvage boat propwash, should not be used in the excavation. Too much would be lost in context. Instead, airlifts with twenty-foot aluminum tubes six inches in diameter, working almost like a vacuum sweeper to remove the sand and overburden, would be used. The contract that Mel had with *National Geographic* required that nothing be disturbed from the site until their film crew arrived. It would be a week before the *Geographic* crew was ferried out to the site with all their gear, and in the meantime the salvage crews began the slow, meticulous job of removing the sand and silt covering the remains of *Atocha*. When they were finished it was like a fantasy world. There were silver bars, artifacts, boxes of coins, and loose coins scattered everywhere.

The pile was gridded with PVC pipe, and a photo-mosaic was made of the wreck site from one end to the other to document everything *in situ*. As the film crew went about its business, the swarm of news and TV media were kept out of the water. They would have to wait their turn.

Mel Fisher, Mendel Peterson, and Duncan Mathewson.

After a week of intense film work, the *National Geographic* crew was satisfied that they had their story, and with their pile of gear safely stowed aboard, they were shuttled back to Key West. This was the moment the salvagers were waiting for. It was time to raise the bars of silver! At first the bars were brought to the surface in cargo nets, often five or six at a time. Kane Fisher found some of the nets had dry rotted, and there was imminent danger that some of the bars might tear through the net and drop on swimmers below with tragic results. Someone came up with the idea that they had been shopping for treasure all these years, why not bring the bars up in shopping carts. It worked very well. From time to time, however, they had to shut down all salvage operations due to the number of divers from the news media and TV stations that swarmed about the wreck for underwater film footage. The media had its day, and the site became one of the most documented in history.

Grace Fisher, Mel, and actor Cliff Robertson.

Bill Moore and Steve Swindell were surveying the extent of the site using metal detectors when they got quite a large "hit" about forty feet to the northwest of the ballast. Steve had just about run out of bottom time, and as the two divers borrowed an airlift from one of the other divers, Steve headed for the surface. Bill moved about a foot of sand over the hit when he saw what appeared to be barrel hoops in a row, or possibly a human rib cage. As he uncovered more of the artifact his airlift nudged one of the oblong-shaped objects...and suddenly he had palpitations of the heartbeat!! The bright glimmer of gold appeared where some of the encrustation had been knocked off.

Normally gold is too dense to be encrusted, so Bill was not prepared to be staring at a row of gold bars. But that's exactly what they were, and as he carefully lifted the sand away more bars appeared. Then gold chains, and gold disk!! He couldn't believe what he was looking at, and it's possible that the airlift was dancing as well. Moore worked on the bottom another 35 minutes before it was time to head for the surface. By this time the hole was about ten feet across, and he could see more bars of gold around the edge. Without disturbing them, he headed for the surface to get his underwater camera. This glory hole deserved to be photographed!

Up on deck Kane asked him, "What are you working on??" Bill thought everyone knew; there were divers close by while he was on the bottom. "Gold bars!" Kane's eyes lit up, "How many?" Bill grinned, "I lost count at twenty." Everyone freaked out. With that, the stern of *Dauntless* was a madhouse as divers looked for spare tanks. They all had a chance to see the glitter of gold as it lay undisturbed on the bottom. It was the greatest gold hole of the *Atocha*. When the area was finally uncovered there lay 77 gold bars, seven gold disks, and seven gold chains. Almost 65 pounds of glimmering gold. Lost in the excitement was the fact that it was Bill Moore's birthday.

The word was flashed back to the Key West office, and Bleth McHaley immediately called the *National Geographic* office in Washington, D. C. As the film crew was ready to deplane at Dulles airport they received a message, "Return to Key West immediately!" They hardly had time to call home and tell their families they wouldn't be home for dinner when they were on the next plane south.

The boxes of coins posed a problem. The boxes were made of redwood, much of which had long been devoured by teredo worms. But there were still a few that remained intact, and finding a means of getting them to the surface required the building of special platforms. Once on the surface they had to be kept wet or the wood would disintegrate within hours. The salvors kept wet blankets covering the boxes until they reached Key West, where fresh-water tanks were built to hold them.

One of the divers got a reading on his metal detector, but the sand was a little deep, and he ran out of bottom time. Kim Fisher was about to drop over the side, and the diver let Kim know where the hit was. Kim reached the sea bed and began airlifting the sand away. The hole was several feet deep when he reached marl bottom. The hit turned out to be an eight-pound gold disk! Under the disk, Kim still got a reading, and he fanned the sand away from...an astrolabe. Now it was getting exciting, because alongside the astrolabe was a cross-staff, one of the instruments with which the pilot takes a reading on the sun to determine latitude. There were other detector readings, including several bags of silver coins, each containing about 100 coins.

As Kim ran out of bottom time he could see the lower portion and sides of what appeared to be a large chest, two feet deep, three feet wide, and about three feet long. Near the bottom was a bag, with a piece of gold chain protruding from beneath. It was part of forty feet of gold chain, and clumped under the chain lay 1-1/2 pounds of gold nuggets and gold flakes. As it later turned out, this was part of the *Atocha* pilot's personal baggage.

There were other days of excitement. Kim was working with an airlift thirty or forty feet west of the ballast pile when he uncovered two salt cellars, both with fancy engraving. As he was airlifting the sand around them he saw a blob of green disappear up the air lift. He shut the air off, then looked up just as the rain of emeralds came down around him. A few even landed in his hair as he reached out to catch them. They landed in the white sand, a pea patch of green Muzo emeralds. It was just the beginning, that first peanut jar full of green treasure. The area would become known as the "Field of Emeralds" when almost 3,000 of the Colombian gemstones would be recovered --possibly the greatest single return on investment Mel's financial backers would realize.

The salvage of the mother lode goes on today, extending out beyond the ballast pile several hundred yards. Still missing... twelve bronze cannons, silver bars, and thousands of silver coins. In 1996, Kane Fisher continues to work the emerald field, recovering hundreds of emeralds during the salvage season. There is a growing feeling that the missing cannon and more great treasure lies beyond the Quicksands. The trail is there, and the hunt goes on.

27...THE FISHER LEGACY LIVES ON

In retrospect, if one could sum up the events and achievements that Mel Fisher has managed to slip between the pages of history, one of the more obvious accolades within the salvage community is that the "little guy" can make a difference. Mel proved that governmental bureaucracy can not always "roll over" someone who stands up for his rights. Time and time again he went to the bar and contested the state's effort to take over a valuable treasure site once his group had spent the time and money to finally locate it. He was successful each and every time.

More recently a few self-interest archaeologists have managed to reach self-centered politicians, and the "Abandoned Shipwreck Act" was passed, over-ruling admiralty law. This gave each state complete control over shipwrecks within their state waters. The *Atocha*, lying some forty miles west of Key West, came under the jurisdiction of the National Marine Sanctuary. No sooner did that occur than the Sanctuary clamped down on salvage operations along the entire string of Florida Keys. Hopefully, somewhere down the road, federal and state officials will come to realize that working with the private salvage community is the only way that shipwrecks can be salvaged and their treasures made available for the public to see and appreciate. If the public can also own a piece of history, what's wrong with that?

After *Atocha*, it would seem that other projects tend to be anti-climactic for Mel. But the world is still full of mountains to climb, and Mel has found a few. He has a gnawing ambition to discover Atlantis, believing as a great many people do, that the city disappeared many years ago into a watery grave. A great deal of research has gone into the project, and he has traveled far and wide with scholars in search of factual evidence that may someday surprise everyone.

Most recently he has been involved in the wealth of shipwrecks at the mouth of the Rio Plata River in Uruguay. He, along with his son, Kim, has spent months searching and salvaging ballast piles under conditions of strong current and zero visibility. And the treasure wrecks are there, as evidenced by the Rubén Collado recovery of almost 2,000 gold coins and gold bullion from the galleon *Nuestra Señora de la Luz* near Montevideo in 1992.

Mel's bout with cancer has been on-going for almost fourteen years now, and his doctor tells him, "Whatever you're doing...keep doing it. It seems to be working." It has slowed him down, no doubt about that, but his spirit and enthusiasm continue to be the fountainhead of the salvage community.

In the meantime, the Fisher family has stepped forward, and they follow in firm footprints. Deo continues as the Executive Vice President of the family corporation Salvors, Inc., and she is on the board of trustees of the Mel Fisher Maritime Heritage Society's museum located in Key West. Dolores' job is keeping investors informed on the various treasure recoveries and sorting out *Atocha* coins that are being sold on the exhibit tour of the Fisher treasures. But more than that, Deo is "there" for everyone. When Mel is out of town, out of sight, out of reach, Deo speaks for the family. She has the time, and patience, to listen, and she may not have all the answers, but everyone feels much better after talking to her.

In 1986, with a great deal of publicity, the Jamestown Corporation bought Treasure Salvors' rights to the *Atocha* and the *Santa Margarita*. This included treasure, the company boats, and the exclusive right to work the two wreck sites. Jamestown put down a large deposit, with a payment schedule for the balance. Much of the treasure belonging to Treasure Salvors was transferred to the Jamestown Corporation, and this was donated to a new entity, the Mel Fisher Maritime Heritage Society museum that was activated in the building at 200 Greene Street in Key West.

Some of the greatest treasures recovered went into the museum as a permanent display. The large gold and emerald cross, the gold poison cup, the *Margarita* gold plate, and hundreds of other unique artifacts were donated to this non-profit museum. With the down payment, Fisher was able to write a check to the IRS for over $1 million to pay for diver and staff payroll taxes, as well as the taxes on the treasure that the divers received in their division.

The following year Jamestown defaulted on the scheduled payments, and the Treasure Salvors group regained the rights to dive *Atocha* and *Margarita*. The treasure donated to the museum was not rescinded and remains there today for the public to see and appreciate. Madeleine Burnside took over the reins of the museum and, through her grants, she has been able to put together an exhibit about the *Henrietta Marie*, a black slaver that sank in 1700. This exhibit is now touring the United States, a tribute to the black heritage of this country.

In 1986, Mel's lawyers recommended dissolution of the company for tax purposes, both for the company and the investors. The total tax against the immense treasure being brought to the surface could very well result in the IRS confiscating as much as 75% of the treasure. In June of 1986, the Board of Directors of Treasure Salvors, as well as the majority of stockholders, agreed to dissolve the company. Many of the stockholders transferred their treasure to the non-profit heritage museum and other museums escaping the IRS ax. Mel donated 1% of his share (which turned out to be the largest emerald recovered to date, a 77.7 carat gem recovered by Kane), to the museum. And so the end of Treasure Salvors, one of the most successful treasure salvaging operations in history, came to an end.

As some marriages have a habit of not working out, Kim Fisher and Jo Stuart dissolved theirs in 1984. Kim was made captain of the *Bookmaker*, a 42-foot Hatteras used primarily for magnetometer surveys of the site. Before long mailboxes were installed on the stern and, when the mother lode was discovered, Kim had the Hatteras on rotation with other the salvage boats bringing up treasure. After the dissolution of Treasure Salvors, many thought that Mel would go into retirement. That would never happen. As salvage on *Atocha* continued to wind down, Mel turned his attention to wrecks along the coast of South America.

In 1579, Sir Francis Drake pinched the Spanish rooster's tail. With only five ships and a crew of 164, he sailed through the Straits of Magellan and into the Pacific Ocean. It was an arduous voyage in which four of his vessels never made it. When he finally reached the Peruvian coast he began raiding the various Spanish ports including Arica and Callao. The Spanish garrisons had never expected to be attacked by the English, or anyone else, and they offered very little resistance.

At Callao, Drake learned that the treasure-laden galleon of the South Sea Armada, *Nuestra Señora de la Concepción*, had just left for Panama. He quickly sailed after her and caught the ship by surprise. There was a brief fight, but the Spanish soon surrendered, and Drake boarded the galleon. He was overwhelmed at the sight of 1300 silver bars, fourteen chests of silver coins, and at least 40,000 pesos in contraband silver in her hold. His crew managed to transfer the entire cargo to Drake's vessel, and he sailed northward with the entire coast of Peru in pursuit.

Kim Fisher and wife Lee.

He was overloaded with the 25 tons of silver, and even a small storm would have capsized the ship. The story goes that as he approached the coast of Ecuador he anchored off Isla de la Plata, where he deposited some of the silver bars on the bottom of the ocean near a prominent landmark...to be retrieved at a later date. He then sailed across the Pacific and arrived back in England in 1580, a national hero. He had no idea at the time that he would some day have a pronounced effect on the romantic life of Kim Fisher.

Lee Wiegand, a gorgeous chiropractor from Pennsylvania, was on the trail of Drake's silver. She had information that in the 1930-40 period a group had traveled to Isla de la Plata and, using a clam shell, had recovered several tons of silver. Based on the Drake documents, there remained quite a bit of silver on the bottom. She was in Key West during the time that Mel was on the trail of the Atocha mother lode, and she asked him if he would be willing to send some electronic gear down to Ecuador and help her find it.

Before long Kim Fisher and Dick Klaudt were on their way south with a magnetometer, metal detectors, and their dive gear. Kim met up with Lee, and together they leased a charter boat to the island. It was during this time that Ecuador was in the throes of a military take-over. The political situation was not the greatest, and with soldiers carrying machine guns standing on every corner, the treasure expedition never really got off to a great start.

When Kim returned to Key West he was starry-eyed. He confided in Taffi, "I've met the girl of my dreams!" The next day he flew back to Pennsylvania, using treasure business as an excuse. After going over a number of updates with Lee, he said, "There is one more thing." She looked at Kim, "What's that?" He grinned, "Will you marry me?" She had only known Kim for a short while, but that was long enough, "Yes!" They were married that weekend. One of the memorable parts of the wedding was Kim throwing Lee's beeper in the river. "You won't be needing this anymore."

Kim and Lee remain an active part of the treasure community. For several years Kim remained captain of the *Bookmaker*, working the 1715 treasure fleet near Sebastian. More recently he and Lee have joined the Treasure Group International, traveling the country --displaying sunken treasure at various locations and selling coins to help support the search for sunken treasure. Kim and Lee may not have found Drake's silver, but they did find treasure. They found each other.

Kane Fisher, wife Karen, and son Dirk.

When you close your eyes and listen to Kane Fisher talk, you would swear it was Mel. When you open them, you see a younger Mel, a spitting image of his father. Tall, red of hair, and with the same driving energy his father gave to the salvage community for so many years. And Kane is dedicated to the hunt. Some call him a "loose cannon" as he ranges up and down the east coast of Florida, but never mistake the dedication for recklessness. Kane is deliberate in the search, and he has the professionalism of a salvor who finds treasure when others fail.

A treasure that has managed thus far to escape Kane is the seventy-pound bag of emeralds that may have been aboard the Atocha when it sank. It provides the magnet that draws Kane back to the ballast pile now lying undisturbed in 54 feet of water. In 1994 and 1995, a large suction dredge was rigged aboard the *Dauntless*, and soon tons of bottom material was being sifted for the green stones. And they began to find some, maybe not pounds of them, but enough to know that they are on the right trail.

Kane, Karen, and their three children Dirk, Daniel, and Farrah have a home in Vero Beach. His brother, Dirk, is buried here in Vero, and Kane feels comfortable being near. Kane also has a number of friends that he grew up with here, and so it's natural that part of the Fisher family carry on the legacy where it all began, here in Vero Beach at 628 Banyan Road.

Have you ever had the immense pleasure of watching a Morning Glory open its petals in the morning mist, fresh and ready to share the day with the whole world? Taffi Fisher fits the picture perfectly. She grew up flitting among the shadows of great treasure hunters. And as she grew older she was accepted by the salvage community as readily as her three brothers were. The Fisher family has been the center of the salvage community in Florida since Mel moved here in 1963, the center of a dream come true. Taffi has had the opportunity to see all sides of the search for sunken treasure, the exhilaration as well as the frustration and heartbreak.

When the rush of *Atocha* treasure was at its peak, Taffi was center-fold, the head of the division committee. The job distributing nearly 150,000 items to the eager stockholders fell on her shoulders. Her group came up with the point values placed on each item, and with the accounting firm of Touche, Ross and Company to audit the division, the computer was readied to match artifacts to investors. Mel asked Taffi to push the button that started the three-day process, which ended in whoops and hollers as the treasure was distributed.

After *Atocha*, the main stage of activity became the 1715 Spanish treasure fleet scattered along the east coast of Florida from Sebastian to Fort Pierce. Taffi became the obvious choice to head up the operation. Her first marriage hadn't worked out, and Taffi wanted her children out of the Key West environment. Josh was old enough to join a Little League softball team, something Key West couldn't offer, but Vero Beach could. It was an easy move for Taffi.

Taffi Fisher. **Credit: Pat Clyne.**

As she became the Area Director of Operations in Sebastian, it gave her a chance to work with treasure divers she knew well, and she brought to the job an understanding of the pressures and problems of on-site salvage operations. There were headaches along the way, primarily from the state of Florida environmental groups. The Bennett Bill was passed, giving Florida jurisdiction over all shipwrecks within state waters. The 1715 fleet of wreck sites were "grandfathered in" by admiralty law, but Florida controlled everything that Salvors, Inc. did underwater.

More than once the entire fleet of salvage boats was left tied to the dock as the result of new rules conjured up by NOAA and DEPA involving turbidity levels and worm reef. And more than once Taffi called the office in Key West and implore whoever answered, "I want to talk to my Mommy!" But through each episode she weathered the storm, became stronger, and today there is no doubt in anyone's mind that Taffi Fisher is as solid as a rock and that Salvors, Inc. is in good hands.

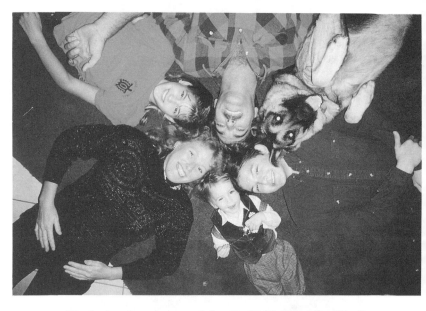

Clockwise from upper right: Taffi Fisher Abt, Nicole, Michael Abt, "Baron", Joshua, and Michael, Jr.

Michael Abt, a perfect stand-in for Tom Selleck, was enrolled in an Orlando stunt school for the movies. A friend of Taffi's was dating the man running the school, and somewhere along the way Taffi and Michael met. That was in 1991, and after Taffi saw Michael do his thing in movies such as *Ghostbusters, On Deadly*

Ground, and *Passenger 57*, she was sure his life was just as exciting as salvaging treasure. They were married on Saint Valentine's Day, 1993. In November, Michael Christopher was born, and between the movies and sunken treasure he will have a tough act to follow.

***Terry and Carla Fisher on their search boat* Gambler.
Credit: Pat Clyne.**

As history will some day be written about the past forty years, and possibly the next ten years or so, they will be referred to as the "Treasure Salvage Years". There has never been a time in our history when the salvage of sunken treasure has so captivated the world audience. Sunken treasure is news, a dream come true for many of us in the salvage community, and a dream for those that would like to recover their own gold doubloons and pieces-of-eight. As we salvage the treasure of the Spanish galleons, it becomes obvious that we will never find it all, that there will be treasure left for whoever has the patience and dedication to continue the search. And as technology advances, the deeper wrecks become a part of the direction the salvage community has taken for rewards exceeding the imagination.

Mel, The Dreamweaver, and Deo Fisher.

The Dreamweaver
and grandsons by Kim Fisher, Sean (L.) and Jeremy (R.).

Even as I write the final chapter of this book, I received through the mail an article from the *Key West Citizen*. "Fisher on the Atocha Trail Again", with a story line recounting the location of the scatter pattern beyond the "Bank of Spain" where Mel feels the remaining ten bronze cannons and the pile of missing silver bars must be. The hunt goes on, the dream goes on, and that is why Mel Fisher *is* the Dreamweaver.

REFERENCES AND SELECTED READING

Search for the Mother Lode of the Atocha by Eugene Lyon. 1995.
ISBN 0-912451-20-3. Florida Classics Library. Port Salerno, FL.

The Search for the Atocha by Eugene Lyon. 1979.
ISBN 0-06-012711-2. Harper & Row. New York, NY.

Treasure of the Atocha by R. Duncan Mathewson III. 1986.
ISBN 0-525-24497-2. E. P. Dutton. New York, NY.

Shipwrecks of Florida by Steven D. Singer. 1992.
ISBN 1-56164-006-9. Pineapple Press. Sarasota, FL.

Florida's Golden Galleons by R. Burgess & C. Clausen. 1982.
ISBN 0-912451-07-6. Florida Classics Library. Port Salerno, FL.

Treasure Hunt by George Sullivan. 1987.
ISBN 0-8050-0569-2. Henry Holt & Co. New York, NY.

Pieces of Eight by Kip Wagner as told to L. B. Taylor, Jr. 1966.
Library of Congress: 66-11563. E. P. Dutton. New York, NY.

The Spanish Treasure Fleets by Timothy R. Walton. 1994.
ISBN 1-56164-049-2. Pineapple Press. Sarasota, FL.

Sunken Treasure on Florida Reefs by Bob "Frogfoot" Weller. 1993.
ISBN 0-9628359-3-5. Crossed Anchors Salvage. Lake Worth, FL.

Famous Shipwrecks of the Florida Keys by Bob "Frogfoot" Weller.
1990.
ISBN 0-9628359-0-0. Crossed Anchors Salvage. Lake Worth, FL.

Galleon Hunt by Bob "Frogfoot" Weller. 1992.
ISBN 0-9628359-2-7. Crossed Anchors Salvage. Lake Worth, FL.

Shipwrecks Near Wabasso Beach by Bob "Frogfoot" Weller and
Ernie "Seascribe" Richards. 1996.
ISBN 0-9628359-4-3. *En Rada* Publications. West Palm Beach, FL.